CONVICTION

SCATTERED STARS: CONVICTION BOOK 1

CONVICTION

SCATTERED STARS: CONVICTION BOOK 1

GLYNN STEWART

**FAOLAN'S PEN
PUBLISHING**

faolanspen.com

All rights reserved. For information about permission to reproduce selections from this book, contact the publisher at info@faolanspen.com or Faolan's Pen Publishing Inc., 22 King St. S, Suite 300, Waterloo, Ontario N2J 1N8, Canada.

This edition published in 2020 by:

Faolan's Pen Publishing Inc.

22 King St. S, Suite 300

Waterloo, Ontario

N2J 1N8 Canada

ISBN-13: 978-1-988035-96-3 (print)

A record of this book is available from Library and Archives Canada.

Printed in the United States of America

1 2 3 4 5 6 7 8 9 10

First edition

First printing: January 2020

Illustration © 2020 Jeff Brown Graphics

Faolan's Pen Publishing logo is a trademark of Faolan's Pen Publishing Inc.

Read more books from Glynn Stewart at faolanspen.com

1

HUMANITY HAD SPREAD to an almost uncountable number of stars. Ships traveled between those star systems in mere weeks instead of the years light took. Gravity could be created, manipulated, set to an exact value. Even the human body and mind itself were now artifacts of human technology and achievement.

And tall men still always thought they could beat short women at basketball.

"She's coming on your lef—*right!*"

The changed warning wasn't as fast as Kira Demirci. The blonde woman ducked under the grabbing hands of the tallest of the three men she was playing against, bounced the ball off the laminate floor— even on a starship, metal wasn't acceptable for a ball court—and planted her feet in perfect position for her shot.

The ball dropped through the hoop as her intended interceptor hit the ground. He'd lost his balance as Kira had ducked around him.

"Shit, sorry, Gregor," she told him as she turned to check on him.

"I'm fine, I'm fine," the big guy told her as he levered himself back to his feet. "*Damn*, you're fast."

"That's three," Kira told Gregor and the other two men. The three were cargo handlers aboard the freighter *Hopeful Future*. They were, in fact, three-quarters of the entire cargo division aboard *Future*.

The ship only had a crew of twenty, after all. She'd been working her way aboard the ship for the last six weeks as an environmental tech, but the clock on the gym's wall told her that her stay aboard *Future* was almost done.

"Now, I believe the bet was on *one* game," she continued with a grin. "Then best of three for double the money. Then best of *five* for double *that*."

She pointed at the clock.

"My schedule says we dock in ten minutes and you three are supposed to be hauling cargo around as soon as we make contact. So, do you want me to demonstrate that I can beat you in under ten minutes or would you rather shower?"

At a hundred and sixty centimeters tall and *maybe* sixty kilos soaking wet, Kira came up to roughly mid-chest height on the shortest of the three cargo hands. She was also faster and stronger than any of the three, which they'd also somehow missed despite working out in the same gym as her for six weeks.

"You need to call it, boys," a new voice said. All four of them looked up to see *Future*'s second officer, Chief Roland.

Even after six weeks, Kira wasn't sure what Roland was Chief of—or whether Roland was the older man's first or last name. He was third in command. That was enough for the cargo hands and the passenger working to pay for her passage.

"Gotcha, Chief," Gregor conceded. "I was about done being run over as it was."

He was grinning as he said it. His friends looked less enthused. Of course, Kira had slept with Gregor—and his friends had not been nearly pleasant enough for her to consider them.

The three of them each rifled through their bags and produced small stacks of hard currency. She skimmed the chips as they were handed to her and smiled. The payment was in funds from at least three star systems, but the credit chips themselves were nearly universal.

"Thanks," she told them cheerfully as she pocketed the coins. "Have fun hauling cargo."

"Sure thing, Riker," one of Gregor's friends said in a *mostly-*accepting tone.

Kira kept her smile up as her friendly several-night-stand and his friends disappeared off to their work, but her actual humor had vanished at the name "Riker." That wasn't her name. It was just the name she'd given when she'd come aboard *Hopeful Future*.

Because Kira *Demirci* had a death mark on her and that was why she was there, over a hundred light-years from home.

"Does the big guy know you're getting off here?" Roland asked, watching *her* as his people trooped off to the cargo bay.

"Yeah," Kira confirmed, still distracted by the reminder of why she was there. "No games there, Chief Roland. He knew what was on offer."

The freighter's second officer snorted.

"Get yourself showered," he told her. "I'm guessing you're already packed, so meet me in my office when you're ready to go."

Kira nodded in reply as she grabbed the duffle of clothes next to her. Kira *Riker* had a few more tasks to complete before she ceased to exist. She didn't have time to deal with Kira Demirci's problems just yet.

EVEN NOW, the standard unmarked shipsuit of a civilian spacer felt vaguely wrong to Kira. It wasn't heavy enough, for one thing. Thanks to its emergency space-capability, it would probably stop most slugthrower fire, but even the cheapest blaster would burn right through it.

The "leather" coat she was wearing over it hung down below her hips and neatly concealed a more modern layer of armor. The jacket *could*, thankfully, stop blasters. She'd had to quietly patch it up in her downtime aboard *Future* because of the proof of that.

It also handily concealed a small blaster of her own. Expensive even back home in the Apollo System, the weapon might be irreplaceable out here in the Redward System.

"Hey, Chief," one of the cargo handlers shouted at Roland as Kira dodged around the edge of the cargo bay. "The big black boxes—we pinged the station net for a delivery address but didn't get one. They're half the damn bay; what do we do?"

Kira managed not to actively shout at the crew to just leave them be for now. She'd have all of that set up within a few hours of getting off of *Future*, but she needed to get *off* the ship to handle that.

"We just docked," Roland shouted back, standing in the entrance to his office and studying the carefully organized chaos filling the big space. "It's also the middle of the night, local station time. Give 'em eight hours to wake up and realize we're here!"

The cargo bay was easily half of *Hopeful Future*'s volume, a hundred-meter-long twenty-thousand-cubic-meter void. *Future* was on the large size of middling for a freighter in Apollo, which meant she was probably massive out here. Redward was supposedly the best-off system out here, but Kira's expectations were low.

"Everything else is in front of them, anyway," Roland continued. "I wasn't an *idiot* when I had you load them in!"

It wasn't much of an exaggeration to say that the six big black storage units took up half the freighter's storage. Each was fifteen hundred cubic meters and Kira had no idea how they'd managed to get aboard the ship. These *particular* boxes were unlabeled, but she knew them by heart and they *should* have been marked with the stylized gold bow and arrow of the Apollo System Defense Force.

"You wanted to talk, Chief?" she asked Roland, shaking off the vagaries of the past.

"Yeah, come in," he told her.

They stepped into his office and Roland closed the door with a gesture in the air. The window changed its tint ever-so-slightly as well, converting to a one-way mirror. They could see out into the cargo bay, but no one could see in.

The sound of the bay cut off as soon as the door closed, and Chief Roland heaved a sigh.

"Those crates worry me," he admitted aloud. "I'll be happier once they're off the ship, which means a missing receiver is making me more nervous than I'm telling them."

"You know what they are?" Kira asked in surprise, then realized that even asking the question was giving away more than she meant to.

"I served in a system fleet coreward from Apollo, yes," Roland said dryly. "And I've hauled military materiel on three ships along the way, though not this one. I know what a damn nova-fighter shipping container looks like, Em *Riker*."

She shivered at his tone.

"And I know you do too," he continued. "I've seen you watching them. But...none of that's my business."

Roland waved a screen alive over his desk.

"You worked your passage, but six weeks' pay for an enviro tech is more than the cost of a passenger ticket on a tramp freighter," he continued. "Captain says you get half, which is honestly a bit unfair to you, but I'm not arguing with her. You going to?"

Kira chuckled mirthlessly.

"No." She'd met Captain Helen Ngo a few times over the trip. For a civilian, she was impressive.

"Thought not." Roland studied her across the desk. "Look, Riker, I know that's not your name. I don't care. What I *do* care about is that the Syntactic Cluster is the ass end of fucking nowhere and you made a more than half-decent enviro tech.

"You're running from something; I can read that much. I'm guessing it's in Apollo, or at least that sector. *Hopeful Future* only ports in that region once a year. You could stay on with us. You'd be safe from whatever you're running from."

She sighed.

"Chief? Those boxes in your cargo bay? They're mine," she told him. How they'd ended up hers was a long story, but the paperwork was loaded into both her headware and the hard datachips in her luggage.

"Yours?" He stared at her. "That's six nova fighters," he noted slowly. "There are, last time I checked, only about two dozen nova fighters in the entire Syntactic Cluster. Those birds make you a target out here while they're in crates."

"Out of those crates, they make me a power to be reckoned with," Kira replied. Only Apollo and Brisingr in her home sector could build nova fighters. Everyone else only had larger ships with more basic nova drives.

And that was part of why Apollo was Brisingr's only real opposition. That, on the other hand, brought up other memories. None of them good.

"If you have the money to run them." Roland snorted. "And now I feel like I wasted my time arguing with the Captain to get you half your pay instead of a third. Still."

He slid a handful of credit chips across the desk to her.

"They're in crests, drawn on the Bank of the Royal Crest," he told her. "The Syntactic Cluster doesn't really have a local reserve currency, so mostly they use the Royal Crest for interstellar trade."

Kira ran through her mental map.

"Aren't they out of the Valerian System?" she asked.

"Not just a sector away but *two* sectors away," Roland agreed. "They'd be just as well off using Apollo new drachmae or Brisingr crowns—same distance and stability—but the Bank of the Royal Crest is actually out in a few places like the Cluster, trying to make a name for themselves as a potential reserve currency. And they're well enough known that most exchanges will take the crest...and most exchanges outside the Cluster haven't even *heard* of most of the Cluster's currencies.

"So, out here, we pay and take payment in crests."

Kira took the coin.

"That's background I didn't have," she admitted. The funds that had come with her and been sent on ahead were all in Apollo new drachmae. She figured the exchanges here would recognize those if nothing else, but it was useful to know the local default international currency of choice.

"Thank you," she told Roland. "It's been a more pleasant journey than I expected, but I didn't come to Redward randomly, either."

"I'm not surprised," he replied. "Good luck...Major."

And that, Major Kira Demirci, Apollo System Defense Force (retired), realized, was the closest the Chief was going to ever come to admitting that *Hopeful Future*'s senior officers had always known *exactly* who she was.

2

THE CONVERSATION in the cargo bay had warned Kira that she needed to take care of her collection of nova fighters before she worried about such minor matters as where *she* was sleeping tonight. It was late enough that most offices would be starting to open, but that meant that Roland's cargo hands would be hitting the net for a recipient for her storage crates sooner rather than later.

She had ended up on Redward intentionally, though. Her previous CO, Colonel Jay "White Cobra" Moranis, had sent her here—and he'd had time to put at least some groundwork in place before he'd died.

Moranis, at least, had died of natural causes. Kira couldn't say the same for the other members of the 303 Nova Combat Group. The Colonel's twenty-four pilots had been at the heart of most of the key battles between Apollo and Brisingr over the last decade or so and had made a reputation for themselves.

Now there was peace…and the Three-Oh-Three's pilots had started turning up dead. The peace was bad enough, since Kira had no illusions about what her government had sacrificed for it.

Her government had bought peace by abandoning everyone they'd promised to protect from Brisingr.

Moranis had suspected the blind eye being turned to Brisingr Shadows operating in Apollo territory had been another part of the deal. No one would have put "we want the heads of your best pilots" in the text of the deal, but the old man had figured it was part of it.

And the Three-Oh-Three had been Apollo's best. *Had been*.

She'd formally handed in her papers. At least two of the people she was expecting to join her out here had outright deserted.

Her brooding brought her to the door of the office she'd been looking for. Her headware was easily capable of running a directional line in her vision, which was handy given that she didn't know Blueward Station at all.

Most orbitals were standard, and Blueward didn't even *smell* different. The only easy way to tell that she wasn't back home was that all of the signs were in Standard Galactic English instead of both English and Greek.

Apollo's desire to be Greek-speaking was more aspirational than actual, but the signs were in both languages anyway. This sign might not have been much different anywhere. It was very straightforward:

Priapus Simoneit and Partners Law.

The door beneath the sign led into a small waiting room with exactly three chairs and a holographic receptionist with a curvaceous female-style body and Old-Earth-suit outfit that had been out of fashion for at least a century in Apollo.

"Welcome to Simoneit and Partners Law," the artificially stupid hologram chirped. "I'm sorry, but you don't have an appointment and you are not one of our regular clients. We only see new clients by previously established appointment. Do you have a delivery?"

Kira smiled thinly.

"I'm here on behalf of White Cobra," she told the digital woman. "I need to speak to Em Simoneit immediately."

The hologram paused, smiling cheerfully at Kira while the computer behind it processed whether that name meant anything to it. Most humans would at least have recognized the name, even this far out. Cobra Squadron had been a *legend* once.

That might have been forty years earlier, but legends only seemed to grow with time. She'd been shocked to discover that one of the actual Cobras was even in Apollo, let alone her commanding officer, when she'd joined the 303 as a flight commander fifteen years earlier.

"Pause, shut down," a voice said clearly before the hologram could respond to whatever the computer dredged up. "Main door, lock."

The hologram blinked out and Kira heard a small *click* in the door. Half-unconsciously, her hand slipped inside the jacket as she turned to face the man who'd entered the room.

He was *old*, easily into his second century, with pure white hair and visible liver spots across his face. The man's suit was a long-tailed white outfit that had been in fashion in Apollo twenty years before but might be cutting edge here.

"I am Priapus Simoneit," the old man told her with a small sad smile. "If you are here alone, I am guessing that Jay is no longer with us?"

"That's a leap, I think, Em Simoneit," Kira said slowly.

"Please, Em Demirci, I know who you are," he replied. "Jay and I corresponded over the years, and there's a reason he trusted me with this affair. He did not expect you to leave Apollo until you either had no choice or he was dead—and he rather expected those two things to coincide."

Simoneit shook his head.

"Come into my office, Em Demirci," he continued. "I know some of what Jay set in motion, but I doubt he trusted it all to interstellar mail. I have resources he put in place for you, but I don't know what his plans for them or you are."

Kira was more than a bit taken back. She'd known the lawyer was supposed to be her first point of contact and was holding funds in escrow for her, but she hadn't expected the man to know Colonel Moranis.

"How did you know the Colonel?" she asked as she entered the office. It was almost painfully stereotypical. Wooden paneling—*probably* fake, but who could tell?—covered the walls and anchored wooden bookshelves. Some of those bookshelves were the usual holographic database interface, but several of them appeared to contain real books.

"I never knew him as a Colonel," Simoneit told her. "He and I met shortly after Cobra Squadron dissolved. We ended up on the same transport heading out to the Periphery and became good friends. We ran a ship together for some years before he met his husband in Apollo and settled down."

The lawyer shrugged.

"He stayed in Apollo, even after Carl passed. I kept going farther towards the edge of known space until the ship broke down here and I hired my now-wife to repair it. Somehow, I just never left after that."

"Colonel Moranis told me that you'd be my contact here," Kira told Simoneit. "He didn't tell me that he knew you."

"That was likely to protect us both," the lawyer said. "Given all that I have heard happened in Apollo, would you disagree?"

Kira winced but had to shake her head.

"When I left, eleven of the Three-Oh-Three's pilots were dead," she said quietly. "I *think* Moranis died of natural causes. Eight of the others are, at least officially, accidents. Two were definitely murdered and someone shot at me before I managed to disappear."

"Moranis knew he was dying when he sent me his last message," Simoneit replied, his voice equally soft. "But he set into motion the safety valve, the escape plan for you and your people. Most of what he sent me was money without much instruction. It's not enough to set up lifetime pensions for you and your people, but it would cover you for a while as you all get set up."

"What to do with it is a question for another day, I suppose," Kira told him. "What I need right now, Em Simoneit, is a specialty storage facility here on Blueward. Ten thousand cubics, high security—and either no questions asked of me or no questions answered for anyone else. Absolute confidentiality."

The lawyer considered.

"I can manage that," he confirmed. "There are several ways, but the one that's going to cost us the least is if my firm puts up a bond that says we know what's in the storage and it is no threat to Redward or the owners of the storage. That, of course, would require me to know what we're storing."

"I need that storage by end of day today,"

"The only way that's happening is if the firm puts up a bond," Simoneit admitted. "So…what did you bring, Em Demirci?"

"Six Hoplite-IV nova interceptors," Kira said flatly. "I need them safely stowed until I either have somewhere else to put them or the people to fly them."

The lawyer was very still for several seconds before he finally, slowly, nodded.

"I assume you have no intention of waging war against Redward or you wouldn't be here," he noted calmly.

"If my main plan falls through, I'll probably end up looking to work *for* Redward," Kira admitted.

"I am familiar with the legal structures involved in mercenary nova fighter squadrons," Simoneit reminded her. "If that is your plan, I can help you set it up. The Syntactic Cluster doesn't have many such, but that would only increase the demand for your services."

"It's a backup plan," she told him. "For now, I need that storage set up so I can tell the freighter that currently has my fighters where to put them. After that, we can have another conversation about what I'm doing next."

"Of course," Simoneit confirmed. "I'll need to make some calls. You can wait here if you'd like, but there's also a nice breakfast place at the corner of the section. By the time you've eaten, I should have everything you need for the storage unit."

Her stomach growled in a reminder that she *hadn't* eaten before leaving *Future*.

"Can I leave my luggage here?" she asked.

"Of course; the office is quite secure," he told her. He paused, studying her. "May I also suggest, Em Demirci, that you leave the blaster behind? Redward is generally quite liberal about firearms, but Blueward Station does *heavily* restrict blasters on the orbital."

She was relatively sure that the lawyer had never seen even a *hint* of the gun—but the man was also over a hundred years old and had apparently been a tramp freighter captain.

"Fair. What *can* I carry?" she asked pointedly.

3

IT PROBABLY SHOULDN'T HAVE BEEN a surprise that the restaurant Simoneit recommended was good. A chunk of its menu was unfamiliar to Kira, but she'd visited eleven different star systems in the Three-Oh-Three and six more on her voyage with *Hopeful Future*.

Redward was the twentieth star system she'd gone looking for breakfast in, and it didn't break the pattern of every breakfast diner having "two eggs over easy with toast" as an option. Someday, Kira would meet a diner that didn't have it.

That day, she'd actually have to think about what to eat for breakfast. Today was not that day.

She returned to Simoneit's office an hour after she left. This time, the hologram had been updated on who she was and turned a bright smile on her.

"Em Demirci, Em Simoneit is finalizing details on the matter you discussed," the digital woman told her. "He will be ready in a few minutes. May I get you a coffee?"

"Please."

The hologram didn't move. The coffee machine was perfectly capable of selecting and brewing a coffee on its own, sliding a cup out onto a saucer for her a minute later.

She hadn't been asked or given a coffee preference, but she was unsurprised to see it was pretty close. Spacers in general were notorious for their taste in coffee, and Kira was no exception.

The coffee was black and strong. That was all she needed. That it was also astonishingly *good* was a nice bonus.

"Where's the coffee from?" she asked the hologram.

"Our machine is supplied by Blueward's Finest Coffee Company," the hologram told her instantly, the required advertising spiel probably provided by the company. "It is currently stocked with Astonishing Orange, a variety of beans grown at particular farms on Redward's South Tangerine continent.

"I can give you contact information for Blueward's Finest or a data file on Astonishing Orange if you'd like?"

"That's fine, thank you," Kira said. The artificial stupid was exactly what the name implied. She'd known what she was getting when she asked the question, but she definitely didn't need more information on the coffee than that.

"Redward grows several surprisingly impressive varieties of coffee," Simoneit told her from the door. "They built their trade empire on coffee first, after all."

He gestured for her to step into his office.

"Come in. I think I have your storage sorted out."

Kira followed the lawyer back into his wood-paneled office and took her seat again, the coffee in her hand.

"Here." He tossed a digital file across the room, their headwares connecting for a moment to transfer the data. "You have a storage bay at one of Blueward Station's top-tier secured cargo bays, run by a group named Transition Storage. They're expecting ten thousand cubics of containers by end of day."

"I'll forward that to *Future*," she told him. That was only matter of moments. There were several queries in the station information network around the cargo, but Roland knew he was waiting on her to get set up, and her response had literally only needed an address.

Grabbing a query from the net and sending the response back was a matter of a few seconds' thought and a hand gesture through an interface no one else could see.

"Now that's handled, I suppose I should find out just what the

Colonel sent on ahead for us," Kira told Simoneit. "Do you have time for me this morning?"

"Fortunately, this morning was scheduled for a long meeting with an old friend of mine," Simoneit told her. "He and I will complete his business over dinner tonight, and I have this morning free for you."

He smiled, only half-humorously.

"My fee for that isn't insignificant, but you are the executor of the funds Jay Moranis 'sent on ahead.' You can afford it."

"Good to know," Kira told him. "How large of a fund *is* that?"

He gave a number and she winced.

"I probably don't want to know where that came from," she admitted. Her own stockpile amounted to roughly the annual operating budget of the 303, and she'd been concerned enough when Moranis had put that in her care.

That had apparently only been a third of the money that her old mentor had sent on ahead.

"Jay also had his own emergency retreat plan set up out here," the lawyer told her. "It was a far smaller-scale thing, but his instructions to me are clear: you're the *executor* for the funds for the Three-Oh-Three's survivors.

"You are his *heir* for the personal funds." Simoneit gestured a picture of an apartment building and what looked like a balance sheet into the air for her. "There's an apartment in Redward's capital city that a service takes care of and about ten million kroner in Redward currency."

He paused.

"Kroner convert to new drachmae at about two to one," he noted thoughtfully. "The reserve produces enough revenue on an annual basis to cover inflation and the apartment. If you were to live solely on those funds, you would most likely dip into the capital on an ongoing basis."

Five million new drachmae was around twenty years of Kira's salary as a ASDF Major. She could live on that for a while, though she *did* have another century or so of life expectancy left.

It was also only about a fifth of the reserve Moranis had set up out there for her and the rest of the 303. The old man had apparently had a *lot* more money to throw around than Kira had ever realized.

"I'll have to think about that," she admitted. "The money I knew about was supposed to be seed capital for our operating as mercenaries out here, putting our skills to use. There's a lot of support personnel that go into operating nova fighters. If we go with the backup plan, we're hiring all of that locally and acquiring a ship."

The ship alone would probably wipe out most of that seed capital. Nova fighters were nova-capable—it was in the name—but their FTL systems were optimized for short jumps. For interstellar trips, they were slower and shorter-ranged than a proper class one nova drive.

She knew how she'd convert a decent-sized freighter into a pocket carrier, but she wasn't sure how many thirty- to forty-thousand-cubic-meter ships were available out there.

"You've mentioned that as a backup plan before," Simoneit noted. "I have no idea what kind of ship you'd need for that—I can help you out with arranging financing for it, but it won't be easy to acquire."

"A forty-thousand-cubic-meter nova freighter," Kira replied instantly. "Preferably one already designed for deep-space cargo transfer; those systems are more easily retrofitted. We could probably refit a thirty-thousand-cubic bulk ship for our needs, but it would be a lot harder."

The lawyer chuckled.

"Redward probably has the most efficient class one nova drive designs in the Cluster," he noted. "But even they are running forty-thousand-cubics as their premium product. This isn't the Core, or even Apollo."

"We're a long damn way from the Core," she agreed. Every colony ship sent out had roughly the same basic fabricator database. Given an iron deposit and salt water, they could set up to build antigrav systems, Harrington coils and class one nova drives inside twenty years.

The standard class one drive was a thousand-cubic-meter unit that could take ten times its own volume into a nova jump with a maximum range of six light-years. Bigger ships required bigger nova drives or more efficient ones that carried greater ratios.

Apollo's top-tier class ones had been five-thousand-cubic-meter units that took twenty-five times their own volume into a nova—but she was a long way from Apollo.

"I'd have to do some research, but I am absolutely certain that the fund that Moranis set up wouldn't cover the cash purchase of your best-case ship," Simoneit told her. "I *might* be able to swing financing, but given the refits needed…"

He shrugged.

"Add in crew costs and operating costs, and I'm not certain we could convince the banks that your mercenary company would be a good investment," he admitted. "Not without a record out here, anyway."

"That's about what I figured," she agreed. "It's a backup plan and not a terrible one, but Jay sent me out here to *meet* someone. We keep the funds set up for the Three-Oh-Three carefully concealed to make sure our people are taken care of, but my first plan is to sign on with an old friend of the Colonel's."

The lawyer studied her for a moment.

"There's only one possible person out here you could be talking about," he said quietly. "*Conviction*."

"Captain John Estanza," Kira confirmed.

Captain John Estanza was the commander of the most famous mercenary ship in the Syntactic Cluster. Few even in Apollo would have heard of him, but he commanded the escort carrier *Conviction* and her wing of mercenary nova fighters.

Exactly the type of people that Kira had come out here to become. Except that *Conviction* was a proper warship, built to carry sixty nova fighters in battle. Of course, she was utterly obsolete even by *Apollo* standards, let alone the fourth-rate power that Kira knew had built her, but out there…

"I didn't know Estanza and Moranis knew each other," Simoneit told her. "Though I've never even met Estanza. I'm not sure I could even get you an appointment with him. My connections don't run in that direction."

"The Colonel left me instructions on making contact with Estanza," Kira said. "And it's not like *Conviction* is here right now. I'm not fully into the station net yet, but even *Hopeful Future* would have picked her up in the system."

"It'll be all over the news when she gets in," the lawyer replied. "*Conviction* is quite famous here—and equally unpopular with our politicians. She shipped out ten days ago. I don't know what her mission is, but there's not much in the Cluster that could see her gone for more than two weeks."

The entire Syntactic Cluster was only about forty light-years across. It was a globular group of stars with thirteen habitable planets, all colonized between two hundred and two hundred and fifty years earlier.

The Cluster was a tenth-rate sector with a single ninth-rate power in Redward. But any nova ship could cross the entire sector in two weeks with only one stop to discharge static buildup.

There were a few places *Conviction* could have gone that would take her more than fourteen days for a return trip, but not many. Redward was central to the Cluster. Most ships would make that static discharge stop at the system's gas giant.

"I'll find a hotel room for a few days and keep in touch," Kira told Simoneit. "Can I trust you to handle folding the cash I carried into the main fund?"

"Of course," the lawyer replied. "I'm on retainer for the fund, Em Demirci. Until you run out of money, I am yours to command."

The codicil there wasn't *entirely* heartwarming, but Jay Moranis had trusted the man.

That was enough for Kira. Not that she had a choice.

4

BLUEWARD STATION WASN'T the main anchorage for the Redward Royal Fleet. There was a small military section at the Station, but the docks that Kira was looking at had clearly been designed to host four of the ten-thousand-cubic-meter gunships that were ubiquitous in human space.

Instead, the RRF had rededicated the four docking arrays to handle a much larger ship. The imagery she was playing in her headware came from the main planetary news network, and the final arrangement just looked awkward.

The locals might not know how atrocious the connections Blueward Station had with *Conviction* were. Kira suspected that *Conviction*'s crew did, but that was probably the nature of mercenary work.

Instead of the ship being nestled against the station in a hard lock, flimsy-looking umbilicals had been extended from the ports intended for the smaller ships. The anchoring connection was a series of cables rather than a hard link, but it was enough.

Kira had to assume it was enough, at least, since the carrier hadn't crashed into or fallen away from the station in the five years they'd been operating from there. And in fairness, at seventy-five thousand cubic meters, *Conviction* was the largest ship in the star system by over twenty thousand cubics. The RRF didn't *have* a dock big enough for her.

Now that the carrier had returned to dock, her largest obstacle to meeting with Captain John Estanza was resolved. The bored-looking Redward Royal Fleet Police standing guard over the entrance to the docking section were her next obstacle, and she had a very simple plan to deal with them.

Bored-looking or not, the RRFP grunts reacted to her approach with appropriate competence. They were covering two entrances, but they were within shouting and headware coms range of each other. Two of the three guarding the entrance she approached stepped back into the entrance, a seemingly innocent movement that put them behind cover if she decided to cause havoc.

She suspected the guards at the other entrance were at least *aware* of her presence, as the third guard, an older woman with cold eyes, stepped out to meet her.

Kira saluted the guard immediately and watched the woman struggle with reflexes and guard duty before slowly returning the gesture.

"This is a secure area," the RRFP noncom told her. "How may I help you, Em…"

"Demirci," Kira replied. "Major Demirci, retired, of the Apollo System Defense Force. I need to speak with *Conviction*'s officers."

Carefully controlled, the truth could open a lot of doors.

The noncom was nonplussed for a moment.

"I see. What brings you all the way out here, Major?" she asked.

"I'm looking for work and *Conviction* seems to be a good place for an ex-pilot to start," Kira explained. She glanced at the woman's stripes and hoped her read of the rank was right. "I don't plan on causing trouble, Petty Officer, but I can give you a message to pass on if you'd prefer."

The MP snorted.

"I'd *rather* send you to Fleet HQ," she said. "Why the mercs, if you don't mind my asking?"

"A favor to an old CO," Kira told her. If she hadn't been following Jay Moranis's plan, she probably *would* have been at Redward's Fleet HQ. Assuming she'd made it out this far, that is.

"It ain't my job to say no for Estanza's people," the MP concluded, stepping aside. She gestured in the air, tossing a virtual business card to Kira.

The Apollon pilot caught it and saved the data.

"That's contact info for an officer at HQ," the noncom told her. "If the mercs give you a cold shoulder, give Sean a call. They'll know what we can do for you."

"Thank you, Petty Officer," Kira replied, touched by the gesture. "I appreciate it."

"Go on in," the PO ordered. "I'd wish you good luck, Major, but you'll forgive me for hoping you end up in our uniform, not Estanza's."

"We're all allowed our biases," Kira said with a laugh.

One obstacle down.

THE NEXT OBSTACLE was the actual mercenary security. There was a large loading and mustering bay between the Fleet security perimeter and the docking tubes and umbilicals that connected to *Conviction*.

From this open space, cargo could be loaded onto the ship, fuel and oxygen lines were controlled, and humans would make their way aboard. A proper dock would have had those three tasks running through three different locks, but the impromptu arrangement here led to this single, massively chaotic space.

Kira wasn't even attempting to hide and she made it over halfway across the dock before anyone noticed her. It was still rapidly clear that she never would have made it to a tube linked to the carrier, as several large troopers in mismatched body armor materialized from multiple directions to converge on her.

Their armor had clearly been fabricated to the same pattern once. It was probably even still cross-compatible if needed, but each of the mercenaries had customized the gear to their own desires. All of the sets were missing panels the wearer had regarded as unnecessary. One of the five converging grunts had painted their entire armor black and then added a fiery red dragon on top of it.

None of them had anything she recognized as rank insignia, but they assembled around her with a speed and efficiency she wouldn't have expected from ASDF Marines.

"Who the fuck are you and what the fuck are you doing here?" the dragon-armored mercenary demanded.

"How'd ye even get in he'e?" another mercenary rapidly slurred. Kira recognized the signs of one of the more infamous combat drugs.

"Fleet's supposed to stop gawkers," the dragon agreed. "So, I repeat my friend's question. *How* the fuck did you get in here?"

"My name is Kira Demirci and I need to speak to John Estanza," she said clearly. All of the mercenaries were bigger than her, and their armor was almost certainly proof against the stunner under her coat.

On the other hand, none of them were visibly *armed,* and in the absence of blasters, she was confident she could evade them long enough to escape. No one there was in any great danger...even if *they* thought they were intimidating.

"The Cap'n don' spek to gawk'rs," the drugged merc told her. "G't g'n."

"My friend's a little under the weather," dragon-armor noted. "But he's right. If you haven't booked something with the Skipper, you shouldn't be here. You aren't ours and you aren't welcome."

"I would expect that he'd want to talk to a potential recruit," Kira offered.

She wasn't expecting that to get her in, but she wasn't expecting the response she got. All five of the mercenaries broke into laughter, like she'd said something utterly hilarious.

"You don't have a fucking clue," dragon-armor told her. "And it's *my* job to make sure no one gets aboard *Conviction* without a clue and a reason...and you don't have either."

"Fine," Kira allowed. "But there's a message he needs to hear if you're not letting me on board."

"No deal he'e!"

The combat drugs were designed to speed a fighter up, accelerating their perception of time and sharpening their nerves. That acceleration was what made it hard to speak, but it also gave the fighter an edge on anyone who *wasn't* drugged up.

The trooper had clearly built up enough of a tolerance to the drug to undermine that edge...and it wouldn't have mattered anyway. Of the five, he'd obviously been the one that was going to take a swing, and she'd been waiting for him to take a swing since he'd first spoken.

He had at least fifty centimeters on her and they were both unarmed, so she hit him with the heaviest object immediately to hand: Blueward Station. She caught his fist, ducked into him, and flipped him over her shoulder.

There was a resounding crash as the mercenary thug hit the deck, then silence.

Dragon-armor looked impassively at their soldier, then shrugged.

"I've seen better, but that wasn't shabby," they said. "I'll give the skipper your message if you get off my deck without breaking anyone's limbs, deal?"

"I'm not going to break anyone I don't have to," Kira replied. "Message is simple enough: White Cobra says hello to Gold."

Dragon stared at her blankly.

"Is that supposed to mean something?" they asked.

"To Estanza, at least," Kira replied. "I have your word you'll pass it on?"

"You'd take a mercenary's word?" dragon asked.

"If nothing else, I think you're curious now," the pilot replied.

Dragon-armor laughed again, reaching down to haul their drugged companion up.

"You're not wrong. I don't know what your message means, crazy lady, but I do want to see just what the boss says. Now get off my deck!"

Kira nodded and inclined her head.

Hopefully, curiosity would carry her words to Captain Estanza—because Kira *did* know what the message meant.

At one point, like Jay Moranis, John Estanza had been a legend. He'd been a nova fighter pilot in the same mercenary squadron when they'd rewritten the politics of an entire sector.

The message meant that John Estanza had been Gold Cobra.

KIRA WAS MAYBE HALFWAY BACK to her hotel when a chime sounded in her headware, alerting her to an incoming message. She stepped off to the side of the corridor, removing herself from the rush of the crowd, then accepted the call.

"Demirci," she answered. If it was who she thought it was, there was no point in concealing her identity—and she doubted any assassins had followed her a hundred-plus light years to the back end of civilization.

"You just roughed up one of my guards and convinced one of my hardcases to carry a message for you," a warm male voice replied. "Does that just about cover your activities?"

"That would be one description," Kira conceded. "Who am I talking to?"

The voice didn't sound right to be John Estanza, who she figured to be a similar age to Moranis or Simoneit.

A second chime indicated the person on the other end was requesting a visual link. Kira sighed and tossed a small drone up and activated the link.

If the man on the other end of the call was John Estanza, he'd been piloting nova fighters in his diapers. The stranger was a broad-shouldered black man of her own fortyish age, with close-cropped black hair and a brilliant white smile.

"Commander Daniel Mbeki," the stranger introduced himself. "I run *Conviction*'s fighter wing for the Skipper. He got your message. Which, given Milani's tendency to be an uncooperative hardass, is impressive in itself.

"You told Milani you wanted a job. Boss says he wants to see you, so I guess it's your lucky day."

"Do I make an appointment to see Captain Estanza now?" Kira asked dryly.

"If you want," Mbeki agreed. "Or you could just turn around and come right back. You'll find a warmer welcome this time, I promise."

5

THE MERCENARY in the red-and-black dragon armor was waiting with the RRFP guard when Kira returned to the dock. They didn't do anything so respectful as salute or anything like that, but they clearly acknowledged her as she approached.

"Milani," they introduced themselves. "Mbeki sent me to fetch you. Seems your message meant something to the skipper after all."

"I knew it would," Kira replied. "You have a rank, Milani? A first name?"

The merc grunted and gestured for her to follow them.

"Squad leader, I guess?" they told her as they led the way across the deck and up to one of the boarding tubes. "Think that's what it says on my paycheck, anyway. My grunts call me boss, my boss calls me Milani. Everyone else calls me 'that terrifying fucker with the dragon armor.'"

"It works for me."

Conviction's crew worked very differently from the Apollo System Defense Force, Kira reflected.

"Is your trooper all right?" she asked as they stepped into the boarding tube. There was a momentary skip of the stomach as they moved out of Blueward Station's main gravity field into the tube's local field. A more advanced station would have avoided that.

"Crush? He's fine," Milani confirmed cheerfully. "Probably needed the wake-up call."

"Is he always drugged?" Kira asked. The tube was only a dozen meters long, and she tensed her core muscles as she reached the end. The transition from the station to the tube had been noticeable where it shouldn't have been.

The tube-to-ship transition was *always* noticeable, and she swallowed a moment of queasiness as she made the transition. *Conviction* and Blueward Station were both running ninety percent of a standard gravity, but the variation between the *exact* settings in play were never good for the inner ear.

Milani was clearly used to it, taking Kira's moment of adjustment to consider her question.

"Not always," they finally answered. "Most the time. No one ever surprises him, though. He's too fast."

"You know that will kill him sooner rather than later, right?" she asked as she looked at her surroundings.

She'd known *Conviction* was old, but it was something else to actually stand on her decks. The boarding tube delivered her into a small open space that did double duty as an airlock or a muster point, depending on what it was connected to.

There should have been lockers or something for spacesuits, but the walls were plain. Anything that had been mounted there was long gone, and spots of rust marked where the steel connectors had been.

The hull was a titanium-ceramic matrix that would never rust. Removing the rust stains from the steel add-ons was *possible* but time-consuming. No one on *Conviction* had ever taken the time.

Milani gestured her through the inner airlock door, past a pair of mercenaries in much the same mismatched gear as the grunts on the loading dock, as they considered her question.

"I know spark will kill Crush sooner or later," they admitted. "Our doc knows and occasionally argues with him over it. Starfires, *Crush* knows. He just doesn't care—and so long as he does his job, it's his problem."

That was so far from how Kira had seen subordinates treated in the past that chewing on it kept her silent most of the way to their destination. The state of the ship was enough to keep her attention as well.

When *Conviction* had been built, someone had etched a decorative wave pattern into the decking. Similar things were common to most starships—the ones that didn't have carpet or another deck surfacing, anyway—but here the pattern only showed where people had been walking for the last century and a half.

In the center of the corridors, the pattern had been worn away by thousands of feet. There was no maintenance that could undo that and it added to the general sense of ancient fatigue of the ship.

For all of that, every *system* she saw was in perfect working order. Her headware was flashing up warnings about needing conversion protocols that weren't currently loaded, but the net was *there,* and the physical controls a warship would rely on by preference were there and functional too.

Some of them looked more worn than she'd prefer, but they all looked like they worked.

Milani still used a headware command to open the heavy security door when they reached it. Kira had just enough time to wonder why they were at a security door before she stepped onto *Conviction*'s bridge.

For all of the ship's age, the bridge didn't even look particularly outdated to her. Apollo ships were easily fifty years behind *Conviction*'s builders still, so she'd only have been a century out of date by Apollon standards, and warship bridges rarely changed on the surface.

Two rows of consoles formed a doubled V pointed away from a large viewscreen. A single seat sat on a dais in the central angle, with multiple screens on levered arms around it.

All of those screens were currently in their rest position, and a broad-shouldered black man rose from the captain's seat to greet her.

"Major Demirci," Daniel Mbeki said with a sweeping bow that seemed out of place on the warship bridge.

"I don't recall giving you my rank," Kira noted as she returned the bow with a smile. The man was vaguely ridiculous—but he was a nova fighter pilot. That wasn't out of the norm by any stretch.

"I looked you up while I was waiting," Mbeki replied. "I thought I recognized the name. The Three-Oh-Three made a reputation for themselves. I wouldn't have expected to see one of their squadron commanders out here."

"Our lives don't always give us a choice, do they?" she murmured. She was flattered by his effort, especially since looking up her history this far from Apollo should have been difficult.

"They don't," he confirmed. "The Captain is waiting for you." Mbeki gestured to a door leading off the bridge.

He turned to Kira's escort.

"Milani, get the rest of your squad awake and on the dock," he ordered. "Our friend here might be gorgeous, but she's also got a death mark. While she's on our turf, *nobody* fucks with her. Clear?"

"Clear, sir."

Kira barely concealed a grimace. She'd hoped that information hadn't made it this far.

AT NO POINT in her career in the Apollo System Defense Force had Kira spent any significant time in the office of a carrier's commanding officer. She'd been a squadron commander, subordinate to the Commander, Nova Group. She'd reported to Colonel Moranis as CNG, so her called-on-the-carpet moments had been in the CNG's office.

She was relatively sure John Estanza's office was almost the same as the equivalent space on an Apollon carrier. The walls were the same material as the main hull matrix. If they'd ever been painted or decorated, that had been thoroughly and cleanly removed to leave only bare metal.

There was a wooden bar tucked into one corner of the office and a large metal-and-wood desk in the middle of the space. The quarter-full bottle holding pride of place on the desk should probably have been in the bar.

There were no visible screens, though she thought she spotted several projectors for holographic imaging built into the ceiling. Anything John Estanza did in there, he was doing with his headware.

Right now, he was studying her like someone had delivered him an unwelcome package...and said package was *ticking*. He held a glass of amber liquid in one hand and leaned back in his chair as she came in, leaving Kira a few seconds to study her host and hopeful employer.

Estanza was younger than she'd expected, but that meant he was probably only seventy instead of a hundred. That was solidly middle-aged, even out there, and she could still see that his shoulder-length hair had once been pitch-black.

Now it was streaked with a mix of silver and dirty gray and partially unkempt. A faint smell of liquor filled the room, and it wasn't just coming from the glass in his hand. His eyes were fixated on her but still vaguely unfocused.

The man she'd come all of this way to meet was drunk.

"Sit down, kid," he ordered. He gestured and a chair slid out of a concealed panel and rolled itself across the room to her. "You've got names to conjure with. I have to wonder if you know what the hell they mean."

"Jay Moranis sent me to you," Kira told him. "He thought we could help each other."

Estanza gestured around him.

"I command the most powerful warship for thirty light-years in any direction," he noted dryly. "I'm not sure how much help I need. I might be able to help *you*, but Jay should know my help isn't free.

"How is the old fucker, anyway?"

"Dead," Kira said flatly. "Metastatic cancer induced a brain aneurysm." She considered her next words very carefully. "Despite the situation, it appears to have been natural."

Cancer could be treated. Even once it metastasized, there were medications and treatments for it. They were hard on the body and grew more dangerous with the patient's age. Careful treatment could still have saved Jay Moranis, and that treatment had been underway. But...an only partially controlled cancer could easily have triggered the blood stoppage that had killed him.

It could also have been induced by the Brisingr Shadows. She couldn't be sure—but there had been a full autopsy done per Moranis's will.

Kira had seen the results just before *Future* had novaed out of Apollo. There were no signs of foul play.

But eleven of the Three-Oh-Three's twenty-four pilots were dead.

"Fuck." Estanza stared at her in silence for several seconds, then drained his glass. "Grab a glass from the bar," he ordered.

After a moment's hesitation, Kira obeyed, and the Captain poured them both healthy dollops of the whisky on his desk. His, she noted, was *much* larger.

"To fallen friends," he toasted, and she joined him in swallowing down the whisky. It was better than she'd expected, at least.

"All right," he told her. "It sounds like you and Jay thought there was *someone* who might have tried to kill him. Who? And why?"

"Brisingr Shadows," Kira replied. "Fancifully named covert action group out of the Kaiserreich of Brisingr. They're actively targeting the pilots of the Three-Oh-Three Nova Combat Group, commanded by Colonel Jay Moranis.

"When I left Apollo, eleven of us were dead, including the Colonel. The survivors are supposed to be joining me out here. Hopefully, we're beyond the Shadows' reach here."

"Few people can send covert action teams a hundred light-years away," Estanza agreed. "Of course, a lot of people can send a few million crests that far to hire an assassin or six."

He sighed.

"I owe Jay. Not as much as I once did—fuck knows, the man always could extract blood from a stone where debts and favors were concerned—but I owe him. What do you need, Demirci?"

"There's what I need and what I can offer," she told him. "I *need* jobs and homes for potentially as many as thirteen fully qualified nova pilots."

"Demirci, I have *eight* nova fighters," Estanza pointed out. "Every one of them has a pilot and a copilot. I don't need new—"

"*I* have six nova interceptors," Kira interrupted. "Hoplite-IVs, Apollo's newest and most advanced nova fighter design. They're mine, free and clear with no legal entanglements.

"I'd be prepared to *lease* those ships to you at a reasonable rate, in exchange for you hiring myself and whoever else of the Three-Oh-Three makes it out here to fly them."

The mercenary captain stared at her.

"You stole six of the ASDF's most advanced nova fighters?" he asked, chuckling as he spoke.

"Technically, we illegally purchased six of them from the manufacturer," Kira replied. "All of the paperwork is correct and legally binding, except that the builder wasn't allowed to sell them. Which is irrelevant out here.

"My ownership papers pass Redward legal standards. I checked." She smiled thinly. "I'll hold out hope that I'll have two pilots per fighter, but the truth is that I might not even have that. The Shadows were hunting my people. Hard."

"You realize you don't even *need* me?" Estanza said dryly. "Six nova fighters. Fuck. The Royal Fleet would buy them from you for enough money to set thirteen of you up for life—and *gleefully* hire you to fly them. Or, fuck, you could set up as mercs on your own easily enough."

"I don't trust the RRF," Kira admitted. "I don't trust any planetary government out here. I *did* trust Jay Moranis, and *he* trusted you. He got the fighters, the funds, the flights…everything that got me out here and should get my people out here.

"I owe Jay Moranis my life and he wanted me to work with you. So, here I am."

Estanza leaned back in his chair again, sipping slowly at his whisky this time as he studied her.

"Like I said, that man could always turn a favor into a life debt," he said dryly. "Look, I can use your birds. If I've got the birds, I can use your pilots. But I'm no white knight. I work for Redward because they're the richest system out here, not because I think King Larry is some idealized benevolent monarch who is going to save everything.

"I'm no crusader. I got that out of my system a long time ago when I was Gold Cobra. Today, I take care of my people, I take care of my ship, and I take care of my bank account. Anything else is a bonus, clear?"

"I don't know enough about the Syntactic Cluster to know if King Larry is a hero or a tyrant, sir," Kira told him. "What I know is that the democratically elected government of my oh-so-enlightened home system just sold out the allies I fought and bled for in public—and appears to have sold me and my comrades out in private."

The Apollo Council of Principals' "Agreement on Nova Lane Security" sounded innocent enough, really. What it *did*, despite that innocent name, was surrender control of the trade lanes in the Brisingr-Apollo Sector to the Kaiserreich. It abrogated every treaty of mutual defense Apollo had signed with other systems in the sector and left every other system in the sector to be forced into tributary arrangements with Brisingr or face the Kaiser's fleet's alone.

The Kaiserreich couldn't invade planets—no one really could, not practically—but they could blockade them until they paid tribute. Apollo had stood against them a dozen times, but the "Agreement on Nova Lane Security" said they wouldn't.

So far as Kira was concerned, the Agreement was an outright surrender.

Estanza snorted.

"Right," he conceded. "I'll have Mbeki and Horn draw up the paperwork, but *my* suggestion is that I hire you as a complete squadron. You can have as many pilots as you want and pay them whatever the hell you want.

"I'll pay you a rate that covers six crewed and equipped nova fighters. We'll cover operational expenses and combat repairs. I'll provide ground crew and security, but you can handle your own flight personnel."

"I'll need to see that rate before I agree," Kira countered. It sounded reasonable enough, especially with the cash reserves that Moranis had made sure she had, but she wanted to build up that reserve working for Estanza, not grind it down.

He drained his whisky again and set the glass down.

"All right, Em Demirci," he told her, and grinned. "Jay Moranis taught me mercenary negotiating. Let's see what he taught *you*."

6

THE CONVERSATION that followed didn't take nearly as long as Kira had feared, and she relatively quickly found herself in a *different* office with Daniel Mbeki as they waited for the carrier's admin staff to finalize the contracts.

She'd need to take them back to Simoneit and get some help from the old lawyer in setting up a properly organized mercenary squadron, but they'd sorted out the important details of what *Conviction* would pay to hire her six nova fighters and whatever pilots she found for them.

Estanza filled Mbeki in on the details, then offered Kira his hand.

"I don't know if it will be a pleasure to work with you, Demirci, but I think it's going to be interesting. Daniel will get everything set up."

Without so much as a goodbye after that, the carrier captain left Mbeki's office. His gait was *just* unsteady enough for Kira to be quite sure she'd never misjudged his sobriety.

"Is he okay?" she asked aloud, watching Mbeki out of the corner of her eye.

"He's no worse than he's been at any point in the last twelve years or so," the man told her. "He can still fly rings around most of us when he gets in a fighter."

"Does he do that often?"

"Nah," Mbeki said. "I think he's got a simulator tucked away in his quarters, but he only flies when he feels like it. Most of the time, he lets me run the fighter wing and Zoric runs the ship."

"Zoric?"

"Kavitha Zoric," Mbeki explained. "*Conviction*'s XO and the only other person on this ship who calls themselves Commander." He grinned. "I guess you'll make three of us, though I suppose you can call yourself whatever you want. Your people will be a separate legal entity, though I doubt any of us will remember that after the first week."

"I doubt it," Kira admitted. "*Commander* will do. *Major* would confuse too many people, from the sounds of it." She shook her head. "What *is* the rank structure here?"

"Commander, Department Chief, Pilot, everybody else," the mercenary reeled off. "Zoric and I have a long list of specialities and skills that we pay extra for, but only the Department Chiefs and Pilots get a title. Too many pissing matches when we tried anything more formal."

"Sounds like a recipe for chaos and even more pissing matches to me," Kira told him. "But I was never a mercenary."

"You are now," Mbeki replied. He pulled a physical tablet from inside his desk, a thin piece of transparent ceramic that was updating with information as he looked at it. "Or at least, you will be once the contract is done and signed. We have a template for this; we just haven't used it in a long time."

"You've based other squadrons before?"

"Yeah, back when I was a dumbass kid with fresh wings and an even fresher medical discharge from the Sorvedo Security Patrol, *Conviction* was anchor to four different mercenary squadrons." Mbeki shook his head. "One belonged to the skipper; the other three were independents. As we moved out to the Periphery, we stopped being able to replace ships.

"Two squadrons ended up bailing and going back coreward. Skipper bought out the other. It's been at least fifteen years since we had an independent squad on the deck. I'm not even sure how many people here other than me will remember it!"

"They'll get used to it again," Kira said. "My pilots are coming from Apollo, same as me. We might be mercs now, but we were military."

"We'll make it work." The attractive black man shook his head. "Assuming your people make it out here at all."

"What do you mean?"

A gesture opened a data window in front of her.

"That's a million-crest bounty on *you*, Kira Demirci, specifically," he told her as she read over the details with a sinking heart.

The window was a glorified classified listing, an entry on a set of bounty boards most people wouldn't know existed, let alone have access to. It stated that one million crests, drawn on the Bank of the Royal Crest, had been placed in escrow with an agency in the Ypres System.

Upon validation of video footage or sensor data providing confirmation of death for one Kira Demirci—image and biometric data in an attached file she could readily pull up with a thought—delivered to either the Ypres escrow agency or to the Brisingr embassy in the Ypres System, the funds would be released to the owner of said imagery.

"That, I'll note, is in addition to *this* posting," Mbeki continued.

The first window slid sideways in the air and a second one opened. That one was more generic on the surface, offering payment for the validated death of any member of the ASDF 303 Nova Combat Group.

Names, images, and biometric data attached.

"My gods," she murmured.

"You're on the list for the second posting," the mercenary commander told her. "There's no *dead or alive*, if you were wondering. There's no reward for delivering you or your people alive at all. It's a death mark—a cool quarter-million for any pilot and I'd guess a full million for any of the squadron commanders, though I only saw yours.

"What did you *do*?" he asked.

"We fought them," Kira said quietly. "Apollo and Brisingr have been fighting for a decade, and the Three-Oh-Three served in fourteen battles over the last five years. I've flown against Brisingr's finest and sent more than my fair share of them home in pieces.

"Apollo caved six months ago. *This*"—she gestured at the bounties —"is just one more manifestation of my government's surrender."

"An expensive one for Brisingr," Mbeki told her. "I mean, it's not enough money that anyone I know would court murder charges out here—too many of the Syntactic Cluster's systems still carry the death penalty on the books for murder—but there will be people looking for you and measuring out what they can pull off."

He reached his hand across the desk and squeezed her wrist gently. His fingers were warm and reassuring in a way she hadn't expected.

"While you're on *Conviction* or under contract with us, we've got your back and we'll provide security," he continued. "You're safe with us, Kira. But I figured you needed to know just what you were looking at."

"Thank you," she whispered. She'd known she was being hunted back home, but the sheer impersonality of the illegal bounty was painful. In Apollo, at least, she was being hunted by people *from* Brisingr. Here? She'd apparently just get killed for a paycheck.

"And on that morbid note, it looks like our contract is finally written up," Mbeki said with an obviously forced grin.

"I'll need to go over it with a lawyer and get the squadron officially set up," Kira told him. "I'll need a day or so."

"Right." The black man's lips thinned in thought—clearly *unpleasant* thought. "Technically, we're not responsible for your security until you're working for us, but we all know that's happening.

"I'll have Milani send a grunt with you. Redward mostly has Blueward locked down, but for the amount of money your old friends have put on the barrel, I'm willing to put some of *our* cash on the line to make sure you make it to joining up!"

7

EVEN IN A LAW OFFICE, physical paperwork was a thing of the past. The contracts and paperwork that Kira were shuffling through were all digital, a mix of holograms projected by the imaging systems in Simoneit's office and data fed directly into her headware.

All of it boiled down to one simple point: once Kira Demirci authorized it all, she would become *Commander* Kira Demirci, sole shareholder and director of Memorial Squadron Limited Liability Corporation.

Memorial Squadron would absorb all of the funds held by Simoneit, providing it with an enviable operating reserve. According to the "papers" Kira was reviewing, her contribution of the six Hoplite-IVs was valued equally to the cash infusion from Jay Moranis.

There was a contract in there that specified that she would hire all survivors of the ASDF 303 Nova Combat Group in exchange for the cash infusion and specified share allowances for those survivors.

"Even if all twelve other pilots survive and make it out here, the fighters were entirely your legal possessions," Simoneit told her as she paused on the sections laying out the ownership proportion of the company and the projected ownership as the rest of the pilots made it out there.

"With three squadron commanders and ten pilots surviving at last report, I allocated ten percent of the funds Colonel Moranis provided to each commander and seven percent to each junior pilot," the lawyer continued. "Since the fighters constitute fifty percent of the opening capital, your minimum ownership would be fifty-five percent, leaving you in full control of Memorial Squadron."

"I'm not sure I trust my people that little," Kira said slowly. Counting the fighters for half the capital, that meant each commander would own five percent of the company and each pilot would own three and a half percent.

"It's not about trust," the lawyer said. "It's about security. Trust but verify, always. This means that if any of the pilots show up and don't want to fly for you, you can buy them out easily enough without risking them causing problems in the operations.

"I'll continue to act as your agent here in Redward and can make sure any arrivals are taken care of if you're out of the system with *Conviction*."

He shrugged.

"The value of the Hoplite-IVs is probably conservative, Em Demirci," Simoneit told her. "You *need* to be certain that you are in full legal control of those spacecraft at all points in time."

"True enough," Kira agreed with a sigh. She scanned through the last few sections and nodded one last time.

"I authorize all documents, authenticate," she said aloud.

"Validate identity for the documentations," a softly female computerized voice replied.

"I am Kira Margaret Demirci, born in Vendel on Apollo, March Seventeenth, Two Thirty Six After Landing," she told the computer. "Data authentication transmitted."

That came automatically from her headware. The computers spoke for less than a second, then the law office's machine beeped happily.

"Identity validated; authorization authenticated. All documents updated and transferred to your headware."

"Congratulations, Commander Demirci," Simoneit told her. "I look forward to working with you on a continued basis as legal counsel for Memorial Squadron."

"Your first job for that is to make contact with *Conviction*'s legal counsel," Kira replied. "I want to have a separate legal team than

Estanza has, but you'll need to talk to his." She waved at the files still hovering in the air.

"If nothing else, we need to make sure that they have copies of all of this. Technically, the contract right now is between *Conviction*'s LLC and me. We'll want that revised."

"Already underway, Commander," he promised. "I expect you to be paying me a *lot* of money over the next few years, but I hope to provide you with far more value from your investment than you expect."

"That shouldn't be hard," Kira said dryly. "My expectations of lawyers are low."

"I think we'll change your mind on that," Simoneit told her. "And to start on that process, I put some feelers out into the station net. A Melissa Cartman and a Sandip Nicastro arrived on a nova freighter two hours ago. They're both on the list for Three-Oh-Three pilots and arrived together, so I'm guessing you may want to meet up with them?"

"Mel and Sandip made it?" she asked, swallowing a loud sigh of relief. "Where are they?"

"They just checked into a hotel two decks down from yours. Catch the address."

Kira caught the data snippet out of the air and nodded her thanks.

"I think I need to be on my way, Em Simoneit," she told him. "Thank you."

"It's my pleasure, Commander," he replied, then smiled and offered his hand. "With the amount of money you've already paid me, I think you call me Pree."

"Then you can call me Kira, Pree," she said.

8

THE HOTEL SIMONEIT'S address brought her to was significantly less nice than her own. It was a serviceable-enough place for spacers between jobs, the kind of place you stayed when you were *hoping* to have somewhere to end up but didn't know how long you'd be waiting.

The lobby was floored in the kind of hard-serving laminate that looked the same in every star system. The chairs and couches tucked against one wall were new but cheap. They were probably comfortable enough, but they readily showed their lack of pedigree.

"Hi! Are you looking to rent a room with the Blueward Green Star Hotel?" an excessively cheerful holographic receptionist asked. "If you require other services, I may be able to assist you or can connect you with a superior agent."

Superior agent did not, Kira reflected, necessarily mean human. In a place like this, it probably meant exactly what it said: a more capable artificial stupid that could handle more complex queries but cost the Green Star more money to turn on.

"I need to pass a message to either Melissa Cartman or Sandip Nicastro," Kira told the stupid. "I'd prefer immediate, but I can leave a recording."

"I'm sorry, Green Star Hotel policy does not allow me to identify clients of the hotel," the hologram told her in the same cheerful tone.

"I don't need you to identify them, just to pass on the message if they *are* here," the Commander said with a concealed sigh. Unless Redward stupids were *much* dumber than their Apollon counterparts, it should be able to do that.

"Oh." The stupid chewed on that for longer than any computer should have to. "I can do that!"

"Tell whichever of them you can get ahold of that Kira is on the station and looking to make contact," Kira told the hologram. A flick of her fingers gave the stupid her contact information. "That's all they really need."

"Of course. Thank you."

The stupid was…exactly what the name implied. With a sigh, Kira gave the image a nod and turned to leave.

At which point, of course, she almost collided with Sandip Nicastro. The younger of the two pilots she was looking for was only a few centimeters taller than her, a compact dark-skinned man with a ready smile.

"Kira!" he exclaimed. He started to reach to hug her, then paused. "We still on hugging terms?" he asked.

"You dolt." Kira swept the man into her own arms. She'd had to smack him down once for trying to seduce her, but that had been a matter of policy rather than dislike. Nicastro and Cartman had an open relationship. Cartman had slept her way through every available man in the 303, and Nicastro had slept his way through every available woman.

But she'd been their squadron commander, which had made his casual pass entirely out of line. That didn't mean she didn't *like* that solidly built man. Just that she couldn't *sleep* with him.

"You and Mel made it okay?" she asked as she released him.

"Nothing like the luxurious accommodations of the ASDF, but, well…" Nicastro shrugged. "The first few systems were the worst. Given everything home *did* give up, I wouldn't have expected to be dodging MPs for as long as we were."

Nicastro and Cartman were neither senior enough nor close

enough to the end of their enlistment terms to be released early. Their presence in Redward was active desertion.

An active desertion Kira couldn't regret, given that the ASDF had been failing to protect their fellow pilots from *assassins*.

"We made it in the end," he concluded. "But we're not bearers of good news. Hughes and Espinoza are both dead. Nova freighter they were on was jumped by 'pirates' in the Sicario System. No survivors."

Kira closed her eyes in a hard wince. That was two more of the 303 dead—and Yngve Hughes had been another of the squadron commanders.

And the loss of a nova freighter meant that the Shadows had killed at least ten other people to kill them.

"What a damn mess," she said aloud. "Did you touch base with anyone else?"

"We were all keeping our routes pretty quiet, even from each other," Nicastro admitted. "I saw the news report with the name list when we passed through Sicario; otherwise, I wouldn't even have known about them."

"Commander," her escort's voice rumbled. "I'm guessing this one's okay?"

There was some amusement in the armored mercenary's voice as Kira released her old subordinate and turned an eye on her bodyguard.

"Sandip Nicastro, this is my current minder, Jerzy Bertoli," she introduced the two men. "He's a ground-pounder off the carrier *Conviction*. I'm under contract with Em Bertoli's captain."

"That's good to hear," Nicastro said. "Got space for two more?"

Kira grinned.

"My contract says I'm to provide six nova fighters *with* pilots and I'm short five pilots. You're damn right I've got space for you and Mel."

She could *see* the tension release from Nicastro's shoulders. Kira had been Moranis's main protégé, which meant she'd been the one with most of the information. Her understanding was that the other Majors had enough to at least track down Simoneit, but there'd been a lot of pieces to the old man's plan.

The pilots had only known to get out there and look for the squadron commanders.

"That's what I needed to hear, I think," Nicastro murmured. "I kept telling Mel everything was going to be fine…but this place is as cheap as I could find in space, and I *know* how long we can afford it for."

"I can front you money if you—"

"DOWN! Both of you get do—"

Bertoli's shouted warning wasn't fast enough. Blaster fire crackled in the plain hotel lobby and a large horse kicked Kira in the back of her long leather jacket. She crumpled to her knees with the impact and stared in horror as Nicastro collapsed against her.

The other pilot hadn't been wearing armor of any kind.

KIRA LET herself fall to the ground with the impact of the blaster bolt. Her jacket could take one hit, but she wasn't confident about *more* than one.

It also took her a critical few seconds to take her attention from Sandip Nicastro. His eyes were glazing over even as they hit the ground together, and a strong smell of burning pork began to fill the air. The other pilot had probably been dead before he'd fallen into her, let alone before they'd hit the floor.

More blaster-fire flashed over her as Bertoli scrambled away from them, cursing loudly as he cleared his own weapon. The mercs were obedient enough to local law that they didn't carry blasters on the station—but Kira would almost *rather* be shot with a blaster than the bead carbine Bertoli produced.

A blaster bolt splattered across the mercenary's armor and then Bertoli opened fire. The carbine was a *far* faster-firing weapon than the blasters their assailants had opened up with, and Bertoli walked his fire across the lobby as Kira finally began to take in the area again.

Four hooded figures had stepped into the lobby while she'd been talking to Nicastro. Each of them had produced a concealed blaster, a stubby energy weapon slightly larger than the sleek carbine the merc was carrying.

Blaster bolts had made a mess of the lobby, with several portions of the wall clearly punctured and others on fire. There was a *reason* blasters were restricted on space stations.

One of the killers took a burst from the bead carbine to the chest, their wavering stance suggesting that they were wearing body armor of their own. The beads, designed not to risk the station, would suffer against any kind of defenses—and while Bertoli's armor had already shrugged off several blaster bolts, it couldn't do that much longer.

Using Nicastro's body as cover, Kira dug for her own weapon. It wouldn't be *much* better against armor than Bertoli's, but she should have the advantage of surprise.

Bertoli, on the other hand, clearly had the advantage of augmented hand-eye coordination. The masks the killers were wearing were designed to thwart facial recognition software.

They were *not* designed to thwart six-round bursts of glass beads. The merc's target's head *exploded* into a spray of blood, brains and fabric.

He had to keep moving as the killers focused on him. He'd made himself a target by engaging, which Kira had to appreciate. He had to think she was dead, after all.

With all three shooters focused on her bodyguard, she had a moment to program their locations into her headware. She didn't quite have the level of augmentation Bertoli had for this, but she made up for it with Apollon military-grade combat software.

She rose from under Nicastro's body and fired three times. Her bead pistol—acquired after Simoneit told her not to carry a blaster—was smaller than Bertoli's carbine but made up for it by firing much larger glass beads.

Two of her targets went down as her shots shattered their faces and sent glass shards into their brains. The third had turned at the wrong time, and her bead shattered on the combination of lightly armored hood and tough skull.

Then Bertoli emptied the rest of his magazine into the killer's head. It would have taken *much* heavier armor to survive that.

As the gunfire slowed, Kira finally noticed the chattering of the holographic receptionist, demanding—in the same bright, cheerful voice—that everyone stop fighting and telling them that the police had been called.

"I need to take care of my friend," Kira said quietly. "Do we need to avoid the cops?"

"Self-defense," Bertoli told her, grimacing at an unseen injury. "Plus, no offense, Commander, but I got shot a lot more than you did, and armor or no armor, I'm not going *anywhere* quickly."

9

THE STATION POLICE were at least fast. Kira didn't know when exactly the artificial stupid had actually called them, but they were in the hotel lobby within minutes. And since the stupid had even managed to get across that there was blaster fire involved, they were there in force.

She had to salute the first wave of responders. There were half a dozen of them, probably the six closest cops, and they were wearing nothing but regular patrol gear and wielding the bead pistols they carried as backups to their stunners.

The next wave had blasters and real armor, but the first wave had none of that. Their patrol gear would have held up better than her leather jacket, and that was about *all* she could say for it.

"You knew the victim?" one of the cops finally asked Kira, gesturing to Nicastro.

"He and I served together in Apollo," she replied. She sighed. "They were targeting me, too. There's supposedly a bounty on our heads."

"And you shot them," the cop asked after she made some gestures in the air, clearly making notes on an invisible screen.

"Em Bertoli is my bodyguard, via a contracted arrangement with

Conviction Mercenary Ops LLC," Kira told the cop. "He shot two of them, I shot the other two."

She gestured at where a white sheet was being pulled over her friend.

"I think it's evident we didn't shoot first, but I'll do whatever is needed," she said quietly. "Em Bertoli's actions were my responsibility."

"Sandip!"

Mel's cry cut through the entire lobby like a knife as she finally arrived. Two of the cops moved to block the dark-haired woman, and Kira held up a hand.

"That's her boyfriend," she said sadly, blinking back tears as she gestured at Nicastro's body. "The killers were probably looking for her, too."

They might not even have known Kira was there. They'd been coming for Nicastro and Cartman, not her. They'd probably thought that they'd lucked out when they recognized her.

"Paid killers," the detective interviewing her snarled, shaking his head. "Mercs are one thing, Em Demirci, but this...this isn't supposed to happen in civilized places!"

Kira kept her opinion of Redward's level of civilization to herself as she dropped to her knees next to Cartman.

"Hey, Mel," she whispered. "It's Kira. I'm here."

"What happen... *How*? Why?" The blonde pilot was a head taller than Kira, but she folded over into Kira's shoulder like her strings had been cut.

"Brisingr," Kira said flatly. "The Shadows put a death mark on us all. Even this far out."

"Em Demirci?" the detective said quietly. "I need you and Em Bertoli to come back to the precinct with me. We'll be moving the bodies as well, so if Em...?"

"Cartman," the sobbing pilot got out. "He was my..."

"We know, Em Cartman," the cop told her. "Em Demirci told us. You can stay with him if you'd like? We'll take good care of him either way, I promise."

"I...I...I don't know," Cartman whispered, and a chilly stone sank into Kira's stomach.

They'd come this far and they *still* hadn't outrun their enemies. *Conviction* needed to be the safe haven Moranis had promised, or this wasn't the last of her friends she was going to have to grieve.

"Stay with me, Mel," she told Cartman. "I've got a place for all of us when we're done with the fine police officers, but I don't want you out of my sight."

And unless Estanza actively kicked them out, neither of the women was sleeping on Blueward Station that night.

SEVERAL PEOPLE INTERCEPTED them at the police sector precinct. Kira hadn't been expecting any of them, so her arrival met with a series of surprises.

First, Milani caught up with them at the entrance with four more mercenaries. As a courtesy to the station rules and the fact they were in a police station, their weapons were obviously slung and were bead carbines, not blasters.

They were still slung on the *front* of the mercenaries' armor, easily to hand.

The detective didn't even blink as she walked up to them.

"You don't get to take them back until I've released them," she told Milani calmly. "You *may* accompany them into the station. Is there going to be a problem?"

The mercenary in the red dragon armor snorted aloud.

"Not yet," they replied. "Not yet. Fall in, people."

Bertoli was on a hover-stretcher by this point. He'd stopped complaining about a second after the paramedic had started the painkillers.

"We need to take this man to a clinic," the paramedic pointed out. "The precinct isn't the right place to examine him."

The merc half-groaned.

"Five blaster bolts," he told the medic. "Four bruised, one cracked rib." He paused as the medic stared at him questioningly. "What? I have internal medware. Not going to turn down some bone-knit and I could use laying down for a day, but I'll be fine."

"Take him to the clinic," the detective ordered. "He's not a prisoner. You." She turned to Milani. "Send *one* trooper with him. All right?"

"Wong."

It wasn't really an order, but one of the troopers stepped to join the paramedic anyway. The white-uniformed man looked up at the merc silently, then shrugged.

"Follow me."

The second surprise took that moment to emerge from the precinct station. A gauntly tall young woman in a matching white suit to Simoneit's stepped out of the doors and offered the detective her hand.

"Detective Mayes? I am Leticia Davids from Simoneit and Partners Law," she introduced herself. "I'm here on behalf of Commander Demirci and Em Melissa Cartman."

She paused, glancing over at Kira, who was still supporting Cartman. The pilot was slightly more coherent now, but she was still quietly weeping.

"That is assuming that Commander Demirci wants me to represent Em Cartman?" she asked.

"Please," Kira instructed. "I don't believe she's in any trouble."

"From my read of His Majesty's self-defense laws, I don't believe *you* are in any trouble, Commander," Davids replied. "Is she, Detective Mayes?"

The cop grunted.

"It's pretty open-and-shut, yes, but I *do* need to book Em Demirci and get contact information, biometrics and a statement," Mayes replied. "As you well know."

"Of course," Davids confirmed. "I'll be with her the entire way, just in case."

The detective grunted again.

"The only people in trouble here are so thoroughly dead, we're doing fingerprint and DNA analysis to ID them," she pointed out. "Em Demirci just needs to give a statement."

"That is, of course, *Commander* Demirci's civic duty," Davids replied.

Kira concealed a snort of her own. She could get used to Simoneit and his partners being at her back. They were handy.

"As soon as you give that statement, Commander, I think we need to get you and Cartman back to *Conviction*," Milani interjected. "You appear to attract too much attention for me to be comfortable without surrounding you with armed guards."

"Right now, Milani...those armed guards sound *fantastic*."

10

MBEKI WAS WAITING when Kira returned aboard *Conviction*. Kira's already-positive impression of the man was improved dramatically by his immediately wrapping Mel Cartman in a blanket and checking her for shock symptoms before saying a word to Kira.

"Em Cartman, I would like to have you checked over by our ship's doctor," he finally told her. "You're not under contract to us, so you don't have to, but I think you're edging into shock and need the check-over."

"I can come with you," Kira offered immediately.

Cartman inhaled sharply and pulled the blanket tighter around herself.

"I can manage, I think," she half-whispered. "Can the big guy come with me?"

She was indicating Milani, who snorted.

"I'd normally complain about *guy*," they observed dryly. "But today, I'll let it slide."

In answer to Cartman's question, the merc scooped her off the ground, blanket and all. Cradling her like a baby, Milani gave Kira and Mbeki a firm nod.

"I'll get her to the doc and to a set of pilot's quarters afterwards," they promised. "She'll be safe."

Kira and Mbeki watched as the mercenary carried Cartman away, and Mbeki coughed slightly.

"I think you might be a good influence on them," he murmured. Then, more loudly to the mercs around them: "Troopers! Fall in and secure the door. Nobody who isn't ours or scheduled enters the dock, let alone boards the ship, without it being run past me, Commander Zoric or the Captain. Clear?"

"Clear."

The mercenaries might not go in for much spit and polish, but Kira had no real concerns about their competence. Anyone who tried to get aboard the carrier was going to have a *very* bad day.

"Demirci, walk with me?" Mbeki asked.

She fell in beside him as he led the way deeper into the ship.

"Our counsel says all of the paperwork is complete," he told her. "I've told my people to stand by for your fighters to come aboard tomorrow, but that's down to you."

"Tomorrow is good," Kira agreed. "I'll be glad to see them out of the boxes. Been a while since I was in a nova fighter…and out here, they're the closest thing I have to home."

"I know that feeling," the mercenary agreed. "I'm from the Sorvedo System, and if you've even *heard* of it, I'd be shocked."

She considered the name for a moment before shaking her head.

"I can't say I have."

"Dependency of the Principality of Breslau," Mbeki told her. "My mother served in the big war in the Griffon Sector." He snorted. "The one we lost, at least partially due to Cobra Squadron."

He was trying to distract her. He was even mostly succeeding, but that didn't mean Kira wasn't aware of what he was doing.

She'd done it herself often enough, after all. The 303 hadn't made it through fourteen battles without losing anyone.

"How'd you end up with Estanza, then?" she asked.

"He was in the region with *Conviction* twenty years ago, doing work for one of the shipping combines Griffon set up after the war," Mbeki told her, waving open a door as they reached what Kira realized was the flight officers' quarters. "I'd just been medically discharged from the Sorvedo Security Patrol, but I had my wings and could fly a nova fighter.

"One of his people decided to retire there, and I was looking for a berth that would put me in a bird." He shrugged. "Everybody won."

The mercenary Commander came to a halt and gestured to a door.

"Here, these will be your quarters. Even with you aboard, we're running two instead of ten squadrons, so we've got squadron commander quarters to spare." He grinned. "I had my people make sure everything was cleaned and working, but they'll be pretty bare. No one's stayed in these rooms in ten years."

"I appreciate it," she said quietly. "Thank you, Commander."

"We're going to be working together, Commander," he told her. "If I'm going into battle with you on my wing, I want you and your people at your best. We'll touch base in the morning as your ships come aboard.

"Cartman will be okay," he continued. "Ailin—Dr. Devin—is a damn fine doctor and he's familiar with shock and grief."

"She's not with us yet," Kira pointed out.

"I know. We'll take care of her either way," Mbeki said. "Don't worry; we'll bill you if Ailin does anything expensive."

She chuckled and thought-clicked the door open. What she could see of the room on the other side was as plain as she'd been warned, but it looked functional enough.

"Thank you, Commander," she said softly. She wasn't talking about the room or Cartman now, and from the way he was looking at her, he got that.

"Please, call me Daniel," he told her. He squeezed her shoulder gently. "But you should rest."

"You're right," she conceded. "But *you* should call me Kira."

He smiled, white teeth flashing brilliantly against his dark skin.

"I can do that, Kira," he promised. "*If* you rest!"

THE QUARTERS WERE LACKING in just about *anything* in terms of amenities, but the mattress had been replaced, and modern self-clean- ing, self-adjusting mattresses were hard to make *un*comfortable. Dreams still bothered Kira, but she woke well rested and studied the space she was resting in.

There wasn't a single piece of furniture that wasn't built into the walls, but a squadron commander's quarters were still a forty-square-meter two-room apartment. Most of that space was the combined workspace and day room with the built-in kitchenette and desk workstation.

The chime from her headware connecting to the coffeemaker was the most glorious sound she'd heard in some time. That had probably been the main thing Mbeki's people had made sure was working, spacers being spacers.

Coffee carried through her issuing the transfer orders to get her nova fighters loaded aboard *Conviction*, but as the cup ran out, she interrogated *Conviction*'s systems to find out where Cartman was.

Even compared to Apollon hardware, *Conviction*'s gear was slow. On the other hand, the ship happily confirmed its own history to her: the carrier was a hundred and sixty-seven years old.

She'd been built for the Starmichael System, a Meridian power seven hundred light-years from Apollo, as a third-tier carrier. She'd served for thirty years and been sold to the Republic of Florin, a star system three hundred light-years inward from Apollo but about thirty degrees around the "rim" of human space.

After serving Florin for over a hundred years, she'd been sold to Estanza thirty years ago. Kira—and Daniel Mbeki, for that matter—had been a teenager when John Estanza had founded his mercenary company.

With the codes Mbeki had given her, she convinced the old ship to disgorge the code-conversion protocols her headware needed to interface with its systems. That was enough for her to sort out that Dr. Devin had sent Mel Cartman to the mess nearest to the infirmary.

A moment's more checking confirmed that there was only one mess running on the carrier. She'd been designed with two enlisted messes, a noncom mess and an officers' mess...but only the larger enlisted mess was being run.

With her weapons stripped when Florin had sold her and only eight fighters aboard instead of sixty, *Conviction* was running at barely forty percent of her list crew. The computers happily flagged that almost a third of the ship was currently locked down—and if Kira read the data correctly, some of those sections had been emptied of air and left in vacuum.

She'd *definitely* seen better days, but those eight nova fighters alone made *Conviction* one of the most powerful warships in the Syntactic Cluster.

For now, Kira didn't need to make any guesses about where Cartman was. If the other Apollon woman was eating, there was only one place she could be!

———

"KIRA!"

Cartman sounded better, at least. Kira suspected the other woman was putting on a brave face as much as anything, but that brave face could be helped with proper headware programming.

Any competent doctor knew to be careful with that kind of headware code, and any sane person knew not to mess with it themselves, but it could certainly help. Right now, it seemed to be keeping Cartman on a level keel as she rose from her breakfast to give Kira a quick hug.

"I'm sorry about Sandip," Kira said quietly as she took a seat at the table.

The redheaded young man at the table took a look at them both and smiled brightly.

"I'm Dr. Devin," he introduced himself to Kira. "I'll leave you two to your chat. If you need me, Em Cartman, the ship can contact me from anywhere until you leave us. If you leave us, that is."

"Thank you."

The ship's doctor vanished with surprising speed, leaving Kira chuckling and shaking her head.

"There goes a medic who understands when friends can do better than doctors," she said aloud. "I know you're not okay, Mel. What do you need?"

Cartman exhaled slowly.

"I don't know yet," she admitted. "Fuck, I don't even know what Sandip's will says or what was even left. We..." She trailed off.

"*You* left Apollo in decent shape," Cartman finally resumed. "Officially resigned, cashed out your pension, the works. *We* ditched an ASDF shuttle during a refueling stop on the edge of the system. We're deserters. Might not be time of war, but that still doesn't feel right and ASDF Command still doesn't like it."

"Sandip said it was hard," Kira agreed. "Fuck, I didn't know any of us were being followed, Mel. I knew there was a death mark on us all, but I didn't expect someone to open fire in a hotel lobby!"

"Who would?" the other woman asked. "I'm glad you found a place out here, but I'm still swinging at loose ends. Sandip was trying to keep me from realizing how short we were running on money, but he was never that good a liar."

"You came out here," Kira pointed out. "What did the old man give you as directions?"

"Get to Redward and look for you or one of the squadron commanders," Cartman told her. "And Hughes is *dead*."

"So Sandip told me." The newly fledged mercenary shook her head. "*My* job out here, Mel, was to set up a place for everyone to run to. I'm under contract with *Conviction*, but not as a pilot."

The younger woman made a "go ahead" gesture. She looked tired, her brave front cracking.

"I'm contracted with them as commander in my own right of a mercenary nova fighter squadron," Kira told her old subordinate. "I have six Hoplite-IVs coming aboard today, but the only pilot I've got is me.

"I need five more. The rest of the Three-Oh-Three is coming out here, but you're the one I've got today. You don't have to decide right now—and there's wheels to make sure you're taken care of if you aren't willing to fly for—"

"I'm in," Cartman cut her off. "Are we going after Sandip's killers?"

Kira sighed.

"They're dead," she pointed out. "And we can't go after Brisingr. We're a long damn way from home, Mel. We have to take the fact that the fuckers who shot him got shot themselves as enough.

"You still in?"

"I've got no money and my only skill is flying a nova fighter," Cartman replied. "I suppose I could go fly a shuttle or sign on with the locals to fly a sub-fighter, but I need *something* to keep a roof over my head.

"I know you, Demirci. I've flown for you before. I've got to fly for *somebody*, so I'll fly for you."

Kira chuckled.

"All right," she told her subordinate. "Looks like the only title you get around here is *pilot*, but catch."

She tossed Cartman the contract.

"Read that, sign it, and you work for me again," she told the other woman.

"Three and a half percent of the company?" Cartman replied. Headware made processing a twenty-six-page contract *fast*. "That's a bit of a signing bonus."

"The money that's underwriting the squadron was the old man's," Kira explained. "He sent it out here to take care of *all* of us, not just me."

"All right." Cartman tossed the contract back to Kira. "Looks like I work for you again, boss. What do we do first?"

"Welcome aboard, Memorial-Two," Kira said with a chuckle. "First things first, our fighters should be arriving later this morning. So we eat, we talk to Commander Zoric to sort out quarters for you, and then we go say hi to our nova fighters."

Kira also needed to check if any more of her people had arrived. Right now, though, she needed eggs, toast…and to touch the starfighters she was going to risk life and limb inside.

If she was unreasonably lucky, *Conviction*'s mess might actually produce an edible breakfast.

11

LOCALIZED gravity control allowed for a fifteen-hundred-cubic-meter box massing the better part of a thousand tons to be simply *floated* down the middle of *Conviction*'s main fighter landing deck. A harness of small rockets had been rigged onto the crate before it had been brought aboard, but most of the control was being exerted by reducing the gravity under it to zero.

"And…down."

Kira stepped up behind the woman giving the orders and studied them for a moment. Her headware said the broad-shouldered chief of the deck was named Angel Waldroup and went by "she."

Given that Kira's first assumption, at least from behind, would have been to assume Waldroup was a man, she was rather grateful for the fact that her headware was talking to *Conviction*'s net enough to avoid that kind of misstep.

"Chief Waldroup?" she asked.

"Boss Waldroup," the woman grunted back in correction. "No chiefs aboard *Conviction*, Commander Demirci. I'm a department head, and that's a bloody useless title, isn't it?"

"Boss Waldroup, then," Kira conceded. "Any questions on getting the fighters out?"

"Standard storage and transport units," Waldroup replied.

"Designed by SolFed three bloody centuries ago. Nobody in the Periphery or the Rim uses anything else." She shrugged massive shoulders.

"I know the damn box, Commander. Your babies will be fine." The "boss" left Kira behind to cross over to the now-settled ten-meter-tall crate.

Kira followed along, unable to keep herself from hovering as Waldroup flicked the codes for the crate to its systems.

The front of the crate slid up and over the top under its own power, revealing exactly what she'd been expecting. Nova fighters traveled in one piece, but they didn't travel fully loaded or on their own.

"Parts fabricator, there," Waldroup said calmly, clearly checking through a mental list. "Detached plasma cannons, there. Refueling and recharging interfaces, there. Fighter itself, there."

The ten-meter-square and fifteen-meter-deep crate had plenty of space for extra storage. Most of the gear that Waldroup was checking off was embedded in a storage matrix underneath the nova fighter that filled half the container.

A storage matrix that Kira was halfway up before she even realized what she was doing. The storage matrix continued into the top half of the storage container, but it went from being a solid block with cutouts for the gear to arching straps and struts that held the Hoplite-IV in place.

The landing deck was brightly lit—there were two more storage crates floating along the deck while Kira was poking at the nova fighter— and even the storage matrix wasn't enough to conceal the gleaming white hull of a factory-new spaceship.

The Hoplite-IV was a deadly-looking wedge of metal with edges that were only smooth at close range. It averaged three meters thick across its length, tapering from an only barely flattened tip to a ten-meter-wide base fifteen meters back.

The access hatch to the fighter itself was covered by the storage matrix, but Kira still laid her hands on the familiar white metal.

"We *do* need to start pulling the birds *out* of the boxes, Commander," Waldroup shouted up from the ground five meters below her. "And it's easier for you to poke around inside her once I've got her on the ground."

"Fair enough," Kira conceded with a chuckle. "I had to touch her myself. Even seeing the boxes, I wasn't quite sure I believed we'd managed to get them out here."

Climbing down took longer than climbing up had, but her heart felt lighter than it had in months. The fighters were there.

"We'll pull them out, install the guns, make sure the fabricators are in our workshops and hooked up to *Conviction*. None of it will be a problem," Waldroup assured her. "Are we keeping them white? Any insignia?"

Kira glanced at where Cartman was approaching the crates in a more sedate fashion and grinned at the deck boss as she dropped to the ground.

"We'll keep them white for now," she told Waldroup. "I'm guessing your people paint them?"

"Whatever the pilot asks for," the deck boss replied. "If you *want* 'em military-standard, I can do that. Squadron, call sign, kill markers?"

"Let's stick with that for now," Kira ordered. "Here."

She tossed the deck boss an image from her old Hoplite-IV back in ASDF service.

"Squadron number gets swapped out for the Memorial Squadron name, but the rest can stay," she told the deck boss.

Waldroup was studying the image she'd sent over.

"Wait, you only have three kills?" she asked. "I thought you'd been a fighting pilot for years."

Kira saw Cartman laugh and gestured to the other woman.

"To avoid bragging, how about you explain it, Mel?" she asked.

Waldroup turned and saw the other pilot.

"All right," she allowed. "It'll stop me having to talk *both* of you down off of boxed fighters!"

"Apollo is a pacifistic culture, by aspiration if not necessarily reality," Cartman told the deck boss. "But fighter pilot tradition says we're aces after three kills and paint the fighter hulls with kill markers.

"ASDF didn't want to glorify killing that much, but they compromised by letting us paint *up to* three markers on the hulls to mark aces. So..." The pilot shrugged. "We color-coded them. Black is one kill. Three black dots says you're an ace.

"Green is two kills. Replace the black dots as you go, count up to six. Orange is four kills. Blue is eight. Red is sixteen."

Cartman shrugged. "Supposedly, purple is thirty-two and yellow is sixty-four, but I've never seen anyone with yellow or purple kill markers."

"Sub-fighters count as half and full nova ships under twenty thousand cubics count as one," Kira concluded.

She knew that the dots she'd given Waldroup were red, blue and orange. The deck boss was clearly doing the math and looked up at her questioningly.

"Eighteen nova fighters, twelve sub-fighters, three gunships and a partial kill on a cruiser," she listed quietly. "I was one pilot out of twenty-four that took out the cruiser, so we all got counted for a single kill-equivalent."

"Okay," the deck boss exhaled. "You want your kill markers or mine?"

"We'll keep Memorial Squadron on Apollo markers for now," Kira told her. "If someone wants to assume I'm a 'mere' ace, I'd rather disabuse them of that notion when it's *far* too late."

The deck boss snorted.

"Makes sense to me. I'll have your birds out and prepped in a few hours. Any idea who's flying them yet?"

"Cartman will be my number two," Kira replied. "I'm heading back stationside to look for the others in a few. Think you'll have my bird ready for a test flight by this evening?"

"Do rocks fall in gravity?" Waldroup asked. "You'll be good to go."

KIRA RAN into Mbeki before she left the fighter bay area, the other Commander looking even darker than usual, with grease smeared over his skin and down a rumpled gray ship-suit.

"What happened to you?" she asked him.

"I like to keep my hand in on the guts of my fighter," he told her. "My nova drive was having some frequency issues, so I was helping my techs track it down." He grinned, the brilliant expression warming Kira's soul a little bit.

"That doesn't normally involve getting covered in grease," Kira noted.

"My copilot could read those displays better than I could," Mbeki said. "I was down in the wiring with the tech. We got it sorted. Want to see them?"

The sudden detour left her blinking for a moment. Mbeki was proving surprisingly pleasant to be around, but she was still getting used to his thought process.

"Them? Your fighters?" she asked.

"Yeah. I looked up the specs on your Hoplites, but you don't even know what my squad are flying. Want to see?"

Kira laughed and checked the time in her headware. She was supposed to meet with Simoneit in about ninety minutes, so she had time.

"Sure."

Mbeki grinned like a kid showing off their new puppy and gestured for her to follow him. That grin was unsettling.

Or maybe it wasn't the grin that was unsettling, Kira admitted, so much as how that grin made her feel. A *smile* shouldn't be making her feel like she'd just chugged a hot chocolate, should it?

Shaking her head against her own idiocies, she followed Mbeki into the fighter launch bay. *Conviction* had separate retrieval and launch bays, a luxury only one of the Apollon carriers she'd served on had shared.

That luxury, of course, was why at peak, she'd carried twelve fewer fighters than an equivalent carrier of her size in Apollo service. It would enable far faster turnaround of nova fighters, but it took up a lot of space.

Kira stepped through the doors into the bay and stopped as she spotted the nova fighters. She wasn't quite sure what she'd been expecting Mbeki's squadron to fly, but part of her had been anticipating the fighters to look like the carrier: solid but worn.

Instead, the eight nova fighters in the launch bay—looking almost lost in hangar spaces designed for *sixty*—were gleamingly sharp war machines. One of them was clearly in the process of having side paneling reassembled, but even there, the fighter was already clean.

Not a single one of the fighters was plain white. All of them carried audacious, even ridiculous, designs and patterns on their hulls. All of that paint was sharp and clean…and the ships were *big*.

"What *are* they?" she asked. All eight fighters were identical, too.

"PNC-One-Fifteens," Mbeki told her. "The Star Kingdom of Griffon's finest…from thirty years ago, I'll admit, but still damn fine fighter-bombers."

The PNC-115s were the same length as Kira's Hoplites, but they were visibly thicker wedges and fifteen meters wide to the Hoplites' ten. They had visible torpedo hardpoints as well, something the Hoplites didn't have the mass or cubage for.

"PNC?" she asked, studying the ships.

"Parasite Nova Combatant," he explained. "The hundred series means they're fighter-bombers. The One Fifteen can carry two plasma conversion torpedoes, one on each side." He shrugged. "We lose a bit in sublight maneuverability if we're loaded with both, but I usually load at least some of my people with one torp."

"Sublight maneuverability doesn't matter *that* much with a nova fighter," Kira said absently. "But then, how often do you need a conversion torp out here?"

Torpedo was an inaccurate descriptor of the system. It did launch out of the ship, but only went a few dozen kilometers at most before detonating. A conversion torpedo was a single-shot version of the heavier plasma cannon mounted on large warships.

Like the class two nova drive that underpinned the entire nova fighter, it was harder to manufacture than the system it miniaturized, but was cheaper if you *could* build it. The two systems combined made a nova fighter with torpedoes a deadly threat to anything in space.

"And now that we have your squadron, we'll have backup next time we need to go up against a full-size warship," Mbeki told her. "We'll lose a bit in maneuvering, but less than you would if we strapped a torpedo to a Hoplite. Best of all worlds."

"I've flown a Hoplite with a torp," Kira replied. "I think I might have maneuvered better without my *engines*."

Mbeki laughed.

"We're better off with my birds carrying them, then," he agreed. "If we drop the torps, my birds can go toe-to-toe with any gunship or nova fighter out here. Your Hoplites would be a challenge for my people, but hey! You're on *our* side."

"Best place for all of us, isn't it?" Kira murmured. The PNC-115s were thirty years old, but Griffon was a more advanced power than Apollo. They were probably just as advanced as her Hoplites.

Most likely, the only reason her fighters had any edge over the PNC-115s was that her birds were more specialized. She'd assumed she had the most advanced fighters on *Conviction*.

She'd been wrong...and hopefully, that would help remind her of the age-old lessons around assumptions.

12

"TWO MORE OF your people arrived around lunchtime," Simoneit told Kira as he collected their coffees. "I took the liberty of hiring private security for them with Memorial Squadron funds. They're on their way here."

"I worry that we're attracting too much attention to you," Kira admitted as she took a sip of the excellent coffee. "I *also* need to sneak a pallet of this stuff onto *Conviction*. I'm going to miss your coffee."

"Astonishing Orange is one of Redward's finest coffees and I'd expect *Conviction* to be stocked with Redward coffee in general. All of which is supposed to be good."

"Every coffee-growing planet has a brand that is the wrecked leftovers of every other growing crop thrown into a grinder together," she pointed out as her headware brought up the contract Simoneit had signed for security.

Ironborn Security was a name she *recognized*, an organization spread across at least half a dozen sectors and probably at least a few million bodyguards and office staff. She didn't even need to check to know that hiring Ironborn was probably the most expensive option—but Ironborn's reputation was, well, iron.

"Ah," Simoneit sighed. "That would be Redward Premium Choice, I suppose. They *claim* to choose their blends carefully, but you aren't the cheapest coffee on a planet that exports coffee by doing things *right*. They can't even get an export license."

"If that's what *Conviction* is serving, I can see why," Kira told him. "The ASDF was legally required to source as much as possible of our supplies on Apollo itself, so all of our coffee was homegrown. We don't *have* any decent coffee-growing climates…and ASDF coffee was still better than whatever it is *Conviction* has."

"I'll give you the card for our supplier," the lawyer said, tossing a virtual datacard between their headware. "You probably want to consider setting an administrative office up here, what with needing to make sure your stragglers get picked up and wanting to arrange supplies."

"I'm not sure when *Conviction* next ships out, but I'll add it to my list," Kira agreed with a sigh. "Not sure how many stragglers I've got left, for that matter. I was waiting on thirteen. If you've got two coming in, I've found three and I know three are dead.

"That's half if we include me. I worry about the fate of anyone who didn't make it out in time."

"You're still going to need a station or planetside office," Simoneit replied. "Your work and funding are going to run through *Conviction* for the foreseeable future, but having a base of operations that's *separate* from Estanza's people is probably wise. At the very least, you don't want to use your *lawyer* to order your coffee," he concluded with a grin.

A chime in Kira's headware told her that one of her bodyguards was opening a channel.

"Demirci," she answered mentally.

"It's Bertoli." The mercenary had apparently been assigned as her permanent bodyguard. Crush was with him today, which Kira wasn't *entirely* happy about, but…*Conviction* provided the bodyguards. The ground troops weren't her people.

"We got a party at the door. Two scrawny peeps who look like pilots and three meatslabs from Ironborn. Trouble or fine?"

Bertoli wasn't supposed to be blocking people from entering Simoneit's office, though Kira could understand his concern at the Ironborn team. Pulling up the video feed Bertoli was providing from his helmet, she recognized the two Apollon pilots—and had to concede the accuracy of the "meatslab" descriptor for the uniformly two-meter-tall Ironborn guardians.

"We're expecting them, Bertoli," she told him. "Send them in. Keep an eye on the Ironborn. Just to soothe my paranoia."

"*My* paranoia was going to require that," the merc replied. "Nobody else dies under my watch."

Kira winced at the reminder and closed the channel.

"They're here," she told Simoneit. "Which I assume you knew."

The law office's security might be automated, but if it wasn't telling Simoneit when people came in, it wasn't worth whatever he paid for it.

FROM THE HELMET FEED, Kira had known who she was meeting in the conference room Simoneit put aside for her. The two 303 pilots—neither of whom had served under her but both of whom *knew* her—hadn't.

Or, least, hadn't believed it. Both stared at her in near-shock and relief as the door slid shut behind them, leaving the three Apollons alone.

"Sit, please," Kira told them. "Hoffman, Patel. It's good to see you."

Joseph Hoffman and Dinesha Patel were both gaunt men of average height. That was where the resemblance between them ended. Hoffman was a fair-haired man with pale skin and blue eyes, where Patel was dark-eyed and dark-haired with skin that looked permanently tanned.

"Tathastu," Patel breathed. "Thank all that is holy. I wasn't going to argue with three large soldiers, but after everything…I couldn't believe we were safe."

"Thank god," Hoffman said, echoing Patel's sentiment if not his exact words. "It's been a hell of a trip."

Kira buried a wince. Her own trip had been pleasant enough, even if the reasons and causes had been nerve-wracking. She'd been shot at before she'd left Apollo, but that had been before her trip.

"Are you both all right?" she asked.

They shared a glance and Patel reached over to squeeze Hoffman's hand.

"We're fine," Patel answered for them both. "Too many others aren't. I think we were the last of the Three-Oh-Three out. Not everyone made it."

"I know about Hughes and Espinoza," she admitted. "Who else?"

"Conroy died back home," Hoffman replied. She realized that he had covered Patel's hand with his own and hadn't let go. If that meant what it looked like, at least *some* positive had come out of their trip. "Spark overdose, the reports said."

"Neither of us was exactly the coroner, so hard to be sure," Patel added.

Kira remembered Denis Conroy. He'd been one of the youngest pilots in the 303 and had only barely made ace before the war ended. He'd been young, earnest…and straitlaced enough to worry her on a warship.

"I'm not sure Conroy even knew what *drugs* were, let alone what spark was," she pointed out softly.

"Me either," Hoffman said with a sigh. Conroy had been his wingman. "I wasn't in touch with the kid and maybe I should have been. I don't know what his getaway plan was, and he was probably the most vulnerable of us all."

"It's not your fault, Joseph," Patel told Hoffman. "We all had our own ways out; it didn't occur to me or Major Cummins, either."

Both men closed their eyes for a moment at the mention of Major Iola Cummins, the last of the four squadron commanders in the 303 that Kira didn't know the fate of.

"Cummins was with you?" Kira asked.

"The three of us left on the ship," Patel confirmed, his voice shaky. "She died to save us."

"Us and two hundred and fifty other people on that ship who'd never done a damn thing to anyone," Hoffman said harshly. "Gunship jumped the liner at a rest point two novas out from Apollo. They'd stripped the colors and IFF, but it was a Kaiserreich ship. I'd know the lines anywhere."

"Our ship was a passenger liner heading to Sophista," Patel said, his voice a soft contrast to Hoffman's. "It was unarmed, but no one was really worried. Brisingr's supposed to be securing the trade lanes now, right? It's what Apollo got from them as a promise in exchange for betraying everyone."

"What happened?" Kira asked.

"Everyone was panicking; the gunship was shooting at the liner. Probably warning shots, since they weren't hitting us, but..." Patel shook his head.

"Major Cummins stole one of the passenger transport shuttles and took it out," Hoffman concluded. "It didn't have any guns, so she did the only thing she could."

"She rammed them," Kira concluded.

"They never saw it coming," Patel whispered. "Neither did we. Crippled the gunship, got us out, but there was no way she survived."

"Damn." She was running the math in her head. That brought the known dead members of the 303 to fifteen. Four of them were here, which meant five were in the wind somewhere. Even assuming all of them made it to Redward intact, her hopes of having two pilots for each of her fighters were long gone.

"Mel Cartman is here," she told them. "Sandip was murdered on the station by hired hitmen. There's only nine of us left."

"And you're the only Major left, aren't you?" Hoffman asked. "We were told to get out this far and find the Majors. I mean"—he gestured at the conference room—"you seem to be doing okay."

"The old man sent a lot of money and resources out this way to make sure we had a fallback position when everything went to hell," Kira explained. "I have the legal structure in place for a mercenary nova squadron flying off a merc carrier—*Conviction*—but right now, I've only got two pilots."

"Pilots will only do you so much good," Patel noted. "My research says that nobody out here can build nova fighters. I doubt the *one* local nova-capable mercenary force is lending us fighters, so, what...we're flying sub-fighters?"

Sub-fighters were the nova fighters' smaller and less capable siblings. They often had everything the nova fighters had in terms of Harrington coils and plasma weapons, but they didn't have nova drives. Apollon nova fighter pilots flew them for the first half of their training, but nova fighter combat tactics relied on that short-range FTL capability.

"No," she told the two men. "Colonel Moranis and I got six Hoplites out here. Like I said, unfortunately I only have two pilots. I could use a few more."

The two men exchanged a glance.

"I'd want to see the pay scales," Patel quipped. "I mean, really, I don't have a comparison out here, but I should probably ask what you're paying first."

"Fixed salary equivalent to ASDF ace pilot rate and three point five percent of the company as a signing bonus," she told him. "No combat bonuses, as we're all going to be part-owners. Moranis sent the money out here for all of us, so we share the company."

"We're in," Hoffman said before Patel could say anything more. "Dinesha is just making noise. A chance to get back in a nova fighter? Neither of us is turning that down!"

She nodded and concealed a sigh of relief.

"I'll have the Ironborn take you back to *Conviction*," she told them. "Cartman is going to be the number two for a while, so she'll see you settled and give you a chance to check out your birds.

"We're going for a test flight this evening to stretch our wings, but we don't have much control over when *Conviction* sails," she continued. "As a squadron, we're contracted to John Estanza, the carrier owner.

"*He*'s under contract to Redward. So, for the moment at least, we sail at King Larry's pleasure."

"A king, huh," Hoffman murmured. "That'll take some getting used to. We staying here long-run?"

"I don't know," Kira admitted. "The extent of the old man's plan seemed to be to get everyone out here and aboard *Conviction*. From there, it's up to us. No one else calling the shots, no high command.

"Just us, six nova fighters, and a starting contract with the most powerful warship out here. We'll see where we go."

"We wait for the rest before anything else?" Patel asked.

"Exactly. We'll probably sortie with *Conviction* before anyone else arrives, but I'll make sure someone is waiting for them to keep them safe until we return."

13

"CONTROL, this is Basketball, requesting clearance for launch," Kira transmitted from her headware.

Her callsign had been hung on her the first week she'd been at the ASDF flight academy, when a tall senior had seen her at the court and challenged her to a "casual pickup" game. He'd been aiming for a different kind of pickup, she was sure, but after she'd run him ragged around the court for twenty minutes, his friends had been laughing too hard for his ego to take it—and her callsign had already been set when she'd logged into her first sub-fighter the next day.

"Basketball, this is *Conviction*. We show all markers green and you are linked into the system."

No matter how casual *Conviction*'s crew took any other matters, this was the one place they could *not* joke around. If the angles on the catapult or the timing on the activation of the Hoplite-IV's Harrington coils was even slightly off, she could hammer the nova fighter into the side of the launch bay at a few dozen kilometers per second.

Conviction would be crippled and she would be *very* dead. Nobody wanted to muck up a space fighter launch.

"I have the ball," she told the control center. "Initiating launch cycle in five."

"We have your metric, Basketball," a different voice replied. Kira smiled to herself as she recognized Mbeki. Of *course* the other fighter squadron commander was watching the first test flight for the Memorials. "You are green."

"Bounce the ball *now*," Kira ordered.

The instruction wasn't directed at any of the humans involved in the process. Once she had the launch system control—the "ball" or the "metric" or one of a dozen other nicknames—the computers were waiting for her order.

Her nova fighter was only fifty-two meters from deep space. Gravity control allowed her to have a clean tunnel of vacuum from just behind her Hoplite to the energy field holding the ship's atmosphere inside—which was good, because she crossed that fifty-two meters in less than a hundredth of a second.

Her Harrington coils kicked live somewhere in the middle of that process, their reactionless impulse taking over when the artificial free fall out of the carrier ended. Unaugmented human eyes and hands couldn't handle that switchover—and even Kira could only keep up with the reports through her headware.

The sequence for a launch took way too little time for even a modern human to exert active control until it was over.

Once it was over, Kira set herself on the planned course. There *was* a physical joystick in her fighter cockpit, but it was currently retracted to allow her to fly the fighter with a virtual one that only existed in her headware and the spacecraft's computers.

No physical lever could keep up with the speed she needed to make changes at to engage in space combat, after all. The physical joystick—like the visual displays hidden behind her current virtual world—was a backup for if the main computer was completely down or she took a head injury.

She was already two hundred kilometers clear of Blueward Station, and she flipped her Hoplite-IV in space to look back at it. It would have been hard to see without magnification, but her headware alone was capable of zooming in on the station and the attached carrier.

"Basketball, this is *Conviction*," Mbeki's voice said in her head. "We have you on the scopes. Clean launch, clean flight. Nightmare is in the tunnel now and has the metric. Launching...now."

Kira was watching the carrier and *looking* for Cartman's fighter. Years of practice made picking out the launch easy enough, but there was no bright flash of light or anything similar. Harrington coils didn't create any visible thrust, after all.

The bright white wedge of a starfighter was clear enough as Mel "Nightmare" Cartman launched into space.

"Nightmare, this is Basketball," Kira hailed her. "I'm at low thrust and waiting for you. If you can't *find* me, I might need a new number two!"

The only response she got from Cartman was a chuckle on the radio—and a noticeable spike in the Hoplite's heat signature as Nightmare's Harrington coils went to full power and flung the fighter out toward her.

Conviction could launch her entire squadron at once—she was designed to launch a *twelve*-fighter squadron at once, a fifth of her complement—but that had a small but measurable risk.

One nova fighter at a time showed up on Kira's screens as Longknife—Joseph Hoffman—and Dawnlord—Dinesha Patel— launched from the carrier in sequence.

Two minutes after leaving the carrier herself, Kira was surrounded by three other nova fighters as she luxuriated in the feeling of being back in open space.

The "cockpit" of the nova fighter was buried at the center of the structure, inside a shell of the only armor the spacecraft had. A second "living" space was accessible through an armored hatch, but that space was barely large enough for the tiny bunk it contained.

The Hoplite was capable of interstellar travel, but it wasn't designed for it. Mbeki's PNC-115s were better off for that, but they still only had one bunk—for a crew of two.

"Basketball, we have all four of your birds on the scopes," Mbeki told her over the radio. "We've cleared a flight path with Redward Orbital Control, you're good to stretch your wings for a bit. ROC has requested that you please not *shoot* anything. This wasn't cleared as a live-fire exercise."

"Understood," Kira replied with a chuckle. A quick glance confirmed that her fighter's guns had never been connected. Right now, her Hoplites were oddly shaped shuttles.

"All right, Memorials," she told her people. "We're going for a leisurely stroll around the neighborhood. Redward-Wardstone Lagrange point two, if you please."

Nonverbal acknowledgements flickered back across the squadron net. Wardstone was the Redward System's star, the inhabited planet having long since taken over as the main name for the tiny monarchy.

"And just for giggles, we're switching to laser coms," Kira continued. "Consider it good practice."

No battlespace would allow for regular radio coms. Directed com-lasers could easily lose lock in intensive maneuvers, but were unjammable.

A two-million-kilometer loop wasn't an intensive maneuver. It was, as Mbeki had described it, just stretching their wings.

KIRA SPENT most of the flight out to the L2 point testing her people's skills in various formations. They were all aces at least three times over, but none of them had been in a cockpit for at least two months.

What little rust existed was easily blown off. By the time they decelerated to a stop at their destination, Kira was comfortable that her people could at least fly. Gun camera exercises would come another day. Right now, she needed to know that they could get a nova fighter around in sublight.

And it wasn't like they were under threat there. L2 was home to the Black Ward, a heavy defensive battle station.

The Black Ward was a ten-kilometer-wide spherical asteroid. Chunks of its exterior had been effectively refined in place to create hundred-meter-thick layers of hardened steel armor that had then been covered in titanium-ceramic hull metal.

With no need to ever attempt a nova, the Ward wasn't limited by the cubage restrictions on a nova drive. The hundred and twenty thousand cubic meter heavy cruisers that had been Apollo's best would have *withered* under the Black Ward's guns.

There was another station at the L1 point and two in orbit. The two in orbit acted as the counterweights for orbital elevators—Blueward

Station was the geostationary midpoint of one of those elevator chains. The fortress at the far end was the Azure Ward.

Redward was somewhat more defended than many planets this far out in the Rim, but most worlds that had been colonized for at least a century had at least one asteroid-based heavy fortress. Conquering worlds was almost impossible. The nova drive didn't really allow for the kind of massive warships necessary to go toe-to-toe with this kind of fortress.

Even in the ugly war between Apollo and Brisingr, none of the actual planets had been at risk. The heavily mapped nova zones that made up the trade lanes had been both the prize and the battlefield of that war.

"Memorial Squadron, Black Ward has you on scanners," a coms officer reached out to her. "Your flight looks clean from here. We're not seeing anything that suggests you have any problems, but I can send you our scan data if you think it would be useful."

"I'd appreciate that, Black Ward," she admitted. "Thanks for the offer."

Her headware pinged with the receipt of the data and she smiled. The locals didn't seem too bothered that she'd signed on with *Conviction* rather than them. Whatever relationship Estanza had with the local fleet seemed warm enough.

"The flight path I have for you has you turning around here," the officer continued. "I don't see any reason to adjust. Starwinds speed you, Memorial Squadron. Always good to see some new faces."

"The welcome is appreciated, Black Ward. We'll be seeing you around." Kira flipped channels to her squadron with a smile.

"All right, Memorials, we've played nice and clean and flown in formation so far," she told them. "Now let's *really* stretch our legs. No novas and no buzzing the locals, but I've got a bottle of retsina for the first of you back to the barn!"

She only had three bottles of the specially made wine, too. Redward had a small wine industry that didn't make anything they bothered to export—on par with Apollo's coffee—but they didn't make the very Greek retsina.

"You'll start your runs...*now*."

Energy spikes flashed on her screen as all three fighters threw their Harrington coils to maximum power, and Kira grinned to herself.

She wasn't convinced any of her pilots actually *liked* retsina...but it was a taste of a home they would probably never see again.

14

"COMMANDER."

"Pilots." Kira returned her people's salutes crisply. The four nova fighters were now nestled back in their hangars, and Waldroup's people were swarming over them for final checkups.

The salutes were far from academy-crisp, but protocol had always been loose for Apollo's nova fighter squadrons. Loose or not, it had *existed*, which made the salutes and titles a reminder of who they'd been.

There'd been no salute from the flight deck crews, and Waldroup's grunt of acknowledgment as she stepped up to the group of pilots barely qualified as paying attention to them, let alone being respectful.

"I'm dumping the birds' computer cores for any problems," the big deck boss told Kira's pilots without any introduction. "If anything flagged for you, let me know."

"I want the guns on those birds in twenty-four hours," Kira told Waldroup. "Couple of civvie ships were flying too close for my peace of mind. Nothing came of it today, but it was a reminder that right now, we're flying glorified shuttles."

"Shuttles can't nova out of trouble," the deck boss replied. "You'll have your guns, Demirci. Anything else?"

She surveyed the pilots, then shrugged and turned to walk away.

Kira exchanged looks with her people.

"That's going to take some getting used to," Patel observed. "Not even sure I can yank her up for it, either."

"You can't," Kira said flatly. "*We* run like we always ran, clear? The rest of the ship runs how it runs and we deal with that, but we stay military."

"Yes, Commander," her pilots replied in a ragged chorus.

"We may end up bringing our own ground team at some point," she continued. "Right now, we're leaning on *Conviction*'s people—which means Waldroup's people. If they can handle the PNC-One-Fifteens, they can handle our Hoplites."

"I'm concerned about turnaround when we take a team that supported eight and ask them to support fourteen," Cartman noted. "Do we have a plan?"

"See how it goes on our first flight out," Kira admitted. "We *have* the funds to bring aboard techs of our own, but we'd have to *find* decent people out here. My guess is that anyone familiar with class twos is either already aboard *Conviction* or working for the Redward Fleet."

Her people got that. Without Moranis's plan, *they'd* have ended up working for King Larry's fleet if they'd gone this far out into the Rim.

"Oh, yeah. Hoffman. You made it back first by enough that *Conviction* landed you first. So, catch," Kira told the oldest of her three pilots. She didn't actually *throw* the retsina to him, but the gesture was implied.

His "desperate" attempt to catch it was intentionally melodramatic and earned a chuckle from her people.

"I was thinking, Commander," Hoffman said as he looked at the bottle. "We didn't get to attend funerals for most of our people. Fifteen of our friends—of our *family*—are dead and we never saw them laid to rest. We should do something…like a wake, maybe? There's a few bars near the dock I think we could rent a room for five or six folks."

"That's a good plan," Kira agreed, looking around at her people. The four of them had come a long way. She was still hoping to see five more of the 303 join them, but her hopes were dimming. For every pilot who'd joined her, she'd heard at least one story of a pilot who'd died at the hands of the Brisingr Shadows or rogue bounty hunters.

"Book it, make it happen," she ordered as she made a snap decision. "We can celebrate our friends who didn't make it and that we did at the same time. We'll remember them best by surviving and *thriving* out here.

"We're Memorial Squadron, people—and that means we *never forget where we came from.*"

HOFFMAN HAD CLEARLY DONE MORE than just *think* about the wake. Kira had a ping to her headware with the address of the bar and a time the next evening before she made it back to her office aboard *Conviction*.

Her office was in the same state as her quarters. It was one of the two wing commanders' offices, designed for the officers who would have led groups of thirty nova fighters in her original service.

Mbeki's people had found her a chair. There *appeared* to be a desk in the middle of the room, but that was the holographic projectors in the room creating a useful illusion. Thankfully, in an era of data packets and virtual paperwork, she didn't need much in terms of physical tools to do her job.

She pulled up the same data that Waldroup would be reviewing. The deck boss knew the engineer side better than she did, but she knew the Hoplite-IV inside and out.

The nova fighters had flown well, as cleanly as any fighter just out of the box ever had. There were adjustments to be made, and Kira started flagging her points of concern for the deck techs as she ran through the recordings.

The four virtual nova fighters paused at a thought as a ping told her that Mbeki was at the door.

"Come in," she told him, ordering the door to open at the same moment.

The broad-shouldered black mercenary stepped into the room, his smile expanding as he saw her in a way that left her questioning her own judgment.

Kira was forty years old. She had no business mooning over a coworker, especially not one where it would be absolutely inappropriate to act on those warm feelings in her stomach. Squadron commanders couldn't be in relationships with each other. Too many risks, too many potential problems—the kinds of risks and problems that got other people killed.

"I saw the test flight," he told her. A moment later, he tried to lean on the holographic desk replacement and stumbled as he discovered the lack of furniture in the room.

He had enough muscle and reflexes to recover before he hit the floor, stabilizing himself with an adorably sheepish grin.

"I *knew* how much furniture was in here," he noted conversationally. "I'm an idiot."

"It's a good hologram," Kira replied with a chuckle and a shake of her head. "But I need to buy furniture and hire an admin team for stationside. The joy of being in charge never stops."

"Advantage: me," Mbeki told her with a chuckle of his own. "I just have to run the squadron. Zoric handles all of that stuff."

"And Estanza?" she asked quietly. "What does he do? I haven't seen him since we hired on."

"He's in command, Kira," he replied. "Right now, that means he's talking to Royal Command and making sure we *keep* our retainer with the King."

"*Conviction* is half again bigger than any of Redward's warships," Kira pointed out. "Hiring us is a bargain."

"I think so. Estanza thinks so. King Larry, presumably, thinks so," Mbeki confirmed. "Some of the King's Members of Parliament, on the other hand, have concerns about the cost-effectiveness of mercenaries and point out that *Conviction*'s fighter group is seventy-five percent under strength."

"Good luck finding another forty-five nova fighters out here," she said dryly. "I imagine if Estanza *could* have, he would have."

"I've served on *Conviction* for twenty years," he reminded her. "At our peak, we fielded thirty-four nova fighters.

"Of course, the other thing they like to point out is that *Conviction* has no real guns of her own. She was *built* with them, but Florin stripped them before selling her."

Kira snorted.

"I mean, if they *want* to sell us heavy plasma cannon to mount on her, I'm sure the mounts are still there."

"Her spine couldn't take the recoil levels that Redward regards as acceptable," Mbeki admitted. "I don't think we could handle even Apollon guns at this point. We'd need to source guns from the Fringe, maybe even the Periphery or the Meridian, to find something with the right power-to-recoil ratios."

The closest Fringe system was over four hundred light-years closer to Sol than Redward. The Periphery was three hundred light-years farther away—and the Meridian was three hundred light-years past *that*.

Conviction had been built on the outer edge of the Meridian, just over three hundred and eighty light-years from humanity's original home. It had been far closer to the homeworld than anyone aboard her, that was certain.

"I doubt you'd need to go farther than the Periphery," Kira countered. "I'm pretty sure *Conviction* is obsolete by even Periphery standards."

"Florin was a Periphery System, so you're probably right," Mbeki agreed. "I don't even know how or when Estanza got her. Sorvedo is in the Fringe, after all."

Kira nodded. Like the carrier she was sitting in, the man she was talking to had been born hundreds of light-years deeper into human-colonized space.

Griffon, Sorvedo…the entire region where the Cobra Squadron had made their legend was mid Fringe, eight-hundred-plus light-years from Sol and over six hundred from Redward. Mbeki was even farther from home than Kira and her people—over *three times* as far.

"I forget you're all that far from home," she murmured.

"*Conviction* is my home," he told her, and his gaze was suddenly very intense. "Her people are my family. I wouldn't be anywhere else, *with* anyone else. There was nothing for me in Sorvedo except taking advantage of my parents."

"There was nothing for me in Apollo but death for everyone I loved," Kira admitted. Mbeki was much closer to her now, and he hesitantly squeezed her shoulder for support.

"I never saw Apollo," he told her. "But making that break from the world you were born on is hard. We're here, though. We make the best of it."

"True enough, I suppose," she allowed with a long sigh. "Did you see anything in the test flights you were worried about?"

"Your Hoplites are more maneuverable than my One-Fifteens, faster on a straight line too," Mbeki told her. "Hard to say how they perform in combat until I've seen them in a jammed battlespace."

"Fourteen battles, thirty-two combat sorties and twenty-eight kills as Apollo counts them," Kira said quietly. "They do just fine."

"Shit," he breathed. "I've been in space a lot more than that, but I think I'm only at thirty actual *combat* sorties." He paused thoughtfully. "I'm not sure how the Apollo kill count works, either. We fight actual nova fighters so rarely, we generally just count everything as a kill, which only puts me at thirty."

"Sub-fighters count as half, gunships count as one, real capital ships count as one for every fighter in the strike," Kira reeled off. She'd had to explain it to a lot of eager young pilots over the years. Three of those pilots were currently aboard *Conviction*.

"Twenty-four," Mbeki noted after a moment to let his headware run the numbers. "I knew you were an ace and I knew you were experienced. I didn't realize you were in the top three on this ship."

"Who's second?" Kira asked, assuming that put her at number three—and that the first was Estanza.

"One of my pilots, name of Boyd Maina," he told her. "Almost sixty, he was the first recruit the boss ever picked up and has stuck it out. He's probably rich enough to retire, but all he wants is to fly. Not command. Not go run a farm somewhere. Just fly a nova fighter."

Kira snorted.

"Can you argue with him?" she asked.

"I'm in charge here, so at least a little bit," Mbeki replied. He shook himself in the same moment as Kira got a ping in her own headware informing her that *Conviction* would be leaving port in fifty-two hours.

She shook her head. It was signed *JE*, and that was the only thing telling her it was from Estanza.

"Well, that makes the party schedule just about perfect," she admitted. "My team is holding a wake for the 303 pilots who never made it out tomorrow. *I* need to see if I can convince my lawyer to hire someone to admin Memorial's affairs for me while I'm gone."

"We've got…like, three people who run an office on Blueward Station?" Mbeki noted. "We can have them cover things for you if you need."

"I need someone to watch for the rest of my people showing up and make sure they don't get knifed in the back," Kira pointed out. "I doubt the accounting team you keep on the station will serve."

He laughed.

"Fair enough. Ask Zoric," he suggested. "She runs that office; she might have some suggestions for people. Have you even *met* her yet?"

Kira paused.

"Other than first coming aboard, I haven't left flight country," she admitted. "I should do that, shouldn't I?"

Mbeki laughed again.

"Yes," he suggested. "In two days, she gets to haul us out to see what we find. Let's make nice with the woman in charge of where we lay our heads."

"All right. I'll invite her to the post-mourning part of the party," Kira decided. "You're welcome too."

She tossed him the details before she could change her mind.

"Give us an hour to get good and morose, then see if you can cheer us up," she told him.

"I do believe, Commander Demirci, that cheering up morose people is one of my *specialties*," he informed her with a broad grin.

15

THE BAR WAS EXACTLY what Kira had been expecting. It was a spacers' bar, within easy walking distance of both the civilian dock and the
military docks taken over by *Conviction* and her crew. The private room
was almost as large as the main space; the drinks and food were both
cheap and solid.

This wasn't the kind of place that had champagne, retsina or fancy
whisky, but they could serve beer, vodka, pizza and spaghetti until
Blueward Station fell off the space elevator.

There was a lot of all four of those in the back room as Kira's people
worked through toasts to all fifteen of their fallen comrades. For the
last one, everyone looked to her as she stood up with a fresh mug of
cold beer and studied the other three.

"You all knew Jay Moranis," she told them. "He was the beating
heart of the Three-Oh-Three. Without him, we never would have made
the name for ourselves we did, and without him, none of us would be
alive out here.

"I flew under him for fourteen years, longer than any of you, and I
looked up to him as a second father. I wasn't supposed to be the only
squadron commander who made it out this far, but he trusted the
lion's share of getting everyone settled here to me.

"I didn't do as well as I hoped, and Sandip paid for it," she admitted, nodding sadly to Cartman. "But we're here and we're as secure as we can hope to be. *Conviction* might not be a long-term home, but it's a place to start. We're a long damn way from the Kaiserreich and the Shadows, so *fuck them*.

"And all of that is Jay Moranis's work." She shook her head. "If we survive and thrive out here, its because White Cobra decided to make a third legend in his life. He flew once with the Cobras, and they became legend.

"He flew once with the Three-Oh-Three, and we became legends at his side.

"Now he's unleashed us to fly on our own and given us every tool, every step up, that he could give us. A legend gives us wings, people—and we're going to take them and fly. We were Three-Oh-Three and a legend in Apollo under Jay Moranis.

"Under me, we're Memorial Squadron—and we will *by gods* be a legend out here. You with me?"

Three mugs of beer were raised in answer.

"Then my friends, I give you Jay Moranis: our Colonel. Our Cobra. Our space dad," she concluded with a grin. "Moranis!"

"Moranis!"

The four of them slammed down solid gulps of their drinks—and the bar staff sent Kira a message informing her the next set of guests were here.

"The rest of the party is here," she told her subordinates. "That's just the Commanders from *Conviction*, so let's play it a *little* nice, people."

There was no coherent response before Mbeki and Zoric entered the back room. Everyone in the space was wearing similar nondescript shipsuits, but Kira knew it would be perfectly clear who the officers were for *at least* five more beers.

"Welcome, welcome," she told the two mercenary officers. Mbeki was looking surprisingly grim initially, but his smile escaped a moment after he saw her. She wasn't sure why he'd been hiding it. His smile was a dangerous animal in her opinion, one that couldn't be safely caged.

Zoric, on the other hand, knew the path to pilots' hearts the way only a carrier's executive officer could: she was carrying a tray holding six more beers and another pizza. Antigrav coils *had* to be involved, Kira was sure.

"They dumped this on us on the way through," the XO told them. "Somebody grab it!"

Patel obeyed, leaping over to retrieve the tray. He and Zoric, despite having been born hundreds of light-years apart, could easily have passed for cousins. Both were dark-haired and dark-eyed. Zoric was taller and distinctly not male, but they looked like relatives.

The tray salvaged, Zoric grabbed a beer of her own and joined the circle.

"Did the guy I sent you to work out?" she asked Kira after her first swallow.

As Mbeki had suggested, Kira had asked *Conviction*'s XO for a suggestion for admin people. She'd suggested a recently retired Redward Army officer living on the station who hadn't been quite sure what to do with himself.

If nothing else, Stipan Dirix was a tad over two meters of walking muscle that fit the "meatslab" descriptor that Bertoli had used for the last round of bodyguards. He could do security on his own.

"Pree Simoneit knew him too, so he came doubly recommended and, unless I miss my guess, doubly leaned on," Kira replied with a smile. "He's aboard. I ran through what we need right now today, but he and Pree are going to be working together pretty closely on this first sortie."

She wasn't sure what that was going to cost her and she probably didn't want to know. She'd checked the old lawyer's hourly rate and nearly swallowed her tongue. The man was *worth* it, but it was a lot of money.

Thankfully, Memorial Squadron *had* that money.

"Hopefully, you won't need to have guards on retainer for much longer, either," Mbeki noted.

"Until everyone is here," Kira replied. "Waiting on five more. Assuming I don't end up holding more of these bloody wakes."

That morose thought led to her staring down into her mug, so she missed Mbeki adjusting the room's music program. An upbeat dance mix broke her focus and she looked up at the black man with a questioning gaze.

His grin grew even wider.

"This is a wake, yes," he accepted aloud. "This is a drinking party, yes. But I was told to come along and get everyone cheered up and rescued from this being a *morose* party, which means that we need to celebrate the dead and drink to the dead...and I don't think *any* of that is best done sitting."

He offered Kira his hand.

"So, Commander Demirci, will you dance with me?"

She snorted.

"I'm a nova fighter pilot, Mbeki," she replied. "I can barely dance by Apollo standards and I don't know this music at all."

"That, Commander, is why it's a good thing you booked a private room," he told her. "Because honestly? I can't dance by *anyone's* standards!"

DANIEL MBEKI UNDERSTATED his dancing skills, even if he wasn't wrong on his assessment of their applicability to any given set of dancing *standards*. Enough beer got Kira and the rest of Memorial Squadron up with him, dancing.

And if Kira Demirci was dancing far closer to the other squadron commander, there was enough beer and cheap vodka in play for no one to think anything of it.

The clock ticked toward station midnight and Zoric made her excuses shortly before she'd have turned into a cabbage. The others followed, and by the end of the night, Kira and Mbeki were alone in the back room of the club when one of the staff stuck her head in.

"We need to shut everything down in ten," she told them. "Station regs. This isn't even last call—that was in your headware ten minutes ago!"

"Come on," Mbeki said. "Let's leave them to their work."

Kira had drunk enough that her augments were noticeably working to keep her walking in a straight line as they exited the bar. A virtual exchange took place on the way out and confirmed Kira's authorization to charge everything to Memorial Squadron's accounts.

"Less than one hour of the bloody lawyer," she muttered to her companion as they made their way into the station corridor. The last of the mercenary grunts from *Conviction* fell in behind them, trailing a discreet three meters behind the two officers as they made their way back to the carrier.

"Cheap bar or expensive lawyer?" Mbeki asked.

"Both," Kira replied with a chuckle. A chime informed her that her headware was being interrogated by the RRFP troopers guarding the docking bay. She hadn't thought they were that close, but her augments were focusing on keeping her moving, not keeping her sense of time intact.

"Thanks, Rona," Mbeki told the guard. "I think I can get Demirci back to the ship from here without getting jumped by assassins."

Kira rested against the wall for a moment, letting the knowledge that they were inside *Conviction*'s security perimeter relax the knot of tension that was always in her shoulder blades on Blueward Station.

"No rest anywhere," she muttered. "It's a bloody mess."

"I don't envy you it," Mbeki told her. "Lean on me."

She did. He was a solid and warm support, even if she didn't *really* need it. Neither of them did and both of them knew it, but they leaned against each other as they headed toward the boarding tubes.

The movement toward a secluded corner *away* from those docking tubes wasn't a planned thing. Kira hadn't been aiming for a private spot. She was quite sure Daniel wasn't guiding her to a private spot. It just…happened, as both of them unconsciously sought one out.

The kiss that followed was equally unplanned, and for one luxurious, amazing moment, Kira greedily leaned into it. In the back of her mind, she already knew how that had to end, so she took every scrap of enjoyment from those few seconds of kissing Daniel Mbeki that she could.

Then she stepped away from him, sighed, and triggered the decontamination decontamination dose she'd loaded before the party and *should* have hit on leaving the bar. Nanites swept alcohol from her blood as she looked at Daniel and shook her head.

"I'm sorry," she murmured. "That shouldn't have happened."

"I… Wait, what?" he asked. "I didn't mean to push, I'm…"

"You didn't do anything wrong, Daniel," Kira told him, firmly. *Very* firmly. "That was both of us. It was nice. I wish it could be more than that, but it *can't*, Daniel. We're squadron commanders. We're going into the line of fire, and if one of us is distracted, people *die*.

"I shouldn't have let this happen, but I did. *We* did. It can't happen again."

"This isn't the military, Kira," he pointed out. "There are no rules against fraternization."

"The rules for my people and for *me* are what I say they are," she snapped. "And there's a gods-cursed *reason* for that rule, you understand me?

"So, I'm sorry. I wanted this, but it can't happen. I'm sorry."

And with the final repetition of her apology, Kira fled into the carrier.

She'd *already* screwed things up. She couldn't make it worse.

16

"ALL SIX FIGHTERS are fully equipped and online," Waldroup told Kira brightly. "Guns are installed, the works."

"How do the power couplings for the guns look?" Kira asked as she paced a slow circle around her own Hoplite-IV. "That was the most common problem with them right out of the box. Seemed like every fourth bird blew the couplings the first time they fired."

"That's because Apollo couplings have a quality control problem," the deck boss said bluntly. "Take a look at this."

Kira bit down an instinctive defense of her home system and stepped over to the work cart the tech was rifling through. The other woman was holding up a solid chunk of ceramic and metal a bit over forty centimeters long.

"I see a power coupling," she conceded. "It doesn't look blown out to me."

"It would if you tried to fire a gun hooked up through it," Waldroup told her. "Hold it."

Kira obeyed, curious now. The mercenary tech had a scanner in her hand and ran it over the device, throwing the data into the air between them as the scanner ran.

"First-check scan, nothing's wrong," the tech noted. "All of our interface patterns and conductivity lines look right, right?"

The pilot studied the diagram for a few seconds, then nodded.

"I'm not familiar with this particular iconography, but it looks right, yes," she confirmed.

"And that's the extent of the check your manufacturer did," the tech told her. "Apollo fabricators are good, most advanced in their sector...but you're still talking a Rim sector, Demirci. Go another hundred light-years closer to Earth and their fabricators are years ahead of yours.

"More importantly, though, they've worked out that even *those* fabricators don't always get it right," Waldroup continued. "The tolerances for a conduit rated for a gigawatt-plus peak throughput are tighter than any fabricator outside the Core can manage.

"Even Griffon, one of the most advanced Fringe powers—and the people who built *Conviction*'s fabricators—still loses one point six percent of their couplings in QC. I downchecked eleven percent of the couplings your birds came with," the tech concluded as she activated a second layer to the scan, zooming the model in to a ten-to-one scale of the coupling.

Kira had never seen the scan Waldroup was doing...but she had enough of an eye for what the conductive pathways through the coupling *should* look like to pick out the point where several of the lines of superconducting ceramic didn't line up.

"And there's your problem," the merc deck boss concluded. Multiple spots in the model acquired red highlights. "This was a bad one, to be clear. Sixteen fracture points.

"None of them are big, but that's sixteen points where you're trying to pulse hundreds of megawatts of energy through as much as ten micrometers of insulator."

The big woman shrugged.

"The coupling blows," she concluded. "In theory, one or two fractures should be okay if you're at less than a dozen micrometers of total misalignment. *This* particular one is a deathtrap that even your people should have caught."

"That makes a disturbing amount of sense," Kira admitted glumly. "I've only seen one nova fighter actually blow up when they pulled the trigger...but I *have* seen it. What do we do?"

"Well, I run the deeper scan and scrap the units that fail,"

Waldroup told her. "Then I run the specifications for couplings for your ships into *Conviction*'s fabricators and make new ones."

She grinned.

"The only things I can't make for your birds are Harrington coils and nova drives. Both of those need gravity to build. If we need Harringtons, we can buy them from the locals."

"And if the class two goes, I'm down a nova fighter," Kira confirmed. That was why her fighters were so valuable out there, after all. Nobody in the Syntactic Cluster had worked out how to build a class two nova drive yet.

Kira knew *some* of the tricks involved—but she also knew a lot of it was having certain fabrication tolerances and very specific tools that the general fabricator didn't have.

The general standard fabricator *could* build a regular class one nova drive. Assuming it had gravity and exotic matter, at least—but the exotic matter itself required *zero gee* to make.

And for reasons that Kira did not have the physics degrees to understand, the gravity requirements for exotic matter and exotic-matter-derived production could not be met with artificial gravity.

"So long as your class twos survive, I can rebuild your fighters from wreckage," the deck boss confirmed. "Lose your class twos and, well…when I came aboard, we had fourteen of the One-Fifteens."

Kira nodded, stepping back to look at all six of her fighters.

"You replaced the damaged couplings, so they're all good to go?" she asked.

"We pulse-tested the couplings we installed and everything looks good," Waldroup agreed. "No fractures that we can detect and they passed the tests. Live fire is always a different question, but I'm as comfortable with them as I can be.

"You have six combat-ready Hoplite-IVs, Commander." She chuckled. "Not that anything else was ever going to happen. We launch in two hours. I wouldn't like what would happen to my paycheck if your birds *weren't* online."

"Thanks, Waldroup," Kira told the other woman. "I'm pretty sure I wouldn't like what happens to my contract rate if I don't have six ships."

"Which does bring up a problem," Mbeki said calmly behind her.

She cursed internally. Her situational awareness was usually too good to let people sneak up on her like that—but she'd been focusing on the fighters to specifically *not* think about Mbeki. That had apparently spilled over into her headware actively ignoring him.

Computers installed in human brains picked up *far* too many of those brains' quirks.

"I only have four pilots," she conceded as she turned to face him. Waldroup clearly registered this conversation as *none of my business* and was calmly trundling the cart with the useless coupling away from the fighter.

"And your contract calls for six fully manned and functional nova fighters," Mbeki agreed. His tone was professional. *Too* professional. He'd been warm and casual with her from the beginning, and almost all of that was gone now.

"I was hoping for more of my people to show up," Kira admitted awkwardly. This wasn't a conversation they really should have been having in the middle of the fighter bay, but Mbeki didn't show any sign of moving elsewhere. "With two hours until we ship out, that isn't happening."

There wasn't even any inbound civilian shipping that could be carrying her people.

"I've reviewed the contract this morning," he noted. "You do remember what the penalties for deploying less than a full squadron are?"

"Yes," Kira finally snapped. If she *lost* a fighter, the contract called for a renegotiation of the fee schedule. If she failed to deploy a fighter she *had*, she was docked twenty-five percent of the fee for that cruise.

"I also don't think is an appropriate conversation to have in the middle of a hangar deck, Commander Mbeki," she continued, her tone still sharp as she intentionally *didn't* use his first name. "My office, if you please?"

"Very well," he conceded with a bow of his head. "Lead the way."

———

KIRA'S OFFICE was exactly halfway between the launch and retrieval decks. Mbeki's office was similarly positioned, a single floor above hers, but he politely followed her to her space.

It wasn't far, but it took long enough to get there for her to regain her calm. Entering the room, she mentally ordered coffees from the built-in machine.

There was still only one chair in the room and neither of them took it. Mbeki accepted the coffee with a nod, then glanced back at the door to make sure it was closed.

"Despite occasional glitches, I'm not your enemy," he said quietly. "I pinned you down to offer a *solution*, not a problem. If you'd actually read my *messages*, I wouldn't have had to track you down on the flight deck."

Kira checked her headware and grimaced. In the ASDF, there'd been a clear template her headware had used to classify her contacts. She was so used to that being done automatically, she hadn't manually classified the *Conviction* crew and officers.

They were all in the *personal acquaintances* group…a group her headware would automatically hold messages from until she wasn't angry at them.

Or, in Mbeki's case, being angry at herself *about* them. Computers followed instructions, after all. Computers that were part of your head followed *all* of your instructions. Even the ones you didn't necessarily mean to give.

"I never even saw that," she admitted. "My headware isn't used to having fellow officers that aren't ASDF. It's getting confused." She snorted. "Which means, I suppose, that *I'm* getting confused."

"I've never met anyone whose headware did anything but make them *more* human," Mbeki conceded.

He exhaled, then took a sip of his coffee as he marshaled his thoughts.

"Your pay gets cut by fifty percent if you don't field those two nova fighters," he noted. "*Mine* doesn't get cut for shit; I'm a part-owner in *Conviction* Mercenary Ops LLC itself."

"Your point?"

"A PNC One-Fifteen needs a pilot and a copilot," Mbeki told her. "If one of my pilots is out, for illness or injury or whatever, I sub up a copilot, and I've got a couple of spare copilots on the payroll who do other jobs around the ship.

"I can put two of my better copilots on 'leave' for this mission," he continued. "They're qualified to fly nova fighters—if I were to suddenly acquire two new birds, they'd be the people I'd put behind the stick."

"And then I temporarily hire them, I presume?" Kira asked. "At full standard pilot rates, plus combat pay, of course."

"Which is why they won't say no," Mbeki agreed. "That's almost double copilot pay without bonuses. Everybody knows up front it's temporary, because you're still waiting on your people, but it gets you six fighters in the air, which gets you full contract payment and puts a nice chunk of change in two of my people's pockets."

"You like that pair, huh?" she asked.

He snorted.

"The greenest crew member on *Conviction* outside your squadron has been here for two years," he pointed out. "I've known all of my people for at least three. There's nobody left that I don't like, and that pair are the best I've got.

"Everyone wins, Demirci."

"So it would seem," she murmured. "Their names?"

He tossed her the data and then leaned against the wall with his coffee while she reviewed the files for the two pilots. Both had been with *Conviction* for five years and earned their nova pilot's wings aboard the carrier. Neither was native to the Syntactic Cluster, but the sector they were from wasn't any better off financially or techno-logically.

They were the kind of people who would sign on to a mercenary ship with no intention of ever coming home. There was no real data in Mbeki's files as to *why* Annmarie Banderas and Shun Asjes had left their home systems behind, but they had to have had a reason.

It might be as simple as they'd wanted to fly nova fighters or as complicated as Kira's own flight from assassins. Either way, there was a *reason* they were aboard *Conviction*.

"All right," she said aloud. "Run it by them, and if they're aboard, send me a message. I promise I *will* get this one."

She'd applied the ASDF fellow-officer template to the other two

Conviction Commanders while they'd been talking. She wasn't going to make *that* much of a fool of herself again.

"I'll need them in simulators by the time *Conviction* makes her first nova," she continued. "They might have their wings, but a Hoplite and a One-Fifteen have quite different performance envelopes.

"You think they're up to it?" She smiled at Mbeki. It wasn't an entirely pleasant expression. "That gets them a shot. But they need to prove they can hack *my* standards and *my* squadron, Commander.

"I'll take the pay cut before I'll send out people in those fighters I don't expect to bring them back. Am I clear?"

"Those fighters are your stock-in-trade, your biggest asset," the other mercenary told her. "That's the rules you *have* to follow. I'll talk to them both; they should be ready to go before we even break dock."

"Good. The sooner I have them in sims, the more likely they are to learn what I want before it's too late!"

17

"SIMULATION OVER."

Kira studied the result hovering above the simulator pod. The first test she'd thrown her two temporary pilots into was a Thermopylae Scenario. They were tasked to protect a convoy until their nova drives recharged against a continuing and growing attack.

If a group of pilots somehow managed to survive and protect the convoy for the *fourteen hours* necessary for the convoy's drives to recharge…those drives would break. Given that the simulation in question would start throwing full Kaiserreich carrier groups at the defenders around hour two, she was reasonably sure it was impossible.

She'd been part of a fighter group that held out in this scenario for ninety-six minutes. That was when the sim threw two full nova fighter wings supported by a pair of cruisers at the defenders.

If nothing else, the *freighters* became indefensible at that point.

"Eleven minutes. They both novaed out," Cartman said quietly beside her. "Abandoned the mission to preserve assets."

"They *lived* eleven minutes, I suppose," Kira allowed. That wasn't particularly terrible, all things considered. Her mental benchmark had been ten—but she'd expected them to go down swinging. "And took down three nova fighters apiece along the way. But as soon as they were outnumbered two-to-one, they bailed."

She didn't bother to wipe the grim expression from her face as the pods opened and the two pilots stepped out.

"Well?" she asked. "Care to explain?"

Banderas and Asjes shared a look.

"Explain what, Commander?" Asjes finally asked.

"Why you withdrew," Kira told them. "The objectives you were given didn't include withdrawal criteria. Your orders were to protect the convoy. As I've traditionally run this sim, *running* is the only way to lose."

"We were outnumbered two-to-one, in the middle of a full multiphasic jamming bubble and unable to maintain more than intermittent coms with each other, let alone the convoy," Banderas said slowly. She was a tall blonde who towered over Kira and was trying very clearly to not obviously "look down on" her new boss.

"The battle wasn't sustainable. Continuing the engagement would have risked our nova fighters for no purpose."

"No purpose," Kira echoed. A gesture opened a holo image of the convoy the two pilots had been supposed to protect. She'd adjusted the sim slightly to make them ships likely to show up in the Syntactic Cluster, which meant it was made up of twenty-thousand-cubic-meter ships instead of the forty- to fifty-thousand-cubic ships she was used to.

"Seven civilian ships were depending on you, pilot," she pointed out. "At that size, average crew of twelve to fifteen. Let's be generous and say you only abandoned *eighty-five* people to their deaths or capture."

"It's capture at worst out here," Asjes objected. "The pirates know that if too many people end up dead, it goes badly for them. They don't even keep the ships a lot of the time. They just strip the cargo and let them go."

"So, your plan was to put the safety of the people paying you on the good will of pirates?" Kira asked. "And this seemed reasonable to you?"

"We're mercenaries, Commander," Banderas replied. "Every time we go out, it's a cost-benefit analysis. Without the fighters we're flying, you've got nothing."

"That's *my* call to make," Kira said flatly. "Which means if I send you out there in real life, you're going to have withdrawal criteria. You'll have *orders*. It's not your place to decide if holding the line is worth your ships, pilots."

"It is under Mbeki."

She wasn't sure which of them had spoken.

"I hear that," she told them. "So, you have a choice. A very simple one. You passed my minimum *capability* standard, so I'm willing to keep you for this cruise as we planned. But *you* need to decide if you work for me—or Mbeki.

"Because I don't run my squadron like he runs his," she concluded. "I run this squadron like it's part of a proper damn military. That we're mercenaries will affect our objectives, but that's *my* call to make. Not yours.

"If you can't live with that, I don't want you on my wing. We clear?" she asked.

"We're clear," both echoed back at her.

"Well?" she asked.

The two pilots shared another look and an almost-synchronized shrug.

"I can get used to anything," Asjes said bluntly. They were looking at the floor as much as at Kira. "I'll do a lot for money and more to fly. I can follow orders."

"It's all a learning experience, isn't it?" Banderas asked with a chuckle. "I'll learn. Can't hurt anywhere along the way, can it?"

"All right." Kira studied for a moment longer. "Fall out. We'll have all six of us in sims in half an hour for one mass exercise, but then we get to hope it was enough as we join the patrol cycle."

Two fighters from each squadron would be in space at all times while *Conviction* was outside the Redward System. Once the carrier made her first nova, there'd be no more chances for squadron exercises.

KIRA'S HEADWARE kept her fully aware of the carrier's position and status at all times. She was halfway into a sandwich after the exercise when *Conviction* finally began to move. There was nothing in the mess hall to suggest that dozens of umbilicals and several large docking and transfer tubes had just detached.

There wasn't even anything to suggest that the Harringtons had engaged. *Conviction* fell away from the station at a rapidly growing pace.

"We're on our way," she murmured aloud. Her headware brought up the cruise route that Mbeki had shared with her. They'd accelerate out from Redward for two hours to get up to a decent velocity and then nova out.

Their first jump would be four and a half light-years and require a sixteen-hour cooldown. That would put them at the first of the "trade route stops," the heavily mapped points in deep space where most ships would stop.

The nova fighters would patrol the area, their faster-recharging drives allowing them to sweep out several light-months in every direction and return in that sixteen-hour cooldown. Then *Conviction* would make a full six-light-year jump to another trade route stop.

The fighters would repeat the sweep over the twenty-hour recharge, the carrier would jump again, they'd sweep again. Then the carrier would jump into the New Ontario System and discharge her drives' tachyon-static buildup at the gas giant there.

They'd return by the same route, this time with a planned convoy of freighters. *That* part of the trip would be the actual dangerous one. The nova fighters would keep close in for the entire trip, running patrols over the carrier and her flock.

Kira had seen dozens of similar patrols over her time in the ASDF. Only three of them had ever been attacked—but on one of those attacks, the 303 had lost their carrier.

They had, however, saved the convoy and got a critical mass of supplies through a Brisingr blockade. She wasn't sure it had been worth it, but it hadn't been her call then.

It *was* her call now. That was the point she'd made to her new pilots, as well.

No matter how many of the missing 303 pilots showed up, she was always going to have a majority stake in Memorial Squadron. They were her fighters, her pilots...*her* mercenaries.

She was going to have to get used to that.

18

"*CONVICTION*, THIS IS BASKETBALL," Kira said over the radio. "Memorial One and Two holding high escort position. I have the rest stop on my scopes and I'm not seeing any signs of trouble."

"Us either, Basketball," Commander Zoric replied. "Launching long-range sweeps in a few moments. Anything for Duck to watch for?"

Duck was Daniel Mbeki. Kira had no idea what the other Commander had done to get saddled with that handle, but she wanted to find out.

Of course, part of her wanted to find out *everything* about Daniel Mbeki, and that part was making her *very* grumpy.

"I think you see what I see, *Conviction*," she replied. "I've got two twenty-kilocubic junkers at the center of the point and nothing as far as the radar with guns except us."

Zoric snorted.

"Be nice, Basketball. This is the Syntactic Cluster. Those 'junkers' might be somebody's pride and joy."

"They're nova ships, *Conviction*," Kira replied. "Doesn't matter where you are; they're someone's pride and joy. That pair, on the other hand? Someone needs a bit more pride and a bit more paint!"

The two freighters in question were small enough to be family or even individually owned and run. Running a freighter with a crew of one couldn't be easy, but Kira knew there were people who did it.

Most of them had more drones than seemed to be the norm out there. And anyone who had labor drones could use the things to repaint the mismatched and battered outer hulls of the two small ships.

"Basketball, we have Darkwing One through Four in the pipe. Final call for clear space."

There were a dozen automated drones flickering around *Conviction*, and Zoric didn't really need Kira's eyes and sensors. On the other hand, in a combat environment, those drones would be rapidly rendered useless by multiphasic jamming. Having the human double check was never a bad idea.

"Space is clear," Kira confirmed.

A moment later, *Conviction*'s launch deck pulsed with gravitic energy and four PNC-115s blasted into space. They took a moment to orient themselves into two two-spacecraft groups, then flashed their running lights in a salute to *Conviction* and Kira's group—and then vanished in a blast of tachyons and Cherenkov radiation as they novaed out.

The patrol wasn't going far, just a light-hour, but they'd sweep the perimeter of the trade route stop to make sure the entire area was clear.

"*Conviction*, confirmed Darkwing deployment and nova," she told Zoric. "Maintaining patrol and escort."

Today, Memorial Squadron had the CSP—Carrier Space Patrol. She'd brought Longknife—Hoffman—out with her and tasked Cartman and Patel with training the temps.

By the time the week-plus journey was over, she was pretty sure the two copilots would be *delighted* to go back to Mbeki's Darkwing Squadron. Nonetheless, they were taking her people's idea of appropriate standards in stride. So far.

They still retreated faster than she liked...but in the quiet of her own head, she'd admit that they were probably closer to the right timing for mercs than she was.

"Boss, one of the junkers novaed," Longknife reported. "Directly along route six. Nothing to worry about."

Redward was not *quite* central to the Syntactic Cluster. It was close enough, however, that nine of the eleven usual trade routes in the Cluster hit a trade stop within one nova of King Larry's star system.

Route six was headed toward Ypres. That was enough to give Kira a moment of pause, but not a big one. Ypres was where the Brisingr ambassador was and where anyone who killed her was supposed to prove it to get paid.

She'd never even visited the system, and she knew the name was going to make her twitchy for a while.

For now...

"I have a Cherenkov radiation spike," she told *Conviction*. "Incoming nova, energy signatures suggest..."

She knew this part of the job. Being a merc, running a squadron with no superiors? Those were new to her—but she *knew* patrol-and-escort in her bones.

WITH THEIR PILOT and copilot setup, the PNC-115s could do a sixteen-hour sweep of the trade route stop without returning to the carrier. The Hoplite-IVs were single-seat fighters, which meant that the ASDF—and now Memorial Squadron, since Kira had simply copied ASDF policies—limited them to six-hour patrols.

Kira and Hoffman waited until Cartman and Banderas were in space, then carefully began to bring their fighters in.

"This is *Conviction*, standing by for automatic control," Waldroup's voice said in her headware. "I have you on the line, Basketball. Vectors are green, contact in thirty seconds. I request control."

For a moment, Kira considered going for a manual landing. It was better to practice it now than under fire, after all.

Her impression was that it would also panic the *hell* out of *Conviction*'s crew. The carrier had no guns of her own, after all, which meant her crew had probably never had to manage landings inside the multiphasic jamming of a battlespace.

"I yield control," she said aloud. Surprising her new comrades with a stunt like that was all well and good, but she'd want to make sure at least *some* people knew what was coming. Probably only Waldroup, now that she considered it.

Kira suspected the deck boss would be entirely on board with spooking her techs.

She felt the twitches of the nova fighter around her as the Hoplite flashed toward *Conviction*. At this velocity, the Harringtons could bring her to a near-complete halt relative to the carrier in a heartbeat.

Waldroup was actually bringing her in faster than an ASDF controller would have in the circumstances, and a moment of panic flashed through Kira before she suppressed it.

If the woman maintaining her nova fighter wanted to kill Kira, she had *far* better options than ramming the fighters into the carrier's retrieval deck.

The maw of that deck swept over the Hoplite-IV and the fighter came to a gentle halt, hovering in the air over one of the transfer platforms for a moment before touching down.

"Contact," Waldroup declared. "Issuing shutdown orders. Welcome back aboard, Commander."

PATEL WAS WAITING for the two of them as Kira and Hoffman exited the fighters. He and Hoffman embraced and Kira concealed a smile. She wasn't *blind*, whatever the two lovers might be thinking.

"Asjes?" Kira asked.

"Sleeping," Patel replied. "They'll do. Not so sure about Banderas."

"She can fly," Kira pointed out. "For this mission, that should be enough. I didn't see anything in the briefing Redward provided suggesting a higher-than-usual threat rating."

"Any escort out here is a higher threat rating than I'm used to," Hoffman pointed out. "I'm guessing you read the briefing on our 'most likely hostile'?"

"Local pirate clans, flying around in gunships built with the basic fabricator database," she confirmed. "I've left *Kaiserreich* gunships in pieces. I'm not going to sweat the Costar Clans."

"Yeah, any one gunship isn't worth much," Hoffman agreed. "But I read the actual report on just who they are." He shook his head. "The important word is probably *desperate*, boss. They're desperate.

"They're a bunch of assholes from asteroid settlements and

marginal worlds and systems no one else lives in," he continued. "The kind of places that start out on a narrow line and, if they're unlucky, never get off it. More civilized places, they get snapped up as dependencies of bigger powers.

"Out here? They band together and take what they need. Brisingr gunship pilots were professionals, like us. These Clans aren't. They're pirates, they're amateurs, and they're convinced that if they fail, their whole settlement dies."

Patel shook his head.

"The margins are *never* that thin," he argued. "I'm from a system like that—one of Apollo's dependencies, obviously. It's not an easy life, but even without Apollo, we'd survive."

"Didn't say the margins were that thin," Hoffman replied. "Neither did the Redward intelligence report. What it *says* is that the Clans' pilots *believe* the margins are that thin. It reads like some damn clever propaganda work on someone's part...but it means that they'll fight like demons.

"They're pirates that think if they fail, everyone they love dies. Hell of a motivator."

"And we'll want to keep that in mind," Kira agreed. "I'd still stack Memorial Squadron up against an equal number of their gunships. Even *with* the temps!"

The two men standing with her chuckled their agreement.

"Not arguing that point, Commander," Hoffman said. "Just... urging caution, that's all."

19

"YOU WANT TO *WHAT*?" Waldroup stared at Kira in surprise.

Memorial Squadron's commander wasn't entirely convinced that Angel Waldroup ever slept. Every time Kira was on the flight or retrieval deck, the massive woman was there somewhere. She seemed to be managing flight control, fighter maintenance, everything.

Kira had caught up with her while she was supervising the functionality check on the carrier's stockpile of conversion torpedoes.

"I want to make a surprise manual landing on the next patrol run, after the nova," Kira repeated. "If we're in the jamming field of an active battlespace, you can't take remote control of the nova fighters. Hell, you don't even have the sensors to guide us in if we're in full multiphasic jamming."

"Nobody is flying this carrier into a battlespace," Waldroup objected. "She's completely defenseless. Zoric's job is to get the hell out of the way while you and Mbeki deal with threats."

"Defenseless?" Kira asked. "Last I checked, if nothing else, *Conviction* has fully functional multiphasic jammers of her own. She might need them to keep herself safe from long-range fire—and the kind of ships that can throw that kind of fire are the kind we'll need torpedoes to kill.

"How do you plan on rearming the One-Fifteens if you can't land them, Waldroup?"

"You're nuts," the deck boss replied. "Nobody *practices* a manual landing."

"The ASDF and the Kaiserreich do," Kira said. "I've made over a hundred practice manual landings—and three real-world ones, under heavy fire each time. I know *I* can land on *Conviction* manually without any problems at all.

"I want to see how your people handle it when I do, but I didn't want to pull that without at least talking to you."

"You're nuts," Waldroup repeated, but Kira could see the beginnings of a wicked grin forming around the technician's lips. "All right." She raised a finger. "Assuming, of course, that the next route stop is clear. Let's not complicate an actual fight more than we need to."

"Of course not," Kira agreed. "It's a drill, Waldroup. I want to do this once to surprise your people, but once your people have their procedures down, I'm going to run all of my *pilots* through it.

"I want to know that, no matter what happens, my people can land on this carrier."

"Going to sell Mbeki on that one?" Waldroup asked drily.

"Darkwing isn't my squadron," Kira said sharply. "They're not my pilots; they're not subject to my training regimen. But the five people whose salaries I'm paying this week?

"They are. And three of them already know this regimen."

And if the other two couldn't hack it, they had no business flying her nova fighters!

KIRA WAS awake and back on the flight deck in time for the nova along route three. There was no noticeable sensation aboard the carrier, even for a full six-light-year nova. Standing on the deck, however, she noted that there were going to be at least four people feeling the ride: two of the PNC-115s were still in space.

The nova fighters were *capable* of a six-light-year nova. Of course, a class two nova drive would need almost forty hours to recharge after that jump compared to a class one nova drive's twenty.

The flip side was that a class two drive could recharge after a one light-minute or shorter jump in ten seconds at most, where a class one drive was looking at a ten-minute minimum recharge time, no matter how short the jump.

A thought command opened her fighter and she clambered into the cockpit.

"This is Basketball, I'm clear to launch," she announced as she strapped herself in. "Who's flying nova escort?"

"Darkwing Seven and Eight," *Conviction* control replied. She didn't recognize who was speaking this time. "Hammer and Fern. They'll land once you and Longknife are in space, Memorial Lead."

"Understood. Proceed with the launch."

The standard back-and-forth followed, but Kira went through it on autopilot as she looked at the plan for this stop. Not much had changed. Memorial Squadron would guard the carrier while Darkwing sent two flights out on twenty-hour patrols.

Different flights than last time, she noted. Mbeki had flown the sixteen hour patrol at the last stop and was leaving his second in command to lead this one.

Space flashed dark around her and she thought an order to her fighter, flickering her running lights at the two Darkwing fighters as she and Longknife took over high escort.

The changeover continued. Shortly after the two escorts landed, two PNC-115 fighter-bombers shot into space. Two more followed a minute later, and then all four nova fighters vanished into their own FTL jumps.

"*Conviction*, anything out here that you're worrying about?" Kira asked over the channel. "I make it slightly busier than the last stop. Four ships, all freighters. Nothing that looks interesting at all."

Three of the ships looked much the same as the twenty-kilocubic junkers at the first rest stop. The last was bigger and in better shape, a Redward-registry freighter of thirty-five thousand cubic meters.

"Nada," Control replied. "We know the Redward ship; she's been part of a few convoys we've escorted. Not well enough that anyone is inviting anyone over for dinner, so no real worries."

Kira snorted.

"Understood, *Conviction*, no need to make friends."

As the unfamiliar voice chuckled and the channel went dormant, she realized one of the things that had been bothering her since they'd left Blueward Station. Really, it had been bothering her since she'd come aboard the carrier.

Where the hell was John Estanza? Gold Cobra owned the carrier and was supposed to be her captain, but Commander Zoric seemed to fill the actual "ship captain" role on a day-to-day basis. She'd seen him to negotiate the contract, and that was *it*. Zoric and Mbeki were the people actually running the carrier and the mercenary corporation that manned it.

On Blueward Station, he'd supposedly been negotiating contracts. What was he doing out there in deep space?

Somehow, she was grimly certain it involved the bottle that had been sitting on the old man's desk when she had met him.

A FREIGHTER DISAPPEARED. Another appeared. It was a quiet patrol for the first hour, so Kira was surprised when her Hoplite informed her that she had a laser-com link from the other fighter.

"Longknife, you see something I don't?" she asked quickly.

"Not out here, no," Hoffman told her quietly. "This is secure, right?"

"It's laser com," Kira said with a snort. "Nobody else out here can even see it. What's up?"

"I had a long talk with Nightmare after her patrol with Galavant," the other pilot told her. "She doesn't think we're going to keep her."

Galavant was Annmarie Banderas's callsign. Kira wasn't even surprised to hear that.

"She didn't seem overly impressed with the training regimen," she agreed. "I'm not sure Mbeki's people take the Costar seriously."

Her wingman snorted.

"I'm not sure *you* take the Costar seriously," he countered. "But you're right. They've fought them and they regard them as practically harmless."

"Which is a terrible classification to hang on anyone who is shooting at you," Kira muttered. "I don't rank them high as threats go, Longknife, but they're definitely a threat!"

"Glad to hear it." She felt as much as heard or saw Hoffman's head-shake. "Banderas seems to figure all of this is a waste of time, and she didn't sign on as a mercenary to get run ragged."

"She's entitled to her opinion, but while she flies under me, she does the training," Kira said. "And then she never flies under me again. That's *also* her privilege."

"Nightmare seemed to think it might come up sooner than that, but neither of us has a feel on how," Hoffman told her. "She wanted to touch base with you, but you were asleep when she landed and then we were novaing."

Timing was everything. Kira suppressed a curse. Secondhand assessments like this were always risky.

"I'll keep my eyes and ears open," she responded. "Galavant's half-decent, so unless she causes trouble, I'll keep her as a temp until this cruise is over."

"Swordheart is fine, according to Dawnlord," Hoffman told her, clearly trying to add some good news about Shun Asjes. "They don't say much, but Dawnlord figures they thought the Darkwings were under-prepped for what's out here."

"I'd agree," Kira said. "But they're Mbeki's squadron, not mine. He can do whatever the hell he wants with them. So long as anyone flies for me, they're going to be ready."

"Oh, I know," Hoffman confirmed. "But Nightmare and Dawnlord wanted those updates on your mind and didn't want to drop a message through the ship."

Conviction was a temporary home for Memorial Squadron right now. That could—almost certainly *would*—change as they stayed aboard and got to know the crew. Right now, the carrier was a stopover and Kiras people only trusted the mercenaries so far.

"We'll worry about—shoot!"

The tachyon pulse that lit up Kira's screens was one of the largest she'd seen in the Syntactic Cluster.

"I have nova," she reported to *Conviction*. "I have *warship* nova," she clarified a moment later. "Forty-five kilocubics; she's running hot and moving to sweep the trade route rest stop."

Almost unconsciously, she brought the fighter's reactor to a higher readiness. Her mental finger rested on the command sequence that would activate the Hoplite-IV's two multiphasic jammers as she waited for the warship's identity codes to register.

At that size, the stranger was a heavy destroyer or light cruiser—and there were only two or three systems in the entire cluster that could have built her. Others might have *bought* her, but...

The ident code didn't really alleviate her fear. She was the Ypres Sanctuary Security Flotilla Ship *Banshee*, flagship of one of the several different fleets run by the disparate factions in that not-particularly-unified star system.

"*Conviction*, are you seeing what I'm seeing on the ID code?" she asked. "What's the Ypres Sanctuary flagship doing out here?"

"Same thing we are," Zoric's voice replied grimly. "Showing the flag and demonstrating the ability to project power. Of course, *we're* doing it for Redward and *they're* doing it for faction number four of a system that could only challenge Redward if they all worked together."

"Threat status?" Kira asked.

"We treat her like a freighter," the carrier commander replied. "Except more so. If I could think of a way to make it *really* look like we don't give them credit, I'd do it."

Kira chuckled.

"I'll keep that in mind," she told Zoric, realizing it was an open channel. Her little drill wasn't going to work nearly as well if the deck crew knew she was coming.

"For now, keep an eye on her and otherwise ignore her?"

"Exactly. And hopefully, she'll return the favor. No one wants to throw down out here, not with real pirates in play. Plus, Ypres Sanctuary doesn't want to throw down with Redward. Period."

Kira apparently needed to do more research on Ypres. She'd registered that it was divided into five different factions—nations, really, by another name—but she hadn't realized that those factions could field real warships.

For now, the patrol was just about up, and that meant it was time to give the retrieval deck white hairs.

"THIS IS *CONVICTION*, standing by for automatic control," Zoric's voice said in Kira's headware as she lined the Hoplite up. "I have you on the line, Basketball. Vectors are green, contact in thirty seconds. I request control."

"Negative, *Conviction*," Kira said calmly as she edged the fighter towards the retrieval deck. "It's surprise-drill time. Prep the retrieval deck for manual landing."

There wasn't really much *to* prep. Mostly, it was just retracting a bunch of the tools and robot arms that ship control could fly her around—but that she wouldn't know the positions of.

"Are you fucking *insane*?" Zoric demanded. Headware meant the conversation was taking place ten times faster than they could have actually spoken, but they still only had so much time.

"Standard training protocol calls for a pilot to carry out a minimum one manual landing drill per month. Carrier crew should be ready for manual landing drill at any time," Kira said sweetly. "I have the ball, *Conviction*. Bay entrance in ten."

They were well past the point where Zoric should have been arguing with her. *Kira* had full faith in her ability to manually land the Hoplite in a retrieval bay that hadn't been prepared for the maneuver.

If *Zoric* had that faith, on the other hand, the mercenary officer was entirely out of line. Kira would never have trusted any of her pilots to make that landing without clearing the landing bay, no matter how many times she'd seen them do it.

It was an unnecessary risk—and Zoric clearly agreed.

Kira slammed her velocity even further down as she drifted into the retrieval bay. The various robot arms were pulling against the walls as she did so, vastly expanding the space she had to work with.

"Landing pad is transfer four," Zoric's voice said grimly in her ear. "If you *hit* my ship…"

"Commander, I haven't hit a ship in a hundred manual landings,"

Kira replied. "I can't speak to random robot arms, but I can guarantee I won't hit the *carrier*."

Grim or not, that got a chuckle from the mercenary as Kira dropped a blinking icon above the transfer pad. A final adjustment on the Harringtons brought the Hoplite to a perfect stop, two meters above the platform.

A tiny push from the coils delivered the nova fighter to the ground, and Kira exhaled heavily.

"*Conviction*, I have contact," she told Zoric. "All systems green, surrendering control to retrieval bay systems."

"All right. You didn't hit my carrier, but that was still *insane*," Zoric replied. "And it made a point to our Yprian friend. So, I'll *consider* letting this slide, this time."

"Good. Make sure your crews are trained for it next time," Kira told her. "I want to run all of my pilots through manual landing drills before we reach New Ontario."

The dead silence on the channel was enough answer for Kira to know that she was going to have a problem.

20

MBEKI WAS WAITING for Kira in her office. Even before he opened his mouth, Kira was glad that Hoffman had warned her that Banderas was going to cause trouble.

"What kind of stunt did you just *pull*?" he demanded. "Zoric is spitting nails."

"I carried out a manual landing drill," Kira said calmly. She walked past him and took a seat in her chair. The coffee machine was already humming, and moving the chair over to sit by it was easy enough.

She took the first of the two cups the machine prepared and leaned back in her chair, studying the still-standing Mbeki.

"A manual landing *drill*?" Mbeki said, ignoring the second cup of coffee. "That's stupid *and* irresponsible. This isn't an Apollon warship, Demirci."

"No, but my nova fighters will keep Apollon standards," she replied. "And my contract with *Conviction* says they'll support me in doing so."

"Your standards are insane," he told her. "Your people are bullying poor Banderas mercilessly. She's a damn fine pilot, but you're treating her like she just stepped into a nova fighter for the first time."

"I'm treating her like she's a damn fine pilot, actually," Kira countered softly. "She's facing the same training and drills as the rest of my people. Which, among other things, means she'll be making a manual landing before we reach New Ontario. I'll talk to her about setting up some simulated runs, but its easier than most people assume."

"Not a fucking chance," Mbeki snarled. "You are *not* doing manual landing drills on *my* deck."

"Then it's a good thing it's not your fucking deck, isn't it?" Kira snapped back, her hackles finally up. She wasn't sure if this was him being angry at her rejecting him or honestly thinking she was over-doing it, but she didn't care.

If nothing else, *she* was angry at *him* for making her need to reject him. She knew it was unfair, but it was still true.

"It's *Conviction's* deck, and my contract says *Conviction's* crew will help me with all reasonable drills and training exercises. So long as Asjes and Banderas fly for me, they'll meet my standards. If they don't want to meet my standards, they can bloody well quit and go back to flying for you.

"But if that's what it comes down to, Commander Mbeki, it's going to become *very* clear, *very* quickly, who the actual professionals on this ship are."

"This is not the goddamn Apollon military," he barked.

"No. But Memorial Squadron is going to be just as damn good as the Apollon military," she told him. "And if you want your squadron to be rusty hangar queens, that's fine. But *my* people will fly with the best.

"Banderas signed a contract that she'd fly with me until we returned to Blueward. She's welcome to buy it out, but she does *not* get to run crying to Daddy to try to get me to change my ways."

Kira shook her head at Mbeki.

"My squadron flies my way, Commander," she concluded. "*I* fly my way and I don't ask them to do anything I can't or won't."

She grinned coldly.

"You're welcome to admit to your people that you don't expect that much of them. I'd recommend against it, though. Being *told* they're second place is always bad for morale."

"You don't have a blank damn transfer, Demirci," Mbeki replied warningly. "*Conviction* doesn't *need* you or your people. Cause enough trouble and you'll be looking for a new berth."

"The Syntactic Cluster doesn't give me the impression that those will be hard to find," she pointed out. "Get out of my office, Mbeki. Unless you have something actually *constructive* to discuss?"

KIRA KNEW what the next step had to be, *if* there was a next step. The only real question in her mind was whether *Conviction*'s hierarchy was sufficiently functional for things to get bounced up that high and get a response.

She was deep into customizing a scenario for her pilots that, purely coincidentally, involved them defending an unarmed carrier against the unexpected arrival of an aggressive forty-five kilocubic destroyer, when her headware chimed with a message.

The message arrived with what the ASDF had called *flag priority*, meaning it came from a superior officer and required immediate response. There was only one person aboard *Conviction* that her headware would recognize as a superior officer.

Estanza's message was short and to the point:

My office. Now.

She saved the simulation and finished her coffee. It seemed that if she raised enough of a stink, *Conviction*'s hermit of a Captain did actually appear.

Straightforward enough. So far, at least.

MBEKI WAS ALREADY THERE when Kira arrived, sitting in one of two chairs positioned facing Estanza across the wooden desk. There was no bottle visible on the desk, but the faint smell of alcohol lingered in the room—and she doubted the amber liquid in the glass the Captain was holding was apple juice.

"Have a seat, Commander Demirci," Estanza told her. "I'm presuming you can guess why we're having this meeting."

"Enough so that I'm surprised Commander Zoric isn't here," she admitted.

"Commander Zoric decided to read the contract before shoving her foot in her mouth," Estanza said bluntly. "She has raised *concerns* with me but also conceded that the contract says she will help you with your drills."

"Your *insane* drills," Mbeki interjected. "Every time we carry out a manual landing, there is a clear and actual threat to this ship. They're best reserved for emergencies, not some kind of misguided attempt at showing off."

Estanza coughed and Kira realized that the other Commander might not have picked his battles correctly.

"Do you mean to tell me, Commander Mbeki, that you *don't* think you could reliably land on the retrieval deck without risking damaging the carrier?" Estanza asked dryly. "That seems rather…confessional, doesn't it?"

"Of course I could," Mbeki snapped. "But it's a risk every time."

"Not if your pilots are as good as they're supposed to be," the old man replied. "In fact, I believe your training when you first reported aboard included a very similar set of drills to what Commander Demirci is suggesting."

Mbeki was silent.

"On the other hand"—Estanza turned to Kira, his gaze managing to be both sharp and strangely dull—"*surprising* the retrieval deck with a manual landing drill *is* dangerous. Even a minor impact with the tools could have caused significant expenses in repairs to *Conviction*—expenses I would have expected you to bear, Commander."

"Had I managed to damage the deck, I would have expected to pay for those repairs," Kira agreed sweetly. "Of course, Waldroup was aware of the drill. I expected her to have things under control."

Estanza started to chuckle but it turned into a coughing fit. With both Commanders watching him in concern, he took a large swallow of his drink.

If the drink was what Kira thought it was, that probably wouldn't have helped *her* with the coughing.

"I don't approve of bullying or overwork as a training method," he told Kira. "I'm not hearing good things from the pilots seconded from Mbeki's squadron. *That*, Commander Demirci, *does* concern me."

"I'm not asking them to do anything the rest of my pilots aren't doing," she told him. "I don't think my people are bullying them, but I can certainly lean on them if that is a concern.

"If Asjes and Banderas feel overburdened, I am prepared to let them buy out their contracts."

"A compromise, I think," Estanza told her. "If one of *my* pilots decides they can't live up to your training regimen, I will accept that as you having made a good-faith effort to deploy your full strength and won't dock your contract pay for being a fighter short.

"*If*, that is, you freely release them from their contract."

The only reason Kira had put in any kind of contract buyout was to reduce her risk of coming up short on her own contract requirement. She nodded her agreement.

"That's fair, sir," she conceded, with an aside glance at Mbeki. It looked like her two temps had ended being almost more trouble than they were worth—and that a lot of people had been carrying complaints up the ladder.

"As for you, Mbeki"—Estanza's gaze turned on the other Squadron Commander—"I shouldn't need to remind you of this, but it seems I must: Memorial Squadron doesn't report to you. You have command authority as Commander, Nova Group, but the daily operations and training of Commander Demirci's squadron are outside your authority.

"You should *not* be complaining to me about her training program without having proven allegations. Am I clear?"

The black man bowed his head in acknowledgement.

"Good. Mbeki, go see to your squadron. Demirci? Remain a moment, please."

All Kira really wanted was to get out of that alcohol-scented room and get back to work, but she nodded her agreement anyway.

Until she ended the contract, John Estanza was her boss. The only boss she had out there.

21

AS MBEKI LEFT, Estanza made a small gesture with his hand that sent the now-unused chair sliding across the office into a cupboard in the wall. That left Kira alone on the other side of his desk, and his strange dull gaze focused on her.

It was weird to her. She was reasonably sure that Estanza was drunk. There was whisky in the glass in his hand, his eyes were visibly unfocused, and yet...

"You two are going to cause this ship more problems than you can possibly imagine," he told her. "The last thing I can afford, Commander Demirci, is for the fighter-jock soap opera to impact the smooth operation of this ship."

"The soap opera?" Kira asked carefully.

"You know exactly what I mean, Demirci," Estanza said. "I am not as old as Jay Moranis was, but believe me when I say I've seen this dance a thousand times. Your emotions and personal affairs are impeding your judgment."

"Are you *kidding* me?" she snapped. "The closest I've come to letting emotions get involved is when I kicked Mbeki out of my office. Are you going to accuse me of showing off now?"

"When my squadron commanders are both *radiating* romantic and sexual frustration and I have this kind of dick-measuring contest going on, what do you expect me to think, Commander?" Estanza asked bluntly. "Too many emotions are getting involved here, and it's complicating the operation of my carrier.

"I won't tolerate it."

"Then talk to your boy Mbeki," Kira replied. "If the hormone-addled *idiot* had bothered to listen to me before going running to you, this situation would already have been resolved. Instead, he 'let personal affairs' impede his judgment, so we end up here.

"If this is how the man handles rejection, I'm not sure *I* would trust him in command of a nova fighter, let alone a full squadron of them!"

She wasn't sure just what Daniel Mbeki had said to Estanza before she'd shown up—and it clearly hadn't succeeded in tilting Estanza's opinion of the actual facts of the situation—but she was so very done with the other squadron commander's crap.

Estanza studied her in silence, a posture that reminded Kira of nothing so much as a slightly bemused Apollon eagle. Then he drained his glass and stood up in the same gesture.

"Stay right there," he instructed her as she began to rise.

With his back to her, Estanza crossed to the bar and poured two glasses of whisky. Returning to his desk, he slid the second across to her.

"Drink, Demirci," he told her. "I believe you that Daniel screwed up. I'll talk to him. The man should know better and *does* know better."

She took the glass of whisky and sipped carefully, waiting for Estanza to get to his point.

"I've known Daniel Mbeki for a long damn time," Estanza said quietly. "Twenty years. I think he overestimates how long I had *Conviction* before he came aboard—easy enough, since he was one of the last of the original crew to sign on.

"He's also one of the last of the original crew *left*. I've watched that man grow from a twenty-year-old with nova wings and a brand-new prosthesis to a man I trust at my right hand, in command of the most valuable combat squadron for fifty light-years in any direction."

"Who apparently can't handle rejection," Kira replied snippily, then paused. "Wait, prosthesis?"

"Several, technically," Estanza confirmed. "He was partially crushed by an idiot tech on a flight deck twenty-two days into his active service at Sorvedo. His left leg and arm are artificial, and a chunk of his ribcage is artificially reinforced.

"The Patrol medically discharged him with a generous pension, but he wanted to fly and I was looking to fill some unexpected holes in my roster." The old man shrugged. "I picked up three people with nova pilot wings on Sorvedo that week. Mbeki was the best of them. His prosthetics are near-perfect replacements, after all."

"So, he'll listen to you, is what I'm hearing," Kira said. "You can talk him up all you want, sir, but the man just tried to start a fight with my squadron because of his 'personal matters.' My enthusiasm is limited."

Estanza sighed and gave her A Look.

"I have seen this dance a thousand times," he repeated. "I can't say for sure where you and Daniel are in the steps, but I know the dance. You're far too angry at him for this to have been a one-way issue."

"Doesn't matter, does it?" she replied.

"You're not a soldier anymore, Demirci," Estanza reminded her. "You're a mercenary now. Even if *I* had rules about on-ship fraternization—and I *don't*—they wouldn't apply to you unless they were in your contract.

"Which they're not."

She shook her head.

"Just because there's no *rules* doesn't mean it isn't a terrible idea," she pointed out. "That rule exists for a reason. Anything between Mbeki and me would be a distraction and a danger to ourselves and our people."

"That's the reasoning behind the rule, yes," Estanza agreed. "I've flown in four mercenary squadrons under three commanding officers. I've been a merc for fifty-three years, and I was a military officer a long way from here for seven.

"In sixty years as a pilot and a commanding officer, I have *never* seen an active relationship between pilots in different squadrons, regardless of the ranks involved, become a problem. I *have* seen a bone-headed determination to do the right thing combined with people mooning over each other get pilots killed.

"Believe me, Demirci, you and Mbeki 'giving in,' or however you want to phrase it, is not going to undermine the chain of command or discipline on this ship. We're mercenaries. We follow the rules that work; we discard the rest.

"A specified number of manual landing drills per month? Probably garbage. Making sure that all of the pilots have done at least one manual landing drill in real space in the last few months? Almost certainly worth it.

"I'm not going to tell you to kiss and make up, Commander," Estanza concluded with a grin. "I'm far too old to pretend I have any business giving personal advice. I *will* tell you that I think your reason for rejecting what *you* want is complete garbage."

Kira had choked down several hot retorts while the older officer had been speaking, and now she took another sip of the whisky while she marshaled her thoughts.

"I haven't seen either in my experience, I have to admit," she finally conceded. In twenty years of service, she was surprised to realize that. It was unlikely that no one around her had ever fallen for a superior or subordinate.

On the other hand, Apollo culture was generally discreet on romantic matters in general, so her comrades might just have had enough practice to conceal affairs they weren't supposed to be having.

"I'm uninclined to throw out rules built on literally millennia of accumulated experience without a better reason than a glorified teenage crush, either," she continued. "I can deal with my own emotions, sir. I'd hope that Commander Mbeki can say the same."

"It's your call," Estanza replied. "I'll talk to him either way."

22

KIRA DID her two new pilots the courtesy of finally finding *chairs* for her office before she called them on the carpet. The desk was still a hologram, but Asjes and Banderas could at least sit down as she stood behind it with her coldest gaze.

"So."

She let the word hang in the air.

"One of you—I do not *care* which—decided you were being bullied and went to Commander Mbeki," she said flatly. "That has led to all *kinds* of entertaining conversations, which I doubt anyone is going to enjoy the results of.

"What's most relevant to *you* is that, since you appear to have been under the impression working for me was going to be a vacation, Captain Estanza and I have come to a compromise agreement."

She watched both of the pilots try to shrink into their chairs. One advantage, it seemed, of the Captain being a near-complete hermit was that coming to his attention was very definitely a *bad* thing for anyone aboard the ship.

"The training regimen we've undergone so far isn't going to change," she told them. "If you fly for me, even temporarily, you will be expected to maintain the training levels and performance standards

I would expect of a pilot in Memorial Squadron—which are those of a pilot in the ASDF's most elite squadrons.

"It appears that wasn't properly communicated to you before you signed on for this contract, so if you want to back out now, Estanza is covering the buyout portion of your contract."

The pilots didn't need to know the exact details of the compromise. That was close enough for their purposes.

"If you stick it out from here, I expect you to stick it out," she said calmly. "We're three novas into an eight-nova trip. Make it back to Redward, you get paid out, everyone wins. If nothing else, you'll probably be better pilots at the end than you were at the start.

"But if you want out, now's the time," she concluded. "I won't hold it against you—and I *am* going to look into the com and video records to make sure my people *weren't* bullying you. It won't happen again, I promise you that."

The two pilots were still sitting in front of her, their gazes fixed on the holographic desk.

"Well?" she asked after a few moments of silence. "We're two hours from the nova to New Ontario. Time to make the call, people."

"I'm in," Asjes said firmly. "If nothing else, rumor has it that we're *all* going to be doing manual landing drills once we're back in Redward. May as well get it out of the way under your watch."

"I'll stick it out," Banderas said, but her voice was quieter. Kira figured she knew who'd complained to Mbeki now—but she doubted that the pilot had expected things to go quite as high and loudly as they had.

"Good." Kira studied them. "I've studied your performance in the tests and training we've done. Both of you *can* hack it. The question was only ever whether you would make the attempt. Am I understood?"

That, it seemed, got under both of their skins in the right way, and she smiled as they finally looked her in the eyes.

"New Ontario is safe space," she told them. "You'll both be making manual landings before we reach orbit. I suggest you go run through the simulator on them.

"It's easier than people who haven't done it think it is, but that doesn't mean it's *easy*," she finished with a grin. "So, go practice."

NEW ONTARIO TURNED out to be closer to what Kira had originally expected of the Redward System. *Conviction*'s base system was reasonably well colonized and industrialized, even if their tech base was still backward compared to Apollo.

New Ontario was...not.

Only one orbital elevator marked the planet's equator. The asteroid counterweight was definitely armed, but it barely qualified as a fortress in her opinion. There was the usual infrastructure around the gas giant for refueling starships and allowing them to discharge the static buildup from their nova drives...and that was it.

No extraction operations on the uninhabited planets. Nothing even in the asteroid belt that stood out to the carrier's sensors. Half a billion people on the planet but almost nothing in space.

"Well, this really is the ass end of nowhere," Kira said aloud. She was standing in *Conviction*'s flight control, running through the prep for the five manual landings she was about to put the poor retrieval deck crew through.

"Yup," Waldroup confirmed. "It's the tail end of this trade route and the far side of the Cluster from the core. Last bastion of civilization before you leave the Rim and get into real empty space."

The Beyond. There were still inhabited star systems and settlements and all of that once you passed the vague edge of the Rim, but there weren't established trade routes and regions with agreements, treaties...or anything.

It probably wasn't as bad as Kira was inclined to think, but even the Syntactic Cluster seemed quiet and backward to her. The trade route stops that Apollo had fought to secure had been physical locations, space stations built from prefabricated sections that provided food and entertainment to the crews waiting twenty hours at each point.

The Cluster, like most of the Rim, had the mapped-out route stops that made for safe trips, but they didn't have that infrastructure. The Beyond didn't even have the mapped-out points.

"What are we even here for?" Kira asked the deck boss.

"Well, we have to discharge somewhere, and New Ontario is the end of the line for the route we were patrolling," Waldroup told her. "So, Zoric is bringing us into Sarnia for that. King Larry has an agreement that lets the Royal Fleet run a base on one of Sarnia's moons.

"They keep a wing of sub-fighters here to watch the base and the refueling infrastructure. They cycle squadrons and personnel in and out.

"We're meeting a couple of empty supply ships and a transport that's carrying a dozen sub-fighters and their crews back to Redward."

"Should send a carrier for them," Kira pointed out. "Then they don't need to send us along to escort them. They've got sub-fighter carriers, don't they?"

"Sometimes they do," Waldroup agreed. "This is only the second time they've sent us. I'd bet that the RRF *wanted* to haul the sub-fighters on *Conviction* but the boss said no. No point launching sub-fighters off our decks when we've got nova fighters to deploy."

Kira couldn't argue with that point. The sub-fighters might be the same size as *Conviction*'s nova fighters and have similar guns and Harringtons, but they'd never pin down an opponent that could be somewhere else at the punch of a button.

"Longknife is on approach," one of the flight controllers cut into the conversation to report. "I make ninety seconds to contact."

"Understood," Waldroup snapped. "Is the deck clear for manual landing drill?"

"Yes, boss," one of the techs reported. "All systems retracted; maximum volume available. Transfer pad one is online and ready to move Longknife's bird off the deck ASAP to clear for Nightmare's landing."

Kira smiled as she considered the timing.

She'd wanted to run all of her people through manual landing drills. It had been *Waldroup* who'd wanted to do all five landings in sequence, two minutes apart.

Her determination to bring everyone up to full speed was apparently starting to get infectious.

HOFFMAN MADE THE LANDING PERFECTLY, coming in just fast enough to make several of the techs in flight control inhale sharply as he slammed to a halt exactly above the transfer pad.

Normally, he'd leave the fighter before the pad moved it out of the way. With another fighter coming in right behind him for a manual landing the pad immediately descended into the tunnels that would move it to its normal resting place.

Cartman's fighter entered the bay exactly two minutes after Hoffman's. The precision was identical, though she didn't cut the velocity quite as closely.

Up next was Galavant—Banderas—and even Kira had to admit she was holding her breath as the nova fighter came in. She could see Waldroup leaning over a console with a full array of controls for the retrieval bay's gravity systems and nodded to herself.

The retrieval bay's systems were fully capable of stopping the Hoplite in its tracks. It wouldn't be great for the fighter—they'd have to downcheck it until Waldroup's people could go over it from nose to tail—but the *carrier* would be fine.

"Velocity is green, green, green," a tech chanted. "Vector is…vector is *orange*. Galavant, raise your angle; you're cutting it too—"

There was no time. By the time the tech had spotted it, it was too late for Galavant to change her vector, and she slid into the retrieval deck easily two meters lower than she should have.

Something got hit and went flying for a dozen meters or more before the gravity systems caught it, but the pilot had control of her fighter's speed even if she'd twitched the angle at the last moment.

The fighter didn't land on the transfer pad so much as *slide* onto it.

"Activate the pad," Waldroup ordered into the silence. There was a pause. "*Activate the damn pad,*" she barked. "Dawnlord is sixty seconds out and I *don't* want a fighter on the deck when he comes in."

The transfer pad started descending and Kira was running over the footage in her head.

"Waldroup?" she said quietly.

"We're fine," the deck boss told her. "She came in with twenty-six centimeters of clearance and hit a transfer pallet that should have been safe…and *still* shouldn't have been on my damn deck."

"The fighter?"

"I need to take a look at it," Waldroup replied. "It *should* be fine. If not, it'll be repairable. Energy signature didn't even blip."

"Dawnlord is in the chute, thirty seconds to contact," someone reported. "Velocity: green, green, green. Vector: green, green, green."

"Double check Swordheart's vector," Kira ordered. "I'm not worried about Patel, but let's make sure Asjes is coming in with the right clearance. I don't need them to bounce a fighter off the toolbox somebody forgot!"

From the way Waldroup winced, whoever had left the pallet behind was going to hear about it. In detail.

"Dawnlord is in, clearance is wide…he's down. No issues."

Kira exhaled.

"And Swordheart?"

"Green across the board," the tech replied. "They should be fine."

"All right," she said calmly. "Well, Waldroup?"

"Your people pass just fine," the deck boss told her. "*Mine*, on the other hand, are pulling a double shift to help fix the dent we just put in your starfighter. Galavant should have been fine."

"I'll make sure to tell her that," Kira said dryly. "From past experience, I can tell you that right now, she feels like she just had a heart attack!"

But she'd made the landing—and Swordheart made his as they were talking—which meant that Kira's little argument over whether her two new pilots could hack it was over.

Part of her immediately asked if that meant she could talk to Daniel yet.

She concealed a snort. The part of her brain that wanted to refer to Commander Mbeki by his first name didn't get a say in *anything*.

Not yet, anyway.

23

CONVICTION RAN her combat operations from two rooms: flight control and the bridge. Both had full access to the carrier's sensors, full suites of both holographic and headware interfaces, and large amounts of old-fashioned visual displays.

What they shared aboard the merc carrier was a strange lack of the Captain. Commander Zoric ran *Conviction* from the bridge. Kira and Mbeki would run their squadrons from their nova fighters.

Waldroup, who glorified in absolutely no title at all, appeared to run flight control. Along with the flight and retrieval decks.

Lack of title or not, Kira was realizing that Waldroup was arguably equal to the three Commanders in authority aboard the ship—which also meant she was a good person to ask questions of.

And as *Conviction* entered high orbit of Sarnia and set her course for the Redward naval base on Canatara, Kira had a few burning questions.

"Who the *hell* lets a bunch of civilians that close to a military base?" was the first one she actually asked. "I thought we were escorting a Fleet convoy."

"We are," Waldroup confirmed. "The rest of them are just tagging along."

It was easy to pick out the three Redward Royal Fleet transports. They were matching forty-kilocubic hulls, rough cylinders that were easy to build and efficient to carry cargo in.

The *other* fifteen ships were a mess. If any two of them were the same, it would have surprised Kira. All of them were far too close to the RRF base on Canatara and the fuel tanks orbiting it.

"Zoric reports we've reached close-enough approach to Sarnia to begin tachyon-static discharge," one of Waldroup's people mentioned. "We have coms with the RRF."

"And who has coms with the rabble?" Kira asked.

"Traditionally, we don't bother to establish coms with them," Waldroup admitted. "We can't really chase them off without getting more violent than anyone wants to, so we let them come along so long as they obey orders we send them.

"And other than that, we ignore them."

"Great," Kira replied. "That's going to mess with my patrol planning."

"It always does," the deck boss told her. "Talk to Mbeki. We've made this run before."

Kira shook her head.

"What a bloody mess. Is everything out here this much of a disaster?"

"I'd say welcome to the Rim, but you never left it," Waldroup said. "But you're from the Mid Rim. This is very much Outer Rim." The big woman shook her head. "They'd *probably* be safe flying on their own, but *probably* isn't good enough when your copilot is your husband and your fifteen-year-old kid is the purser."

"I didn't say I didn't sympathize," Kira conceded. Waldroup sounded like she knew the situation more intimately than Kira, too. "But I don't see any coordination or security sense going on here. Even if Canatara Base brought up their multiphasic jammers, most of those freighters are *still* in range to shoot it."

"No one at a planetary base worries about people shooting them with plasma guns, Commander," the other woman pointed out. "They worry about people ramming starships into them. Canatara Base will be *very* happy to see that convoy on its way."

Waldroup shrugged.

"We can't be rid of them, Commander," she concluded. "We may as well find some pleasure in that we're helping people who *need* the protecting."

"Fair." Kira shook her head. "Time to go shred a mission plan and start from the bottom. Let me know if anything comes up I need to worry about!"

"YOU PINGED ME TO SWING BY?"

Kira couldn't see Daniel Mbeki, but she had at least known he'd entered her office this time. She was facing away from the door, studying a massive holographic image of a formation based around *Conviction* and their flock of fifteen individual sources of trouble.

"I did. Thanks for coming," she told him. "I'm looking at our escort formation plan. I was assuming we were only seeing the three freighters RRF said we were picking up."

He'd stepped up closer to see the hologram, even as she could tell that he was sidling sideways to respect her personal space. The man didn't even need training—at least when he wasn't *actively* being an idiot.

"I was expecting some extras," he admitted. "I was not expecting twelve. What are you thinking?"

"*Conviction* is functionally defenseless, which means she and the freighters are all in roughly the same boat," Kira noted. "That gives us sixteen escortees and we only have fourteen fighters. Short of an outright emergency, we can't field them all at once."

"Agreed. Suggestions?"

"We did the security sweep on our way out," she reminded him. "So, we don't *need* to do it on the way back—which is good because we just plain don't have the nova fighters for it.

"We have to deploy by wings of two. I'm thinking one wing of mine, one wing of yours. We rotate your birds to keep your crews rested and provide us with a ready reserve of the One-Fifteens.

"Nova fighters that are out use the Patterson-Five sweep and

141

nova," she continued, thinking the icons in the display into motion. Patterson-Five would see the four fighters carrying out a figure eight sweep around and through the formation of their charges, using novas to cross the main axis at random intervals.

"Why Five?" Mbeki asked. "Most of the Patterson sequences call for novas."

"The novas are at a random interval in Five. It keeps even people watching closely guessing," she said. "That way our Costar Clans friends won't know exactly where we are in the sequence at any given moment."

"You think we're being watched?" he asked.

Kira chuckled.

"Look at those ships, Daniel," she told him, gesturing at the ragtag collection of extras. "At *least* two people in there are trading intelligence for immunity from Clan raiders. Probably by an automated program that any Clan ship can trigger by laser, so we can assume that if the Costar Clans show up, they know everything we've been doing."

He was silent for a moment.

"You're probably right," he conceded. "It's a good plan. Four birds up, six in reserve, four crews off?"

"Exactly."

They were both silent, studying the hologram for a minute.

"So, it's Daniel again, is it?" he finally asked, his voice warmer than it had been.

That warmth sent a shiver down her spine, and Kira very pointedly told her body to get over itself.

"Never said you couldn't call me Kira," she told him. "Don't make too much of it, Daniel. Everybody on this ship—including us!—is better off if you and I get back to where we were before we decided to turn into hormone-addled messes.

"So, let's shelve *that* particular problem until we get back to Redward, at least, and try to get back to working together. Sound good?"

There was a long silence and she turned to look at him. The dark-eyed black man was studying her, and his gaze was back to being intense again.

"It does, actually," he conceded.

"Not least because something about *this* convoy makes my neck itch."

Kira nodded her agreement. Behind that nod was the irritated realization that a very eager part of her did *not* want him to stop looking at her like that.

24

"PATROL PATTERN CALLS for nova across the formation in ninety seconds," Kira said to Galavant over the com channel. "Darkwing flight, do you confirm?"

"This is Gizmo; I confirm your nova course," the pilot in charge of the two PNC-115s holding the other half of the shifting figure eight of the Patterson-Five patrol.

The two Hoplites flipped in space as they reached the far end of their current loop. After almost twenty hours in the first rest stop system, the gaggle of civilian freighters weren't even spooking away from the sweeping nova fighters anymore.

Sooner or later, the flock stopped spooking at the scent of the sheepdog, Kira reflected with a grin. None of the freighters had caused the slightest problem when Zoric had calmly issued them all positioning instructions.

Conviction still hadn't even officially acknowledged that the non-RRF freighters were even *there*, but Kira's patrol plan had required the freighters to be in a particular formation. So, the freighters had been told to get in that formation.

If there'd been a dozen extra slots in that formation, oops?

"I have the course," Galavant replied. "I make a four-hundred-thousand-kilometer nova in forty seconds. Confirm?"

"Confirmed," Kira replied. A nova that short would only shut down their drives for a few seconds, but it would also cross that distance in *far* less time than their current velocity would take.

A timer ticked down and she didn't give the other woman any new instructions. She'd had the younger pilot on her wing for six hours now on this patrol and she'd done just fine. Few non-combat missions called for novaing quite this often, either. It was good practice.

The final call was mostly made by the computer based on the instructions Kira had given, but the line where a headware-augmented human ended and their computer began was…vague at best.

Time.

Nova.

The clocks always said that a nova was instantaneous. Kira had seen enough of them from the outside to even *believe* those clocks.

Inside a nova fighter it always dragged on for her. And it *hurt*, like the worst menstrual cramps she'd ever had, as her guts tried to turn themselves inside out in rebellion against the strange not-space she found herself in.

A class one drive with its ten-thousand-plus-cubic-meter field and its larger ship didn't have this effect in a nova. It was unique to the class two drive in her experience.

An experience only nova fighter pilots shared and that no one else would ever understand.

Then her Hoplite plunged out of the nova into regular space, on the opposite side of the formation.

"Basketball, this is *Conviction*," Mbeki's voice said in her headware. "We've got a full charge on the drive and the RRF freighters report the same. I'm pulling everyone back aboard for the nova."

"Plan calls for us to nova with the carrier, *Conviction*," Kira countered.

"And if you nova with the carrier, four of our birds can't nova for forty hours," the other squadron commander said reasonably. "I didn't think of it when we wrote the plan, but my skin is crawling today, Basketball.

"Let's take the risk at the nova to help cover the flock."

She *could* argue. Technically, the only person she answered to was

Estanza—but Mbeki was the official Commander, Nova Group—and he was the man in flight control with all of the data.

"Understood, *Conviction*," she replied. "Basketball and Galavant headed back to the barn."

She considered the dozen freighters that *Conviction* wasn't validating the charge status of before she novaed.

"Anyone care if I drag my feet so our lost sheep get a few extra minutes to charge their nova drives?" she asked.

Mbeki chuckled, the warm rumbling that kept sending heated ripples down her spine.

"Not at all, Basketball. Take your time, Memorial Lead."

KIRA WASN'T GOING to argue with Mbeki's crawling skin. She wasn't on *quite* the same page, but given all of the things in play, she couldn't argue with the paranoia. It had been a while since the Clans had jumped one of these convoys, there was a significant bounty on *her* head in particular, and she was damn sure at least one of the freighters was a Costar plant.

That meant there were no real space drills. No manual landings. Only the patrol regimen designed to keep sixteen ships safe.

She came in last, after the two Darkwings and Galavant.

"I yield control," she told Waldroup. "Everything looks clear out there, but everyone is huddling close to us."

"I would in their place," the deck boss replied as the computers took over flying Kira's fighter. "I hear Mbeki on the crawling."

"Out of curiosity, do we know how many sub-fighters they have on that transport?"

"Thirty," the deck boss replied instantly. "Next time we pull this stunt, can we *please* talk the boss into letting us haul them? At least if they're on our decks, they can go out and shoot somebody if needed instead of sitting in a box."

"I don't think we're transporting the pilots," Kira pointed out. "And we don't have thirty spare pilots floating around, even if you could convince any of us to fly something without a nova drive."

"Prima donna," Waldroup replied as the fighter touched down.

"Get out of that fighter and grab a coffee. We'll refuel her and have her ready to go for your next shift."

Kira snorted. The plan had been for them to swap patrol wings right after the nova, so she was technically off-duty until her shift as a reserve pilot. The Patterson-Five patrol was fuel-draining, which meant her bird was already down forty percent of fuel. If she'd novaed with the carrier, she'd have been at her combat reserve.

Of course, "combat reserve" was enough to fight and combat-nova for about thirty minutes and still get back to the carrier.

"How fast can you turn them around?" she asked Waldroup as she dropped out of the fighter. Transferring the conversation from the fighter system to her own headware was almost entirely unconscious.

"I was planning four hours, to have them ready well in advance of your reserve shift," the other woman replied. "Why?"

"Do a combat turnaround, Waldroup," Kira replied. "We're ten light-years into the black, as far from both New Ontario and Redward as we're going to get. I want my nova fighters."

"I can have them up in five minutes without risking anything quite as dangerous as a full combat turnaround," the deck boss replied. "Go get that damn coffee, Demirci.

"By the time you're done, you'll have six fighters ready to go." She paused. "And before you say a *word*, I'll have Gizmo and Migraine's birds ready on the same time frame."

THE FLIGHT ready room was as full as it ever got. Either Mbeki's paranoia was infectious or, well, it was shift changeover and no one was currently asleep or in a nova fighter. Fourteen pilots and eight copilots were strewn around the tables in a room sized for a wing of thirty.

There was another ready room on the other side of the launch deck, but this was the one everyone was using today.

Mbeki's headware had obviously given him enough warning to have a coffee ready when she stepped in.

"Busy today," she murmured. "Wait, did we nova yet?"

"We should be—"

The world rippled.

"Right now," he concluded with that damn chuckle. "Second rest stop on our trip, which means that I and a few friends need to get out to our fighters. Enjoy the coffee, Kira."

"Thank you," she said softly, then held up a hand as he headed out. "Hey, Daniel?"

"Yeah?" He looked back over his shoulder.

"Fly safe. Fly true."

"I will," he promised with a smile and a small bow.

Cartman and Patel followed him out, trading nods with Kira as she drank her coffee and linked in to the sensors.

Their lost sheep had followed them through the nova as a block. Four fighters would be in space to guard them shortly—and enough of the pilots were gathered there to provide a full scramble in under a minute.

"There's a second cluster at ten light-minutes," Zoric's voice said in the back of her head. "Looks like half a dozen civvies."

"What?" Kira asked back, keeping the conversation in her headware.

"You wouldn't be half the officer I think you are if you aren't looking at the sensor feeds right now," the carrier XO replied. "There's us here and there's a bunch of civvies at ten light-minutes; vector is one-oh-eight by two-thirty-five."

Kira focused her mental attention. There they were. Far enough away to not be a major concern.

"Numbers look pretty vague," she told Zoric. "You're not wrong on what I'm looking at, I'll admit."

"Yeah. It's odd. I'm focusing sensors now but…no, that's *not* right."

The data they *were* getting on the cluster dissolved into garbage, and Kira understood *exactly* what Zoric was talking about.

"That's an active multiphasic jamming field," Kira snapped. "Someone is jumping those ships."

"They're not our escortees, but I'm not going to sit here and watch them burn, either," Zoric replied. "What do we do?"

"The only thing we can, Commander Zoric," Kira said firmly. "Call battle stations and order a full scramble. Everything we're seeing is ten minutes out of date—their lives ride on seconds."

"Go!" Zoric urged, the single word hanging on the channel like an anvil.

Kira yanked her attention back to the ready room.

"Everyone!" she bellowed, gathering their eyes and ears. "Combat scramble *now*. Briefing on the way, but you need to be in your fighters *now*."

Mercenaries or not, every pilot in the room was moving before the alarm started flashing ten seconds later.

25

KIRA'S HEADWARE said it had been *exactly* five minutes, but her fighter was already in its dock waiting for her. The indicators the spacecraft downloaded to her headware told her it was fully refueled but that the regular service checks had been abbreviated.

Not quite a combat turnaround but pretty damn close—and exactly what the situation had turned out to need.

By the time she finished reviewing the indicators, she was already in the fighter and initiating the start-up sequence.

"Memorial Lead, this is *Conviction*," Zoric said in her headware. "We have no further information on the target zone. Multiphasic jamming continues. Stand by for full deck launch in sixty seconds."

That was risky...but not as risky as rushing the preflight checks or *not* having their entire fighter strength in space.

"Memorial Lead, this is *Conviction* Actual," John Estanza's voice sounded a moment later. "Darkwing Lead, this is *Conviction* Actual. *Conviction* Two is on the channel.

"We can't uncover the carrier, but I agree that we must respond to the situation," Estanza told them. "Darkwing Lead, hold your squadron in close escort around *Conviction* and the convoy. Memorial, the strike is yours.

"*Conviction* Two's analysis of the scans suggests four to ten gunships, almost certainly Costar Clans. If they're Clan, take them out."

"And if they're not Clan, sir?" Kira asked. "What if they're someone else's gunships?"

"Then fuck them," Mbeki said harshly. "Our contract says we counter piracy in all forms, sir. We only specifically get paid for Costar kills, but we are authorized and required to protect any shipping in the region."

"Agreed," Estanza said after a moment. "Regardless of their colors, Memorial Lead, you will protect civilian shipping by any means necessary." He snorted. "We just get paid better if they're Costar Clans."

"Understood."

A ten-second timer started on her headware. Right now, Mbeki was in space with three other fighters. When that timer hit zero, ten more nova fighters—including Kira's—would be in space.

"Ambushes are not outside the Costar Clans' methodology," Estanza continued. "Darkwing Lead, you need to keep the convoy and *Conviction* safe."

The timer hit zero and acceleration gently pressed Kira back into her seat. Her Harringtons activated as she cleared the carrier, and she twisted her fighter around to point at where they'd identified the ongoing attack.

"Memorial Squadron, form by wings," she ordered as she established laser coms with her people. "We have six civilian ships under attack by unknown forces at ten light-minutes. You should have the waypoint on your scopes.

"Dawnlord, Longknife, form on Nightmare. You'll nova to the waypoint plus two hundred thousand kilometers and catch them from the other side. Multiphasic jammers online as soon as you emerge from nova.

"Galavant, Swordheart, form on me. Nova to the waypoint on my command and hold formation to sustain laser coms in the jamming.

"Everyone understand?"

Wordless acknowledgments responded and her fighters fell into formation.

"*Conviction*, Memorial Squadron is deploying. We'll be back in time for dinner."

"We'll keep it warm for you. Good luck."

Kira nodded, inhaled sharply.

"Memorials...*nova*."

THE WAYPOINT she'd set up based on *Conviction*'s scans brought *her* wing back into real space just outside the multiphasic jamming field. The three Hoplites were in a perfect position to see as much of the situation as physically possible—even if it was slightly hampered by all three of them bringing their *own* multiphasics online.

Radio coms ended instantly, but that was why they were in formation. Multiphasic jammers badly limited the range of laser coms and laser sensors, but they didn't render them as useless as many other sensors and communicators.

"Memorial Wing, I read six gunships," she told Banderas and Asjes. She'd kept her two temp pilots with her for a reason. "That's enough for both of you to make ace if you want us old hands to hold back for you.

"We're probably better off taking them as a team," Banderas—Galavant—said calmly. "Your orders, sir."

"Flagging a bogey for each of you, but we all know how useful that will be once we lose coms."

They were hurtling into the gunships' jamming and their targets had *definitely* seen them. Headware and computers meant the conversation was happening fast enough to be safe, but they were still running out of time.

"Once we break formation, you're on your own. If they're shooting at the civvies, return the damn favor."

The civilians were in pretty rough shape. The last ten minutes hadn't gone well for them, but they were still intact. That looked to be mostly due to one larger ship whose owner appeared to have heavily invested in defensive armaments.

Those weapons were mostly wreckage and metal vapor now, but they'd held the gunships off long enough. Now that six nova fighters were in play, the gunships were ignoring the freighters in favor of the hostiles.

No more time.

"Hold your targets until they're done," Kira told her wingman, hopefully an unnecessary order. "Memorial wing, *break and attack*."

Her fighter happily informed her she'd lost coms with her compatriots almost instantly. As soon as the three of them were moving randomly to avoid enemy fire and close with their targets, the multiphasic jamming rendered communications impossible.

Even the best scanners in the galaxy could only get vague details out of the worst multiphasic jamming at any significant range. Visual scanning—well, optical scanning by computers with a dozen cameras —was the best tool a pilot or ship had once battle was closed.

Coms were down. Sensors were down. Even visual wavelengths of light were badly distorted at a distance from the effects. The multiphasic jammer had been the end to the dream of remote-controlled drone warfare in space at the same time as it rendered most long-range weaponry nearly useless.

Kira had a gunship in her sights and she dove for the ship *fast*. The sooner this engagement stopped looking anything like a fair fight, the happier she'd be—and given that the gunships were ten-thousand-cubic-meter ships twenty times the size of her nova fighters, that wasn't happening anytime soon.

Plasma fire flickered through space around her as she dodged forward. The pulses were enough slower than lightspeed to add a time delay to even fighting at this range. A hundred and fifty thousand kilometers. A hundred and thirty...the range was dropping fast and she was watching *everything*.

In a moment like this, a nova fighter pilot *became* their fighter. Headware lived in the brain and the fighter's computers lived outside your skull, but the integration had been updated and revised for centuries now.

A computerized part of her mind tracked the entire battle, watching the optical pickups and tracking the fate of her people and the freighters. Most of her mind was focused on her target and its desperate attempts to bring its much heavier guns to bear.

They were *far* from good enough and she hit her mental triggers. Her first set of plasma pulses missed.

The second didn't, walking a line of fire up the seventy-meter-long spine of the gunship. It was a flat-looking thing, wider than it was high to enable two gun turrets on each side.

Her fire walked right through *both* of the turrets and tore them to shreds. Secondary explosions rippled through the ship, but her crew was still moving. Harrington coils flashed energy into space, and the gunship rotated to bring her second set of turrets to bear.

Kira was feeling vaguely generous toward the Costar Clans—she could understand, at least intellectually, how desperation and a desire to help your people could put someone in that position.

She wasn't feeling *that* generous. The gunship never completed her rotation as Kira slammed on her Harringtons to hold her line of fire on the gunship for three full seconds.

The fighter danced around that line, but she still put over sixty plasma packets into the gunship and watched it disintegrate into a hundred pieces.

Then part of her mind watching the rest of the battle noted a warning, and she slammed everything to full power, flinging her ship almost a dozen extra kilometers forward in a moment as plasma fire flashed through where she had been.

That moment of focus on her attacker's part cost *them* more than her focus on their compatriot had cost her. Galavant's fighter swept in at the momentarily immobile ship and emptied a two-second-long salvo into the gunship's engines.

The engines ruptured, and secondary explosions gutted the gunship in a spectacular explosion. Kira threw a mental salute to her temp pilot and surveyed the battlespace.

The gunships might have been twenty times bigger than her fighters, but they'd been utterly outclassed regardless. As she watched, Swordheart micronovaed past the gunship she'd tasked them on. Plasma flashed into empty space as the gunship's turrets flared—and then Swordheart hammered his target with fire.

Kira could have intervened to finish the gunship off, but she left the kill to the temp as she checked on her old hands. She apparently hadn't even needed to worry. The last of the gunships came apart under Dawnlord's guns as she turned her attention.

Two seconds to double-check that the zone was clear, and she shut down her own jammers. At least one of her people still had them up, and the now-former-battlespace was still a mess for several more seconds.

Then the last jammer came down and Kira exhaled. She'd had no worries about her old 303 hands, but Swordheart and Galavant had come through without a scratch. Head-on with an equal number of gunships wasn't *exactly* a fair fight, but the gunships were a serious threat to their smaller cousins.

"Memorials, report in," she ordered. "Damage, fuel, ammo."

Kira wouldn't have needed the second half of the order if she just had her old hands. Her temps had done well enough to earn her respect, but she still had to account for potential shortcomings.

"Swordheart here. No damage, fuel at ninety-two percent, ammo at forty," the first temp replied. "Transferring reaction mass to recharge ammo supply."

"Galavant. No damage, fuel at ninety-three percent, ammo at sixty. Recharging guns."

"Nightmare here. No damage, fuel at ninety percent, ammo at eighty."

"Dawnlord is present and watching," Patel said in an excessively formal voice. "Minor damage; I took the corona of a couple of shots when somebody got clever. Fuel at ninety-one percent, ammo at sixty."

"You lot talk too fast," Hoffman complained. "Longknife. No damage, fuel ninety-four, ammo sixty."

"Ammunition" on a nova fighter was a ready capacitor full of superheated plasma. It was the same reaction mass as provided fuel for their fusion reactor, but held at a higher-energy state. Refilling the ammunition capacitors took time—time that was hard to take when a fighter battle rarely lasted long. A second of sustained fire emptied ten percent of the capacitors, and that same ten percent took twenty seconds to recharge.

The entire fight with the gunships had been over within two minutes of Memorial Squadron's arrival. It had been a perfect first battle. Kira couldn't have asked for a better initial test of her people.

She was honest enough with herself to regret that they'd just killed thirty-odd people—but *she* hadn't decided that they were going to attack civilians.

"All right. Watch my back, people. It's time for my least favorite part of the job."

"Talking to the civilians?" Nightmare asked.

"Yeah. And to make it even *more* awkward than I'm used to, this time I should probably hit them up for money!"

"CIVILIAN SHIPS, this is Memorial Squadron leader," Kira opened on a wide channel. "Please confirm your status. The gunships are neutralized and we should be able to stick around for a little bit to make sure you all get out of here safely."

"Memorial Squadron, this is Captain Davies of *Man Forgotten*," a gruff voice replied after a few seconds. "I think I speak for all of us to say that I was not expecting you. I was trying to protect everyone, but when the second trio of gunships showed up, I knew I was a dead man.

"How can I possibly repay you?"

Kira forced a chuckle.

"Memorial Squadron LLC is an active mercenary corporation registered out of the Redward System," she pointed out. "Our intervention here was under our contract with the government of the Kingdom of Redward, but I won't turn down recompense to cover our expenses in coming to your rescue."

"You just saved my life, Memorial," Davis told her. "Replacing turrets and such isn't *cheap*, but I think I can come up with something to have made the detour worth your while. As can the rest of you, *right*?"

That was directed at the other ships who were also on the channel. Several audible chuckles on the line suggested more of them had tuned in than Kira had suspected.

"I home-base in Redward, too," Davies continued. "I'd be delighted to personally buy you and your pilots dinner if we're ever home at the same time. Your timing is *impeccable*."

"I'll keep that in mind," Kira promised. There'd been a moment when she'd thought he was offering to buy *just* her dinner, and she'd had to bite back a retort saying she was taken.

Which she wasn't. Right? Just what *was* her brain doing to her?

"*Man Forgotten*'s drives are at seventy percent," Davies continued. "We'll need six more hours to get our nova drives ready to go."

"The rest of you?" Kira asked, directing her question more widely.

The answers came back, ranging from needing four hours to needing ten.

"I'm also sharing responsibility with *Conviction* to escort another convoy," she told them. "If you're all capable of sublight movement, I suggest we start meandering in that direction to meet up with them. Some of you will be able to nova before we get there, but it keeps as many people as safe as possible for as long as possible."

The confirmations came back and she got them all accelerating in the right direction. Some of the freighters were damaged enough to really slow things down, but everyone would get to *Conviction* in under six hours.

Once she'd rendezvoused with Darkwing Squadron and the carrier, she'd feel *much* happier about everyone's security. Plus, she'd be able to talk to Daniel again.

And *that* particular thought had sneaked in there without her planning it, and Kira shook her head. Cooling down their not-quite fight, combined with Estanza's comments, seemed to have put that overly eager part of her brain into overdrive.

It was *still* a bad idea; that was the frustrating part. Sooner or later, she was going to have to convince herself of that—but she could already tell that even getting laid would be a problem until she did.

Shaking her head at her own idiocy, she assembled a databurst summarizing everything and fired it back to *Conviction*—just as her own fighter launch showed up on her lightspeed scanners.

The speed of light was hardly *slow*, but when she'd novaed ten light-minutes away, it caused all kinds of interesting results. She got to watch her own fighters nova out ten minutes before, and knew that the carrier would now be seeing the beginning of the battle.

And about thirty seconds after her fighters novaed *out*, someone *else* novaed in. At least a dozen ships appeared on her screens a second before multiphasic jamming turned the long-range sensor data into complete garbage.

"Memorial Squadron, check your long-range scopes," Kira barked. "Anyone have a clean read on *Conviction* or the convoy?"

"Negative, negative," Nightmare replied instantly. "I have multi-phasic jamming covering home base. Your orders, ma'am?"

"We'll come back for the freighters," Kira barked as she dropped a new waypoint onto all of her subordinates' computers. "Form on me, combat formation. Stand by to nova."

She spent ten precious seconds making sure her people were aligned on her so they'd have coms on the other, sighed, then exhaled a terrified breath.

"Memorial Squadron, *nova!*"

26

THE UNIVERSE CAN CHANGE in ten minutes. When Kira and her fighters had left the carrier, everything had been perfectly orderly. There'd been no known threat and local space had been clear. They'd had all of Darkwing Squadron out, but that had been almost entirely paranoia at the presence of hostiles in the region.

Memorial Squadron returned to an ongoing battle. With multiphasic jamming covering the entire region, she could only guess at how many ships were gone, but she could see how many of the attackers and defenders were left.

All of the escortees, from *Conviction* herself to the fifteen freighters, were intact. Only six fighter-bombers were still actively defending them, a number that send a cold chill down Kira's spine as a full *dozen* gunships swarmed in for another attack run.

The Darkwings were tied down defending the convoy. They'd clearly done enough damage that their opponents were respecting their presence, but their careful allocation of weapons fire told Kira everything she needed to know.

Mbeki had smashed the crap out of the first few strikes, but his people's capacitors had to be drained now. He was using whatever recharge they'd managed since the last clash, and it wasn't going to be enough, not when he was down two fighters.

Unfortunately for the gunships, Kira and her people were there.

"Memorials, nova and attack!" she barked over the laser-com link to her other fighters. She didn't wait to see if her people obeyed her—she *knew* they would.

The nova was only a hundred and fifty thousand kilometers, a distance that wouldn't have been worth the fuel to jump across in other circumstance. *Today*, however...

That nova brought her in behind the attacking gunships, barely *ten* thousand kilometers behind the trailing warship—and *her* guns were fully charged.

Five seconds of sustained fire burned half of Kira's ammunition—and left a gunship scattered across a thousand kilometers of empty space before the attackers even realized they were caught.

Her people were right behind her. Their formation wasn't intact enough for her to hold coms with them, but she *saw* the results of their arrival. Plasma fire hammered into the formation in a crashing wave, and half of the Clan gunships were gone before they even knew the tide had turned.

One moment, they'd outnumbered the defenders two-to-one and had run the nova fighters out of ammunition. The next, the *gunships* were outnumbered two-to-one and *Conviction*'s pilots were very, *very* angry.

Kira tried to flip to a new target, only for that gunship to flail away from her, already being flayed by one of her compatriots' guns. Her fire was only insult to injury, and she switched her focus to the entire battlespace.

The jamming made tracking everything hard, but she could get the overtone of the fight. Mbeki's One-Fifteens were sortieing now. Their guns weren't any better than her Memorials' guns, but an extra six sets could make all of the difference.

Four more gunships came apart before the survivors hit their own nova drives, vanishing into the night just as completely as the destroyed ships.

Her jamming dropped and she tried to ping the Darkwings. Only more jamming answered her for a few seconds, then the various jamming fields slowly came down.

"Darkwing Lead, what's your status?" she barked. "Duck, what's going on?"

"Memorial Lead...this is Gizmo," someone else answered. "Duck's gone, sir."

THE WORDS DIDN'T PROCESS. For a second, *nothing* processed.

But while Kira's headware might have cooperated with that refusal to function, her nova fighter's computers were less a part of her brain. They cold-bloodedly IDed the surviving Darkwing fighters.

Duck—Daniel Mbeki—was missing. So was Cataphract, though she'd barely met that pilot and her copilot.

"I need an update on your ammunition, fuel and damage status," a long-trained part of her reeled off. "Can Darkwing's fighters maintain patrol?"

A silent thought brought her Squadron and *Conviction* into the loop.

"*Conviction*, do we have status updates on our lost sheep?" she asked. "*Officially part of the convoy* just became irrelevant. Do any of them need assistance our fighters can provide? I need to deploy at least some fighters to bring the other convoy into our immediate patrol shell."

"We're linking with the transports now," Zoric's voice replied. Her tone was just as stiff and formal as Kira's. She'd known Mbeki for even longer.

"Commander, I need you to do something," Waldroup's voice joined. "I've got retrieval birds on the deck, but multiphasic jamming is a bitch. I need to know where Duck and Cataphract's fighters are.

"We might get lucky with them. We might not," the deck boss cautioned. "Either way, I need their nova drives or we're permanently down two fighters."

Kira bit back a shout. Waldroup *wasn't* being callous, not really. She was right—they needed to retrieve the fighters. There was a chance that someone had survived. It was a miniscule chance, but it was something to latch on to.

"Understood," she said grimly. "Gizmo, you've got live data from the entire fight. Do you have a vector cone?"

"I think so," the pilot replied.

"Take whoever has the most fuel left from the Darkwings with you and find those ships," Kira ordered. Technically, she wasn't in command of Mbeki's people, but no one was going to argue right now.

"Nightmare, take Galavant and nova back to the convoy we rescued," she continued. "They probably won't like being dropped down the priority list, but they'll deal. Bring them home."

"Do we let them nova?" Cartman asked grimly. "This is *not* looking incidental to me, boss."

Kira grimaced. No one could see her, so there was no need to appear as calm and level as she had to sound. Everything had been too perfect. This had been a trap—a trap targeted at a carrier.

Which meant *Conviction*. One of Redward's carriers, stuffed full of sub-fighters, would have taken hours to intervene in an incident they saw at ten light-minutes. They might have novaed in closer—and the same trick would have worked with a smaller distance scale without nova fighters.

"We want full IDs on everybody," she said grimly. "Order them to return to *Conviction* and tell them that we'll be interviewing everyone.

"Anyone who *runs* is probably a lot less innocent than we'd like them to be. Try not to kill anyone, but you're authorized to shoot to disable," she concluded. "I want answers, people."

"On it."

Thirty seconds later, Nightmare and Galavant vanished as she went through the status reports from Darkwing Squadron.

"Kitsune, Hammer, Oglaf," she reeled off after going through the data. "Get your birds back aboard ship and into Waldroup's hands."

Oglaf had somehow managed to get her ship under forty percent fuel in the firefight. Kitsune and Hammer had gone the more traditional route to being sent home of being shot to pieces.

It was a sign of how off-balance everyone was that none of the three argued with her. The three PNC-115s dropped into landing formation with prompt alacrity.

The four Hoplites were now in a flattened diamond around the main plane of the convoy, as secure a formation as Kira could arrange. The ships were too concentrated under *Conviction*'s metaphorical skirts for a full patrol pattern to be possible, let alone needed.

"Basketball, we've got a solid count on our flock," Zoric told her. "Minimal damage; a few people took stray hits, but I don't think these guys were expecting to run into a full squadron of nova fighters."

"They thought you still only had one squadron and they were off saving the innocents," Kira said. "It was a trap, *Conviction*. They were aiming for us. Who else has nova fighters?"

"They hit us with sixteen gunships and a pair of corvettes, Commander," Zoric replied. "If Mbeki didn't launch with a torp on half his fighters by habit, we'd have been screwed."

Kira had forgotten that the Darkwings did that. It made sense—he'd said that carrying one torpedo didn't impede his fighter-bomber's maneuverability much, and it would have been worth every scrap of lost dexterity when two thirty-thousand-cubic corvettes had jumped them.

It would have been a shock to those corvettes to suddenly find themselves facing conversion torpedoes at close range. Mbeki's habit had probably saved the carrier.

"Basketball, this is Gizmo," the Darkwing pilot reported in. "We've located Cataphract's fighter. One of the corvettes put a heavy plasma cannon right through the center of the ship. Guns are trashed, cockpit is *gone*.

"Nova drive *might* have survived."

"Tag it for *Conviction*'s shuttle and keep searching for Duck," she ordered.

"Migraine just tagged him," Gizmo said, his voice very quiet. "Or at least, what we think is the biggest piece. We're basing a new vector cone from it, but that chunk doesn't have the nova drive in it."

"But it's got half the cockpit."

She winced.

"Send me your video," Kira ordered. "Then keep up the sweep."

"Understood."

She had to see. It was a *terrible* idea, she was sure, but she *had to see*.

The footage from Gizmo's external cameras and sensor data crossed the link in moments, and she studied it with the harsh eye of a woman who'd seen over two hundred wrecked nova fighters across the years, two dozen of them shattered by her own hand.

She could tell the difference between a nova fighter where a pilot could potentially be retrieved, one where the pilot had died in agony… and the ones where the pilot had never even known they'd been hit.

Mbeki's fighter was the last. If the Clan followed common logic, the two corvettes would have each brought a pair of real guns to the party, heavy cannons that rivaled the force of a conversion torpedo but capable of sustained fire. The cockpit hadn't been sheared in two.

The forward half of it had been *vaporized.* Anyone inside the central brain of the nova fighter would have been burnt to ashes with it, quite possibly before their nervous system even had time to register pain.

Daniel Mbeki had died about as cleanly as a nova fighter pilot could die.

But he had died.

And Kira Demirci had never quite decided what she was going to do about him.

* * *

DESPITE THE ORDERS she'd given, Kira was somehow unsurprised to see her two Hoplites appear out of nova less than five minutes after she'd sent Cartman to retrieve the freighters.

"They were already gone, weren't they?" she asked Nightmare without preamble. The light from those novas would probably be reaching them in the next few minutes, even if her long-range scanners still showed her the theoretically civilian ships.

"Got it in one," Nightmare replied. "*Fuckers.*"

"Whole thing was staged," Kira concluded. "Davies—or whatever the hell his name actually is— didn't save the convoy. He and the gunships had been staging that fake duel, occasionally turning the jammers on and off, for a while. Definitely hours. Probably not days, if only because we were here only a few days ago."

"Commander, I suggest we pull at least a third of the fighters back aboard," Zoric told her. "The ones who were just patrolling at the last rest point, if nothing else. You've basically been in the cockpit for eight hours now, Basketball.

"You *need* to rest."

Kira didn't want to do any such thing. She wanted to find the sons of bitches who'd killed Daniel Mbeki and burn them to pieces. Intellectually, she knew that he'd killed his own killers, firing his torpedo into the corvette even as its main gun had vaporized him.

"All right. Nightmare—assume command," she ordered.

They'd have to sort out who was in charge of Darkwing Squadron going forward, but that was Estanza's problem. Not hers.

Her problem was how to deal with losing a man she had no real reason to call hers.

27

INSOMNIA WAS as unlikely to happen to a human with modern head-ware and vaccines as the common cold. *Nightmares,* on the other hand, were hard to get rid of without long-term damage.

Kira was asleep the moment she hit her bunk and woke up exactly seven hours later...drenched with cold sweat from dreams she could only vaguely remember. She was grimly certain, from the fragments that she recalled, that her subconscious had spent most of her seven hours of unconsciousness accusing her of killing Daniel Mbeki herself.

Several new messages flagged as high-enough urgency for her to push through them as she showered and dressed. They had success-fully novaed to the next stop on their route without any further problems.

To help everyone relax a bit more, one of Redward's ships was already there. *Armed Sedation* was a forty-five kilocubic heavy destroyer, easily a match for the one Ypres ship they'd seen on their trip and more than a match for any half-dozen gunships.

If *Sedation* had been subjected to the same trap *Conviction* had faced, she'd have been obliterated. Combined with *Conviction* and her squadrons as backup, Zoric had felt the destroyer was enough to stand all of the nova fighters down.

Everyone was aboard and asleep now, which was probably a good thing, in Kira's opinion.

The next message was from Waldroup, including Kira on a note meant for Estanza and Zoric. They'd recovered enough of both Cataphract and Mbeki's fighters to allow for the deck boss to build new fighters. *Conviction* had the complete schematics for the PNC-115, after all—but they needed new Harrington coils they'd have to buy from Redward.

That was probably good news, but it was so clinical that it left Kira's skin crawling. There was no mention of the crews in Waldroup's message, and Kira didn't even need to ask why. She'd seen the footage from Cataphract's fighter as well.

There hadn't been enough left of any of the four Darkwing officers to bother burying.

The last note informed her that Zoric had called a senior officers' briefing in an hour. Estanza was *supposed* to be there, but given the carrier commander's complete absence from the communications since Mbeki's death, Kira wasn't sure she believed it.

Searching through the rest of her messages, Kira found the note she was *looking* for as she finished dressing. The funeral for the dead officers was scheduled for one hour before they novaed to Redward. There were no bodies to bury, so there was no concern about *where* to bury them at least.

More memorials and wakes. After mourning the deaths of every pilot killed in the fight against Brisingr—and then the deaths of over half of the 303 in the aftermath of the war—Kira would have thought she'd get used to it.

But she hadn't. And Mbeki's funeral was going to be particularly hard to face.

If she'd known then what was going to happen, she would never have controlled herself after that damn kiss.

IT WASN'T until she was in the meeting room that Kira realized that the call Zoric had sent out had been the *first* senior officers' briefing she'd seen so far aboard *Conviction*. There were three people in the room that she'd *never met*.

She wanted to write part of that off as "mercenaries are weird," but she was starting to suspect that it was specifically *Conviction* that was weird and a little bit broken.

Her assessment that Waldroup was more senior than the deck boss gave herself credit for was bang-on. She and Zoric were the only two people in the room Kira actually recognized. The other three were new to Kira.

Headware meant that she could at least ID them as she took a seat. The terrifyingly gaunt and pale officer at the far end of the table was Lakshmi Labelle. They ran *Conviction*'s engineering department and were responsible for keeping the old ship running.

Oddly, the starship's database had very little data on Labelle beyond their role aboard the carrier. Privacy was one thing, but that kind of blank on the personnel database could only be intentional.

A similarly pale but far beefier man sat at Labelle's right. Caiden McCaig was probably the largest person Kira had met aboard *Conviction*...if not ever. The leader of the mercenaries' small ground and security contingent was easily two and a quarter meters tall and massively broad with it.

Sitting to the engineer's left was another man who was a study in contrast with both of the other strangers. *Maybe* a hundred and fifty centimeters tall, Purser Yanis Vaduva was a swarthy man whose teeth were spread in what looked like a permanent grin.

Somehow, Vaduva's grin managed to not seem particularly opposed to the overall chill tone of the room.

"Captain Estanza will not be joining us," Zoric told them all as Kira took a seat, last to arrive. "He's busy arranging the funeral later today." She shook her head. "For the moment, Ruben 'Gizmo' Hersch will handle command of the Darkwing Squadron, until Captain Estanza officially promotes someone to fill Commander Mbeki's role."

"What's this about, Zoric?" McCaig asked. "I thought briefings were kept to the end of the mission so Estanza could show. Otherwise, we'd have actually introduced everybody to the new Commander, wouldn't we?"

He nodded to Kira.

"Commander," he added in extra acknowledgement.

"That was my request," Vaduva told the platoon leader. "I ran our gun-camera footage and so forth by Captain Shaheed aboard *Armed Sedation*. Her tactical department has reviewed them and she's signed off on the bounty payments.

"While our pay scale was based around the known vessels available to the Costar Clans, there was an entry included for vessels such as the corvettes Commander Mbeki destroyed."

The purser's smile widened.

"The bounties on twenty gunships and two corvettes dramatically outstrip our payment for the nova-lane patrol or the escort run from New Ontario." The numbers downloaded to everyone's headware as they spoke.

"Even with the additional expense of covering the reconstruction of two PNC One-Fifteens, this will have been one of our most profitable missions in some years," Vaduva concluded. "That will trigger almost all, if not all, of the bonus criteria in the crew and pilot contracts, which I wanted to discuss with Estanza and you before we released that to the crew."

"I'm on the 'bonus criteria in the contracts' side of this discussion," Kira pointed out humorlessly. "Mercenary or not, I have to admit that the financial aspects of this fall far below the fact that we just lost four of our people."

Vaduva nodded unhesitatingly.

"I agree," he told her. "I knew Daniel Mbeki for four years. He was a respected coworker and a personal friend. But *we* are responsible for the function and operation of both this ship and the corporation that runs it.

"If nothing else, Commander Demirci, you need to be aware that the other pilots will be receiving bonuses after this mission, and that may be a factor in your discussions with your own people."

"I have my own arrangements for that," she said coldly. The fact that her people owned three point five percent of the company apiece made that pretty straightforward—her current plan was to pay out that percentage of whatever was left after fixed salaries and expenses after each mission.

And there *were* bonuses built into her contract if *Conviction* brought in additional bounties.

Still…

"I don't really have a place in a financial discussion around *Conviction*'s corporate structure," she continued. "If that's all we have to discuss…?"

McCaig chuckled loudly.

"I like this one, Zoric," he told the carrier XO in a thick, throaty accent. "And she's not wrong. My people are just sitting around right now, but everyone else in this room has work to do. I'll keep the bonuses in mind, but was there more to this?"

"Of course there was," Zoric said sharply. "The announcement that Hersch would be running Darkwing was important. We also need to consider the effect on our people's morale of what just happened.

"There are no idiots on this ship, people," she continued. "Anyone who hasn't already worked out that we just walked into a trap that *would* have killed us all without Commander Demirci's squadron will do so shortly. We've fought the Costar Clans under contract before, but this is more targeted. More personal. It may get under our people's skin, realizing that the Clans are now specifically hunting *us* as a target."

"We'll want to raise security at port," Kira said with a sigh. "I know you did some of that when my people came aboard, but if we're *all* being hunted, then we need to plan around that."

"Redward should still be safe enough," McCaig said. "But you're right. Buddy systems, moving with guards." He shook his head. "I've got twenty-three grunts. I can't provide individual escorts for all hundred and fifty-six crew and pilots."

"Which will, once again, hit our people's morale," Zoric concluded. "Talk to your people, everyone. Keep a finger on the pulse of what's going on. If anyone wants out, there are always clauses in their contracts for that—and big bonuses are when we'll usually see people buy out.

"I need to know if we're going to lose anyone critical and have to plan to replace them. *Most* skillsets we can pick up in Redward, but there's a few we'd have to train up from near neighbors."

The room was quiet.

"And we need to consider that while funerals are essential for *long-term* morale, morale *tonight* is going to be in the shit," Waldroup told them all bluntly. "I'm pushing my people to get the last repairs we can do finished before that, but we can't even start the rebuilds until we're back in Redward."

"Four hours to the nova, two hours after that to dock," Zoric told them. "I don't think we'll be launching for at least a week after that, but that's down to the Captain and the client."

"Plan for worst cases, plan for losing people after we pay out the bonus, plan for recruiting to fill holes ASAP." The carrier XO shook her head.

"I don't know about the rest of you, but I want to go after these fuckers before they come at us sideways again. I think the Captain does too, so it boils down to what we can convince Redward to pay us for."

Kira was silent now, considering her own people and considering what kind of mission going after the Costar Clans entailed.

Even with the body blow the Clans' deployable forces had just taken, there was *no way* that *Conviction* alone could take on whatever home base the pirates had.

And that was assuming they even knew where to go.

28

THE GRAVITIC FIELD at the end of the launch deck always had a slight ripple to it, just enough for the human eye to catch the process that kept breathable air *inside* the ship despite the open end of the deck.

The massive hatches that closed the end of the deck outside of flight operations were visible on either side of the opening. The gravitic field kept ninety-nine percent of the air in, but there were inevitable losses when you opened a thirty-by-forty-meter portal into open space.

There were no bodies or coffins to fire into space today, but the hatches were open anyway as the fighter squadrons and much of *Conviction*'s crew gathered to say goodbye to four of their pilots.

"Attention to arms," McCaig's voice bellowed, drawing everyone's attention to where a thin line of mercenaries had formed on the edge of the deck, looking out into the void.

In front of them stood John Estanza, and Kira shivered at the sight of the mercenary captain.

It had been mere days since she'd seen him, but it looked like he'd aged years. He held an open whisky bottle in one hand, passing it off to Zoric only as everyone's attention gathered to him.

"Our job sucks," Estanza told them all. Kira was relatively sure she'd never seen him sober…but she'd never seen him *this* drunk. "We get up each day and we do our jobs. Our paychecks are high, but there's a reason for it.

"This is the reason for it." He gestured at the long tables with the food and drink in the room. "Four of our own died yesterday. Were we a national military, I could tell you they died righteously, fighting for what they believed in or for some grand cause.

"We're not a national military," he reminded them, his voice slurring slightly. "We're a mercenary company. So, I can't tell you that Daniel Mbeki died doing the right thing. I can't tell you that Lita Oberto died with honor at his side, or that Dhaval De Santis honored his ancestors, or that Adrienne Lehmann 'held the line' against some great threat."

Quiet overtook the entire room as the Captain now had everyone's full attention.

"It's not my place to bullshit you," Estanza told them. "We all fight for money. Many of us fight for our own stubborn or crazy or bullshit reasons that swept us away from home and world to this cold deck and these scattered stars.

"I won't tell you lies about courage or honor or duty. But I knew Daniel Mbeki better than any of you. I knew Lita and Dhaval and Adrienne as well as any of you did, and I can tell you why all four of them died.

"They *fought* for money…but they didn't die for it. They died because if they didn't launch those bombing runs, *Conviction* died."

Zoric pressed a glass of wine into the Captain's hand, and Kira realized that, harsh as the opening of Estanza's speech had been, the whole thing *had* been planned. It wasn't *just* that he was drunk—though from the slurring, he was *very* drunk.

"Daniel Mbeki, Lita Oberto, Dhaval De Santis and Adrienne Lehmann died to save this ship and this crew. And they succeeded in doing so. Because of their actions, their determination, we all stand here today to remember.

"I hope that's enough for them," Estanza concluded. "Because it would be enough for me."

He raised the glass.

"Platoon, attention to orders," McCaig barked.

"I give you Daniel Mbeki," the Captain intoned.

"*Fire!*" McCaig ordered. Twenty-one blaster rifles fired as one through the gravitic field at the end of the deck, the *hiss-crack* of the energy weapons an undertone to the response to Estanza's toast.

"I give you Lita Oberto," Estanza continued.

"*Fire!*"

"I give you Dhaval De Santis."

"*Fire!*"

"I give you Adrienne Lehmann."

"*Fire!*"

Four twenty-one-gun salutes echoed through the launch deck, and John Estanza lowered his glass.

"Remember our friends, people," he told his crew. "Thank you."

APOLLO-STYLE WAKES WERE FAR MORE energetic than the subdued affair that *Conviction*'s crew had put together. No one was lining up shots of vodka for groups to take at once, the music was quiet and the food was limited to small snacks.

To Kira, the affair was almost as depressing as her state of mind. She could be a cheerful, if controlled, drunk at a wake. At this more-formal affair, she wasn't quite sure *what* to make of herself and ended up the ghost in a larger conversation among the fighter pilots.

If she was quieter than the average, she wasn't the only one. Kira might have been considering sleeping with Mbeki, with a potential relationship definitely in the cards, but she'd still only known him for a couple of weeks.

Most of the people here had known him for years—and the person who'd known him the *longest* was Captain John Estanza.

Thinking of the man drew her attention to him and she watched as he brushed off Vaduva's attempt to say something to him. Estanza wasn't even *walking* straight, she noted grimly, and realized it wasn't just the purser he was rudely dismissing.

The man was physically present at the funeral, but he didn't seem to be emotionally or mentally present—and, drunk as he was, probably creating more problems than he was solving.

Excusing herself from the cluster of pilots—it wasn't like she'd been paying attention to the conversation in any case—she delicately dodged her way across the funeral to Estanza.

She got there just as he grouched *something* at Kavitha Zoric that made the carrier XO turn about as pale as the woman could and step backward away from him.

The Captain had reached the edge of the room and was standing in the door as Kira stepped up beside him.

"This is *really* how you're going to honor Daniel's memory?" she asked. "Drinking beyond even *your* tolerance and alienating your senior officers?"

"What do *you* care?" Estanza barked. "You didn't know him. You don't know anyone here. Don't play your little games with me, Demirci."

"I care because he would have," Kira told him softly, almost unconsciously edging them both out into the corridor and closing the door behind them with a thought. This wasn't a discussion that they needed to have in front of Estanza's crew.

"These were his people, his friends and family, and they looked up to you *both*. Treat them like this and you betray *him*."

"What do you know?" the old man told her. "I've buried more friends than I can count. You fought *a* war? That's cute. I've fought a dozen. Daniel Mbeki fought a third of them at my side. He shouldn't have died like that.

"He *wouldn't* have—if he hadn't been distracted! By *you*."

Kira had *not* been expecting that, and she spent a moment torn between recoiling from Estanza or *punching* him.

"Or maybe he was distracted by the fact that his mentor and *friend* was drinking himself to death and never emerging from his quarters," she countered. "Maybe he realized the fucking ship was *falling apart around him* and his so-called boss was only looking for answers in a whisky bottle.

"Did you throw that muck at Zoric, too?" she demanded. "Is there anyone aboard this ship you *haven't* accused of killing Daniel? Are you so determined to deny reality that you will tear your ship and crew apart to find some *scrap* of reason why he died?

"Or are you just terrified to look in the mirror? Or maybe, just *maybe*, after sixty fucking years of war, you should realize no one was to blame—least of all Daniel—and war comes with a shit set of odds we can't beat forever."

She glared at him.

"You can say I distracted Daniel. I can say he distracted me. I can say you distracted him. We can say that every *fucking* person on this carrier distracted everybody else, and it's all true. And it's all lies.

"Does it really matter?"

The corridor was silent for several seconds.

"You have no damn clue what you're talking about or to who," Estanza told her, but there was no heat in his voice. Just a massive, bone-deep exhaustion. "You don't know what I need to forget—or what I can't afford to become.

"Daniel did. He was the only one. He had a full damn pension on Sorvedo, a quiet life without needs if not necessarily full of luxury. And I talked him into coming out here with me. And dragged him into all of my messes.

"So, yes, Demirci, I know half the blame is in the mirror. But he'd flown with that blame a thousand times. *You*, though. That distraction was new."

"Even if you hang it on me, it doesn't change anything," Kira said gently. "It doesn't change that you can't afford to burn this crew down around you and you can't afford to disrespect Daniel's memory. You need to hit a de-alcoholizer, go back in there, and fix the bridges you just tried to burn.

"Because Daniel didn't die to save this ship so *you* could wreck it. Sir."

Estanza stared at her. She could *see* the moment he triggered the emergency routine stored in his bodyware. *She* would have had to go get a dose from the medbay, but it appeared that the Captain kept a de-alcoholizer in his system.

He closed his eyes. There was a *reason* Kira only had a de-alcoholizer loaded into her bodyware when she expected to need it. The nanite purge was *not* pleasant.

"You're a bitch, you know that?" he said conversationally.

"I've been told that before," she agreed. "Right now, no matter *what* else, you owe it to *Daniel* to keep this ship together. He did it for you. I don't know how long he did it for you, but I'm guessing years. Long enough for you to drink yourself into hermitdom.

"He's gone now. You're going to have to be the Captain now. *Captain.*"

29

RETURNING to Redward was as uneventful as they could have hoped. *Armed Sedation* was planning on staying at the rest stop for another twenty-four hours, which gave *Conviction* a clear conscience as they novaed back to the Redward System.

Redward itself was almost sacrosanct. There were asteroid fortresses above the planet and the gas giant with the refueling infrastructure, each of them capable of engaging an entire fleet of nova-capable warships.

But a ship had to leave the weapons range of those fortresses to enter nova, and the heavily mapped trade route stops were the safest places to nova *to*. Redward was rich by Syntactic Cluster standards but poor by any more objective one. It was still almost immune to direct assault—but an enemy with the power to engage and defeat her nova-capable forces could trap her civilian shipping behind those forts.

The six hours that *Conviction* took to discharge her tachyon static at the gas giant Lastward were enough for messages to flow back and forth with the planet, which meant that Kira had a chance to review the video from Simoneit and Stipan Dirix in private.

The lawyer and the current admin manager for Memorial Squadron were an interesting study in contrasts, one slim and one as broad as a brick wall. She was, however, surprised to see them in the same room in the recording.

"Commander Demirci, we wanted to give you an update on where things stand on Blueward Station," Dirix told her. "Em Simoneit has been more essential than any of us hoped, as we've...had some problems."

"What Em Dirix is trying to brush over was that he didn't make sure he had a valid bodyguard license before getting involved in a fire-fight on Blueward Station," Simoneit noted primly. "*Technically,* he's been released to your jurisdiction until after his hearing, with myself acting as your agent, but the situation is under control. While it wasn't open-and-shut self-defense, Redward law does recognize the concept of immediate defense of others at a similar level."

A firefight? That was bad...but on the other hand, it almost certainly meant that a 303 pilot had made it to Redward.

"I have a reputation with the local bounty hunters," Dirix said grimly. "Not one I'm proud of or one I really want to talk about how I acquired, but I 'knew' they'd back down. The people who came for Bardacki were *not* local."

Kira didn't like the sound of that. She *did*, on the other hand, like the idea of having Evridiki Bardacki on her side. Bardacki had been the single most experienced pilot in the 303, a man who'd been transferred over from another combat group that had been smashed.

He'd been next up on the list for a squadron command of his own if the 303 hadn't been forced to flee.

"My guess is that your enemies have an even longer reach that we thought, Commander," the Redward native continued. "Em Bardacki is under lock and key now, behind a squad of Ironborn. That security isn't cheap, but I don't go to jail for it, either."

"Em Bardacki is the only one who made it through, Commander," Simoneit concluded. "I've put out inquiries, but it looks like the five of you may be it, Demirci. Every other member of Moranis's NCG I can find is dead. There are two or three I can't find any trace of, but I wouldn't hold out hope.

"I'm sorry. Bardacki will be here when you arrive. You and Dirix will need to decide how much of a shore establishment you want at the point where we know everyone is either here or not making it."

"I'll see you when you land, boss," Dirix told her. "I'm restricted to Blueward Station for the foreseeable future, but inside that, I'm yours to command."

The recording ended and Kira shook her head to clear the video feed. Had Brisingr's Kaiser sent Shadows *this* far? From what she understood of the Kaiserreich's goals, they'd really been achieved the moment the 303 had dissolved into flight and desertion.

The 303 Nova Combat Group wouldn't fly against Brisingr again. She was grimly certain there would *be* another war—Apollo had conceded her *allies* but hadn't agreed to pay tribute herself. The oligarchy that ruled her homeworld would never do that, not without having it forced down their throats.

And the Kaiser would demand it. Apollo was the wealthiest system in the region, so they would be forced to bend the knee. The Council of Principals clearly hadn't agreed with Kira on that, obviously, or they would never have signed the treaty they had.

Today, her answers were on Redward. Tomorrow, they might be somewhere else. For now…well, she had more messages.

As Vaduva had told her, payment had been sorted out for *Conviction*'s mission. That fee, with the additional bounties included, had triggered a significant bonus payment for Memorial Squadron that she'd need to distribute to her people.

She had salaries to pay and bonuses to calculate, even if both of those things were new to her. There was really only one thing she'd want to buy for Memorial Squadron and, well, it didn't look like she'd have pilots for them even if she could find someone able to *sell* her nova fighters.

And there was no one who could do that within fifty light-years.

30

THEY WERE PREPARING to leave Lastward when Kira got a ping asking her to meet Estanza in his office. She didn't have much to do with moving the ship, and it wasn't like she could *ignore* the Captain, so she followed instructions.

The biggest surprise was that Estanza wasn't *in* his office. He was on the bridge, presumably relying on the fact that she had to step around at least the edge of the ship's control center to reach his working space to intercept her.

The old mercenary was standing next to the command chair, one hand supporting himself on the back of the seat and the other gesturing through an interface display only he could see. It might have looked strange if everyone *else* on the bridge wasn't doing much the same thing.

"You have the course laid in?" he asked the carrier's helm officer.

"Seventy minutes' thrust at fifty percent, one ten-light-minute nova, seventy-eight minutes deceleration to bring us in to Blueward Station," the woman replied crisply. "All vectors are coded in. Unless there's trouble, we should be fine."

"Less than twenty minutes of that course is outside the range of the forts," Estanza replied. "We'll be fine."

He turned to face Kira.

"Thank you for coming, Commander Demirci. I think everything is finished up here." He glanced around with an oddly bemused smile.

"You have the conn, Officer Stefanidis," he told the helmswoman, then turned back to Kira. "My office, Commander?"

Kira was more than a bit bemused herself. Every time she'd seen John Estanza before, he'd had the dull edge to his eyes of someone who was at least partially drunk. Today, that edge was completely gone and replaced with a hard glint she'd only seen on a handful of people in her life.

One of those people had been Jay Moranis. There'd always been hints that Estanza had come from the same mold that had produced her war-hero commander, but this was the first time *Conviction*'s Captain had truly put on the cloak of his role.

It looked *damn* good on him.

"Of course, sir," she told him. "You've piqued my curiosity, I must admit."

Estanza chuckled and led the way. The door slid closed behind him and she *watched* as some of the aura of command slipped. His shoulders drooped slightly and he closed his eyes for a long sigh.

"I'm out of practice," he said aloud. "Coffee, Commander?"

"Please."

It was only as she watched him draw the cups from the machine that she realized what had changed in the office: the bar was gone.

"The bar moves?" she asks.

"On its own, actually," Estanza confirmed. "Wheels, stupid-brain, the works. I *do* trust my self-control, if you were wondering, but it seemed wiser to put the bar in my closet rather than have it close to hand."

He placed two black coffees on the table.

"I'm terrible at admitting when I'm wrong and I'm worse at apologies," he told her. "But I was wrong and I apologize. I was out of line and you called me on it in a way that no one who knew me better would have dared."

There was a smile dancing around his lips as he drank. It didn't entirely reach his eyes and there was a sad edge to it, but Kira understood that.

"If I kept on going the way I have been going, I would have failed

Daniel," he conceded. "I won't let that happen. I won't let his death go unavenged."

"I'd rather not myself," Kira agreed. "Though I understand that he *did* take out the ship that killed him."

"I checked the footage," Estanza said. "He put his conversion torpedo right through their main power core. They never stood a chance—they were already dead when they fired the shot that killed him. They just didn't know that."

He shook his head.

"But groups like the Costar Clans don't fade away after one failure. More interestingly, I'll note, is that the Costar Clans are *extremely* protective of their limited corvette strength. They have the fabricators to build the nova drives, but most of their population lives in habitats and asteroid colonies.

"They don't have the *gravity* to build Harringtons and nova drives in significant numbers. To build a bigger nova drive for a corvette costs them time and resources better used building a gunship squadron."

"So, they *really* wanted *Conviction* dead," Kira noted.

"Which feels damn personal," Estanza replied. "And that may well be the core of it, too, in which case I at least have some answers as to what's going on."

He shook his head and took a long sip of his coffee.

"I'm getting ahead of myself," he noted. "That's either the third or fourth thing I wanted to talk to you about."

"You have an agenda, sir?" Kira asked.

His smile hadn't reached his eyes but his laugh did.

"Apparently, Commander Demirci, you're as good for me as Daniel Mbeki was," he said after a moment. "It's a good thing I was planning on keeping you.

"I needed to apologize, which I believe I've done with my usual half-assed disaster of an attempt," he continued. "But I have an update for you as well. I received a message from a friend that you'll be interested in."

"Sir?"

"Shang Tzu commands a pair of mercenary destroyers," Estanza told her. "He headquarters them out of Exeteron, a system that makes New Ontario look rich, because Exeteron is so desperate for help, they basically don't charge him taxes or licensing fees so long as he keeps money in the bank and swings his destroyers through every couple of months to show the flag.

"The message I got from him was out of Ypres," he continued. "You know the system?"

"Gateway to the cluster, factional clusterfuck, home to the Brisingr embassy and a bounty on my head and all of my people's," Kira reeled off. The name of the system made her twitch. "What was Shang Tzu saying that was relevant to me?"

"I *may* have intimated to my mercenary friends in the cluster and the next couple of sectors that there was a reward for making sure any members of the Apollo Three Hundred and Third Nova Combat Group made it to Redward alive and unhurt," Estanza said dryly.

"That said, Ypres is a hotbed of backstabbery, and it appears that some of Tzu's crew decided to involve themselves when they saw a pretty young woman being followed into a dark alley." The carrier Captain shook his head.

"It did *not* end well for the people following her—and according to Tzu, not just because of his people. I believe you know Evgenia Michel?"

Kira blinked back both surprise and tears. More of her people were alive?!

"She was one of mine," she confirmed. "Even more than the rest— she flew on my wing for the last two years." Then she chuckled at the thought of anyone who thought Michel was vulnerable in a dark alley.

"Also a black belt in some grotesque martial art involving knives and dirty tricks," she remembered aloud.

"All Shang Tzu said was that while he was pretty sure his people's help was *useful*, he wasn't entirely sure it was *necessary*," Estanza concluded. "And because of my note, he offered her and a friend a ride.

"He wasn't coming straight here, but I think they thought traveling on a nova warship was much safer than hopping economy class on a liner. From the note I have from Tzu, Evgenia Michel and Abdullah Colombera will arrive with him in about three days."

Kira had to close her eyes to hold back tears of relief.

"We thought everyone else was dead," she admitted. "One more is waiting for me at Blueward, but we'd only lost track of three." Michel and Colombera—Socrates and Scimitar—were an inseparable pair of jokers, the youngest of the surviving pilots now, and she'd be *glad* to have them.

If her last lost sheep showed up, she'd be ecstatic, but her hopes were low. To get Michel and Colombera was more than she'd dared hope.

"Well, they'll be here in three days," Estanza repeated. "Though I'd prefer not to pay the reward I promised myself, to be clear."

"We'll take care of it," Kira promised. Memorial Squadron was more than capable of matching the bounty posted for her people's heads, which seemed a "nice round number" to pay someone who helped get someone home.

"Good. My understanding is that neither of them knows more than 'get to Redward,' but Shang Tzu did. I doubt they've had a pleasant trip."

"They're not alone in that," Kira confessed. "We didn't plan this as well as we could have."

"You were *expecting* to be betrayed to foreign assassins by your own government?" Estanza asked with an arched eyebrow. "Even Jay's paranoia wouldn't have been planning for that until it started happening.

"Seven out of twenty-four might feel like a failure, Commander Demirci, but against the resources of a major interstellar power, that is a victory you should be proud of."

"Too easy to remember the dead, sir," she confessed.

"I know," he agreed. "Drink your coffee, Demirci. You look like you need a moment."

The carrier shivered around them as her Harringtons came online. Estanza closed his eyes, clearly checking reports and data as Kira took that moment he'd offered to regain her composure.

Two more survivors were *everything*...and they were nothing. Seventeen of her comrades—her friends and family—were dead. Seven pilots would fill out her squadron, but the number would also remind her of how much she'd lost along the way.

SHE FINISHED her coffee and Estanza took her cup away, replacing it with a freshly full one. The Captain's mannerism hadn't *completely* changed now that he was suddenly sober, but it was still strange to watch him move without the slight imbalance of being constantly drunk.

"So, now we know that Memorial Squadron is going to have six pilots," Estanza noted. "That helps with my plans for the near future. If nothing else, I unfortunately now have pilot slots to put Galavant and Swordheart into on my side.

"But that brings up another problem that I'm facing: the most senior surviving pilot is Lozenge: Boyd Maina. He doesn't want the squadron command, would be mediocre at the job at best, and doesn't command the respect of the other pilots.

"On the other hand, I have Gizmo: Ruben Hersch. Two pilots in addition to Maina are senior to him, but he'd be *good* at the job and he has the respect of all of the pilots, including those who've been with the company longer.

"But." Estanza held up a finger. "Hersch is young. He celebrated his thirtieth birthday shortly before you came aboard. He needs seasoning, but I don't have smaller commands for him to practice on. He can do the job, but starting out will be rough for him...which means that while he can command the Darkwings, I *can't* make him *Conviction*'s Commander, Nova Group."

Estanza pulled a virtual document out of the air and tossed it to Kira.

"I need a second contract with you, Kira Demirci," he told her. "Separate from but dependent on the contract between *Conviction* and Memorial Squadron. *That* contract explicitly says you have no command authority over *Conviction* personnel except as required to support your squadron.

"*This* contract brings you fully into *Conviction*'s chain of command as Commander, Nova Group," Estanza explained. "You'll have complete authority over Darkwing Squadron as well as Memorial Squadron for training, recruiting, organizing—everything. I'll maintain oversight, of course, but the nova group will be yours. You'll share authority over the flight deck with Waldroup, but in space you answer to me and God."

He smiled.

"The extra contract is, of course, remunerated appropriately," he told her. "That won't go through Memorial Squadron, even if, as I said, this contract is both legally and functionally inextricably linked to the contract for the Memorials."

Kira exhaled slowly as she reviewed the contract. The legalese agreed with everything Estanza was saying. The salary was higher than she'd expected, especially given that he was already paying for Memorial Squadron to employ a squadron commander.

"I'll have to run it by Simoneit, but it looks good. What's the catch?" she asked.

Estanza sat there in silence for several seconds, studying her.

"The catch?" he said softly. "The catch is that I'm done running and I'm done hiding. If that attack happened for the reasons I think it did, I'm about to go to war, Commander, and hitching your star to mine will make you enemies forever."

"I'm already hunted everywhere I go," Kira said dryly. She wasn't sure just who or what Estanza was talking about, but it couldn't be *worse* than having the dictator of an interstellar power personally signing kill orders for you.

"I know. It wouldn't change much for you, but it would still be a change," Estanza warned. "You need to understand who I am and what I've done before you sign that contract—and who Jay Moranis was and what he'd done, too.

"Tell me, Kira, did Jay ever tell you anything about the Equilibrium Institute?"

31

KIRA COULD ONLY STARE BLANKLY at Estanza.

"No," she finally conceded, though the name sounded vaguely familiar. "I think he might have mentioned the name once or twice, but he never explained anything about them."

"Makes sense." *Conviction*'s Captain rose to his feet, a thought turning the wall behind him into a virtual window showing the gas giant Lastward slowly shrinking away behind them.

"It was an unspoken deal," he told her. "We didn't reveal what we knew of Equilibrium and they let us go. No pursuit, no knives in the dark. Cobra Squadron just ceased to exist."

"What does Cobra Squadron have to do with this Equilibrium?" Kira asked.

"Everything," Estanza said bluntly. "The Griffon Sector wasn't the first time Cobra helped someone rise to dominance over a region. It was the *fourth*. Our involvement was easy to miss: we were just one mercenary flight group, operating out of a couple of freighters. Nothing special, except in our numbers.

"Except that we were at the turning of the tide of a dozen wars," he continued. "Always in favor of turning the arc of history to where the Equilibrium Institute said it should go. Take the Star Kingdom of Griffon, for example.

"They were wealthy and technologically advanced. They didn't claim any great degree of pacifism; they just had far better things to spend their money on than fleets and didn't feel the need to enforce hegemony around them.

"So, the Institute arranged for a massive pirate fleet to raid the system. They had *just* the right amount of firepower, timing and inside assets to seize control of the refueling infrastructure for a day or so before Cobra Squadron 'coincidentally' arrived. We threw the balance in favor of Griffon, drove the pirates out.

"The fleets started building up then. There was a not-quite-legal change of government, and suddenly Griffon was aggressively expansionist and massively powerful. Two of their local rivals challenged them. We flew for one of those rivals for long enough to get it unavoidably involved, then ended up flying for Griffon as they smashed them into the ground.

"Griffon became what the Equilibrium Institute wants: a regional hegemon powerful enough to prevent war among the other star systems. They imposed trade deals and tariffs, seized military control of the trade routes, the works. Much as Brisingr is doing right now in your home sector."

"But why?" Kira asked.

"The Equilibrium Institute's goal is peace for all humanity," Estanza said quietly. "The goal is hard to argue with. The image of a humanity at peace—still disunified, but at peace—was tempting and convincing as all hell.

"We might have officially been mercenaries, but we were an Equilibrium Institute special ops team. Those 'freighters' we were flying around in were Heart World–built escort carriers with fake plating on top. We kept the fighters local, but our support infrastructure outclassed everything else in the sector.

"We were the unexpected knife that built four hegemonies from nothing, creating regional powers that would enforce peace. It was only in Griffon that we saw the *other* side of the Equilibrium Institute's plan."

"Which was?" Kira asked, stunned at the grand scope of what Estanza was telling her. She wasn't sure if it was his paranoid conspiracy theory or an *actual* conspiracy she was stunned by, but the scope was mind-boggling either way.

"To stabilize regions, they needed their local hegemons," he explained. "But to keep their precious *equilibrium,* they needed to make sure that none of the powers they'd propped up and made expansionist were powerful enough to get *too* expansionist.

"They wanted people who could enforce 'peace' within one or two nova recharges but lacked the strength to end up in conflict with the *next* designated hegemon over. So, when Griffon started looking at expanding beyond what the Equilibrium Institute thought was their *appropriate territory*, they sabotaged the shipyards."

Kira looked past Estanza at the image of Lastward behind him. At this distance, the Redward Royal Navy shipyards were just shiny dots above the moon they used as an anchor, but she knew there would be millions of people on the stations and the moon beneath them.

"Fourteen million dead," Estanza concluded. "Maybe…six people in the galaxy who weren't involved knew enough to put together all of the pieces. Four of them were Cobras. I was one. Moranis was one.

"We told the rest of the squadron."

"And?"

"We *liked* Griffon," he admitted softly. "Compared to some of the people we'd supported over the years, the Star Kingdom had more than just greed in mind when they'd turned expansionist. A lot of their expansion at this point was even peaceful—they'd pick a nova stop, move in and secure it, then cut trade and protection deals with the local governments.

"Their carrot was money and they had a lot of it. Their stick was their carrier fleet…and they had a lot of that, too. With the shipyards wrecked, they stopped, pulling their ships back to defend the areas they'd already secured.

"Expansion was contrary to their general political discourse. Once it stopped, it never really restarted. Another victory for the Equilibrium Institute…and a couple dozen of their best assets looking in the mirror and realizing how much damn blood we'd shed in pursuit of a goal that couldn't really *be* achieved."

"So, you abandoned them?" Kira concluded.

"I think some of the Cobras stayed," he told her. "But at least half of us deserted, abandoning ships and fighters in the night. We had money and reputation. Turning that into new options for us was easy enough.

"And the Institute didn't come after us, not initially. I think they were watching and waiting. They knew we'd been loyal, so what would we do now that we'd run? We kept their secrets...and they let us go."

"And now?" she asked. "I thought Redward was trying to do just that kind of setup here."

"King Larry is trying to negotiate a trade and mutual protection association," Estanza said. "There's no illusion that Redward wouldn't be first among equals, but the goal is to get everyone signed on voluntarily and working together."

"So, exactly what do they want? Why do you think this Institute is involved now?"

"Because their 'Seldonian Analyses' tell them that mutual-benefit associations don't work," the old mercenary told her. "There's a bias in their numbers, in their calculations. I worked with one guy who went back and reanalyzed the reports they'd done, and they figured that the Institute had twisted Seldonian social-projection analysis pretty badly so it always produced the answers they wanted.

"In the absence of a key power prepared to become a military hegemon, the Institute will *create* one," Estanza concluded. "One of the methods they'll use to encourage whoever they work with to play along is to arm the local pirates. So, right now, I'd bet money that there are Equilibrium agents negotiating with at least three governments in the Cluster.

"But most importantly, the Costar Clans have become more aggressive in recent months and years, and more willing to use their heavier ships. *That* tells me that they're not as concerned about their ability to *replace* those ships.

"Something has changed and it stinks of the Institute. I have spent thirty years running from them, Kira. Thirty years trying not to be a threat, intentionally not opposing their operations.

"I'm done. If they're behind the Costar Clans' new aggression, then the Clans need to be broken. And nobody knows the Equilibrium Institute better than me."

"Why tell me all of this?" she asked softly.

"Because Daniel knew it," he replied. "Because if you sign on for this fight, they'll mark you as an enemy—and because if I'm *right*, someone other than me has to know what's going down. I'm only one man."

"And if you're wrong, sir?" she asked.

"Then at least one more person knows about this galaxy's most aggressive societal cancer and we go kill pirates for shits and giggles," Estanza concluded. "Nobody loses. You're right in having Simoneit review the contract, but I'd like a verbal answer now. We can sort out details later."

"I might ask you for more money after *that* lecture," Kira countered.

"Then that's one of those details," he confirmed. "But are you with me, Kira?"

Either John Estanza was crazy paranoid or he'd encountered one of the most dangerous conspiracies in the galaxy and learned how it operated. Both options were concerning, but neither really impacted whether or not Kira would help the man hunt pirates.

"I'm with you. Sir."

"Good. Sort out the contract with Simoneit and check in on your pilot who landed. We'll have a few days while Waldroup rebuilds my fighters and I talk to the RRF, but I suspect you and I are going to be sitting down with Redward Command before the week is out.

"If the Costar Clans can now produce corvettes reliably enough to *expend* corvettes, we need to act decisively and quickly. *Conviction* can't do that alone and won't do that for free, so if everything breaks right, well…"

He grinned.

"I'm pretty sure King Larry will be *more* than happy to pay for our revenge!"

32

KIRA HAD ARRANGED to bring Cartman with her on her trip aboard station, keeping with the "buddy system" requirement that McCaig had ordered. Both of the women were armed with bead pistols tucked away under armored leather jackets.

The outfit that Kira had adopted on her way out to the Redward System was extremely practical for their current situation, and she'd grabbed a few equivalent jackets for her people before leaving Blueward Station last time.

She was comfortable enough with that level of armed and armored that she was surprised to find two of the more heavily equipped mercenary troopers waiting in the docking bay—one of them in Milani's distinctively painted red dragon armor.

Kira hadn't seen the mercenary *out* of the armor yet. She wasn't even sure she'd seen their face, as the handful of times she'd seen Milani aboard ship, they'd still been wearing the gear.

"What's this, Milani?" she asked the trooper.

"We're your escort," they replied, gesturing to themselves and Bertoli. "The whole ship is in watch-your-back protocol, but we know there are *extra* assassins gunning for you. *You*, Commander, in particular.

"Rest of the Memorials can buddy-system it if they want, but we've got a note up to be ready to provide armed escorts for them if they ask. You don't get a choice."

Kira shook her head.

"And who do I argue with over that?" she asked.

"Right now, me. And you aren't winning," Milani replied, their voice cheerful. "And since you have an appointment to keep with a five-thousand-crest-an-hour lawyer, I suggest we don't have that argument.

"Since you'll lose," they repeated.

Kira studied the armored merc with their licensed blaster—the weapon she *couldn't* carry aboard Blueward Station and distinctly felt the lack of—for several more seconds, then sighed.

"Fall in, Milani," she told them. "You don't get to come into the meeting—and please exchange the minimum necessary glowers with the Ironborn."

"That's still a *lot* of glowering and one-upping, sir," Milani pointed out. "Just so you know."

"When we're back, I'm raising this with Estanza," she warned them.

"That's fine," the merc replied. "Where do you think the order came from?"

Kira grimaced. There were downsides, it appeared, to convincing the Captain to finally leave his office.

GLOWERING OR NOT, the mercenaries split off to secure the waiting room at Simoneit's office. The young woman sitting in the space—presumably a client for one of Simoneit's junior partners—looked taken aback by the pair of armored men.

Taken aback or not, Jerzy Bertoli had her smiling cautiously as he offered to grab her coffee before Kira and Cartman stepped into the meeting room where Dirix waited for them.

"Stipan," Kira greeted the broad-shouldered man. "Where's Bardacki?"

"He'll be here in about half an hour," her administrator told her. "I wanted to run through the basic details of what your shoreside operations are looking like first."

"All right. Simoneit will be joining us?" Kira asked.

"In half an hour," Dirix said with a chuckle. "He knows most of this."

"Are you still technically under arrest?" she asked.

Dirix sighed and bowed his head.

"Not quite," he pointed out. "I'm under *bail terms,* not arrest. I can't leave the station until I face a tribunal that's set for just over three months from now. I'm not allowed to carry weapons or act as a bodyguard, either. Once the tribunal is over, I can reapply for those licenses and—so long as I'm cleared—I should get them easily enough."

"Which is what you thought the first time and got yourself in this mess, yes?" Kira prodded.

"Yes, sir," he confirmed, military habit kicking in.

"All I want from you, Stipan, is honesty," Kira told him. "You saved Evridiki Bardacki's life by all accounts. That's what I hired you to do. I just need you to be entirely up-front with me."

"I understand, sir," Dirix conceded. "What do you need?"

"You wanted to go over our shore establishment, and we'll get to that, but I need data first," Kira said. "In your message, you said Bardacki's attackers weren't local bounty hunters. Do you know who they were?"

"They weren't local at all," he replied. "I've got a few ins with Station Security and they can't ID them. The first group you collided with wasn't from Blueward Station, but Security knew them. Expensive in-system talent, willing to kill for coin.

"Most bounty hunters aren't," he explained. "The Cluster isn't organized enough for any kind of interstellar police. There's no SolFed Marshals out here."

"There's no SolFed Marshals within a thousand light-years of here," Kira pointed out.

The Solar Federation was nearly a legend this far out. They were one of the few known true multistellar states, a union of the forty or so stars closest to Sol. Treaties and agreements gave their Marshals authority well beyond their borders, with the organization acting as an interstellar police force across almost the entire Core.

Respect for their role, authority and sponsor carried their effective authority to the edge of the Heart—and probably beyond that. A SolFed Marshal had no authority in Redward, but that didn't mean anyone would *stop* them from arresting someone and dragging them back to the Federation to face trial.

"Fair enough," Dirix conceded. "But my point stands, sir. Without formal extradition treaties, bringing criminals back to face justice is hard. Even Redward posts bounties, but even a dead-or-alive bounty is rare and only valid in the system that posts it.

"Mostly, it's extrajudicial rendition," he concluded. "Glorified kidnapping, but because the targets are criminals, people have just grown to accept it.

"There are always a few people who will go for the dead-or-alive bounties with the assumption that if they kill someone, they can sneak themselves and the body out to avoid charges. It's still legally murder, but most of these groups are interstellar in nature and will just go somewhere else to avoid the charges.

"The hunters who came for you two and Nicastro were a local branch of one of those groups." Dirix glanced over at Cartman and clearly decided not to delve more into *that* particular topic.

"The people who came after Bardacki were something else entire-ly," he concluded. "Blueward Station Security is chasing shadows."

"*Shadows* is a word with particular meaning to us," Kira pointed out. "The Shadows are the Brisingr Kaiserreich's black operations team."

"They didn't come that far," Dirix said with a forced chuckle. "But you're looking at the same kind of thing. I should have been more clear. BSS doesn't know who they were. *I* have a pretty solid guess."

"That I'm guessing you didn't want to put in a recording?" Kira asked.

"These people killed my boyfriend," Cartman said grimly. "They keep trying to kill our friends. Who the hell are they?"

"It's all the bounty, Em Cartman," Dirix replied. "The people who came after Bardacki and I have clashed before. Not...everything I did for Redward was aboveboard, Commander Demirci."

"Given that the Royal Army has never officially done *anything* outside the Redward System, I'm not entirely surprised by that," Kira said. "Who were they, Stipan?"

"Special forces of the Ypres Hearth," he said simply. "Not the elite assassins they like to pretend they are, but still solid dark-side operators. I recognized the gear and the combat style."

He shrugged.

"They might not be Hearth," he conceded. "But they're Ypres special forces and they *fought* like Hearthers. They were from one of Ypres' factions."

"I'm really starting to hate that system, and I jumped right past it on my trip here," Kira concluded. "What do they have in for us?"

"I don't have a clue," Dirix admitted. "Each of the Ypres factions thinks they're a major player in the cluster because *Ypres* would be a major player in the cluster if it was actually unified. Because it's five separate factions, they're mostly ignored."

"And I'm guessing all of them are sucking up to Brisingr," Kira said grimly.

Or worse, they might even be sucking up to Estanza's "Equilibrium Institute," if that organization actually existed.

"It would follow," he confirmed. "Ypres was the payout point for your bounties." Dirix shook his head. "Right now, I'm using Ironborn for security on your people, but as we go forward, Memorial is probably going to want to hire some security of our own."

"That makes sense to me," Kira conceded, glancing over at Cartman. "I don't want to end up at the point where our shore office ends up mostly managing security for our shore office. Am I clear?"

"Well, that brings us back to just what you want the shore office to do, Commander."

"How about you start with laying out what you've *been* doing?" Kira suggested. "And if needed, we can continue the conversation after we speak to Bardacki."

"Of course," Dirix agreed. "First things first, of course, I am currently sourcing a physical office here on Blueward Station…"

33

BARDACKI HADN'T CHANGED A BIT. He was still a solidly built man well into his fifties. Age hadn't slowed his reflexes or rusted his skills, and it had brought a level sense of calm equanimity that Kira had always prized in a squadron's second.

He hadn't been *her* second, but she'd been impressed with him regardless. Now, as the Ironborn bodyguards settled into the apparently-required glower-off with her *Conviction* bodyguards behind him, he took in the occupants of the meeting room with an amused smirk.

"Figured that Moranis had put the lion's share of fixing this mess on you, Demirci," he told her. "Guessing the old man buried a pile of money out here and smuggled nova fighters out? The lawyer strikes me as his type."

"Depending on how you mean that, both yes and no," Simoneit agreed as he stepped through another door concealed in the wall of the meeting room. Kira hadn't even *noticed* the concealed entrance, and she stared in surprise at the opening.

"Jay and I were never lovers, but we were good friends for a very long time. He asked me to make sure there was a fallback point for him out here—for him and his husband, initially."

Bardacki grunted.

"So, Moranis's *suggestion* to me was to get out here and make contact with the Majors, which I'm guessing means you now," he said. "I'm assuming you have some offer for me. I'm not interested."

Kira blinked. That was the *last* thing she'd expected to hear.

"I haven't even said a word yet," she pointed out.

"You've got nova fighters," Bardacki repeated. "Presumably, you want pilots. I'm guessing it's a mercenary show, but it doesn't matter. I've flown enough, Demirci. Left enough pilots dead in my wake to make a name for myself—and lost enough friends to truly understand what that name cost.

"I don't want to be a nova fighter pilot anymore, and I don't know what else you've got to offer me. I appreciate the assist with the bodyguards while I was here and I wanted to see you lot, know how many of the Three-Oh-Three survived, but I'm not signing on."

"Including you, seven," Kira said softly. "The three of us. Hoffman and Patil. Michel and Colombera. That's it. Everyone else is dead, Evridiki."

He grunted.

"Figures," he finally said. "Anyone who rides with you, Demirci, is going to end up the same way. Nova fighter pilots die. It's what we do. I'm done. I have my own reserves and I'm going to keep going."

"Going where?" she asked, fumbling through her mental script as she tried to pull herself together. "Even if you won't fly combat for us, there are other roles we can offer with the Squadron."

"A long damn way from anywhere where anyone knows me, knows Apollo, or knows Brisingr," he told her. "I figure bounce around the Rim for a year or so, then head coreward a long way from home. I'm sorry, Demirci, but I'd rather not tell you where I'm going.

"And I can't stay. Even if I just joined Em Dirix here and ran admin for you, the urge to ask me to fly when you needed me—and the urge for me to do so—would be irresistible for us both. I don't want to be the emergency pilot.

"I just want to be done."

"Okay," Kira accepted in a sharp exhalation. "I won't pretend I wouldn't rather have you on my wing, Evridiki, but I can respect what you want. And I can help with that, too."

"And how's that?" he asked.

"Pree?" she gestured to the lawyer. "You set it up."

"Jay Moranis sent the seed capital that set up Memorial Squadron with the intention of making sure all of his pilots were taken care of when they made it out here," Simoneit told Bardacki. "Simply by arriving in the Redward System, you became a part-owner of the Squadron.

"If you don't wish to become one of the Squadron's pilots, the incorporation articles require that you accept a buyout based on the initial valuation of those shares," the lawyer continued. "Functionally, this is Memorial Squadron honoring the intent of the original source of funding that these funds be available to you."

"How much?" Bardacki asked cautiously.

Simoneit gave him the number and the pilot studied him in silence.

"Is that enough to buy a ship out here?" he finally asked.

"Not a great one," the lawyer admitted. "I could probably pull some strings and manage to acquire, say, a fifteen-thousand-cubic-meter small-crew freighter for that. It will only be Redward-level systems and tech though."

"If it can nova and get out of this system, I can keep her running after that," Bardacki said flatly. "What're those strings going to cost me?"

"Memorial will cover Simoneit's time," Kira told him. "You may not want to keep flying with us, but you're still family. We'll buy out your shares and help you get a ship. Seems the least we can do."

"Fair." She could see him relax. "Sorry, Kira. I was worried you'd take this harder than you did."

"I'd rather you stayed," she told him. "But I'll take picking a friend up and helping him go his way under his own power over another damn message telling me he died. You get me, Evridiki?"

"I get you, Kira," he conceded with a chuckle. "Once I have my ship, I'll have to have you aboard for dinner. All of you, if it has a big-enough dining room."

"I've been on ships that size," she warned him. "You might be aiming too high with *dining room*."

***

"YOU'LL TAKE care of everything for him?" Kira asked Simoneit after Bardacki had left.

"Of course," the lawyer promised. "That's what you pay me for."

"I *know* what we pay you, and I'm still not sure we're worth the hassle you get with us," Kira said with a chuckle. "I appreciate it, Pree. All of it."

"I know," the lawyer said with a smile. "It will be *easier*, of course, to get a good ship for Em Bardacki if the budget is more flexible?"

"A *little* flex," she said, holding her fingers up a centimeter or so apart. "We'll put a bit of extra money behind making sure he's okay, but we also need to watch for the rest of us.

"I'm not sure we'll get to keep Michel and Colombera now," she admitted.

"They're younger," Cartman reminded her. "And I'm not sure either of them would ever be willing to give up flying, not for anything."

"We'll find out in a day or so, I suppose," Kira agreed. "They'll be coming directly aboard *Conviction*; we shouldn't need any immediate help from you, Pree."

"You found two more?" the lawyer asked. "Thank gods."

"Captain Estanza found two more," Kira admitted. "He put out a call in the mercenary community—which reminds me of what I *do* need. What's the best way to pay a merc for bounties? Estanza apparently promised I'd pay for safe delivery of my people, and I see *every* reason to keep that promise."

"Same way you brought money here," Simoneit told her. "Bearer cred sticks, though I'd suggest crests not new drachmae. The Bank of the Royal Crest did an incredible job making themselves the reserve currency of choice around here."

"All right. Dirix—there's a quarter-million-crest bounty for the head of any of my pilots. I want six hundred thousand crests drawn from Memorial's accounts into bearer sticks by end of day tomorrow. Can we manage that?"

"I'll need your imprint on the forms with the bank," Dirix replied. "It might be easier if the three of us go visit the Bank of the Royal Crest here on Blueward together."

He blinked.

"Three hundred thousand a head?" he asked.

"And if you want to put that number out to the bounty hunting community, feel free," she told him. "We should have thought of it when we first got set up—if Brisingr wants to offer a quarter-million for my people to end up dead, I can fucking outbid them for safe delivery."

She sighed.

"Easy enough, too, since even in a best case, there's only one more of us out there."

34

COMMODORE SHANG TZU was one of the few people Kira had ever met who made her feel tall. The mercenary commander was of distinctly Asian descent in a way few people were this far out into the Rim, but he was barely a hundred and fifty centimeters tall.

Some of his lack of height was made up for by one of the largest and bushiest beards she'd ever seen on a human being. Despite the scale of the thing, Shang's beard was neatly trimmed and managed.

It was just bigger than the rest of his head.

"Commander Demirci," he greeted her cheerfully with a two-handed handshake. "Captain Estanza said good things about you!"

"And I'm sure 'she'll pay you for saving her people' was one of the more important ones," Kira replied with a chuckle as she saw Evgenia Michel and Abdullah Colombera emerge from the docking tube onto the flight deck behind Shang.

Each was escorted by a mercenary in mismatched armor who peeled off at the edge of *Conviction's* deck.

"It was definitely mentioned," Shang confirmed. "And I won't turn down the money, either. But I'll admit that knowing my boys roughed up some Hearthers didn't hurt."

"We appreciate your intervention, Commodore Shang," Kira told him, and produced the cred stick. "Unless it's been updated, the death mark on my people is a quarter-million crests apiece. This stick is for twenty percent *more* than that."

The mercenary paused with his hand on the bearer stick.

"That might actually be too much," he said slowly, some of his bright cheer fading. "I didn't save your people for money, Commander Demirci. My people saved them to be good sports. All I offered was a ride."

"Share it with the troops who saved them, please," Kira replied. "But I want the word out there—someone might be paying for my people's deaths, but I will pay *better* for helping them.

"And you helped without being certain of a reward. That's worth a lot all on its own."

Plus, the entire reward was less than Memorial Squadron's payment for the last operation. A two-week patrol with an admittedly nasty firefight near the end had paid out over two million crests for the six nova fighters she'd deployed.

She had to pay salaries and bonuses out of that—and that had been with bonuses for the bounties—but two million crests were a million new drachmae, and *that* was four times her old annual salary.

For two weeks' work for six people.

"All right, Commander," Shang finally told her, taking the bearer stick. "If that's your attitude, you're going to make a lot of friends among mercenaries. Not all of them will be true and many will try and use you, but at least you'll *have* those friends."

"I might pay well, Commodore Shang, but I'm an untrusting bitch," she replied with a smile. "But it's hard to argue you *didn't* rescue my people when they're right behind you."

Shang bowed, folding himself so completely, his beard nearly brushed the floor.

"Then I will leave you to catch up with your friends. I am pleased to have helped put Ypres Hearth in their place and gladdened to reunite companions sundered by the vagaries of war and politics." He smiled brightly. "I am *ecstatic* to have done so and been paid well for the privilege. I look forward to working with you in the future, Commander."

If Kira understood Estanza's plan, that would be closer than the mercenary thought. She smiled and inclined her head.

"Thank you again, Commodore."

Shang saw himself out and Kira crossed to face her two latest lost sheep.

"Socrates, Scimitar," she greeted them. "How are you two doing?"

"She got us this far by sleeping with a man I'd be charitable to compare to a hairy dog," Colombera said bluntly, the dark-skinned man still standing so as to shield Michel from threats. "I'm all right, but it's not been a good trip for either of us."

"I made that choice, Abdullah," Evgenia Michel said softly. "I won't pretend it was as fun as it might have been, but Roger was a far more delicate partner than his appearance might suggest. He just didn't shower as much as I would have liked."

The young woman's smile was forced, but her determination *not* to be made a victim shone through regardless.

"I'm glad Shang's people found you, even if I'm told the muggers were already having a rough day," Kira said.

"You and Evgenia here have left me forever terrified of tiny women," Colombera noted.

Michel was about three centimeters shorter than Kira and even more lightly built. There was a *reason* she'd trained in an armed martial art.

"Large men will always assume they can take small women, even *after* you produce a knife," Michel said grimly. "Those three weren't the first people I'd killed since leaving Apollo. Dear *gods*, Demirci, what did we *do*?"

"Nothing," Kira told her. "Brisingr was hunting us, people. For being effective against them, nothing else. So…here we are." She shrugged.

"Not your carrier, I'm guessing," Colombera said gruffly. "Whose?"

"A friend of Colonel Moranis's named John Estanza," Kira replied. "I wear enough hats here to call it home. We're running a mercenary nova fighter squadron with money and fighters Moranis arranged for.

"If you want to fly, I've got berths for you. If you don't, I can still arrange safe harbor here."

"I will move worlds and stars and Olympus itself to be in a nova fighter again," Michel said grimly. "I am *so* sick of not being in control of the world around me."

"Inshallah," Colombera added. "I'm with her. And you, Major."

"It's Commander now," she told them. "No real ranks among mercenaries. If you're in, you're in. That makes you pilots and co-owners in Memorial Squadron, our own personal mercenary company."

"If you've got a nova fighter, I'm in," Michel repeated.

"My dear Evgenia, I have *Hoplites*," Kira told them with a broad grin. "It'll feel just like home."

Michel closed her eyes and half-slumped against Colombera.

"I'll settle for *safe*, sir," she admitted.

"You're on *Conviction* now," Kira insisted. "You're safe. I promise."

FOR THE FIRST time since Kira had come aboard *Conviction*, Memorial Squadron's briefing room was full of familiar faces. She knew every one of the pilots sitting in the chairs like the back of her own hand.

Only three of them—Cartman, Michel and Colombera—had flown in her squadron. There had been four squadrons in the 303, after all.

It didn't matter. They were all Apollon, all survivors of a mad purge that *still* made no sense to Kira. Thanks to Jay Moranis and a dozen helpful people along the way, some fragment of the Apollo System Defense Force 303 Nova Combat Group survived.

And as their new name suggested, they would remember the ones who hadn't made it.

"All right, people," she said loudly. "So, today, we have a full Memorial Squadron of ex-Three-Oh-Three pilots, as we always planned." She shook her head. "I wish—more than words can really express, I think—that I had the backup pilots I'd hoped to. I wish that the fact we only got six nova fighters out here was actually going to be a problem for us.

"But we're here. Six of twenty-four—and Bardacki's alive, too. He's chosen a different path, but we'll all meet up with him before he leaves on it." She smiled. "We picked up a few strays along the way in our temps, and I wanted to make sure that everyone knows they're not suffering for us finding our own, either.

"Banderas and Asjes are back with the Darkwings and are being bumped to full pilots," she told them. "Banderas made ace in that scrum around *Conviction*, too—and Waldroup tells me she's planning on using Apollo-style kill markers on her fighters as a sign of thanks to us.

"I don't know what *Conviction*'s next mission is going to be yet," she continued. "There's a good chance it will look a lot like the last one —sweeping the nova lanes and playing convoy escort is most of what Redward's Fleet does, and we're backup for the RRF until the retainer ends."

Estanza might want to do something more spectacular about the Costar Clans, but that hadn't been decided yet. She doubted he was planning on taking *Conviction* into a war all on her own. Not without some answer for the carrier's lack of guns and understrength fighter group, anyway.

"Regardless, the last word is that we're going to stay at Blueward Station for at least four days," she told them. "Waldroup will have the last two PNC One-Fifteens online before that, hopefully, so we'll have time and space for some real-space exercises to knock everyone's rust off before we jet out.

"Your next two days are yours. After that, we're back to ASDF-standard dockside activities."

She grinned wickedly.

"And yes, that means you're going to be spending a *lot* of time in simulators. We did okay last time out, but our training up to date has focused on anti–nova fighter tactics. I'm not going to discount those or remove them from the cycle, but we need to refocus.

"Over a third of the known nova fighters in the Syntactic Cluster are aboard this ship, which means we're not going to be fighting many dogfights. *I* didn't account for that as I ran the training schedule prior to the last op, but I'm planning on it now."

The room chuckled in anticipation and she joined in.

"So, enjoy your two days, people—and make sure you bring your capital-ship-killing pants with you when you're back on duty. Because you all know how I train."

And that meant that if she threw her people against the defenses of a spaceborne rogue colony and its pirate shipyards, they'd hold together. Nobody out there had nova fighters.

Everybody out there had gunships and corvettes. Which meant her people needed to be completely comfortable with fighting ships twenty times bigger than theirs.

Unfortunately for her enemies, with the right pilots, nova fighters were more than capable of doing just that—and Kira Demirci knew damn well her people were the right pilots.

35

IT WAS in the quiet moments when there was nothing demanding her attention that it hurt the most.

Kira didn't *get* many of those moments, of course. That was a conscious choice right now, but it was also true of her life in general. Those few weeks aboard *Hopeful Future* had probably been the quietest part of her life for at least twenty years.

This one had sneaked up on her, a few moments when the paperwork seemed under control and no one was messaging her or knocking on the door of her office. A video feed from the launch deck caught her by surprise, and she caught herself half-expecting Daniel Mbeki to step out from behind the PNC-115, settling in to his old spot.

When Annmarie Banderas did so instead, it was like she'd been punched in the gut with his death all over again. The fighter the younger woman was inspecting wasn't the ship that Mbeki had ridden to his death...but it shared the same heart. The class two nova drive that propelled the newly rebuilt spacecraft had once rested in Mbeki's fighter-bomber.

It was a necessary thing. Without a fabrication plant for class two nova drives in the Cluster, they needed to retrieve and reuse the systems if they possibly could. Waldroup had amply demonstrated her ability to build the *rest* of a PNC-115 from parts, but she couldn't replace the nova drive itself.

And, Kira had to admit, it wasn't like she was silently crying because she knew that particular One-Fifteen had the parts from Mbeki's fighter in it. *Any* of the One-Fifteens could have set her off.

She'd never even had the chance to see if they could disprove her assumption that fraternization rules existed for a reason—or to even see if he was interested in more than a one-night stand, for that matter.

"It's never easy," a voice said behind her. Kira spun around, glaring at the intruder as her hand fell to the blaster she carried aboard *Conviction.*

Estanza's words were soft and gentle, his tone muffling her anger. The Captain probably *had* pinged for admittance, too. She'd just been too distracted to register it.

"I've lost three pilots I'd call my children," Estanza told her, stepping up to look at the video feed with her. "Four lovers, too. I can take solace, I suppose, in that I parted ways with the woman I meant to marry to protect us both from Equilibrium.

"Friends...god, I've lost count," he admitted. "People I'd shared meals and laughs with, whose weddings I would have stood witness at. I can remember all of their names and faces, but I'd need to consciously use my headware to count to tell you how many.

"Subordinates?" He shook his head. "Even more than friends, even if I'd call most of the pilots who died under my command friends."

"And Daniel?" Kira asked softly.

"Was a son to me, and I wish I'd told him that more often," Estanza admitted. "We always do when it's too late. We always feel guilty for what we didn't say—or wish we'd said it more, even if we did say it."

"At least he didn't die with us mad at each other," Kira said. She wasn't sure she could put into words how grateful she was that she'd managed to rebuild that bridge. Daniel might not have died her lover, but he *had* died her friend.

"It's not enough, I know," her Captain told her. "But it also has to be enough. You've danced this dance before; I can *see* it, Kira. And in the quiet moments, it burns us all the harder for setting it aside the rest of the time."

She'd dried her eyes while they were talking, and she shook her head now to clear the last stubborn tears.

"And we go on," she said firmly. "We miss him. We mourn him—and the others, too. I didn't know them as well as Daniel, but you knew them better than I did."

"I did," he confirmed. "Not as well as I should have. My plan to make myself look nonthreatening had unintended consequences for the quality of my command."

There was a thin smile on Estanza's face as she turned to look at him.

"And now?" she asked.

"Now I am very, *very* angry," he admitted. "If the Institute is behind the Costar's new aggression, we have a big new problem. If we don't, I have enough information now to know who was behind that particular attack, and I have every intention of blasting the bastard and his little pocket dominion into ashes."

"We have a plan?" Kira asked.

"Not yet. What I have, Commander, is a target."

He tossed her a file and she threw it up on the screen that had been showing the launch deck. The image was a man in a gray shipsuit marked only by a single crimson stripe across the right shoulder. He was probably in his forties or fifties. Younger if he was from the Costar Clans, she reminded herself—but potentially older, too, if he came from deeper toward the Core.

"Anthony Michael Davies," Estanza introduced the figure. "Currently rejoicing in the *fascinating* title slash nickname of 'Warlord Deceiver.'"

"Davies," Kira echoed. "The captain in charge of the convoy that baited us out of position was called Davies."

"From what I've come up with from Redward Intelligence and my own contacts, that would almost certainly have been him," her boss confirmed. "All of his operations that we can identify are in a similar vein: some kind of distraction, combined with a sucker blow that probably would have been enough *without* the distraction.

"We smashed his deployable forces. The losses we inflicted on the Clans would have crippled most system fleets out here. Redward Intelligence figures that he's currently running around stabilizing his position and bartering alliances to rebuild his strength."

"And you figure?" she asked.

"I figure the trap was made for us or one of Redward's three junk carriers," Estanza said quietly. "Even sub-fighters could have ruined his people's day. He risked what he could afford to lose—which means that two corvettes and twenty gunships was an *expendable* force.

"So, he's got a shipyard and a nova-drive fabricator and a reliable source of money, materiel and crew." The carrier Captain shook his head. "It's not that the Costar Clans really lack in raw materials to work with. What they lack is food and tech, not metal.

"If someone is supplying Warlord Deceiver with money and tech, he might well be able to replace his losses in weeks at most. It might not be the Institute, either," he noted. "Even one of the Ypres factions could see the value in undermining Redward and the new trade association they're trying to build."

"Okay. So, what do we do?"

"That's why I'm here," Estanza told her. "You inherited an apartment down on the surface, right?"

Kira had to pause and call up her headware memory to confirm that. It had been just one part of a *very* busy series of days.

"Yeah, Jay Moranis's bolthole," she admitted. "I'd forgot. Wasn't really important to me."

"Well, since you gave your people a couple of days off, I think it would be a *great* time for you to go check out your new digs," he suggested. "And I'd be delighted to accompany you to make sure you get there safely."

She gave him A Look.

"And what is actually going on?" she asked.

"We need an excuse for the two of us to go down to Red Mountain," he told her. "Having an address where people can meet us that isn't an official RRF office would be handy, too.

"Since you *have* that apartment, it should make solid cover for us to meet up with a few senior officers in person and have conversations that we can't have recorded. I knew Jay. I think I can assume the place would hold up to a decent meeting?"

Kira dug into her headware.

"I got a keycode and an address," she told him. "It's a mid-floor apartment, only the fifty-eighth level."

Estanza chuckled at that and she glared at him again.

"What?" she asked.

"This isn't Apollo," he reminded her. "Sixty stories is a good sized building in Red Mountain. What's the address?"

She tossed him the data and his chuckle became an outright laugh.

"That's the fifty-eighth floor of the Reginald Forsythe Tower," he told her. "The Tower is *exactly* fifty-eight floors high and is one of the four Founders' Towers, named after the original primary funders for the colony."

"Your point?"

"Your *apartment* is a penthouse in what I believe is the third most luxurious apartment developments in the capital city," the Captain explained. "Certainly among the top ten developments on the *planet*."

"Oh." Kira mentally checked the math on an offhand comment Simoneit had made. "That would explain why it's eating all the interest on ten million kroner in upkeep, wouldn't it?"

"Yes, yes it would," Estanza chuckled. "Now, I don't know Priapus Simoneit well, but I *did* know Jay Moranis. Unless I'm severely mistaken, you won't quite believe what he's set up here until you see it."

"I saw his manor on Apollo," she pointed out. "That was a mansion with fifteen acres of manicured grounds. And concealed anti-air missiles."

"That sounds like Jay," the Captain agreed. "Now realize that *you* own something that he regarded as acceptable. I want to see this *apartment* myself now."

"And if we manage to sneak in a meeting with your Admirals, everyone wins?" Kira asked.

"Exactly. And, helpfully, I think at least one of said Admirals lives in Reginald Forsythe Tower."

Estanza grinned again.

"Though I don't believe that *she* lives in a penthouse."

36

THE FOUR FOUNDERS' Towers weren't large enough to earn the key mark of a gold-standard top-tier development on Apollo: none of them had a shuttlepad on the roof. The *complex* had a shuttlepad behind the towers, shielded from weather by a flank of the mountain the city was named for, and Kira tucked the spacecraft into the pad with delicate ease.

The Towers were...well, they were small and quaint, if she was going to be honest, but the grounds were decorative enough. The four buildings were spread out across several acres of neat paths and carefully managed gardens.

Kira's own tastes ran more toward untamed forests and wild moors, but she'd grown up in a village of shepherds on Apollo. The sheep might have been genetically engineered to shed three times in a standard year, and the herding might have been done as much by drone as by dog or staff, but sheep still flourished on much the same kind of terrain they always had.

This kind of manicured setup made her look for the concealed weapons systems.

The Founders' Towers weren't quite up to that standard of "luxury," but they were still acceptably ridiculous. A transfer drone contentedly moved the shuttle Estanza had lent her into a stacked parking garage of similar vehicles. Holographic signs discreetly directed her to the correct tower, where doors carved from the local stone slid silently aside to let them in.

The doors showed a bit of wear on the outside, easily missed as they slid open, and that seemed to be the tone that Kira was picking up. The Towers were *very* well maintained, but they were also old.

Her headware happily confirmed that the complex had been among the first few luxury developments on the planet. For it to still hold itself among the top ten was impressive.

The security was slightly less so, though at least there *was* security once she entered the lobby of the tower. Her experienced eye picked out concealed sensors and what were probably closets holding security bots.

It even took her a moment to realize that the attractive young male receptionist was a holographic artificial stupid rather than a real human. The projection was as good as any she'd seen in Apollo and, she suspected, had cost an arm and a leg out there in Redward.

"Em Demirci," the hologram greeted her as she arrived. "We weren't informed that you would be coming home today, but our records show that both the cleaners and security team were through your apartment yesterday.

"While we don't have access to your food-storage system, we project it highly unlikely that you have foodstocks on hand. Would you like us to arrange a chef service for your dinner this evening?"

Kira managed to *not* tell the computer to go to hell.

"I'll be fine," she told it. "If you could forward a list of recommended *delivery* services, that would be appreciated."

"Of course, Em Demirci," the image replied. "Should we advise your cleaning and security teams of additional services required?"

Kira took a moment to check what level of service she was currently getting. Once-a-week cleaning and security sweeps for an empty apartment?! No wonder the place was eating half a million kroner a year!

"The regular service should suffice," she murmured. She was going to have to take a closer look at just what services the apartment was using. The security sweep was probably necessary, but she wasn't sure an empty apartment needed the toilets scrubbed every week.

"Of course. Reginald Forsythe Tower's staff and artificials are ready to assist you with anything you need, Em Demirci."

She shook her head.

"Right now, I need an elevator to my apartment," she told the AI.

"Of course," the hologram said cheerfully. "If you step to your left and circle around the mermaid fountain, you will see the express penthouse elevator and the security panel there. Provide your keycode to our systems and you will have access to your unit."

"YOU SHOULD GET USED to the finer things in life."

That was what Jay Moranis had told Kira almost every single time she'd stayed at his sprawling manor estate on Apollo. Usually while plying her and the other squadron commanders with wine that cost far too much.

In hindsight, Kira should probably have wondered where the old man's money had come from—and why a man with that much money spent his time flying a nova fighter instead of sitting on his estate, drinking retsina.

Even from beyond the grave, it seemed he'd found a way to make one final argument in his case on converting Kira from the shepherd peasant's daughter she still semi-identified as.

The penthouse was, at least, not the *entire* upper floor of the building. It was one unit of four that divided the top *two* floors between them. The exterior walls were entirely transparent aluminum, armored against light blaster cannon fire, according to the brochure she'd finally extracted from Simoneit's files.

There were five bedrooms in the penthouse. *Somewhere.* Kira couldn't see any sign of them as she stepped out into the main living area, staring at the immediately visible view out over the city of Red Mountain. The bedrooms were probably upstairs, in the loft that covered half of the open living area.

A sprawling kitchen—fit for the chef the stupid had wanted to send her—filled one corner. An elegant-but-functional dining room table that could seat sixteen marked another. A third corner had a similarly plain sitting room setup, and the fourth was simply empty, a massive expanse of local hardwoods.

"Jay came from money and brought it with him," Estanza told her as he surveyed the apartment next to her. "He spent most of his life on starships or in nova fighters, but everywhere he laid down an anchor, it looked like this.

"And the Equilibrium Institute paid well—even *before* you factored in what being legendary mercenaries made us. I bought a *carrier* with what I stashed away on my way out," he noted, then shrugged with a laugh.

"And a few other things I acquired afterward. But still. Compared to what I spent on *Conviction*, this is nothing. Or so Jay pointed out when I challenged him on his 'little luxuries' after buying her, anyway."

Kira laughed softly. For all of the scale of the space, even she could tell it was plainly decorated for its nature. There was no art, simply the native stone and wood paneling of the walls. The empty parts of the main space could have held another three sitting or entertainment areas.

Shaking her head, she checked the cupboards and storage. Like the hologram had predicted, there was no food. There was a neatly organized set of dishes and utensils to feed sixteen people, plus a set of cooking gear well beyond her skills.

"We have to stay here at least tonight to make it look good, I suspect," she told Estanza. "Go confirm that there are actual *beds* in this place for me, would you? I'm going to look at that delivery menu."

He coughed delicately.

"You may want to take the Tower staff up on that chef," he told her. "I've confirmed with my guests and they're heading in this direction. They'll be here around dinnertime, and much as I think he'd find it *hilarious*, I don't want to feed the King of Redward takeout."

Kira stopped in mid-thought to round on her Captain.

"The King," she snapped. "Are you serious?"

"King Larry, also known as King Lawrence Bartholomew Stewart, His Royal Majesty, First Magistrate and Honored King of the Kingdom of Redward."

Estanza smiled.

"I could meet Admirals on Blueward Station," he told her. "They have reasons to be in space. King Larry doesn't. He only leaves the planet with multiple destroyers in escort. There's no subtle movement for the king of a star system, not once you leave his capital."

"But in his capital?"

"He can move covertly with only a handful of bodyguards," the Captain confirmed. "And the staff at the Founders' Towers are *very* cleared. The chef can be trusted."

"More than the takeout place, I assume," Kira conceded with a sigh. "All right. I'll make the call."

37

KIRA HAD SEEN his picture in a hundred places since arriving in the Redward System, yet it was still a shock to meet King Larry in person and realize just *how much* he looked like the kind of man who would go by "King Larry."

The system's monarch was the fifth person to enter the apartment, which made him the first after the security detail. Almost two meters tall with shoulder-length hair, he wore a dark green suit that had clearly been tailored *not* to hide his girth. He had the smile lines of a man who smiled easily and often, and laughed just as readily—and the stress lines of a man responsible for three billion souls.

Large and cheery as he was, there was also a presence to the man that drew the eye. It took Kira a few seconds to even realize that the King was wearing a crown—a simple gold circlet that rested at the top of a flushed high forehead.

"Kitchen shutters are down," the guard reported as King Larry entered. Kira hadn't even *realized* that the kitchen had walls that could come down to conceal staff if needed, but there they were. "We've engaged the security field. One of the team is talking to the chef, but he already passed the background check a few months back."

There was a smile in the man's voice as he continued.

"Dinner will be ready in fifteen minutes, sir."

Kira didn't put a *lot* of stock on royalty—for all that Apollo was explicitly an oligarchy with a restricted franchise, her people didn't really believe that kings and queens had been good for humanity. It was still rather flustering to find herself in a room with a monarch.

She'd never even been in the same room as one of Apollo's Principals, the elected councilors who ruled her homeworld, after all.

Estanza, on the other hand, seemed to take everything in stride. He stepped forward with a small bow to exchange a handshake with the King, then gestured to Kira.

"King Larry, this is Commander Kira Demirci," he introduced her. "She commands Memorial Squadron, who I've subcontracted to work for me, and is also my new Commander, Nova Group."

"A pleasure, Commander," Larry told her as he offered her his hand. He was clearly used to people being a bit taken aback by him.

"I heard about Commander Mbeki," he continued. "I know you and he were close, Captain Estanza. You have my condolences."

Kira had heard a *lot* of politicians give condolences over the years. King Larry was one of the few who seemed to actually *mean* it.

More people were coming through in the King's wake, and it spoke to the sheer presence of Redward's monarch that Kira had failed to notice the arrival of three *Admirals*.

The two women and the man trailing behind King Larry all had stars on their collars. One woman had three; the other woman and the man both had two. Admiral and Vice Admiral, if Kira remembered her briefings on Redward's fleet correctly.

"Please, let's get everyone inside," the senior bodyguard told them all. "Team two is holding the lift, but the neighbors are important enough I hesitate to cause trouble, sir."

"They can wait a few minutes for an elevator," Larry replied dryly. "Even CEOs can afford to lose time, Richard."

Despite his argument, however, Larry ushered the three flag officers forward to clear the entryway.

"The table will work best," Kira suggested, not quite sure how to handle the mix of both being the host and being the most junior person actually involved in the discussion.

"Agreed." Larry led the way, indicating each of his companions as they passed by. "Captain Estanza knows everyone here, but

Commander Demirci doesn't. This is Admiral Vilma Remington, the senior officer of the Royal Fleet, along with Vice Admirals Ylva Kim and Shi Abreu."

Both of the Vice Admirals were carrier group commanders, in charge of the freighters the Royal Fleet had converted to deploy sublight fighters. Those carrier groups also came with real, if small, cruisers as well as smaller ships. The strike forces that reported to each of them might be a joke by Apollon standards, but they represented real firepower out here.

"Most important of all is this introduction," King Larry continued, gesturing to the woman in a long black dress who'd just entered the apartment with the second security team. She matched the King in height but was gaunt to his cheerful bulk.

"Sonia is my wife. She is the most decorative Queen my system has ever had, runs the charitable efforts of the Crown with an amazingly deft hand and, most relevant to today, runs my Office of Integration."

She stepped up beside him and kissed his cheek.

"It's a tiny, intentionally misnamed office," she told Kira. "My team's job is to take all of the information that comes in from both civilian and military intelligence and create a complete intelligence picture that goes back down to both teams.

"We try and catch the gaps in each group's expertise while avoiding territorial pissing matches." She waved a long hand delicately. "We do not always succeed, but it helps to have someone no one expects running the intelligence apparatus. I would say someone out of the public eye, but my public role is *very* public."

"I forwarded you all of the data I extracted on our Warlord Deceiver," Estanza told her. "I hope it made its way through the appropriate channels."

"It did," the Queen confirmed as she took a seat next to her husband. "Larry didn't break the evening free *without* asking me what I thought of your assessment of the situation."

"And?" Estanza asked bluntly.

"We now believe that you are correct," Admiral Remington said, equally bluntly. "Someone is supplying Davies with tech and funds to allow him to expand his forces. He has become a drastically expanded threat and one that must be neutralized."

"We will need to locate him first," King Larry pointed out. "I can't afford to send any of you off on a wild goose chase."

"There will be no wild geese," Sonia told her husband and the officers. "Please, let's get everyone seated and then I can go over what I've assembled from our intelligence and Captain Estanza's."

"Cleared as the chef is and solid as those shutters are, we're probably better off continuing this conversation after the food is served and he has gone on his way," Larry agreed.

KIRA WAS REASONABLY sure that the chef had been expecting to serve the meal he'd plated up himself, but the security team took over that task. The polite young man was ushered out of the apartment by equally polite *armed* young men who promised to handle the dishes.

Once the door closed behind him, Kira checked her security system and flicked the status update over to the King's senior bodyguard.

"The system report probably makes more sense to you," she told the man with a chuckle.

"Probably," he confirmed. "Toews, check the third bedroom upstairs. The Tower system is blocked but the apartment system is still picking up a radio signal."

The suited guard turned to the table.

"I think we do have a small bug," he told them. "Give my team a moment and we'll have it neutralized." He cocked his head, listening to a voice no one else heard. "It wasn't transmitting before. It seems that your prior conversation hit the keywords for an emergency message."

"The overwatch should have intercepted it even if we didn't block it," the Queen said quietly. "We'll trace it. That was part of why I wanted to wait, too. Just in case."

The guard nodded to her.

"We've found and neutralized the device and two more," he reported. "Your Majesties, you may want to take a look at this."

An image appeared above the table as the security man linked to the apartment's holoprojectors.

There was nothing in particular that stood out to Kira about the zoomed-in image of the electronic device.

"Solid-state molecular-circuitry device," the officer noted. "We couldn't build that bug, Your Majesties. No one in the Cluster could. That's Meridian tech, at least."

Kira exchanged a glance with Estanza as a chill ran down her spine. From what he'd explained, there was *definitely* someone out there who would have wanted to bug Jay Moranis's emergency bolt-hole.

"How long as it been there?" Queen Sonia asked.

"Hard to say exactly, but definitely months, not days," the nameless security man confirmed. "It wasn't placed to intercept this meeting."

"Do another sweep," King Larry ordered grimly. "Push your scanners to their limits, Captain. If there's three Meridian-tech bugs..."

"There are more," the man confirmed. "I suggest you refrain from discussing business until after dinner, Your Majesty. We should be certain by then."

THE TOWER, it seemed, had known enough about either Jay Moranis or Kira herself to have arranged a meal plan that at least resembled Apollon cuisine.

Of course, since Apollo was a *long* way from Redward, the standard of cuisine they were trying to follow was a vaguely remembered passed-on stereotype. Dolmades were quintessentially Old Earth Greek, so Kira could see the thought there, but the stuffed vine leaves had never been an Apollon staple.

The roasted lamb with mint sauce was *far* closer to Apollo standards, the chef having done a surprisingly good job with a dish that Kira had grown up on.

Her father's lamb had been better, but that was to be expected. Her parents had been shepherds, even if their village had been on hills with an excellent view of Apollo's largest spaceport.

At a table with three Admirals and the royal couple of an entire star system, she had no idea what to contribute to the conversation and ate in near-silence until she was done.

She was spared trying to think of social conversation by the return of the senior bodyguard.

"I don't know who you pissed off, Commander Demirci," the bodyguard told her with a soft chuckle. "But I *want* their resources. We only found four more bugs, but they were all well beyond anything we could build. Seven molecular-circuitry listening devices."

He shook his head.

"I think if I spent my entire team's annual listening device budget, I might be able to import *one* of these guys. Anyway, they're all disabled and being packaged into neat Faraday-cage boxes to go back to the office for analysis.

"The apartment is clear. I apologize for missing them the first time around."

"Nothing was discussed that would betray our plans or our intentions, Captain," Queen Sonia told him. "We were worried about the chef, not bugs that don't belong on this planet, but the discussion was safe."

She smiled thinly as she gestured for Kira to give her control of the holoprojectors.

"The rest of tonight will not be," she said flatly. "Everything that will be discussed here is classified Top Secret Orange Topaz. If you review your contract, Captain Estanza, you will note that a violation of any security classification above Top Secret results in a voiding of your contract and seizure of your ship."

Kira didn't even need to look at Estanza to know what the carrier captain was thinking: *Good luck with that.*

It was, notably, the heaviest threat they could realistically level.

"I want the sons of bitches who killed Commander Mbeki," Estanza noted, his voice chilly. "I haven't made a career of betraying the trust of the people who hire me, Your Majesty."

"I know," Queen Sonia conceded. "But some of what we are to discuss is intelligence that Redward did not acquire ourselves but came through the channels that are developing around the SCFTZ."

Kira's headware happily expanded the initialism: the Syntactic Cluster Free Trade Zone. An organization that didn't officially exist so far but that a quarter of the Cluster's systems were committed to creating and another quarter were negotiating toward.

Back channels between the four systems who'd already signed on to the draft agreement made sense. They'd presumably been allies for a long time to agree to the concept so readily.

"Other intelligence comes from assets we cannot afford to expose or methods that, frankly, would not hold up in our courts," she continued. "All of this data, plus Captain Estanza's trawling of the knowledge of the local mercenaries, ended up in the Office of Integration.

"My people did their jobs and we now have a relatively solid image of just what Warlord Davies is up to," she concluded.

A wave of her hand brought up the Syntactic Cluster. It was a roughly globular collection of sixty stars forty-three light-years across. Seventeen of the stars held habitable worlds, all of them settled. All seventeen of those systems, Kira saw, were highlighted. Redward was gold, three others were green—the tentative members of the SCFTZ—with five orange icons presumably marking the systems negotiating for entrance. The remaining eight systems were highlighted in silver to mark them as inhabited.

"We have always had a relatively solid grasp of the physical locations of the Costar Clans," the Queen noted. Ten systems on the map flashed crimson. None of them were systems flagged as having inhabitable planets.

"They represent a mix of outposts from the other systems, daughter colonies from spaceborne settlements closer to the Core, ships that ended up in the wrong place, and in the case of the Crysty System, a planet that suffered a tectonic realignment while the colony ship was en route," she explained. "All of them are struggling-to-marginal.

"I have a deep and abiding sympathy for the people of those systems," she continued. "But I have *no* sympathy for their willingness to embrace raiding and violence as a cultural touchstone and answer to their status.

"Nonetheless, we and most of our partners have generally followed a two-pronged approach to deal with the Clans: on the one hand, we have escorted our critical convoys, swept trade routes, secured the entry and exit points from our systems and generally worked to thwart the actual raiders as thoroughly as possible and as violently as necessary.

"On the other, both private and system-level charitable efforts have dug into many of these systems to try and resolve the underlying problems. This project has been ongoing since before I was Queen. Since before I married Larry, in fact.

"But over the last thirty years, we have been seeing success. Several systems that would once have proudly proclaimed themselves Costar Systems now bar the raiders from their ports and have turned their shipyards to building freighters and futures."

"A success that has been bought with the blood of hundreds of our spacers," Admiral Remington noted. "I don't disagree with the approach, Your Majesty, but I have always felt that a certain degree of direct action into their systems against key facilities would be wise."

"And traditionally, the Crown has disagreed with you and your predecessors," King Larry said comfortably, this clearly being a well-worn argument. "For our efforts to bring these systems in from the cold, they needed to trust us.

"But it has always been clear in my mind and my mother's, when she was Queen before me, that there would be times we needed to strike at the Clans directly. To keep the trust we were trying to foster, we needed to make sure that even the *Clans* would agree that someone had gone too far.

"I believe we may have reached that point," the King finished. "Please, Sonia."

"We know that Warlord Deceiver is based out of the KLN-35XD System," the Queen of Redward said firmly. "Known to the locals as the Kiln, it's an uninhabitable hellhole with a vast quantity of rich asteroid belts.

"Cluster systems have always been up for trying to exploit the Kiln, but no one really has the resources to do so successfully or to really defend a claim there," she continued. "There were a lot of failed mining outposts, and not everybody left when their home companies tried to pull them out.

"The Kiln became a Costar Clan system. Enough resources are present there to make everyone in the system rich, but they've never had the tech to exploit it on their own or a partner they trusted to help them do it. So, they started stealing that tech."

Sonia shook her head.

"Of course, telling you that the Warlord is in the Kiln System isn't helpful," she noted. "A star system is a large place, and there are multiple factions even in the Kiln System. What has drawn our attention more and more to his operation is that he has become increasingly aggressive over the last two years.

"The attack on *Conviction* was his largest operation to date, but it wasn't his first strike that was well out of scale with normal Clan resources. The Deceiver clearly feels he has the resources to risk significant losses for significant victories.

"That suggests that he has an outside partner who is enabling him to properly exploit the resources of the Kiln," she told them. "Our current suspicion is someone on Ypres, but I suspect we're talking one of the embassies, not one of the factions."

"Like Brisingr," Kira suggested. Or the Equilibrium Institute Estanza was worried about. Either would be a problem.

"Brisingr isn't high on my list of potential troublemakers, but they're on it," the Queen confirmed. "The two key points are that Warlord Deceiver must have a large, recently expanded mining-and-construction operation somewhere in the Kiln System.

"One that he built with somebody else's help. We believe that we can strike at this facility and, so long as we stay within reasonable laws of war, it won't be held against us."

"You don't pay me enough to ignore atrocities, let alone commit them," Estanza said grimly. "Even knowing what we're looking for, a star system is not a small place."

"And that brings us to why I needed to be completely certain that this meeting was private," Queen Sonia agreed calmly. "We have highly placed assets inside the Costar Clans. Some of them, I am certain, only work with us to undermine their rivals. Others are at least partially aligned with our objectives for their systems."

The *partially aligned* was probably key, Kira suspected. She assumed that the systems that had left the Costar Clans were now economic dependencies of Redward or another system. They were almost certainly better off...but they definitely weren't going to be anything a former pirate colony would call *free*.

"You know where he's based?" Estanza asked.

"I know where he's based," Queen Sonia confirmed. "I also am absolutely certain that he has spies in this system and has potentially acquired assets at the highest levels of the Redward Royal Fleet. Some of that may be his new friends. Some of that is definitely him.

"Any attempt to actively move against Warlord Deceiver's main base is going to find empty stations and abandoned mines. There is no way this man hasn't prepared for a full-on evacuation of his facilities on twenty-four hours' notice or less.

"If we follow the nova lanes, Kiln is eighty hours from here. If you have someone mad enough to do unmapped six-light-year novas, you can reach Kiln in three jumps."

Kira was checking the routes as she listened. Kiln was seventeen light-years from Redward. A jump to the nova lane, three jumps— eighteen light-years—along the most convenient nova lane, a jump to the system.

Five jumps, four twenty-hour waiting periods. Eighty hours. But a direct route would be *three* jumps, with two twenty-hour waiting periods. The only real *good* news was that Davies definitely didn't have *Conviction* penetrated—if he had, his plan to take the carrier out wouldn't have foundered on the presence of Kira's squadron.

"They probably have mapped a number of points outside the nova lanes," Kira pointed out. "I know Apollo had an entire secondary set of mapped nova stops through the entire cluster for our fleet if needed."

"Fuck me," Remington replied in a heavy breath. "We have...a few fallback points around Redward mapped. We never even thought to expand a shadow network that far."

"Think about it," King Larry ordered. "Get me a plan, Admiral. We'll talk about it later."

"Of course, Your Majesty."

Every so often, Kira almost forgot that she was a long way from home and that a hundred light-years farther out from Sol could make a *huge* difference. And then she had the reminders that things she'd assumed were the case...weren't out there.

"But we don't have that network now, and I hesitate to send a significant force via unmapped long-range novas," Remington noted. "Do we have information on the defenses?"

"No," the Queen admitted. "It seems that we can safely assume at least twenty gunships and two corvettes, that being the force he sent against *Conviction*. I would suggest assuming at least twice that."

"*Conviction* could handle a large portion of that but not all of it," Estanza noted. "I'd be remiss if I didn't mention that Commodore Shang Tzu is currently in the system as well, with two destroyers. No one has wasted resources infiltrating *our* command structures."

"A carrier and two destroyers are unlikely to suffice," King Larry said calmly. "Remington, we need Captain Estanza and Commodore Shang, but the mercenaries will not be enough.

"You need to send *Perseus*."

"Sir, *Perseus*—" Remington argued, gesturing at Vice Admiral Ylva Kim.

"Carries the Lancer Squadron, I know," the King interrupted. "That's why we need *Perseus* and Admiral Kim's group."

"If I'm deploying the Lancers, we should at least advise Captain Estanza of their nature," Vice Admiral Kim said delicately. The flag officer had been quiet to this point, and her voice was soft as she spoke.

"Lancer Squadron is six Royal Crest–built Cavalier-II medium nova fighters," Estanza told her. "They're fifteen years out of date, and Crest didn't even bother to downgrade them before selling them to you. They *claimed* that was because they trusted you, but it was actually because the Cavalier-III was a vastly superior design and they knew the II had severe issues.

"As, I understand, your test and training flights have uncovered," the Captain said with a grin. "I believe you've managed to find answers for most of them, but those birds were *born* to be hangar queens."

The table was silent for a moment.

"How many of our secrets do you *not* know, Captain?" Queen Sonia asked.

"I don't know," Estanza said with a chuckle. "I made it my business to know everything I could about nova fighters in the cluster. With the Lancers alongside us, we'll have twenty nova fighters. The Cavalier-II has maintenance issues, but if you've kept them up, they're solid fighters.

"Barring any significant phalanx of capital ships, I'd take that nova group against anything in the cluster."

"We'll hire Shang and send the full *Perseus* group," King Larry ordered. "That'll be a cruiser and four destroyers, backing up your two carriers."

"Neither carrier is armed," Remington noted. "Protecting them will be a challenge."

"That's Admiral Kim's job," Larry told her. "And your mercenary COs'. The biggest issue is going to be avoiding giving away our hand."

"The oldest of problems with the oldest of solutions," Estanza suggested. "Sealed paper orders. Captain's eyes only, opened after novaing out. Admiral Kim already knows the mission, so unless *she* is compromised, you send out her carrier group individually and use sealed orders to have them converge at a particular nova point with no further details.

"From there, Admiral Kim gives the direction to proceed to the Kiln System and the target. Shang's orders are to accompany *Conviction*, and I bring us to the same rendezvous and place ourselves at her disposal."

The mercenary captain smiled grimly.

"I know this dance, officers, Your Majesties. I suspect I know our enemy, but that's a problem for another day. For now, sealed orders and a handful of people in the know will get our forces where they need to be."

Seven warships. Even by Apollo standards, that was starting to sound like a real task group to Kira. They might all be tiny, obsolescent or *both* by her standard, but it was still a real force.

Deceiver was going to *regret* coming after *Conviction*.

38

THE REDWARD PARTY left the apartment shortly afterward, leaving Kira and Estanza alone with their thoughts.

The two mercenaries sat in silence, watching Wardstone set over the system's capital city. As the sunlight faded, the apartment automatically sensed that there was someone inside and brought on lighting around them.

"I didn't know Redward had nova fighters," she finally said, as much to fill the silence as anything else.

"There are twenty-four nova fighters in the Cluster that aren't aboard *Conviction*," Estanza told her. "Redward has six. The Ypres factions have five between them. Bengalissimo has four. Serengeti has three. There's four in 'private ownership' scattered around, and the Hassani System has the last two."

She snorted.

"And how public-knowledge is all of that?" she asked.

"The twenty-four-nova-fighter number seems to be surprisingly public," the mercenary captain admitted. "The breakdown, specifically? I suspect most of the major systems have an idea of at least *who* has nova fighters, if not how many."

Kira nodded. A thought brought up what was publicly available on the Cavalier-II. It had been built as a medium fighter, theoretically more heavily armed but less maneuverable than her interceptors. Both ships could carry a single conversion torpedo, but the age of the design meant that the Hoplite-IV's technically lighter guns were just as powerful.

And even with a torpedo attached, her interceptors could fly rings around the Crest fighter. Still…a nova fighter was a nova fighter, to a large degree.

"I'm guessing you figure the bugs were Equilibrium?" she asked after another few minutes of silence.

"Who else would be putting Meridian-level tech in an apartment in an Outer Rim system?" he asked. "I know you don't entirely believe me, Kira, but who else would put those resources into bugs on Jay Moranis's contingency hideout?"

"I'd say Brisingr, but I don't think they have the resources for that kind of gear," she admitted. "I don't *dis*believe you, either, boss. It's just a lot to swallow, to believe there's this shadowy organization in the background trying to influence astropolitics on that level."

"Honestly? I thought they were bullshitting me on the scale for the first few years that *I worked for them*," Estanza admitted. "The scope, the sheer audacity of their intent…it didn't seem like it could be real. How do you organize something like that across *three thousand light-years* of known space?"

He shrugged.

"I'm still not sure, to be honest," he said. "What I encountered was a cell structure with access to seemingly infinite accounts and large, but not infinite, quantities of Meridian and Heart tech. Communication was by couriers who spoke for vague 'higher-ups' but had access to even *more* infinite amounts of money—couriers nobody questioned."

"Sounds like a classic bad movie conspiracy," Kira countered.

"It's classic because it works. I only ever knew the name of one person outside of Cobra Squadron with the Institute, but I saw their handiwork again and again. I had no reason to disbelieve their existence, shadowy as they felt even to people on the inside."

"It just all seems mad, that's all," she admitted. "Molycirc bugs in my apartment? It's just…"

"I'm not convinced that whoever set the Institute in motion *isn't* insane," Estanza told her. "I'm not even a hundred percent convinced every day that *I'm* not insane. I'm almost grateful that Queen Sonia's people found those bugs.

"It helps me be sure this *isn't* some paranoid delusion."

"Or in your delusions, you planted them while you were checking the bedrooms," Kira said slyly.

She almost instantly regretted it as Estanza clenched his hands together and stared at them.

"Sir, they said the bugs had been there for months," she pointed out gently. "They were installed when Jay bought the apartment, not today."

"Right, right," he agreed, unclenching his fists. "It's weird, let me tell you, to remember having worked for a massive organization that the rest of the galaxy doesn't know exists. I don't know if they're here, Kira.

"But those bugs suggest it. The resources being funneled into this Warlord Deceiver suggest it. It would be their usual mode, too. In their mind, augmenting the Costar Clans will create a situation where Redward must either become more aggressively expansionist or will be replaced by someone who *will*."

"Aggressive expansion doesn't seem to be Redward's style," Kira acknowledged.

"I once told you I didn't work for King Larry because I saw him as the best hope for the Cluster," Estanza reminded her. "I work for him because he's about the only person in the Cluster who can afford me. That he's *also* what I see as the best hope for the Cluster is a very nice bonus."

"But the Institute says his model will fail?" she asked.

"Exactly. So, they'll undermine him and create a self-fulfilling prophecy. Either Redward will change or Redward will fall. That is what the Equilibrium Institute demands. Today, the agent of that change is this Warlord Deceiver."

"If that's the case, how heavily *are* they likely to have equipped him?" Kira asked. "I mean, from what you've said, they could have equipped him with Meridian-level tech."

"They'll be working through proxies this far out," Estanza said with a shake of his head. "I suspect we'll see Crest Sector or Brisingr-

Apollo Sector tech at worst. More likely, we'll see the standard 'high tech' for the Cluster."

"He's probably kept anything more advanced than the Clans would normally have at his base, too," she noted. "Both for secrecy and for the security of the base. If we run into anything powerful, it'll be there."

"I'm guessing they've mostly given him industrial tech," her Captain told her. "Mining-droid and refinery schematics for the fabricators they already have. A better supply of raw materials into the systems he already has would be enough to dramatically expand his ability to replace ships."

"I'm worried about worst cases here," she said. "What are we thinking? A Brisingr carrier group equivalent?"

Estanza had been taking a sip of water and sprayed half of it across the table. Shaking his head, he grabbed a cloth and mopped it up while he thought about it.

"I don't think *anyone* who was backing him—whether it's the Institute or an Ypres faction or Brisingr—would give Deceiver that much tech or support. My worst case would probably be a few Brisingr-Apollo-tech-level destroyers. Maybe... No."

"Boss?" she challenged.

"If it was Brisingr or someone more local than the Institute, they probably have their own people and defenders on hand," he pointed out. "If they're smart, they'd have an evac transport for those people and a small force of nova fighters to protect that transport.

"*If* those fighters existed, they wouldn't field them against us. Not if we show up with enough force that they run."

"But they might exist," Kira replied, running scenarios in her head. "So, we're looking at a worst case of, what, three destroyers and a dozen nova fighters backed by ten corvettes and thirty or so gunships?"

Estanza winced.

"That would be the equal or superior of half the system fleets in the Cluster," he pointed out. "So, yeah, I'd say that's a solid worst-case scenario."

"All right," she said cheerfully. "Once we get back aboard ship, I'll start running the fighter group through that scenario. Without the *Perseus* group for backup."

Estanza was silent for several long seconds as he stared at her.

"I gave you authority over the entire fighter group," he conceded. "I won't stop you. But I'm starting to realize why Brisingr's crews and pilots kept coming up short against their Apollon counterparts!"

39

"WHAT. THE FUCK. WAS THAT."

Kira couldn't keep herself from laughing aloud at Melissa Cartman's precisely emphasized question as the other woman stepped out of the simulator. The other pilots were slower in getting out of the pods, but the shocked expression on the Asian pilot's face was mirrored across the board.

"That was three Brisingr Kaiserreich D9C heavy destroyers, ten Kaiserreich CV5 corvettes, sixteen Kaiserreich Weltraumpanzer-Fünf nova fighters and thirty-five Costar Clan gunships," she reeled off. "For those of you who *aren't* veterans of the Brisingr-Apollo war, that's a Kaiserreich heavy cruiser group without the cruiser but with the cruiser's fighters.

"Plus a Costar Clan assault wing," she added thoughtfully.

"And we were expected to take that with fourteen fighters," "Gizmo" Hersch replied flatly. "We almost lost the damn carrier."

"But you didn't," Kira told him. "I'm actually impressed," she admitted. "I expected the first time I threw you at that list, I'd see a complete wipe. Instead, you successfully covered the bombers delivering their payloads and got *Conviction* out, smashing two destroyers on the way."

Of course, only three of the Memorials and *none* of the Darkwings had survived to rendezvous with *Conviction* after her nova.

"To your advantage as well, though I didn't point this out in advance, *my* fighter was being flown by an AS subroutine and I was running the OpFor," she continued. Controlling the over sixty individual ships of the Opposing Force in the sim had been a pain, but the simulator software was designed to make it as easy as possible.

She might still try to borrow Estanza or Zoric to run the opposing force next time. Sixty-four combatants was a little too much for one person.

"Is this something we're remotely likely to encounter, sir?" "Galavant" Banderas asked, her tone clearly that of a woman who'd hoped she'd escaped Kira's idea of training.

"I can't give you details at all," Kira replied. "But this is close to the worst-case scenario for a mission we have agreed to take on. *If* everything goes according to plan, we will not be facing that OpFor alone.

"I don't believe in things going to plan," she continued grimly. "So, we're going to plan and train for the absolute worst-case scenario. Now that I've massacred everybody in one mass scenario, we're going to split into groups.

"Most of you are getting a ten-minute break, then you're going back in the simulator to practice anti-nova-fighter and anti-capital-ship tactics by flights.

"Gizmo, Nightmare, you're going to join myself and Commander Zoric in a sealed conference room and we're going to wargame how fourteen nova fighters take down a fleet."

She smiled grimly.

"I'll admit I'm not certain it will be a particularly *productive* session."

IT WAS a weird feeling for Kira to have her headware actually cut off. Security mode was one thing—she'd had multiple extra layers of encryption running on her signal when they'd met with King Larry, for example—but in the secure conference room, she had *no* signal.

She was alone in her head without access to even *Conviction's* datanet. The only other time she would be cut off from a general datanet was when she was in her fighter, and then she was linked to the fighter's databases.

It wasn't a *new* feeling. She'd been in secure conference rooms before, after all. But it was not a comfortable feeling.

At least, unlike Zoric and the two pilots she'd brought with her, she'd known who everyone in the meeting was supposed to be. The other three were just starting to settle down when Estanza joined them.

"Good afternoon, everyone," he said cheerily. "I've activated the full seal on this room and I want you all to find and activate the classification functions on your headware.

"Everything discussed in this room stays in this room until we've left the Redward System. Am I clear?"

Kira had already activated those functions. They didn't *prevent* her from talking about whatever she'd marked as classified—her headware literally *could not* do that—but it could make sure that she never even thought about the topics without being reminded that they were classified.

Gizmo clearly took a moment to even find the system and looked vaguely surprised that it existed. Darkwing Squadron's new commander was still quite young and out of practice at all of this.

"I understand that Kira ran the flight group through a scenario from hell that resembles our worst everybody-fucked-us-and-all-our-fears-were-right case of the mission on the table," Estanza continued. "We're going to come back to that in a minute, but first the two of you need to know what's going on.

"In thirty-six hours, we and Commodore Shang Tzu's destroyers will be jumping out to the route six nova stop," he told them. "Once we're there, I will open a sealed physical envelope, which will provide us with rendezvous coordinates where we will meet the Redward Royal Fleet Carrier Group *Perseus*.

"Those coordinates will be within one nova of the Kiln System, where we intend to assault and capture the primary shipbuilding facilities belonging to Warlord Anthony 'Deceiver' Davies, the man behind the attack on *Conviction*."

Cartman whistled silently.

"And we believe he has Brisingr backing?" she asked.

"We *know* he has support from somebody who is providing him with industrial and mining technology to allow him to expand his fleet," Estanza told her. "Most likely, they have also provided ship-building tech if not outright ships.

"In some ways, we are better off if it's an out-of-cluster source like Brisingr," he continued. "They are more likely to have provided ship-building *tech* but less likely to have provided actual ships. If we're looking at, say, an Ypres faction, we might see some Ypres corvettes in play, but we won't see heavy ships or nova fighters."

"But we're expecting nova fighters," Zoric concluded aloud. "Someone coreward."

"We think any nova fighters will have the priority of protecting the partners' personnel," Kira said. "They may or may not actually engage us in the opening moves of the fight but are unlikely to press the battle once it's clearly lost.

"With the Redward carrier group and Commodore Shang's destroyers, we *should* outnumber and outgun any force that Davies has. We have to assume that everything he's holding at home base has been upgraded—at *least* to equivalency with the RRF."

Kira saw Estanza wince. It was the logical conclusion of his own theories. If it was the Equilibrium Institute—which she doubted he was willing to suggest to the other officers—tech to upgrade the Clans' ships would have been their biggest offering.

"Demirci is right," the Captain conceded. "That is why we're exercising the fighters against the worst-case scenario. Zoric, I want the crew to run through similar scenarios. If anyone has some suggestions on making *Conviction* herself a little less defenseless within thirty-six hours, I'd love to hear them."

He shook his head.

"Most of the time I've commanded *Conviction*, we've had reasons to want the carrier herself to appear as inoffensive as possible," he told them. "I won't go into it, but those reasons are no longer valid.

"I've spoken to Labelle about it, and to mount new plasma cannons, we're going to need either yard time or some serious long-term internal bracing work. The plan is the latter," he noted. It sounded like he'd hoped for a better outcome from his chat with the carrier's chief engineer. "But that means that it'll be weeks or months before we can put actual guns on the old girl.

"Alternative suggestions are welcome."

"Torpedoes," Gizmo told him with a shrug.

Everyone in the room, including Kira, adjusted slightly to stare at the Darkwing pilot, and he flushed and shrank into his chair a bit.

"A torpedo duplicates a capital ship plasma cannon with a shorter range," he reminded them all. "We've got almost three hundred in inventory and can fab them to order. Boss Waldroup has at least half a dozen fighter torpedo launchers in inventory at any given moment.

"We'd probably want to rig some kind of launcher that sends them more than a few thousand klicks into space for a longer-term system, but if you want a last-ditch surprise…the ship should be able to handle six torpedoes firing, especially if we tie them into the reinforced infrastructure around the flight bays."

"I've never heard of anyone mounting torpedoes on anything bigger than a gunship," Kira said slowly. "But that's because putting in real guns is unquestionably superior. But we *can't* mount real guns on *Conviction*, not right now."

From what she understood, they *never* could have mounted guns with as bad a recoil-to-power ratio as the Cluster could produce. With the carrier's age, they might not have been able to fire her original guns.

"Zoric, talk to Waldroup and Labelle," Estanza ordered. "You three, keep the pilots' noses to the grindstone. I suggest we don't throw them against the full worst-case scenario every time. We need them to think they can *win*."

"Not my first choreography," Kira replied. "They'll be ready, sir."

"Good. Remember, the details are under lockdown until we're out of the system," the Captain told them all. "Redward Intelligence thinks the military is full of holes and the system is full of spies—and everything *I've* seen suggests they're right. Carrier Group *Perseus* is leaving on a training cruise to the Exeteron System. Assuming everything goes right, they might even complete that cruise."

He shook his head.

"Given that I don't believe Exeteron even knows the cruise is coming, I don't think Their Majesties are expecting that."

40

"NOVA COMPLETE."

Kira still didn't spend much time on *Conviction*'s bridge, but she'd made an exception today. Still, she'd seen novas at a far more *personal* range than the carrier's viewscreens which made the nova itself a non-event.

There wasn't even much activity on the bridge. Zoric ran a nine-person bridge watch for most non-combat situations. There were consoles on the carrier's command deck that didn't look like they'd been used in years, too.

If Estanza got his guns, that would change. For now, Kira suspected that control of whatever defenses had been improvised rested in the Captain's seat.

A seat currently occupied by John Estanza, still an odd sight after weeks of him hiding in his office. Kira suspected it was even weirder for the bridge crew than for her. *They'd* had years to get used to the Captain never being on the bridge.

That oddity wasn't why he was the focus of everyone's attention. The reason for that rested on the left arm of his command chair, a plain manila envelope slightly larger than a side plate.

"Do we have Commodore Shang on the coms?" Estanza asked aloud.

"Reestablishing link now," one of Zoric's people confirmed. A moment later, the bearded destroyer commander appeared on the screen.

"So, got your envelope, Estanza?" the man asked brightly. "Are we going to make a grand show and tell of the cloak-and-dagger?"

"I do believe so, yes," the mercenary captain replied. "Is this new to you, old friend?"

"I'm not sure I've ever had someone issue a mercenary contract with sealed orders," Shang replied. "Redward put enough money on the barrel for me to be curious and was straight-up about high risk."

He shook his head.

"I'm here because I trust you, Estanza. Let's not fuck it up, hey?"

"Agreed," *Conviction*'s Captain replied, holding up the envelope. "Shall we, Commodore?"

Both men tore the envelopes open simultaneously. The paper inside Shang's clearly included more text than Estanza's—Kira could *see* that all that was on Estanza's was a set of coordinates, but Shang was still reading.

"These coordinates aren't anywhere *near* where *Perseus* is supposed to be," Shang observed. "But the orders say to escort *Conviction* to those coordinates and place myself under Admiral Kim's command. What's going on, Estanza? I can *see* that all you have are coordinates."

"I've been more thoroughly briefed, yes," Estanza confirmed coolly. "I recommended you for this mission. I wouldn't trust anyone else at my back, but there's still aspects of this we want to keep quiet for a little while longer.

"You're correct that we're rendezvousing with Carrier Group *Perseus*, escorts and all, which means Admiral Kim wasn't going to Exeteron. As for where we *are* going..." He shrugged. "Admiral Kim will brief us."

Shang glared for a moment, then laughed.

"High risk it is. All right, Estanza." He waved a finger at the carrier CO. "I'm apparently *still* trusting you. It's a good thing you've always been straight so far, I guess."

"So it seems," Estanza murmured.

NOW THAT MORE OF the mission had been announced, Kira updated the simulations to include Shang's destroyers. From the exhausted expressions of her pilots as they gathered in the mess, it hadn't been as optimal for them as she'd hoped.

She, on the other hand, was grinning from ear to ear.

"You all look like you're feeling damn sorry for yourselves," she told them. "Anyone want to make the counterargument?"

Silence was the answer. And a few glares from people who didn't control themselves fast enough.

"I don't think it's really breaching classification at this point to tell you that we're rendezvousing with someone else," she said. "So, we're not going up against the go-to-hell scenario without more backup.

"I can't tell you *what* backup yet, but I can tell you this: with two destroyers and fourteen nova fighters, you fought sixty-four enemy combatants to a standstill."

They hadn't *won* the scenario. But they'd earned a handy draw, extracting all three of the friendly capital ships intact and leaving the theoretical Costar force badly mauled. If it had been a real-life scenario, it would have been a tactical draw—if a strategic defeat.

"With the reinforcements we're meeting in a few novas, I'm starting to feel comfortable about this fight," she told them. "So, we're going to ease off on the training. Of course, once we leave this nova stop, we're not under the protective guns of the RRF, either," she warned them.

"We're back to a standard patrol regimen in five hours. You all get those five hours off, but the reserve flights are going to be expected to be in the simulators for at least half that shift.

"You Memorials were the best the ASDF had to offer," she reminded them. "Daniel Mbeki handpicked every pilot of the Dark-wings, which means he thought—and *I* think—you can be just as damn good as the Memorials.

"We're going to train far harder than we ever hope to fight," she continued, feeling a twinge of grief over Daniel—and guilt over using her people's grief as a goad. "We're going up against an enemy with unknown resources. I think what I've put in these sims is overkill, that the enemy won't field a force this strong.

"If I'm wrong, it falls to all of us to haul *Conviction* and everyone who shows up with us out of the fire. Because we're the best damn nova fighter group in this Cluster—and if you don't believe that, people, get back in those simulators until you do."

She grinned.

"Because if this mission goes the way I *expect* it to, *everyone else* in the Cluster is going to."

41

"NOVA COMPLETE. LAUNCHING FIGHTERS."

Kira blinked and *Conviction* was gone, her Hoplite-IV flung into the void.

"We've got lots of contacts on the scopes, Commander," Zoric's voice said in her headware. "We're on the edge of the mapped nova stop, too."

"Please tell me they're RRF," Kira replied as her fighter's scanners began to pick up the contact as well. There were a dozen small signatures hurtling toward *Conviction* already and, as Zoric had said, a lot of bigger signatures behind the sub-fighters.

"I don't think anyone else out here bothered to put sub-fighters on a carrier," *Conviction*'s XO pointed out. "Plus, Bogey Bravo? That's a cruiser. Only three other systems in the cluster have cruisers at all, and none of them should be here."

There was a pause and Kira followed the data as Zoric's people put it together.

One bulk freighter, fifty thousand cubic meters. Except the power levels were wrong for a freighter. Some kind of reactor modifications were definitely in play, and there were guns on her upper hull. That made her one of Redward's escort carriers, almost certainly *Perseus*.

One serious warship, the first Kira had seen in the Syntactic Cluster outside of the Redward System. She'd probably seen *this* warship in the Redward System, she realized. Apollo would have called the fifty-five kilocubic warship a light cruiser.

Out here, she was one of the most powerful warships around—and as Kira was comparing her to what she was used to, *Conviction*'s tactical department IDed her. *Last Denial* was *Perseus*'s companion cruiser, exactly the ship she'd expected to see.

Four Redward-built destroyers and six corvettes filled out the group. The six sub-fighters had been flying a loose patrol that had converted into a much *less* loose strike formation at the emergence of unknown contacts.

"We have made contact with *Perseus* and her escorts," Zoric told Kira after a few seconds of them both watching the sub-fighters lunge towards them. "Sub-fighters are falling back into regular escort formation momentarily.

"Estanza says maintain CSP for now as we tuck into formation. Six hours until anybody's going anywhere."

"Understood," Kira replied. She'd scheduled herself to fly the first CSP at the rendezvous point intentionally. The "body language" of how the two groups of ships interacted with each other was going to tell her a *lot* about how well or badly this mission was going to go.

So far, so good. The reaction time on the sub-fighter wing had been acceptable, and they were turning around within an equally acceptable time frame of the recall orders.

All fifteen ships were starting to move together as well. The carrier group would inevitably be better at flying in formation with each other, but the mercenary ships needed to be incorporated too.

Kira's patrol was scheduled to be short. She'd hover above the fleet as they rendezvoused, but if Admiral Kim wanted to call a big briefing, Kira would need to be there.

BY THE TIME her turn on patrol wrapped up, the combined fleet had assembled in something resembling a logical formation. *Conviction* and *Perseus* floated together at the heart of it, the two carriers drifting ten thousand kilometers apart. *Last Denial* was above them, with the five destroyers spread out below and the corvettes in front and behind to complete the rough globe formation.

With six sub-fighters filling the same role, she arguably didn't need to have two of her nova fighters out in space. She was still planning on keeping a flight in space at all times. Just in case.

Kira trusted Redward, but she was learning that a good mercenary didn't trust *anyone*. She could see where Estanza's fear of paranoia was coming from. If the Institute had Redward so well infiltrated they could make sure no strike force hit their minion by surprise without extraordinary efforts, what was to say they couldn't have infiltrated someone onto *Perseus* or *Last Denial* to turn their weapons on the mercenaries?

That lovely image carried her through her landing cycle. Cartman was waiting for her as she exited her fighter, her second-in-command looking harried.

"Fucking military," Cartman said bluntly. "Wait, wait, wait, *hurry up!*"

"What happened?" Kira asked.

"I don't think Admiral Kim considered that our CNG might be in the fighters flying patrol," the other woman told her. "You have exactly *three* minutes to shower and change before you need to be on a shuttle toward *Perseus*."

"Then why are we wasting time cursing her out?" Kira asked, already heading toward the ready room. "I've done that before!"

She couldn't shower and change in that time, but hell…she *could* fly the shuttle, and she had every confidence in her ability to shave a few minutes off the expected flight time.

42

"WAS THE RUSH REALLY NECESSARY, COMMANDER?" Estanza asked dryly as Kira left the shuttle cockpit to join him. "My clock says we are now two minutes *early* despite leaving three minutes late."

"I should have rushed less, I suppose," Kira acknowledged as she doffed her flight helmet and quickly adjusted her hair. "But we didn't want to be late. Not today."

"Agreed," he conceded. "This is their ground. Kim is a competent officer but not always the most adaptable one. *I* wouldn't have picked her for this mission—but sending anyone else would have deprived us of the Lancers."

Kira nodded. Six nova fighters was worth a lot. They were almost certainly worth having a decent Admiral instead of a great Admiral.

Assuming that Redward *had* a great Admiral.

"Come."

Estanza led the way out of the shuttle onto *Perseus*'s combined retrieval and launch bay. For most affairs, the ship had a smaller shuttle bay toward the rear of the ship. Today, there was a shuttle on the deck for every ship in the assembled task force.

Even carriers only had one place to stick fourteen shuttles!

Several shuttles were still cycling their way aboard, but *Conviction*'s craft had been transferred to an offloading area separate from the actual *landing* area. *Perseus*'s crew had even managed to line the shuttle ramp up with a dark blue unrolled carpet.

Control of the platform made that easier, but it was still an appreciated effort on their part. There was no formal escort on the carpet. A pair of troopers in dark blue armor saluted as Kira followed Estanza off, and a single officer waited for them past the soldiers.

"Captain Estanza, Commander Demirci," that individual, a tall black man with bright blue eyes, greeted them with a bow. "As you can imagine, we're having all kinds of fun organizing greeting parties for everyone.

"I am Captain Saif Abiodun, commanding officer of the carrier *Perseus*," he continued. "I know she's a pale imitation of what either of you are used to, but she's my baby."

"I've flown off worse," Estanza told him. "Redward did a good job when they refitted the class. She might not be as large as *Conviction*, but she has the advantage of being much, *much* younger."

Abiodun chuckled politely.

"I appreciate the concession, Captain, but I've seen *Conviction*'s scans," he pointed out. "She might be old and a tad battered, but your ship can still outmaneuver mine *and* process fighters faster.

"I'm glad to see her and your fighters." He turned his attention to Kira and bowed again. "Commander Demirci, your reputation precedes you from two services now. It would be remiss, I think, for any carrier commander within a hundred light-years of Apollo not to know your name."

"Last I checked, Captain, there was a million-crest bounty attached to that name," she pointed out. "I'd almost rather go unrecognized."

"I understand. No one on this ship will attempt to collect that bounty, I can assure you," Abiodun told her. "If you wish, I can have these two Marines escort you for your entire stay. It won't be that much of a burden," he assured them. "My understanding is that the briefing should only take a couple of hours at most."

"That would be reassuring to *me*, at least," Estanza cut in before Kira could reply. "Commander Demirci is critical to the operation of my ship and our plans for this mission. Losing her at this juncture, well."

He smiled. There was no humor in the expression at all.

"If something happened to Commander Demirci, I might have to burn down a few planets to make a point."

Perseus's Captain blinked. He didn't—quite—step backward from Kira's Captain as Estanza let the anger boil to the top for a moment.

"You will be perfectly safe aboard my ship," Abiodun assured them. "I have only recently been briefed on the full scope of our mission, and we will need every nova fighter pilot we can muster."

"We will," Estanza agreed. "But we are going to burn Warlord Deceiver's little base to ashes. I think everyone can agree that is going to be a vast improvement to the Kiln System's esthetics."

PERSEUS MIGHT HAVE BEEN BUILT as a freighter, but Kira wouldn't have guessed it from her interior. It was completely crisp and clean, lacking the wear that marred *Conviction*'s martial impression. Every edge was sharp, every panel clean. Uniforms and salutes abounded.

For the first time since leaving the ASDF, she really felt the lack of a proper uniform and insignia. Everyone aboard *Perseus* clearly knew who she was, but she was an outsider there in a way she'd never been aboard a warship before.

Even on the rare occasions she'd been aboard other nations' warships as an ASDF officer, she'd still been an allied military officer. That was a position, it seemed, that drew more respect than a "mere" allied mercenary.

Estanza clearly wasn't letting it bother him. He was probably used to it. Even when he'd been more than a regular mercenary, no one outside his organization had known he was a member of the Equilibrium Institute.

For Kira, it was new and unpleasant. But she followed his lead as he stalked through *Perseus*'s corridors like an allied head of state. Captain Abiodun led them to a large room with a circular table in the center of it. Twenty seats had been laid out in the room.

All of those seats had names appear above in Kira's headware. She and Estanza were at the far end of the table—directly to Admiral Kim's left hand. Just past them were Shang and his second captain, then the two senior commanders of *Perseus*'s fighters.

She followed the Captain to their seats, barely beating Shang, and watched as everyone else filed in.

The outsider feeling didn't really abate, even as she noted that Shang and his companion were probably getting it worse. *Conviction* might be a mercenary ship, but they'd been working with the RRF for a while. *Most* of Kim's officers seem to feel that the long-term retainer at least made them *reliable* allied mercenaries.

It was still a step down from allied military officers. On the other hand, it was probably better than an ASDF officer would get on the ships of the nations Kira had once visited as an ally. Betrayal didn't do much for people's opinions of your military, even if the officers hadn't been involved at all.

Vice Admiral Ylva Kim's arrival interrupted her thoughts, an unsubtle announcement chime drawing every eye in the room to the tall blonde admiral.

Kira instinctively rose with the actual Royal Fleet officers. It wasn't until she was on her feet and braced to attention that she realized the other three mercenaries weren't rising.

A couple of seconds of awkwardness followed, then both Shang and Estanza rose simultaneously. Something in their body language told her that they were rising to support *her*, not show respect to Admiral Kim.

That lack of respect was intentional. A power game that Estanza hadn't thought to brief her on.

"Sit down, everyone," Kim ordered as she took the seat at the head of the table. A hologram of the task force appeared in the middle of the circular table.

"First formalities," she continued. "Carrier Group *Perseus*'s officers know each other, but we have some guests." She gestured. "Most of you know Captain John Estanza of *Conviction* by reputation. He is accompanied by Commander Kira Demirci, his Commander Nova Group. We are also joined by Commodore Shang Tzu and Captain Somchai Wattana of Shang's Squadron.

"With their three ships and *Conviction*'s nova fighters augmenting our strength, Carrier Group Perseus has been subsumed by Redward Royal Fleet Task Force Thirty-One. I remain in command, but the use of the TF 31 designation allowed us to draw up instructions and operational plans without them being attached to the carrier group."

Kira hoped that the Royal Fleet had relied on more layers of deception than *that*. Otherwise, they were probably going to be attacking an empty base.

"Only a portion of you have been briefed on our mission here, but before I get to that, I want to make certain that our chain of command is explicitly laid out and accepted," Kim continued. "Commodore Shang and Captain Estanza report directly to me and will assume formation and maneuvers with the rest of the Task Force.

"All sub-fighter and nova fighter forces will report to Major Teige Sagairt," she continued. "Commander Demirci, your ships will be subordinate to Major Sagairt's command."

An officer with six nova fighters and thirty sub-light jokes. That was *not* Kira's understanding of how this was supposed to be organized. She was stunned enough that it took her a moment to gather her thoughts to respond to that.

A long-enough moment that someone *else* interjected.

"Sir, I have six nova fighters and less than ten years' experience flying and commanding them," a brilliantly copper-haired slim man at the far end of the table noted calmly. "I have only flown six nova fighter combat missions—because keeping our nova fighters secret has always been the priority.

"Commander Demirci is a twenty-year veteran pilot and commanded a nova fighter squadron involved in the active war between Apollo and Brisingr," Sagairt continued. "I don't know her numbers for combat missions or kills, but I would not be surprised to discover that she had over *ten times* my experience in nova fighter combat to go with her double my experience in general nova fighter operations.

"Speaking for myself alone, I cannot reasonably or logically expect Commander Demirci to operate under my command. I strongly recommend that we place Commander Demirci in charge of the nova fighter component of the task force."

That was a conversation that should have taken place in private, but Kira suspected that Admiral Kim hadn't even considered the possibility that *her* officer was not only far less experienced than Kira but willing to *admit* that lack of experience.

There was a long silence.

"Far be it from me to argue with a man willing to surrender authority," Admiral Kim said coldly. "Very well, Major. Lancer Squadron will be placed under Commander Demirci's authority."

Sagairt, Kira was grimly certain, was going to suffer for that suggestion. She'd have to make *very* sure that it was worth it.

"The rest of the chain of command will operate as normal," the Admiral noted. "Which brings us to why you are all here."

The image of the task force floating in deep space vanished, replaced by an image Kira recognized from repeated discussions since the meeting with King Larry.

"This is an asteroid cluster in the Kiln System," Kim told them all. "While its residents presumably give it a name, the only identifier we have in our records is a catalog code from when New Ontario attempted to exploit this part of Kiln forty-eighty years ago: Cluster Sixty-Five-X-Nine.

"The failed New Ontarian base became home to one of the more aggressive Costar Clans some time ago. Like the rest of their kin, they weren't a major threat. Recently, however, the settlement in Sixty-Five-X-Nine has become the home base for an alliance of Clans under an individual known as Warlord Deceiver.

"Deceiver has been responsible for multiple attacks on our shipping and military vessels over the last six months, and we have decided it is time to make an example."

More data began to fill in around the asteroid cluster, marking additional stations: shipyards and fabrication facilities.

"Our target here is to destroy Warlord Deceiver's defenders to neutralize his fleet; and to either destroy or capture all shipyards and military fabrication facilities.

"We are at all costs to avoid damage to civilian habitat stations," she noted, "and our official priority is capture over destruction of fabrication bases. Their Majesties wish to take control of this facility and use it as a wedge into rehabilitating at least a portion of the Costar Clans."

And if Estanza was correct, the Institute might have even given

Deceiver more advanced tech than Redward possessed. Seizing the facility made sense, but Kim's tone wasn't promising.

"It is not my place or our place to defy Their Majesties' orders or intentions," Kim said. "It is our place to make tactical decisions in the moment. I am not prepared to risk our brave Marines attempting to storm active Clan facilities. If the locals surrender, we will secure surrendered bases, but our priority is to neutralize the threat."

Kira smothered a grimace. The Admiral might not even be *wrong*, but it still felt vaguely wrong to plan to ignore the orders from their superiors.

It wasn't her problem, anyway. The nova fighters would be tasked with dealing with hostile spacecraft, not shipyards and fabricators. As the briefing moved forward toward *that* part of the affairs, she started to assess what they knew of the asteroid cluster the fight would take place around.

At the end of the day, she was being paid to follow Admiral Kim's orders. Outside of that, the only thing she was going to insist on was scattering "Warlord" Davies' flaming pieces across a few thousand kilometers.

43

"NOVA COMPLETE. LAUNCHING FIGHTERS."

They'd practiced it exactly once since Kira had come aboard, but a full-deck launch was entirely automated. With fourteen fighters clearing the launch bay in seconds, it *needed* to be.

The most she'd seen launched in a single wave was forty-five fighters. Today was a third of that, and *Conviction*'s launch bay was just as large as the one aboard *Perseus*.

The launch went off without a hitch and her Hoplite-IV was back in space where it belonged. The sluggish feel of her Harringtons as she maneuvered away from the carrier was both new and old. She'd made sure she spent simulator time on anti–capital ship missions, but this was the first time she'd been in real space with a real torpedo in over a year.

Her fourteen nova fighters carried twenty-two torpedoes. The Lancers carried another six, and the Redward nova fighters slotted into her command network and formation as she watched.

Half of the sub-fighters also had torpedoes, but they were hanging back as a defensive perimeter around the carriers. The first pass would go to her people.

"Task Force is formed up, escorts advancing," Estanza said in her headware. "First pass is yours, Commander. Time to show the locals what twenty nova fighters can do."

There was enough activity at the target for Kira to be grimly certain they'd got there ahead of any evacuation order. It wasn't resolving into easily identified targets—they were still almost ten million kilometers away—but there were definitely ships over there.

In a few seconds, the defenders would see the light from TF 31's arrival and the activity would become chaos and then vanish behind multiphasic jammers. The first step was data.

"Nova group, form on my wing," she ordered. The order was mostly unnecessary, but she noted a couple of the Lancers twitching their alignment slightly.

"First pass is scouting," she continued. "Don't waste your torps until we're sure of what we're looking at, but don't hesitate to put plasma on anything that's armed. Any questions?"

She gave them about two seconds—more than enough time for people with headware linked into nova fighter computers.

"All nova fighters," she addressed them crisply. "*Nova.*"

The world *curved* around her as her nova drive pulsed. Ten million kilometers vanished in the blink of an eye, and an automatic countdown started in the back of her brain.

A thirty-four-light-second nova would take her drive three seconds to cycle. It wasn't much, but in a combat environment, it could be life or death.

"Jammers are silent," Sagairt barked on the general channel. They'd have had coms either way. They'd come through the nova in neat-enough formation to maintain laser links.

The moment the jammers came up and they *broke* that formation, they were on their own. Right now, twenty fighters formed a distinct line in space as they swept through Warlord Deceiver's home base.

It was bigger than the data they'd seen. Not just new shipyards but new hab structures, too. The cluster had to have at least three times the space—if not necessarily three times the *people*—as the latest Redward intelligence suggested.

The yards had expanded too. They'd expected ten yards capable of building gunships and one capable of building corvettes. Those were all *there*, but three corvette-sized yards had been added—and so had two clearly capable of building *destroyers*.

Because they *were* building destroyers.

"Those ships are *not* live," Kira barked. "Ignore the slips; find me the warships"

Gunships were bringing their Harringtons online, probably reacting as much to the light arriving from TF 31's appearance as the unexpected arrival of nova fighters in their midst. Several of them sent plasma skittering across Kira's formation, earning themselves massed return fire from half a dozen of Kira's craft.

A gunship died. Then another—but that was incidental.

"We have the data. Nova group—*nova!*"

THE CLOSE-RANGE DATA was critical to planning the next phase of the mission. By the time Kira and her fighters had regrouped around the task force, multiphasic jamming had consumed the area around the Deceiver's base.

But the nova fighters' close-range pass meant they had data from before the jammers had come up, and they knew what they were facing.

"That's a *lot* of gunships," Sagairt observed as the data flickered between the ships and the fighters. "I'm reading at least forty, plus *six* corvettes."

"We can take that," Kira told him. "I was expecting worse."

The power signatures suggested the corvettes were more advanced than the Clans had been fielding before, but they didn't make it up to even Redward standards.

"All right, people," she continued, widening the channel. "I don't know about the rest of you, but I hate flying around with a torpedo strapped to my hull. And my data shows this set of six nasty little ships I don't want within a million klicks of my carrier.

"We're going in and we're going in hard and hot this time," she told them. "Multiphasics online with the nova. Target is the corvettes, but I'm not going to cry too loudly if you put a torpedo into anything with guns, clear?"

"Yes, sir!"

A chorused reply, but it was what she needed to hear.

"All right, people. Range is dropping; this is only a twenty-light-second nova. Do not—I repeat, *do not*—spend more than ten seconds in the battlespace. We can stick around once the task force catches up. Darkwings, keep a torpedo for later, just in case.

"For now, burn those corvettes and haul for home. Clear?"

She didn't wait for a response, spending her time checking that her own multiphasic jammers and nova drive were online.

"All right. Lancers, Memorials, Darkwings." She grinned as she reeled off the squadrons under *her* command. She was in command of a nova combat group. Understrength and divided, with one of "her" squadrons flying obsolete trash, but *hers*.

Hopefully, she could live up to Jay Moranis's long-standing claim that she could do his job just as well as he could.

"Nova and attack."

COMS DIDN'T SURVIVE the transit. They might have had the formation for laser coms for a few milliseconds after emergence, but it wouldn't have been worth the effort. Kira was off her emergence vector in under a quarter-second, her own multiphasic jammers adding to the chaotic mess that any scanner would see.

Only close-range visual detection was meaningful in a modern battlespace, but her computers could at least help with that. After twenty years of practice, she knew where her prey *should* be and dove toward where the largest group of corvettes had been.

It took a critical two seconds to find them, two seconds that the corvettes and their gunship escorts spent filling space with plasma.

She deked around their fire with contemptuous ease, and she wasn't the only one. Her fighters were weaving in and out of her awareness as she closed with her prey. There was no way to distinguish which corvettes any of her people were aiming at, but she wasn't even the first to fire.

A corvette on her screen died in a blaze of fire as two of the Darkwings focused their torpedoes on the ship. Counter-fire came near the fighter-bombers, but the gunners were slow.

The gunners were just plain *bad*, she realized. They had no idea how to handle a properly managed nova fighter strike. They had *known* she was coming, but too many of their weapons were clearly expecting less-maneuverable enemies.

Kira ducked "under" a salvo of fire from the corvette's heavy main gun and clicked the mental trigger. Her torpedo snapped free of her hull as she vectored up and away, watching the weapon close with a quarter of her brain.

The torpedo only existed for about a tenth of a second after she released it, anyway. Then it vanished into a cone of thermonuclear flame as the shaped warhead detonated. The plasma blast hit her target like a hammerblow and punched through its hull.

She didn't wait to see the final result. Even as the torpedo's plasma blast was burning into her target, she was bringing her nova drive online.

Kira had been in the battlespace for ten point two seconds. The last thing she needed was to set a bad example!

44

"MEMORIALS, check in. Darkwing Lead, Lancer Lead, check in with your pilots and advise," Kira barked as they returned to formation with the rest of the task force. "Cross-reference visual data and confirm kills.

"We have the time."

"Nightmare here. No damage, fuel at seventy percent, ammo at eighty," Cartman reported immediately. "Torpedo expended. Recharging guns."

"Longknife here. Same as Nightmare."

"Dawnlord. No damage, fuel at seventy-five, ammo at sixty," Patel continued. "Torpedo expended, recharging guns."

"Socrates. Ditto as Nightmare but ammo at thirty-five," Colombera reported.

"Geez, Socrates, did you turn your guns *off?*" Michel asked. "Fuel and ammo both at seventy, torpedo expended."

Michel's question was probably a good guess as to what Socrates had done, Kira reflected. Emptying sixty-five percent of his magazines would have taken six point five seconds of sustained fire—in a battle-space pass that lasted less than ten seconds.

"This is Gizmo," Hersch said on the command channel. "No damage across the squadron. Fuel averaging sixty-five percent, ammunition at seventy. We'll recharge ammo before the nova, and everybody's got a torpedo left."

"This is Helmet," Sagairt's voice added. "No damage to Lancer Squadron. Fuel averaging seventy percent, ammunition averaging eighty percent with torps expended." He paused. "I haven't flown a nova strike like that before, but did it seem weirdly easy to anyone else?"

"I expected better from veteran pirate gunships, but you might have put your finger on it," Kira said slowly. "If *you*, who commanded the only complete nova fighter squadron in the Cluster outside of *Conviction*, haven't flown a proper high-speed nova strike before…who in the Cluster would have seen the other side of one?"

The range between the main task force contingent—whose rapid advance was far from as slow as it felt—and the enemy base was shrinking by the minute. Over half of the distance was gone.

"Demirci, this is Admiral Kim," the Redward flag officer's voice cut in, overriding Kira's main channels. "Camera footage suggests you've taken down the corvettes, but there's still over thirty gunships out there, and analysis suggests fixed defenses on several of the new stations.

"I need you to get back in there and kick those pirate scum in the ass again. Move, Commander."

Kira ran timelines in her head as she studied the fuel numbers for her combat group.

"Sir, if we go in again without refueling, we'll be entering the final crunch at minimum combat reserves for fuel," she warned. "And no torpedoes except the ones Darkwing saved."

"The destroyers will clean up at that point, Commander. Can you do it or not?"

"We can do it, sir," she confirmed with a mental sigh. Flag officers, it seemed, were the same the galaxy over. "Just warning you that we'll be short on fuel and bombs if we do it."

"Cut those gunships down to size, Demirci. That's an order."

The channel cut and Kira swallowed a curse.

"All right, people, good news," she told her pilots with forced cheer. "Any of you who haven't made ace yet get a second chance.

We're going back in ahead of the escorts. We'll hold until we have full ammo charges, but then we nova in and hit the gunships.

"Flag wants the numbers brought down to a more reasonable level, and I can't say I disagree with her."

She wasn't sure another unsupported nova fighter strike was the *right* answer, but she couldn't argue with Kim's wanting to face a more reduced gunship flotilla.

"I make it three minutes to full charge on everyone's guns," she concluded. "That's about enough time to take off your helmet and grab two sips of coffee, in my experience.

"Do whatever floats your boat, people. Because in three minutes, we go kill some more pirates."

"NOVA AND ATTACK."

The thrill of giving the order to an expanded command had already worn thin, Kira realized as she punched the controls and flung her Hoplite back into the battlespace. The task force she was leaving behind would be bringing up multiphasic jammers in the next minute or so. There wasn't going to be much in terms of clear space or communications until the battle was over now.

The gunships were showing *slightly* better coordination this time. They'd assembled themselves into something resembling an anti-fighter formation, but they still looked like they were following a play-book they'd never practiced.

Kira yanked her fighter into a line on one of the gunships and emptied half a second of sustained fire at the ship before dodging around again. Her own maneuvers were almost unconscious, and she barely registered that the gunship had evaded most of her fire as she studied the battlespace.

The gunships weren't veteran crews. It didn't make any sense to her, but it was obvious. Their gunners were slow and their pilots were worse. These weren't the elite crews she'd expected to be guarding Davies's home base. These were the kind of third-line raw recruits she'd expect to see at a minor refueling base.

Two of those raw crews tried to catch her in a crossfire, holding her attention for a handful of seconds as she dodged around streams of plasma and then dumped two seconds of sustained fire into one of the gunships. The hundred-meter-long warship disintegrated and Kira was out of time.

Nova flashed around her, twisting her stomach as she tried to hold on to her thoughts. The attack had flashed by in the designated ten seconds, and every one of her people had broken clear again.

It hadn't been a *complete* clean pass this time, she reflected as her people aligned on her and the reports trickled in. Several of the Lancers and Darkwings had taken solid hits and were down weapons and scanners…but everyone was still combat-ready.

They were also less than a hundred thousand kilometers behind the heavy strike force and following the capital ships in. The destroyers, at least, were large enough to sustain solid communications through the fight.

Most of the sublight fighters were hanging back with *Conviction* and *Perseus*, and a chill ran over Kira as she watched the main duel begin. There *were* guns on the asteroids, heavy installations with heavy guns that were probably more powerful than the destroyers'. The sub-fighters would be enough to handle them, she concluded—and watched as the pilots agreed with her and swarmed forward.

Something in the entire situation felt off. If this was the Warlord's main base, it was missing the elite crews she'd expect from Davies's protectors. Was he off somewhere else with his best? The sheer size of the yards suggested that this was exactly the main base Redward Intelligence had thought it was.

"Sir, does this seem odd to you?" Gizmo asked. "It seems like they're missing their best pilots and gunners."

Pilots.

Pilots.

Why did that sound important to Kira's brain?

…because *gunship* pilots were the only people a Costar Clan warlord would have been able to put behind the stick of a nova fighter.

"All fighters, form for nova," she barked. "Set your course for *Conviction* and *Perseus*."

"Sir?"

"Just do it," Kira snapped. "Nova. *Now.*"

Because if Davies' best pilots weren't aboard his best gunships, it was because he'd found a better use for them. And *that* meant that the Costar Warlord had nova fighters—and if he'd let Kira rip his corvettes and gunships to pieces, he'd done it with a plan.

The exact same plan he'd tried to use to destroy *Conviction* once before.

45

EVEN IF SHE'D guessed wrong, the main strike force had a dozen sub-fighters, six destroyers and half a dozen corvettes. They could handle the fixed defenses and less than twenty gunships Kira's strikes had left behind.

At the point the heavy ships hit the battlespace, the nova fighters' role was mostly done. Fourteen more fighters would *help*, but they'd already hammered the defenders as much as they were going to.

She hadn't guessed wrong.

The nova fighters had probably been inside the base's fighter hangars when she made her first pass, and then they'd novaed out under cover of the multiphasic jamming, waiting for the moment when the attackers' escorts brought up their own jamming.

At that moment, no one in the battlespace could see what was happening at *Perseus* and *Conviction*. Only a hunch could bring anyone back to the carriers before it was too late—but Kira had had that hunch.

Her fighter squadrons emerged directly behind thirty-two Weltraumpanzer-Fünf heavy fighters. The sub-fighters they'd left behind to protect the carriers were sortieing to meet them, but they were both outnumbered and individually outclassed.

The Brisingr-designed nova fighters had their jammers online at maximum power. No one aboard the carriers or sub-fighters could call for help. They outnumbered the defending fighters almost three to one. Neither carrier was heavily armed.

They *knew* they'd won—which gave Kira a precious handful of seconds to act.

"Nova fighters—*break and attack!*"

The Weltraumpanzers had no business being out there. They were superior fighters to anything in Kira's flotilla, too. Only her Hoplites could outmaneuver them—but the heavy fighters had the guns to tear *Perseus* or *Conviction* apart even without their torpedoes.

The laser-com links broke before Kira received even a single response from her pilots, every one of her people acting before she'd even finished speaking. Twenty nova fighters dove at thirty-two, and Kira *knew* what the response would be.

Every nova fighter had the response drilled into them from the first day of basic training: if you're spooked, *be somewhere else*. A fifty-thou-sand-kilometer nova didn't even take you out of the battlespace, but it sure as hell screwed up someone's attack run.

She was expecting the emergency escape nova so thoroughly, she almost didn't fire when her sights settled on her target. The Weltraumpanzer was paying *some* attention: he was evading, he was flipping in space to bring his own guns to bear on her...but all of her maneuvers were sublight and her interceptor's plasma guns shredded the heavy fighter across several hundred kilometers of space.

That was the end of her few seconds of shock before sparkling stars around her warned her that plasma fire was coming her way. She decided to be somewhere else.

A ten-thousand-kilometer nova put her in the middle of the sub-fighters, a stunt that only earned two near-misses instead of the four or five she was expecting before the Redwards realized who she was.

She flipped in space and spent a second and a half surveying the dogfight.

Only three of her fighters were still in the scrum, and they short-novaed out as she watched. Thirty-plus of Brisingr's most advanced nova fighters had been reduced to fourteen in a single six-second engagement.

Plasma fire from *Perseus*'s heavier guns reached into the midst of the nova fighter formation as Kira watched, and the idiots finally, *finally*, novaed away from the killing zone they'd found themselves in.

That was what she'd been waiting for. Years of practice meant that she and her computer could take the minimal data she could pick up through the multiphasic jamming and guess a distance and destination.

She was only right three times out of four or so—but a computer on its own was only right one time in three.

And the fact that the course she estimated put them right on top of *Conviction* was all the confirmation she needed. A half-second of calculation and *she* novaed after them.

She emerged into an already-disintegrating fighter strike. The pilots weren't bad—she'd bet her own fighter that they were the original pilots of the gunships her people had shredded at the main base—but they didn't know nova combat.

Conviction had been waiting for them, and Gizmo's idea had worked like a charm. Six torpedoes had been mounted on the hull, and when the nova fighter strike had begun, Estanza had pulled the trigger.

He'd only actually *hit* four nova fighters, but it was enough to disrupt their formation and leave the attack a mess as almost half of the remaining Weltraumpanzers novaed out.

They were learning—but they'd left six of their friends behind, and Kira wasn't the only pilot in her combat group capable of following a short nova.

There was no way to give orders in an environment that blocked sensors and coms alike, but that was why they trained. She *knew* her Memorials were on her wing—and a moment's attention confirmed she had two Darkwings and a Lancer, too—as she went after the nova fighters that were trying to press their attack.

One survived to launch a torpedo. Kira stared at it for an eternal quarter-second...and then her computer finished its calculations.

It missed, a gout of flame that would give *Conviction* problems with its sensors for days but didn't even touch the hull.

She flipped her fighter again and surveyed the battlespace. It was clear. There were still four Weltraumpanzers out there, but she could leave those to the intact sub-fighter formation.

Hopefully, the rest of her pilots saw the same thing. The carriers couldn't lower their jamming, not yet, but she had an agreed rendezvous with her people for just this situation.

Home base was safe. Now it was time to see how the *mission* was progressing.

IT TOOK a good fifteen seconds for everyone to nova into the rendezvous point after Kira arrived, by which point she and the squadron commanders were on a rapidly flowing information hookup.

"Those fighters shouldn't be out here," Cartman, acting as commander for the Memorials, said first. "Those are—well, were—Brisingr heavy fighters. *Good* ones."

"I haven't flown against Kaiserreich pilots, but I'm guessing they're better than that," Hersch replied. "They knew what they were doing, but it felt like they'd never flown a nova fighter before."

"Gunship crews," Kira told them. "The gunships we fought were missing pilots and gunners. We just ran into them here. They hadn't seen a real nova fighter scrum yet and you could tell, but they were learning *fast*. Those last four birds have me worried."

"I didn't put together that link," Sagairt said slowly. "Damn. You just saved *Perseus*, Commander. We owe you."

"I saved *Conviction*. Your ride home just happened to be in the same area," Kira replied. "Status report on your squadrons?"

The reports were instant—the entire conversation was taking place in seconds as thoughts were sent between ships with no need to actually *vocalize* anything.

"We lost *nobody*?" Kira demanded. A number of the fighters had taken damage. Migraine's Darkwing was a wreck that she wasn't sure should have novaed to the rendezvous point, and two of the Lancers weren't in much better shape…but everyone was still there.

"Two of the sub-fighters didn't make it," Sagairt said grimly. "But we're all still here. Is it…over?"

"Jamming field is still up over the main battlespace," Kira replied. "Computers are trying to resolve visuals, but I'm not getting shit."

A new set of data came out of her fighter's attempt to resolve anything through multiphasic jamming thirty light-seconds away.

"But either that's corrupt data or we have a real problem," she said grimly. "Because I'm reading *nine* destroyers and we only sent in six."

The command channel went silent.

"We go in?" Cartman finally asked.

"We go in," Kira responded. "You have fifteen seconds, people. Assess which of your fighters can't be risked and send them back to the carrier—Gizmo, that's *definitely* Migraine, but I need as many of the Darkwings as we can manage."

"Sir?"

"The Hoplites and Cavaliers only carried one torpedo apiece, Gizmo," she reminded him. "Your One-Fifteens have the only torpedoes left, and we're about to go destroyer-hunting."

"Memorial and Lancer squadron are covering fire," she continued, aware that her subordinates would be making the call she'd ordered as she spoke. "Darkwing has the torps, Darkwing is the killer blow."

Silence hung for several seconds and she watched as four of her fighters disappeared, Migraine leading half of the Lancers back to the barn.

"My people are getting the shit kicked out of them," Sagairt said bluntly. "But if I'd been in command, we'd have lost the carriers. I'm with you till the end of the line, Demirci. Your orders?"

"Lancers and Memorials, form on the Darkwings," Kira told everyone. "Form your laser links. We'll lose formation quickly enough, but remember: there are hostile capital ships in the zone. We cover the bombers, all the way in."

She took a deep breath, settling into her fighter and the network with her comrades.

"All fighters, you have your orders. Nova and attack!"

46

THE VERY NATURE of multiphasic jamming meant that any long-range scans of a zone under active jamming were vague at best and dangerously useless at worst. There had been a chance that Kira's computers had drastically misinterpreted the badly distorted heat and visual signatures that were the only *useful* data out of a battlespace.

She'd hoped that her computers had made up contacts. *That* had been too much to hope for, but at least the errors had still been in her favor. Mostly.

There were ten contacts still in play in the ugly melee her people novaed into the middle of. *Last Denial* was clear on short-range visual scans, which also allowed her to break down the nine "destroyers" she'd seen as *seven* destroyers—and two large corvettes.

The *problem* was that only five of the destroyer contacts were friendly and *none* of the corvettes were. One of the RRF destroyers was just…gone. One of Shang's ships was a reeling cripple, with gouts of burning atmosphere occasionally flashing out of breaches before being smothered by vacuum. All six of the RRF corvettes were wreckage and debris scattered across the battlespace.

The four active ships were covering the crippled mercenary destroyer and falling back toward *Last Denial*, but they were badly outmatched. Everything Kira had left behind was gone, gunships and fixed defenses alike obliterated by the destroyers and corvettes before the new ships had arrived.

The enemy ships were something out of Kira's worst nightmares. She'd fed a Brisingr battle group into her people's simulations because she *had* the data necessary to use Brisingr heavy destroyers in the sims.

She hadn't actually expected to face a pair of D9C heavy destroyers. She didn't know the corvettes—they were neither Costar nor Brisingr designs—but they were definitely up to par with the two Kaiserreich destroyers.

Forty thousand cubic meters of more advanced technology, a D9C heavy destroyer was more than a match for *Last Denial* herself. The regular destroyers were outgunned and outclassed.

And dying. A massive gout of flame burst from the RRF destroyer closest to the closing Brisingr ships as Kira spent a precious fraction of a second tracking the fight. The deadly precision of the closing destroyers' fire told her the worst part of it all.

Either Davies's absolute best were on those destroyers and were even better than she thought...or those two ships *did* have Kaiserreich crews.

"Gizmo," she said softly over the laser link. "All One-Fifteens on the trailer. Leave the lead for *Last Denial*. Go."

The Redward cruiser was badly outmatched in firepower per cubic meter, but she was almost half again the D9C's size. She'd been hanging back to provide long-range fire support before but was now lunging forward to cover her smaller sisters.

She couldn't take *both* of the Brisingr destroyers between her and the nova fighters—and Kira had no intention of making her try.

Seconds after her order to Gizmo, her entire formation broke up into a chaotic swarm.

A chaotic *attack* swarm—headed for the trailing Kaiserreich warship.

IN THE ABSENCE of gunships or fighters, the enemy ships had limited options to respond to the nova fighter attack run. Both of the corvettes moved to block her incoming fighters with admirable speed, and the targeted destroyer redirected a portion of her guns toward Kira's people

They could only spare so much of their firepower from pounding the Redward capital ships. Kira's allies might not have been giving as good as they were getting, but they were definitely still in the fight. *Last Denial*'s heavy guns were starting to have an effect too, and the lead destroyer's power signatures were fluctuating.

If they split their fire, they were doomed.

If they *didn't* split their fire, Kira was going to shove every torpedo her Darkwings had left up the closer destroyer's exhaust port.

There were no orders left to give. She'd trained her people on this and she had to hope that the Lancers had paid attention to the briefings they'd managed to throw together. The PNC-115s had to get through to their destroyer target without using their torpedoes, and that meant that the lighter fighters had to take down the corvettes.

With just guns.

Tally-ho!

Kira led the way, with eight other fighters in her wake as she charged the closest destroyer at maximum thrust. This crew *did* know what they were doing for anti-fighter tactics, and she dodged through a tight mesh of *perfectly* coordinated fire.

A Lancer fell, their old Cavalier coming apart under the corvettes' fire. A Memorial—Longknife, she was grimly certain—took a hit and went spinning off into the void.

Her own guns spoke again and again, white flashes of superheated plasma that burned away chunks of the corvette's armor and hull. The ship only *had* four real guns, and she focused on them.

So did the rest of the Memorials. The last of the presumably Clan warship's guns fell silent as she broke past Kira's formation. The corvette wasn't attacking now. With her guns disabled, she was *running*—and leaking atmosphere from her brutalized hull.

The second corvette wasn't as lucky. Three of Kira's pilots formed on the Commander in an unplanned wedge formation. They couldn't sustain it for long, not with the corvette and the destroyer flinging plasma their way, but they held it for long enough to focus the guns of four Hoplite interceptors onto a single ten-meter-square section of the warship's hull for at least two full seconds.

They burned clean through the armor and triggered secondary explosions inside the corvette. For a second, Kira thought they'd disabled the ship—and then the fusion core overloaded, a ball of newborn starfire to add to the confusion of the multiphasic jamming.

If she'd ever doubted the degree to which Mbeki had trained and encouraged his people before, she would never doubt it again. Gizmo led his seven PNC-115s *into* the fireball of the corvette's death, covering them from the destroyer's visual scanners for a handful of critical seconds.

The seconds he needed to get his bombers into range. Five torpedoes flashed in the night, hammering battleship-grade plasma into the destroyer. Two missed, but three hammered directly into the destroyer.

Three direct hits *wasn't* survivable, but the destroyer didn't seem to agree with Kira on that! She was struggling, but she was maneuvering to try to escape the enemies she'd been pursuing a moment before.

But even as Kira was about to curse the Darkwings for not firing *all* of their torpedoes, two of the fighters emerged from the fireball on a *very* different vector.

And then novaed.

The fireball had given Gizmo *just* enough cover to realign two of the fighters—one of them almost certainly his own—on the *other* destroyer, and their nova brought them to within five hundred kilometers of their new target's hull before they launched their torpedoes.

There was no missing at that range, and the torpedoes were designed to be lethal at twenty-five *thousand* kilometers. The destroyer, already heavily battered by the duel she had been fighting with the Redward fleet, was *gutted*.

The surviving warship had somehow survived the body blow Gizmo's fighter-bombers had inflicted, but it was now *Last Denial*'s sole focus.

The destroyer's captain chose the better part of valor. As Kira's fighters swarmed toward the surviving enemy ship, it vanished in the bright blue flash of a full-power nova.

47

SILENCE FELL ACROSS THE VOID. For the first seconds, it was just the lack of gunfire. Then, ever so slowly as each combatant made the call for themselves, the multiphasic jammers started shutting down.

This had been the final place where pure combat AI had failed. The human controllers couldn't *tell* the AIs to shut down their multiphasic jammers…and a far-too-large proportion of them just hadn't. Unable to communicate with their armed creations, the controllers had been left with no choice but to destroy them.

Most people agreed AI combatants were a terrible idea now. There was always *someone* trying, Kira suspected, but most of those attempts would end very badly.

She had time for that introspection. It took over ninety seconds until the last multiphasic jammer—aboard Shang's crippled destroyer, which likely didn't have functioning sensors—finally shut down.

Even the defenders had shut down their jammers. It was hard to beg for mercy when no one could hear you.

"Commander Demirci, this is Captain McNee aboard *Last Denial*," a vaguely familiar female voice told her within moments of coms becoming possible. "You have no idea how grateful I am to see you. Or how terrified I am of your predictive abilities, given what I heard of your training scenarios.

"Sir, I threw in D9Cs because I had sim files for them," Kira admitted. "I wasn't actually expecting them." She exhaled a long sigh. "They had nova fighters, too. A full combat group of Weltraumpanzers jumped *Perseus* and *Conviction*.

"That's why we were late."

A long pause followed.

"My scans show they're both still intact and their jammers are up," McNee told her. "I don't have rearming bays for fighters, Commander. If I did, I might have been able to save our sub-fighters."

Kira grimaced. McNee, it sounded, would be spending some time talking to therapists about survivor's guilt. The lighter units of the main strike force had been completely wiped out, fighters and corvettes alike.

"Most of the fighters with *Perseus* are intact," she told the other woman. "Both carriers are undamaged, and I only lost fighters here."

Part of her mind was already going over her losses. One of the PNCs was just...gone—she wasn't sure who yet. It had been Longknife's fighter that had been hit, and she had only the vaguest idea of his vector.

"I have vectors on a lot of wrecked fighters and escape pods," McNee replied. "I *think* we got a solid visual on the Hoplite that went down, too," she continued, as if she'd heard Kira's private thoughts. "If you can cover them against potential risks, I can get search and rescue up."

"We need the drive cores even if we can't save the pilots," Kira confessed sadly. "We'll cover them until everyone comes home."

There was another pause.

"I have an update from Admiral Kim," McNee told her. "The carriers are coming in at full speed now, along with the attack transports. We're to flag targets for Marine landing forces and see if we can negotiate surrenders."

"That's on your side, I think, Captain McNee," Kira replied as she checked her people's fuel. They were down to fumes, basically. They could nova once or recharge their guns twice...but the sublight Harringtons didn't need much fuel. They were still more maneuverable sublight than the capital ships, which meant they still had a role to play.

"I'll babysit the search and rescue. There are still at least four hostile nova fighters out there. They're *probably* smart enough to keep running, but I can't count on that."

"Agreed. You keep my people safe, I'll go be diplomatic," the cruiser captain confirmed. "And Demirci?"

"Sir?"

"Thank you. Again."

KIRA HAD DONE damage cleanup over a dozen battlespaces over the years. Losing Hoffman *hurt*, after everything they'd done to get everyone this far out, but it was an old, familiar pain. It was worse, but it was the same pain.

And she couldn't argue that the victory hadn't been worth it for Redward, at least. With more time to study them, she could confirm that the two destroyers under construction were both D9Cs. The two heavy destroyers alone would make a huge shot in the arm for the Royal Fleet, and if the fabricators and schematics were taken intact, Redward had the resources to do *far* more with them than Warlord Davies had.

The sheer scale of the facility felt off to her. Whoever was backing Davies—she wasn't quite buying the Institute theory just yet, but *someone* had put a lot of money and tech into a pirate warlord—had thrown *way* more resources into his base than was reasonable.

From Davies' perspective, it made sense. With these yards, mines and factories, he could build an *empire*. A fleet of D9Cs and Weltraumpanzers, even if the nova fighters were operating on their own and strategically slow, could conquer the entire Cluster.

But it would have taken years to build that fleet. Davies had lacked the numbers of laborers needed to turn what he'd been given into what he needed. *Redward*, on the other hand, could make massive use of what he had.

Which…fit disturbingly well with Estanza's conspiracy theory. They armed Davies with the tech to build a fleet, and either he conquered the Cluster himself—or everything they gave him fell into the hands of a bigger power like Redward.

With that shot in the arm to their fleet, she had to wonder what King Larry would do. He didn't seem the type to turn into an all-conquering warlord, but given the *power* to do so...how would Redward's monarch jump?

She snorted at her woolgathering and opened a channel.

"S&R–Six, finding anything?" she asked quietly. That shuttle was following the vectors for her fighters.

"We were just about to call you, Commander," the shuttle responded. "We have located Darkwing-Five's fighter. Scans suggest multiple life forms aboard. It looks like Megavolt is still with you, sir. We're beginning extraction now.

"S&R–Seven is continuing to sweep the vector cone for Memorial-Three," the pilot continued gently. "We have not located the fighter yet."

"Understood, S&R," Kira noted. "Thank you."

Two fewer deaths on her conscience. That made Hoffman the *only* person she'd lost.

The RRF hadn't been as lucky as *Conviction*'s crew in that sense, and those losses stung—but they hadn't been her people. She'd grieve the RRF's and Shang's dead more than she'd grieve the Costar Clans' dead, but she'd grieve them all second.

She flipped her fighter, coming back around for a second patrol sweep across the zone. Her new angle brought the destroyer slips into the center of her view, and she shook her head again as she studied the two-thirds-complete warships.

Kira was about to ask if anyone had IDed the design for the corvettes building in the smaller slips when the first destroyer exploded.

THE UNDER-CONSTRUCTION SHIP was only the beginning. Explosions—presumably pre-planted nuclear warheads—tore through the entire shipyard complex. Both destroyers vanished in the first moments, rapidly followed by the corvettes.

The industrial nodes feeding the yards followed suit, and Kira was grimly certain no one had properly evacuated them. Rolling mills for hull plating, smelters for the asteroid ore, large-scale fabricators…an industrial site to rival many small systems' entire capacity went up in a series of explosions the Redward fleet could do nothing about.

"Change in orders," Admiral Kim's voice interrupted every channel in the system. "Priority is now search and rescue. Colonel Brigham, take your transport to the habitation stations and impose order.

"The rest of you Marines: sweep the largest debris pieces for survivors. We can search for usable tech and machinery later. Right now, we need to save 'Warlord Deceiver's people from his petty revenge."

Of course. The Equilibrium Institute had intentionally set it up so that Davies' whole campaign would end up benefiting whoever brought him down more than him—and he'd done the math and decided he wasn't going to stand for that.

"Nova fighters, begin close-in sweeps with your scanners," she ordered her people. "We can get in tighter than anything except the shuttles themselves, and our sensors can confirm if anyone is left.

"There would have been thousands of people on those stations," she continued grimly. "Let's save as many as we can."

She was already on her way as she transmitted, bringing up her fighter's full sensor suite as she dove into the wreckage of the shipyards.

The Costar Clans might be the enemy most of the time, but at this point, it didn't *matter* who was drifting in space. Anyone aboard a wrecked space station was a fellow human being.

A fellow human being with minutes or hours to live at best without help.

48

IN SOME WAYS, the aftermath of the bombs was more chaotic than the battle itself. The debris from the starships and fighters wrecked in the fight was joined by the wreckage of industrial platforms, some of the pieces as large as the corvettes lost in the fight.

Kira slipped her fighter slowly through the mess, training her sensors on debris after debris and flagging the sections that showed up as having life signs aboard.

Assault shuttles were on their way to follow up on those flags. The spacecraft had been brought along to insert Marines onto the space stations to capture them. Now they were running with partial Marine contingents as they prepared to take aboard as many survivors as they could find.

Kira's sensors couldn't say how long any given group of survivors had. She was flagging life signs, but the Redward forces had almost no ability to prioritize. The shuttles could only start at the edge and work their way in.

Hopefully, the larger pieces closer to the center of the disaster had more air and would buy people more time. *All* of those were showing at least some life, but they'd get swept last.

As she flew closer to the heart of the wrecked base, she realized that at least *some* modules appeared to be undamaged. An entire section of the fabricator portion of the shipyards was intact.

Intact enough that warnings went off on her systems as sensors dialed in her fighter. Grimacing, she tapped a command to send a transmission.

"Unidentified station, either use your sensors for search and rescue or shut them down," she ordered. "Keep them locked on me and they're going to cease to exist."

She wasn't certain what to expect as a response, but to her surprise, she actually received a request for a coms channel.

"This is one of Captain Estanza's fighters, correct?" a skittish voice asked. "I need to make contact with the good Captain."

"I don't know who you are or what you think is going on," Kira replied. "But you're in the middle of a disaster zone triggered by an asshole with a pile of nukes. Captain Estanza is a bit busy. My scans suggest your life support is intact, so hold tight and we'll get to you."

"We are surrounded by enough debris that the continued intactness of this facility is at risk," the voice told her primly. "You do not want to allow damage to this station, pilot. Please connect me with Captain Estanza."

"This is Commander Demirci, Captain Estanza's Commander Nova Group," Kira told the voice, goosebumps running down her arms as suspicion hit her. "He doesn't have time to spare for you, but I can afford a few seconds."

The man behind the voice spent those seconds hesitating, she suspected.

"My name is Cameron Burke," he finally said. "Captain Estanza and I worked together, a long time ago. I have eleven technicians and twenty-two security officers aboard this station. We apparently succeeded in preventing our erstwhile host from planting bombs aboard our facility, but we have no shuttles or docks."

"We will get to you," Kira promised with a sigh. "You can talk to Captain Estanza then. You are far more secure than many people currently in danger."

"Yes, well, you're going to move this entire module immediately, and it is safer to do so without us aboard," Burke told her. "I have a self-destruct command for the fabricator on this station, but I am prepared to trade it for the immediate extraction of myself and my people and our transfer to the Ypres System."

She knew. There was only one thing in the mess that would fit on one standard module that would be worth that effort.

She had to push back anyway.

"I repeat, Em Burke, that you are more stable than anyone else in this wreckage. We will extract you and discuss repatriation later," she told him. "If you are external parties who have been arming Warlord Davies, that may resemble POW negotiations."

"Commander, this facility is a fabrication line for class two nova drives," Burke confessed in a rush.

Kira had figured. Its position relative to the larger asteroids suggested very careful alignment to create the *exact* amount of "real" mass-based gravity required for the process. A normal nova drive required in excess of point three gees to manufacture.

A class two nova drive required between point zero five two and point zero five eight gees. Kira didn't understand *why*, but she knew what the range was.

"I am prepared to trade the fabrication line and associated software and manuals for safe passage for myself and my personnel to Ypres, aboard *Conviction* specifically," he repeated. "But the longer this module remains in the center of this mess, the more likely it is that the fabricator will be damaged."

The fabricator wouldn't build the hulls, guns or Harringtons of a nova fighter—but Redward could build all of those already. If they could arrange the gravity and build the nova drives, Estanza's clients would suddenly become a *true* carrier power.

And that meant she had to talk to her boss.

"WHO?" Estanza demanded.

"He says his name is Cameron Burke and he is in charge of a team of techs and security officers, presumably from our 'outside supporter,'" Kira repeated. "He's in control of the class two nova drive fabricator, sir."

"Fuck me," the Captain murmured. "And he's in the middle of that mess from your scan, which means the facility is in danger. I don't want to prioritize that over people's lives, but...*fuck.*"

"I don't know about the One-Fifteens, but the Hoplites have tow cables," she pointed out. The hypertensile nanotube cables took up very little mass or volume, little enough that any Apollo fighter carried two ten-kilometer lengths.

"Seriously?" Estanza asked. "That's... Okay. That's useful. You can't tow that station with people aboard it."

"That was what Burke said," she agreed. "My assessment is the same. We *could* leave him there until we've finished evacuating everyone else."

"We'd risk losing the fabricator," her boss admitted. "Burke? Really?"

"You do know him?" she asked.

"How well do you know Waldroup's second munitions technician?" Estanza replied. "Because that was his role—on the Cobras' *other* carrier. We've *met*, I think, but I wouldn't say I know him.

"What I *do* know is that if he's out this far, after this much time... he's Equilibrium, Commander."

"And he wants a ride on our ship as part of his price for handing over the fabricator, sir," she reminded him. "He seemed to think his name would open doors with you."

"Most likely because he realizes I'd guess he had to be Equilibrium," Estanza replied. "It's not like we knew each other." He made a wordless sound of disgust. "Keep the EI angle under your hat, Commander. I'm looping in Kim."

A moment later, the Redward Vice Admiral's mental voice joined the conversation.

"This better be good, Estanza. We're coordinating search and rescue across a rapidly expanding AO with thousands of lives on the line."

Despite her earlier suggestion of ignoring the spirit of King Larry's orders, it seemed that when push came to shove, Vice Admiral Ylva Kim shared her leaders' general concern for human life.

"Demirci, brief her," Estanza ordered.

"Sir, there were outside contractors running Davies's fabricator for the class two nova drives," Kira said crisply. "They had their own security and prevented bombs being deployed on their station.

"The fabricator is intact but aboard a station module in the middle of the debris zone," she continued. "Davies likely believed that the destruction of everything *around* it would take care of the fabricator.

"There is a self-destruct code in the hands of the head contractor. He's prepared to turn the fabricator over to the RRF in exchange for immediate extraction and transportation to Ypres aboard *Conviction*.

"If we want to retrieve the fabricator, we need to move the module ASAP, as the odds of it taking critical damage increase by the second—and we can't move the module with people aboard.

"Not without killing them, anyway, and I *suspect* they'd trigger the self-destruct at that point."

There was silence on the channel for several seconds, an eternity in headware coms.

"The last thing I want is to rescue our outside operators as a priority over Clan civilians," Kim noted. "Even the most innocent of those techs is more responsible for this mess than the poor bastards Davies dragged into building his war machine.

"But we need that fabricator. How many people?"

"Under forty," Kira said.

"That's one shuttle's passenger capacity, even if we're treating them as prisoners," the Admiral replied. "But one shuttle can't move a space station."

"Five Hoplites can if you remove the passengers," she said. "We have nanotube tow cables, ten-kilometer lengths. Hooking up might take longer than more specialized vessels, but we can get the station module out of the debris zone."

They couldn't nova it. The module itself was the size of one of the RRF destroyers. They'd either need to extract the fabricator in pieces or bring in a bulk freighter of a rare size for the cluster.

"I'll have the shuttle redirected," Kim decided aloud. "Start hooking up your cables now, Commander. We'll meet the bastard's terms."

"They also insisted that their transport to Ypres be aboard *Conviction*," Kira pointed out. "I'm not sure they trust Redward."

"Consider yourself contracted, then, Captain Estanza," the Admiral snapped. "I may not like it, but we need that damn fabricator. *Move.*"

"WHAT ARE YOU *DOING?*" Burke's voice asked, his pitch rising to a near-squeak of fear as Kira's fighters swept in and launched the first round of tow cables. Ten nanotube cables shot into space.

Roughly in line with Kira's expectations, six hit and only four actually managed to form a magnetic connection.

"We are beginning the irritating-as-*hell* process of hooking your station up for towing while we wait for your extraction shuttle," Kira told him. "Redward has agreed to your terms."

She *could* have told him that before she started shooting magnets at his space station, but she wasn't feeling *that* generous.

Six cables slowly retracted and Kira concealed a bitter chuckle as she realized that both of *hers* had missed but the rest of her people had landed a cable apiece.

"Oh. That's acceptable, then," Burke told her. For a member of a galaxy-spanning conspiracy, he was surprisingly trusting. There wouldn't be much warning when Kira's fighters brought their engines online to tow the station clear.

There'd *probably* be enough time to fire the self-destruct code off if he was ready. But only probably. She'd have been more argumentative in his place—and probably even set up a dead-woman switch in her headware.

The computer would survive the organic portion of her brain by at *least* two or three seconds, after all.

"Your shuttle will arrive in a little over sixty seconds," she continued as her cables shot out again. This time, both of hers hit...but only one made the connection. Still, they had seven of ten cables connected now.

"Get everyone grouped together and have your security people leave their weapons behind," she ordered. "You are potential hostiles on an enemy station. Any resistance or appearance will be met with lethal force."

"Right," Burke squeaked. "I'll let them know."

By now, she was certain that either he was the most optimistically naïve conspirator she'd ever known—or a superb actor who was attempting to play her. Her guess was somewhere in between.

The final connections latched on as the Marine shuttle was supposed to arrive. They were late, which was the last thing she'd expected.

"RRM Shuttle K-Two Seven Six, what is your status?" she transmitted, attempting to locate the spacecraft.

"Apologies, Memorial Actual," the shuttle pilot told her. "We picked up a life sign on a weird vector and no one else was in position for pickup. A detour seemed justified."

"Fair enough, K-Two Seven Six," she conceded. "New ETA?"

"Forty-two seconds and counting," the shuttle pilot replied. "And we just IDed the bogey we pulled aboard, Commander. Looks like a Hoplite-IV ejector seat. I'm pretty sure the relieved idiot *waving* at my cameras is yours."

Kira exhaled like she'd been punched in the gut.

"You picked up Hoffman?" she asked.

"I'll have Gunny ask his name once she's done cutting him out," the pilot replied. "But last I heard, you'd only *lost* one pilot, so I'm guessing."

"Thank you, Two Seven Six," she said. "What's your name, pilot? I owe you and your entire crew beers when we're back in Redward."

"Lieutenant Brynhildur Ó Foghladha," the woman replied. "Part of the service, sir, but we're not going to turn down free beer, either."

"I make it twenty seconds to contact, Lieutenant Ó Foghladha," Kira told her. "They're supposed to be waiting for you unarmed, but move as quickly as you can. We're keeping the area clean, but I'll be happier when we can get this chunk of metal moving out of the debris zone."

None of her pilots were even consciously involved in that process. The fighters' guns had a *lot* of flexibility and were currently using all of it, rotating them around to hit any chunks of debris approaching the station with minimum-energy shots.

"Oorah, Commander. Gunny's got it in hand."

49

IT WAS over eight hours after they started towing the fabricator station out of the debris field—and over ten since they'd initially launched to sortie against the Clan base—when Kira finally shepherded her fighters home.

There were no manual landings today. *Last Denial* and the combat-capable destroyers hovered over the carriers and the damaged ships like angry eagles protecting a barely hatched chick.

Today had been both the worst losses ever suffered by the Redward Royal Fleet and said Fleet's greatest single victory. There'd be stories told about today, Kira was sure.

She was also grimly certain that the role of the mercenary destroyers and nova fighters would be talked down in those stories. Give it ten years and the mercs would barely be mentioned. Thirty, and they'd be a footnote in the history-book list of ships present at the battle.

Today, however, she knew what her contract and *Conviction*'s contract said for payouts for this mission. She trusted Redward to pay their obligations—and those obligations were huge.

If she was lucky, they'd even let her buy a class two nova drive from the new line. She could fabricate all of the other parts to replace

Hoffman's fighter, but they hadn't succeeded in retrieving the nova drives this time.

Two of the fighters they'd lost today were gone forever, with no way for *Conviction* to replace them. Kira now *fully* understood how the carrier had gone from over thirty nova fighters to eight.

With only eleven other fighters on the transfer pads, the retrieval bay felt disturbingly empty as she dropped out and looked around. The only other vessel present was what looked like a Redward Royal Marines assault shuttle.

She'd barely registered the shuttle before Hoffman was there, wrapping her in a bear-armed embrace.

"Gods above and below, I thought I was a goner," he told her.

"We thought you *were* gone," she replied. "We never found your fighter, even."

"Power core overload," he said grimly. "She was breaking up even as I spun out, and there was nothing I could do but eject and hope I got clear. It stayed intact long enough that I didn't see her go, but it was a matter of minutes, not hours, sir."

Kira saw Patel drop out of his fighter, the younger man staring at Hoffman like he wasn't sure the pilot was real.

"Get over here, Dinesh," she told him, stepping back to allow the two lovers to embrace. "Someone was listening to our prayers," she told both men. "The Marines picked you up in passing on the way to grab the contractors. You okay?"

"A bit flash-frozen around the edges, but the ejection pod worked perfectly," Hoffman told her. He hadn't let go of Patel yet—but it didn't look like Patel was planning on letting go of *him*, either. "Kept me warm and breathing. We might want to check the beacons on the other ships. I was *fixing* it when Two-Seven-Six found me, but it didn't work when I told it to."

Apollo's education program for the pilot academy included enough secondary courses to be generally accepted as both an electrical and spaceframe engineering degree *and* an electrician's apprenticeship. Kira had *very* few fond memories of the academy, but she admitted that it left her pilots able to rewire most of the things in their fighters that weren't molecular circuitry.

"We'll have Waldroup triple-check them all," she promised. She glanced past Hoffman to the assault shuttle. "We still have Marines aboard?"

"Helping McCaig secure our not-quite-guests," the deck boss's voice told her. Kira glanced up to see Waldroup emerge from behind a moving array of tools. "I caught the word on the beacons."

She grimaced.

"Fuck checking them," she concluded. "That's a tiny piece that we can't afford to fail. I'll replace them all."

"Agreed," Kira allowed, looking around the retrieval deck. "Need anything from me, Waldroup?" she asked. "Because I don't think there's a pilot that just came aboard that should be going anywhere except a shower and a bed, *hopefully* in that order."

Most of her people were on their way to their quarters in a familiar exhausted shuffle.

"I don't, but I think the Captain was waiting for you to get aboard."

Kira got the chime from Estanza in the middle of the deck boss's sentence and sighed. She checked.

Report to the bridge as soon as you can.

"Not much of one for detailed instructions, is he?" she asked rhetorically. "All right. Hoffman, Patel—get the hell off Waldroup's deck.

"Waldroup, check those emergency beacons and get at least four fighters prepped for relaunch."

"You're not planning on launching anytime soon, are you?" she asked. "I don't think there's a bird on the deck that doesn't need a six-hour run-through at *least*."

"And you'll give them that," Kira agreed. "*After* you crash-prep two Hoplites and two One-Fifteens for a security blanket. Get me?"

"Security blanket sounds nice, gotta say," Waldroup conceded. "Go see the Captain, boss. Deck is under control; your people are going to go fall over. Situation normal."

Kira snorted. She knew how *that* sentence usually ended.

TO KIRA'S SURPRISE, the bridge was actually guarded for the first time since she'd come aboard the mercenary carrier. Milani, distinctive as always in their red dragon armor, flanked one side of the door, with another armored grunt on the other side.

"Do I need to show ID?" Kira asked dryly.

"Nah, we're just making sure our guests don't get any ideas," Milani replied. "You can go right on in, Commander."

"We're letting them roam randomly?" Kira said.

"*Officially*, they're passengers," the merc pointed out. "But no, not that I know of. But McCaig said guard the bridge, so here I am. For now, at least."

She snorted and gave the other guard a nod as she stepped onto the bridge.

"Ah, Demirci, good," Estanza greeted her. "Get up here."

She stepped up to stand next to his seat and saw that he was already on a visual call with several other officers, including Shang and Kim.

"Commander Demirci, it's good to see you," the Vice Admiral acknowledged her. "I didn't have time earlier to speak to you directly; but thank you. Your actions may have completely changed the course of this battle."

"None of us expected the bastard to blow the entire facility," Captain McNee, a flat-faced and pale-skinned woman, noted harshly. "That's a degree of sheer viciousness we don't normally see from the Clans."

"Davies appears to have been unusual for the Clans," Kim agreed. "The final count, people, is that we extracted sixty-two hundred and eighty-five people from the wreckage. Their friends and family aboard the hab stations are ecstatic to have them back but worried about what happens next."

She sighed.

"The locals are now being extremely cooperative, which means we now know that there were just over *eighteen* thousand people working in the shipyard complex. Anthony Davies just murdered about twelve thousand people.

"*His* people."

Kim shook her head.

"Worse, we've confirmed that he was aboard the destroyer that escaped. We're still in the process of sorting out where the destroyers came from, but the two we engaged were *not* built here."

"Couldn't we just ask the contractors we pulled off that fab module?" Kira asked.

"In exchange for disabling the self-destruct code, we promised safe transport to Ypres," the Admiral replied. "We have confirmed that the contents are exactly what Em Burke said they were, which means he has handed us a critical component of a new strategic balance in the cluster.

"I hate where it came from, but we'll honor the deal," she concluded. "You're welcome to ask him questions on your way to Ypres, but an actual interrogation would violate the *spirit* of our promises."

"Which leaves us with very few answers as to where Davies got his hands on multiple Inner Rim warships," Estanza said. "What do you need from us, ma'am?"

"At this point, this area is now effectively Redward territory," Kim replied. "*Perseus* and *Last Denial* basically can't leave until that is official and unquestioned, but I have cripples we need to send home, and I want Em Burke as many light-years from anything I want to keep intact as possible.

"So. Commodore Shang: there's nothing in your contract for this level of damage to one of your vessels," she told him bluntly. "We *did* commit to regular repairs and munitions costs, however, and I do not believe the spirit of the contract would be honored by leaving you with a wrecked ship. Can *Zheng Chenggong* make nova?"

"Not much more, Admiral, but yes," Shang answered carefully.

"If *Liu Bei* will join *Grumpy Cat* in escorting our damaged vessels back to Redward, I would be grateful and pay your full rate," Kim told him. "Regardless, I will provide secured and validated orders for our yards to carry out full repairs and as many upgrades as possible to *Zheng Chenggong* at Their Majesties' expense.

"I am also activating *all* contingency bonus payments in your contract. Some of them weren't technically fulfilled, but the scale of our accomplishments today justifies them.

"I know money isn't much of a trade for your people's lives," she said gently, "but it's what I have available to recognize your efforts and sacrifice."

"You're right, but we are mercenaries," Shang Tzu told her. "I appreciate both the money *and* the recognition it represents. We would be honored to help escort our wounded comrades home."

"Thank you," Kim replied, then turned her attention to Estanza. "I've issued the same orders for you, Estanza. All of your contingency bonuses will be paid. I don't believe you have any damage that will require a yard for repairs, correct?"

"Correct," he said. "There are conversations we'll need to have about that fabricator when we all get back to Redward."

"You might beat it back there," the Admiral admitted. "The RRF only has two ships capable of hauling that facility, and I hesitate to take apart the fabricator without a *lot* more study. Commodore Shang will be carrying my reports home, and I expect to see one of those ships here in a few days.

"Your trip to Ypres will be faster."

"I hope so," Estanza said calmly. "I'm not enjoying our guests."

There were layers to that only Kira understood, she suspected. It had to go against the grain for Estanza to have people he was certain were Equilibrium Institute agents aboard. What choice did they have?

Burke had demanded his ride be on the carrier, so the carrier it was.

"Using a carrier to haul thirty-odd hostile contractors annoys me as well," the Admiral replied. "If you'll allow it, I'd like Gunny De Soto and her people to remain aboard *Conviction* until you return to Redward. An extra twenty Marines will make me feel much happier about their security team."

"I won't turn them down, Admiral," Estanza said. "So long as they follow orders."

"De Soto is under your command until you deliver her to Redward. She's already been made aware of that," Kim told him. "Any other concerns, Captain?"

"Many, but they are irrelevant to the topic at hand," Estanza said with a chuckle.

50

THERE WAS STILL no alcohol in Estanza's office, a lack that his body language suggested he was feeling as he led the way in and took a seat.

"Equilibrium," he snarled. "I knew it was a possibility, but I didn't expect it to be *quite* so obvious."

"It wouldn't have been if they hadn't had someone from the Cobras out here," Kira pointed out. "In the absence of that, I would have assumed we were looking at a Brisingr operation."

"We might still be," Estanza conceded. "Or, fuck, *both*. The Kaiserreich has every sign of being fully in bed with the Institute. The fact that *somebody* had two of Brisingr's destroyers to throw around suggests that the Kaiser is at least involved."

Kira grimaced.

"Should I be worrying that Burke's people are going to try and knife me in the back?" she asked.

"Unlikely. They were here for one mission, and that didn't include you except *maybe* as a target of opportunity." The Captain snorted. "And they're not dumb enough to start a fight on their ride home."

He sighed, looking back to where the bar would have been for a long moment.

"Coffee?" he finally asked.

"No thanks. I need to *sleep* sometime soon," Kira pointed out.

"Fair enough. Sorry, I needed you to hear at least some of that briefing, and I needed to touch base with you, as well."

"I'm at your disposal," she said. "Falling asleep in the chair here, but at your disposal."

She was exaggerating. Her headware wasn't going to let her fall asleep by accident, even if the chair felt a *lot* more comfortable than it had in the past.

"You can go rest soon enough," Estanza conceded. "Sorry. I need you to field Burke, Commander."

"Define 'field Burke,' sir," she asked slowly.

"He's already made two requests to meet with me, and he's been aboard for five hours," the Captain told her. "I need you to meet with him and keep him under control. Ypres is a long way from here and we'll have to stop along the way to discharge static. That's at least three days I have the man aboard my ship.

"If he has something of value to say, I'll talk to him. Otherwise, I want him to sit down, shut up and be a good passenger. I'm pretty sure you can get him to do that."

Kira snorted.

"If he needs to still be breathing afterwards, that's a soft maybe," she told her boss. "All right. I'll talk to him once I've slept. He can wait until then."

"He most definitely can," Estanza agreed. "Right now, I want to put a bug in your ear. You need to think on something as we make this cruise."

"Sir?"

"The schematics and fabrication plans we have for the Hoplite and its parts are copy-protected," he reminded her. "That kind of military-grade security is hard to breach, but it *can* be done. You could potentially sell Redward the design for the Hoplite."

Kira swallowed a harsh immediate response. That would be, inarguably, treason. On the other hand, Apollo's Council of Principals had made very clear what they thought of *her* loyalty to *them*.

The attempt would risk slagging one of the fabricator terminals she had. On the other hand, she'd brought a parts fabricator for each fighter, so she now had one to spare.

"I'd have to think about that," she admitted.

"I know," he agreed. "That's why I raised it. We spent a lot of time over the last twenty years breaking the encryption on the data I have for the PNC One-Fifteen. I have every intention of selling those designs to Redward in exchange for a refit of *Conviction*, new-built PNCs for my own use, and a *fuckton* of money.

"As my CNG, you're going to get a dramatically expanded fighter group out of that...but as things currently stand, the Memorials will become a much-reduced portion of that group."

Where if she did what Estanza was suggesting with the Hoplite design, she could expand the Memorials and the Darkwings equally. *Conviction* would be better served with thirty interceptors and thirty fighter-bombers than five interceptors and fifty-five fighter-bombers, that was for sure.

"Without doing *something*, your Memorials will shrink over time," he said gently. "So, do you want them to forever be just the six of you and those five fighters? I'll happily lease you a One-Fifteen for Longknife once I've acquired more, but it's a question for you, Kira.

"Do you want to go forward as my Commander, Nova Group first and leader of the Memorials second? Or do you want to keep the Memorials half the weight of this carrier? I'll back you either way and adjust contracts to match, Kira, but you have to decide whether you're willing to hand that data over to Redward."

"A nation whose enemies appear to be supported by Apollo's greatest enemy," Kira admitted aloud. "I have to think about it," she repeated.

"Given what we learned on the PNCs and the fact that you have officer-level access codes for the ASDF, Waldroup can probably crack open the copy protection in three or four days," Estanza told her. "I *won't* do it without your permission. It's up to you. I think you should," he admitted. "But I won't tell you what to do or go behind your back. Good enough?"

"For now," she conceded. "I need to sleep on it, sir. No question about that."

"Fair enough. Go," he ordered. "Zoric and I have the watch. We'll probably nova out to the trade lane before you're awake.

"I want these Institute engineers *off* my ship."

51

KIRA MAY HAVE PROMISED NOT to interrogate anybody, but she hadn't said anything about not using the interrogation *rooms*. She'd gone so far as to dig up more comfortable chairs, but that was her sole concession to making the steel-walled room any less intimidating.

Burke wasn't any more prepossessing in person than he had been over the com. He was a small man of roughly her own height, but vaguely pudgy with faded brown hair and watery blue eyes.

He didn't look like he'd been expecting her, but a glance back at the mercenary escorting him resulted in a sigh before he stepped into the room.

"When they told me someone senior wanted to speak to me, I was hoping Estanza was finally responding to my message," he admitted, but he took a seat in the empty chair.

"He is. He sent me," Kira told him. She gestured with her coffee cup to the full one on the table. "There's coffee if you want it. I'm Commander Demirci."

"The Apollo pilot, yes?" Burke asked as he took the coffee cup.

"Yes," she confirmed. "I'm surprised you don't know more about me. There seems to have been *some* effort to pretend you were a Brisingr team, but there's no way anyone from the Kaiserreich navy would be so uncertain about me."

"I'm from deeper towards the Core," Burke conceded. "That's how I know Captain Estanza. I just wanted to catch up with an old friend since fate brought us together."

Kira sighed.

"Interesting that you don't say that you were or weren't working for Brisingr," she noted. "How about we cut the bullshit, Em Burke? I know you're from the Equilibrium Institute."

She'd been reasonably certain that the nervous engineer was an act. He might have been a munitions tech once, but today Burke was running a thirty-person covert mission to secretly deliver arms technology to a pirate warlord.

The speed at which he recovered from her namedrop proved that he was a *good* actor. He just wasn't good enough not to react at all.

"That's not a name you hear much out here," Burke countered gently, but his voice had changed ever so slightly. Some of the nervous pitch was gone.

"But I imagine it was one you heard when you worked for the Cobras, yes?" Kira pushed.

Burke chuckled, but he never took his gaze away from hers.

"I did," he conceded. "It's hard to argue with the vision, isn't it? A peaceful galaxy, kept that way by Seldonian analysis and careful balancing of the galactic powers.

"There's not much point in arguing with the woman who can decide I suffer an unfortunate accident before we reach Ypres," he told her. "Yes, I work for the organization that Captain Estanza knew as the Equilibrium Institute. Some of my people are from the Institute. Others are exactly the kind of minimally questioning contractors we were all supposed to be.

"I don't expect you to understand what we were out to achieve here, but I assure that our goal is not what you think it was."

"Your goal was to make Davies enough of a threat that Redward or one of the Cluster's other significant powers had to smack him down," she replied. "In doing so, they'd take possession of the shipyards and fabricators, giving them a shot in the arm you expected to encourage them to turn militarily expansionist.

"By controlling that expansionism, you expected to turn them into a regional hegemon to maintain stability in your particular model of Seldonian analysis."

Kira smiled.

"Am I close?"

Burke had frozen with his coffee cup nearly at his lips.

"Surprisingly," he conceded. "I see that Captain Estanza has been very free with our secrets."

"I'm a special case," she assured him. "I don't know what you plan to say to Captain Estanza, but you can say it to me."

"I suspect you can guess," Burke pointed out. "We want to recruit him—and I wouldn't blink at recruiting you—to help us guide this Cluster towards stability."

"King Larry and his Syntactic Cluster Free Trade Zone seem to be a huge leap in that direction," Kira said. "I'm surprised to find you opposing him."

"Who says we are?" the Institute agent asked. "The RRF was the most likely candidate to move against Warlord Deceiver, and everything we set up in the Kiln System would have fallen into their hands."

He snorted.

"We were *not* expecting Davies to rig the entire place to blow, I'll admit."

"Ass-backwards way of helping someone out," she said. "A lot of dead people to get to that point, even if it worked. Why not just offer King Larry help?"

Burke sighed.

"In its current form, our Seldonian analysis projects that the SCFTZ will successfully take shape—and then slowly disintegrate over twenty years, precipitating an economic and political crisis that will trigger a no-holds-barred war over most of the Sector.

"We're looking at an eighty-five percent probability of a war with minimum casualties measured in the *billions*, Demirci," he told her. "We've seen it happen; we trust the analysis. This kind of free-trade structure buys some time but only at the cost of major long-term violence.

"The only solution that reliably works is a strong hegemon forcing the rest of the region to behave. King Larry has so far refused to let Redward become that hegemon."

"So, you try to make him," Kira concluded.

"Exactly." Burke shrugged. "Either Redward becomes the Syntactic Cluster's unquestioned leader, or someone else has to. It's the only way to avoid the war that will come."

"So, building a peaceful trade alliance can only end in war?" she asked.

"I don't do the Seldonian analysis," he admitted. "I'm an engineer. This kind of tech-lift? It's what I do. It's what I've done for the Institute for thirty years."

"And what if the analysis is wrong?" Kira asked. "What if you've already killed hundreds—*thousands*—and created the very crisis you're trying to prevent?"

"That's not what the analysis says will happen," Burke said calmly. "There are very smart people running those numbers, Demirci. *Very* smart people—far more capable than you or I. They know what they're doing, they know what they're seeing."

"So, you blithely hand Redward nova fighters?" she said.

"Part of my job was to make sure at least some of this tech stayed in the Cluster ecosystem," he agreed. "It's not like Redward can do anything spectacular with them. They'll have to go through the same rough edges of developing nova fighters everyone else did.

"They'll learn, Demirci."

"And how many people die along the way?" she demanded.

"As few as possible, as many as necessary," Burke said bleakly. "It would help us a lot to have you and Estanza on board. Very clearly, King Larry trusts Estanza and Estanza trusts you. Even if he won't speak to *me*, you can carry my message."

"I could, but I already know his answer," Kira told him. "I already know my answer. Tell me, Em Burke, how much did the Equilibrium Institute have to do with the Brisingr-Apollo Agreement on Nova Lane Security?"

The room was silent.

"We've helped Brisingr, yes," he conceded. "The Council of Principals represents the worst kind of oligo-capitalism: self-centered, grasping, and unwilling to exert the control necessary to maintain peace.

"Better a dictator than a self-satisfied oligarch."

"I'm not sure the worlds now forced to pay tribute would agree with you."

"Their children who will live in peace might," Burke told her. "It is always for the future."

"I don't believe in your future," Kira replied. "I don't believe that tyranny trumps democracy, that hegemony trumps association. Larry might be a king, but he's bound by law and an elected government. Redward isn't perfect, but they're better as leaders than as masters.

"I won't fight for your Institute and neither will Captain Estanza. If you want to spread your tendrils into the Syntactic Cluster, well."

She smiled thinly as her decision on the fighter schematics and everything else fell into place.

If Cameron Burke was representative of Estanza's old employers, she *knew* her enemy. This self-satisfied little man, this *fanatic* in service of an imaginary calculation...he was an example of the worst humanity had to offer. He'd do anything in service of his cause and could never be swayed from it.

"If the Equilibrium Institute wants to pick a hegemon out here, they're going to have to go through Redward to pull it off," she said sweetly. "And I don't think you're going through Redward without going through *us*."

JOIN THE MAILING LIST

Love Glynn Stewart's books? To know as soon as new books are released, special announcements, and a chance to win free paperbacks, join the mailing list at:

glynnstewart.com/mailing-list/

ABOUT THE AUTHOR

Glynn Stewart is the author of *Starship's Mage*, a bestselling science fiction and fantasy series where faster-than-light travel is possible–but only because of magic. His other works include science fiction series *Duchy of Terra*, *Castle Federation* and *Vigilante*, as well as the urban fantasy series *ONSET* and *Changeling Blood*.

Writing managed to liberate Glynn from a bleak future as an accountant. With his personality and hope for a high-tech future intact, he lives in Kitchener, Ontario with his partner, their cats, and an unstoppable writing habit.

VISIT GLYNNSTEWART.COM FOR NEW RELEASE UPDATES

f facebook.com/glynnstewartauthor

OTHER BOOKS
BY GLYNN STEWART

For release announcements join the
mailing list or visit **GlynnStewart.com**

STARSHIP'S MAGE
Starship's Mage
Hand of Mars
Voice of Mars
Alien Arcana
Judgment of Mars
UnArcana Stars
Sword of Mars
Mountain of Mars
The Service of Mars
A Darker Magic
Mage-Commander (upcoming)

Starship's Mage: Red Falcon
Interstellar Mage
Mage-Provocateur
Agents of Mars

Pulsar Race: A Starship's Mage Universe Novella

DUCHY OF TERRA
The Terran Privateer
Duchess of Terra
Terra and Imperium
Darkness Beyond
Shield of Terra
Imperium Defiant
Relics of Eternity
Shadows of the Fall
Eyes of Tomorrow

SCATTERED STARS
Scattered Stars: Conviction
Conviction
Deception
Equilibrium
Fortitude (upcoming)

PEACEKEEPERS OF SOL
Raven's Peace
The Peacekeeper Initiative
Raven's Course
Drifter's Folly (upcoming)

EXILE
Exile
Refuge
Crusade
Ashen Stars: An Exile Novella

CASTLE FEDERATION
Space Carrier Avalon
Stellar Fox
Battle Group Avalon
Q-Ship Chameleon
Rimward Stars
Operation Medusa
A Question of Faith: A Castle Federation Novella

SCIENCE FICTION STAND ALONE NOVELLA
Excalibur Lost